In the Shadow of Lies

In the Shadow of Lies

a mystery novel

M. A. Adler

She Writes Press

Published 2014
Printed in the United States of America
ISBN: 978-1-938314-82-7
Library of Congress Control Number: 2014930012

For information, address:
She Writes Press
1563 Solano Ave #546
Berkeley, CA 94707

For William, Benjamin, and Nicholas Ardine,
my father and his brothers, who went to war.
Two came home.

Everyone sees what you appear to be,
few experience what you really are.

Machiavelli

Author's Note

It is difficult for me to think certain words found in this book, let alone write them. You will find them where they would have occurred in real life: in the dialogue and thoughts of characters whose actions are motivated by the ugliness of racism and prejudice.

The book is set in a real place and time. The characters are my invention, save Thurgood Marshall, an extraordinary and courageous attorney, and General DeWitt, a man who acted ruthlessly against the people the United States had labeled "enemies."

1941

Chapter 1

Ribbons of ebony crows streamed across the cobalt sky. They landed on redwood boughs and sidled along needled bridges to the centers of the trees. The trees seemed to lift and fall as the flock settled down for the night, rustled and murmured, closed their eyes, dreamed their corvid dreams.

Blue deepened to purple. A screech owl rattled and glided through the dusk, hunting for a hapless rodent scratching for dinner along the edge of the dry meadow.

Maude Fleming walked out onto her porch, breathed the hot bay smell lingering from the ridge trees, and considered whether she would have the strength to get up from the steps if she sat down on them.

Late tomatoes next. The jars of vegetables would be welcome when winter came, but she was tired of the tyranny of things ripening all at once and dictating how she spent the hot fall days. The work would become harder after Ellie started seventh grade next week. Maude would miss her daughter's help but more her singing spirit, her chatter that made the work go faster. She had to find time this weekend to make up those plaid yard goods into a back-to-school outfit for her. The child had surely earned it, scraping and slicing, cutting the beans, watching her brothers, when all she wanted was to finish *The Wizard of Oz* before she had to return it to the library the next day. She would probably hide under the covers with a flashlight tonight, struggling to stay awake.

The children should be coming back soon. Maude had sent them with a picnic into the woods by the creek, where the boys could play in the trickle that was left of it and Ellie could read the book she had slipped into the dinner sack. Before bedtime, they would eat pudding and listen to the jar lids pop, Ellie and Joe jumping in their chairs as if the pings startled them, reducing Sammy to giggles. They must have gone to that blackberry island in the middle of the hill and lost track of time.

She leaned on the post, half asleep and half dreaming about a summer kitchen where she could work outside and feel the afternoon winds that blew inland from the Golden Gate, although the breeze setting the glass chimes dancing felt more warm than cool.

Something wasn't right. She smelled smoke. Who would have a fire on a night like tonight? A sudden cry and the clatter of crows broke the night quiet; they wheeled and swirled in the air, a huge black cloud that erupted into the sky, circled and gathered, then screamed away from the ridge. The hairs on the back of her neck stood up.

The children should be back by now. She grabbed a flashlight from the kitchen and hurried toward the woods.

Shadows flickered against the sere hills as the make-shift cross whooshed into the sky and burning shards exploded into the darkness. Last year's rains had soaked into the ground, and grateful seeds had flourished, grown lush, luxuriant. The grass had rippled like young wheat in the breeze, and then spring had come, dry as summer, and the grass had turned brittle in the hot sun that bronzed the hills.

A spark landed in the dry meadow. First a whisper, a rustling, as embers ignited the long, thin stalks that danced and swayed at the edge of the clearing. Then the flames crackled like locusts as they gobbled through the grass, leaving a charred funnel that grew longer and wider. White smoke billowed in front of the fire, and yellow and orange flames raced toward the ridge and rounded the curve of the hill, moving almost ten miles an hour and heating the air to more than a thousand degrees.

At first Ellie thought the noise was the wind rattling the bay trees. She looked up at the ridge, then turned to look at the hill behind her. The sky on the other side of the hill seemed foggy, blurred gray and white, like a low cloud. Orange and yellow flickers flashed through the gray and a burst of wind carried the smell of smoke to her. She picked up Sammy and screamed at Joe to run. She saw fear whiten his face when he turned to look at her. He tried to help her with Sammy.

"No, run! Run as fast as you can, and don't look back. Run!"

Joe hesitated. Ellie screamed at him. "Go. Get help!" She faltered for a second as the world of Oz slid to the ground, then she held Sammy tighter and ran toward the woods, the boy clinging to her, his eyes closed against the smoke and soot that was beginning to swirl around them. He whimpered, a baby again. Ellie tried not to breathe the ashes that floated on the wind. When she coughed, Sammy's grip loosened, and she almost dropped him. The heat scorched the backs of her legs as she stumbled through the smoke overtaking them. Her eyes smarted and burned, and she ran blindly for home.

The men in the pickup truck heard the firehouse bell before they made it back to Point Richmond. When the truck turned onto the main street, they saw people pointing toward the hill they had just left. A fire raged through the meadow.

The driver swore and turned off between some stores. He stopped and jumped out of the cab, told the men in the back to lie down and be quiet.

"We cleared the area. It wasn't our fault."

"Shut up."

He wound through side streets until he got to the garage.

"Everyone in the back room. Get out the cards."

"But . . ."

"Shut up. All of you. We didn't do this. Have no idea who did. Do you understand? We were all here playing poker."

"Why?"

"That fire could spread to the houses up there. You want us to be blamed for that?"

No one argued, they rarely did with him, but they didn't try to hide their resentment. He'd get some women over later, give them something to celebrate.

"What about the others?"

"They have alibis. Been drinking at the Stop. I'll call there, let them know where we are. And don't you worry—you'll be having some fun later on."

The phone rang as he reached to pick it up. What a surprise. He listened to the other man rant.

"What the hell was that? You set the whole goddamned hill on fire."

He lit a cigarette and blew out the smoke. "I think you got more than you bargained for tonight. I hope it was worth it to you."

"You expect me to pay extra for your incompetence?" The voice spoke to the implied threat.

"I told you we should have put the cross in front of the house that uppity professor was buying."

"It wasn't safe to do that. The fire might have spread to the other houses."

"Yeah. *Your* houses." He flicked tobacco from his tongue. "Seems to me you have a lot more to worry about if we don't keep on enforcing things for you. One gets in, and there goes the neighborhood. Only people want to rent next to one is other trash. You need us. So when things get complicated, you pay a bonus. No later than tomorrow."

Chapter 2

Joe stumbled out of the smoke, coughing and crying, the meadow like thunder behind him, and ran almost into his mother's arms. She looked at him and then at the woods.

Neighbors rushed to the meadow to help beat back the fire, some when they smelled smoke and saw ash swirling in the air, some when they heard Maude screaming for Ellie.

The men brought shovels, rakes, and hoes, dug at the dirt to clear a break, and beat out the sparks that leaped it. They gathered Maude and Joe and forced them to go to the hospital, swearing they wouldn't stop looking for Ellie and Sammy.

They searched along the edges of the fire, calling the children's names, probing the line for a way in. The moon spilled a cooling light on the meadow, but smoke still rose from the smoldering ashes. The firemen tried, but, helpless and too late, they didn't know where to direct the scant water they had. They worked to get in front of the fire and protect the homes but had little heart for the job. In the end, only an abandoned shearing barn burned, prompting one weary firefighter to lament that the damned sheep weren't still around to keep the hillside grasses short.

As soon as they could, the men stepped into the smoking meadow, bleakly hoping that the girl had escaped the fire. Flashlight beams crisscrossed the charred earth as the men called her name. A fireman stopped dead when he saw a mound not far from the edge of the woods. The heat penetrating his boots forced him to pick up his feet, one after the other, with no place to go but toward what he knew was the girl. She might have made it on her own, but it looked as if she had carried her brother until the smoke and the heat had overcome her. He didn't think this child, as brave as she was, could have stayed sheltering her brother if she had been alive when the flames reached them. At least, he hoped not. He knew he had to tell the others what he had found, but when he tried to speak, he couldn't. They would have to wait, just for a minute.

Chapter 3

The wily old fox had timed it perfectly: the rainy September day, the cemetery, the weeping mother huddled with her son under a black umbrella, a clichéd study in grays and blacks that evoked a memory of another coffin's descent into the earth, a memory that stirred Oliver Wright's guilt and made him so deeply tired that he slid into the thankless habit of trying to please his father.

They had barely returned from the Fleming children's funeral when Oliver's father summoned him to the study.

"Not the dog, Oliver."

"Harley, go find Zoe." He sent the German shepherd off with a wave of his hand, and the dog bounded away, tail high and nose to the floor, on the trail of Oliver's niece.

Judge Wright motioned his younger son to a chair.

"It is fortuitous, Oliver, that circumstances have brought you back to Richmond at the time you are needed."

Fortuitous? The word reminded Oliver that his father had no more empathy than a hanging judge should have. He drew back in his chair.

The judge seemed unaware of Oliver's reaction. "Everyone knows the Klan set the fire that killed the Fleming children, but we didn't know why until a Negro professor at Berkeley received a threatening note. It warned him to stay where he was, or his children would be next. It was signed with a drawing of a cross in flames. He decided against moving into a white neighborhood in Richmond."

"You can hardly blame him. Did he receive any support from the community?"

"The community is part of the problem. The Klan has been terrorizing people for years, but no one spoke out against them. This time, a witness came forward—someone who chanced to see the men who set fire to the cross. We believed this time we could persuade a jury to convict."

"And?"

"The witness disappeared."

"Who else knew about him?"

"That's a bit unclear. The witness approached my clerk, who told no one else, and I personally took the information to Buonarotti, the prosecutor. We think someone in law enforcement had to have leaked the information, perhaps to protect a family member."

"Maybe the witness told the wrong person what he was doing."

"No. He was too frightened to do that."

"Anyone on the force active in the Klan?"

"Not to our knowledge. Normally, people don't hide their Klan affiliation. Hell, they marched up the middle of MacDonald Avenue on the Fourth of July—without hoods." He shook his head. "They're proud of themselves, keeping America for Americans, and a lot of people sympathized with them. But now they've killed the children of a longtime Richmond family—white children—which has finally turned the community against them."

"Who might have an interest in passing on the information about the witness?"

"Several local families have been involved in Klan activities for years. Perhaps they've secretly infiltrated the police force, or Buonarotti's office." His father leaned across the desk. "That's where you come in."

"Me?"

"We need you to find out if it is someone on the police force. We'll never clean things up until we know who is passing on information. The police commissioner suggested hiring you. It makes sense. You could have decided to move back home, be a homicide detective here instead of Seattle. Nothing suspicious about that." The judge looked pleased. "I insisted that they start you at your same rank and salary."

Oliver smiled to himself. The judge hadn't changed one bit. *Here's what I want you to do with your life, and while you're at it, you can be grateful.*

"I'm sorry about the children, Judge, but I'm leaving Sunday."

The judge held up a hand.

"Seattle can wait. If you go back there now, you'll just sit around feeling sorry for yourself."

"Feeling *sorry* for myself?" He looked at the judge, who seemed to realize he had gone too far. "I'm leaving now." He nodded at his father and walked toward the door.

"I need your help. Please."

Oliver turned around. How had those words escaped his father's mouth? The judge looked away, then reached for the decanter on the table behind his desk and half filled a crystal tumbler with whiskey. He held the glass toward Oliver, who shook his head.

"It won't work. I'm an outsider; plus, they know my father is a judge and my brother is a prosecutor. Who in his right mind would let me in on the big secret?" Oliver sat on the edge of the chair. "You need to turn someone already in the inner circle or find someone who has a network of informants. I'm not the right person for this."

The judge drank deeply and touched his lips with his handkerchief. "There's something else."

Right. Now his father was probably getting to the part that really mattered to him.

"The witness who disappeared might have been killed. We think anyone who talked to him could be at risk."

"For example?"

"Your brother."

"Ah." Oliver smiled at his father. "I see."

The judge colored, the broken veins across his cheeks and nose flaring against the pink of his face.

Oliver was twelve again, watching blood drops splatter the principal's white shirt as he shook Oliver, asking why he couldn't be more like his brother. Oliver knew Peter wouldn't have risked getting dirty, let alone hurt, sticking up for the new kid outnumbered by bullies. Right then, with his head whipping back and forth, Oliver vowed to leave Richmond one day and make a life where being a Wright meant nothing.

"Oliver, please. Do it for me. Do it for your mother."

Oliver wasn't sure whether to admire the judge or detest him for invoking the memory of his mother, who had wished Oliver had been closer to Peter. And to his father. If his brother were at risk, his father might be, too. Oliver knew he couldn't count on Peter to protect himself, let alone the judge. His captain had told him to take as much time as he needed before returning to Seattle. *This is for you, Mom.*

"I'll stay till the end of December, but then I'm going home."

He turned away, regretting his promise before he reached the door. He looked back and glimpsed the satisfaction on his father's face.

Chapter 4

The seventh of December, a week into the last month Oliver had promised to his father. The detective ran on the hard-packed sand, one foot in front of the other, trying to tire his body, hoping to quiet his mind. He had given himself until the end of the year to uncover a Klan connection in the police force. He was beginning to think there wasn't one.

As he rounded the point, he heard music coming from the gaping doors of cars pulled up along the edge of the highway. Men in suits and women carrying high heels crossed the sand, moving toward the water. Oliver stopped a man and asked what was happening.

"The Japanese attacked Pearl Harbor this morning. They didn't even have the guts to declare war first."

"How bad?"

The man shook his head and his voice broke. "Bad. It sounded really bad." He raised a hand, then turned and hurried after his friends.

Another war. Germany and Italy would be forced to join their ally, and once again Americans would die in Europe. And the Pacific.

Oliver looked toward Hawaii. He could imagine the horror of the attack, men waking to shelling, to flames, to the screams of their shipmates. How many men had been murdered this morning? How many families were waiting to find out if their loved ones had survived?

What Japan had done would not be forgiven. Not in his lifetime. He could feel the anger and hatred in the people around him. They were here to see for themselves whether Japs were landing on the beaches. Some had weapons, ready to defend the coast, ready to avenge the dead at Pearl Harbor. Men on cliffs scanned the kelp beds, lifted binoculars to the sky, and listened for the sound of planes coming out of the sun.

But most of the people seemed to be mourning the men of the Pacific Fleet, California's own. They lit candles by tide pools and cast flowers on the gunmetal swells. They pressed against the water's edge, against the thousands of miles of uncaring ocean that stretched between them and Honolulu. They wanted to help—to tend the wounded, to shroud the dead. This was as close as they could get. What was left of Oliver's heart went out to them.

Michael Fiori sat in Alfred's living room, wondering what he was doing there. Each time the phone rang, Alfred's mother crossed herself and her husband snatched up the receiver, the interrupted bell echoing in the darkened house. They'd heard nothing; they had to keep the line free. In case. In case someone, somewhere, knew something about their son who was stationed at Pearl Harbor.

Michael had gone to see the Aiellos as soon as he'd heard about the attack. He had thought he could help but now realized he brought them pain, not comfort. They were too polite to turn him away, so he made an excuse and left, scorched by their silent accusation: Why was he there, and not their son?

He walked through the dense night, missing the porch lights and lamps whose brightness used to flow to the sidewalks. He picked up his pace, suddenly wanting to be home with his father and sister, who would have been torn with worry like the Aiellos if his dad hadn't talked him out of enlisting with Alfred.

"Aiuto, aiuto."

Cries for help. In Italian. Michael looked up the hill and saw two men pushing another man into a car. It was Mr. Posto, his grandfather's friend from Italy. Michael yelled and tore up the hill.

"Hey! What are you doing?"

One of the men brushed his coat back, flashed the revolver on his belt, and stepped between Michael and the car.

"You don't want to get mixed up in this. Go home."

"Mixed up in what? Where are you taking him?"

The tall man turned toward Michael.

"Who are you?"

"Michael Fiori. Who are you?"

"How do you know this man?"

"He's a family friend."

"Get lost, kid. Just stay out of it." The shorter man looked at Michael intensely and flicked his head to the side, as if he were trying to get him to leave. "Get yourself home."

"But where are you taking him?"

The tall guy started to shut the door, and the old man called out to Michael in Italian.

"What did he say to you?" The man kept one hand on the door but turned to Michael with one hand on his gun.

"Nothing." Michael backed away. "Just to go home."

The men looked at each other. The shorter one shook his head, but the other one ignored him. "Get in the car."

"No."

"I said get in the car." The tall man grabbed Michael's arm. "You're so damned worried about him, you can go with him."

"Let him go. He's a kid, and he's not on the list. Besides, we have enough to do tonight."

"You don't know what the old man said. Could be telling him to do something. Warn the others. Blow something up."

The shorter man shook his head. "Should've left when I told you, kid."

When Michael tried to pull away, the taller man smacked his head against the corner of the door. Michael fell to the ground. The last thing he heard was a forceful whisper.

"Look what you've done. We're supposed to be arresting them, not killing them."

The scent of the night flowed through the open door and filled Oliver's living room. The day had run long into the small hours of the morning, the precinct switchboard jammed with calls about Japanese planes over San Francisco and rumors of invasions. Oliver had almost felt as if he belonged with the other Richmond cops as they patrolled the streets and reassured people who had left dinner cooling while they sought the comfort of neighbors. He quieted their fears, told them they were safe, although he knew little more than they did.

Now he sat in the armchair that faced the bay, rested one hand on his sleeping dog, and let his breath find the rhythm of the chest beneath his palm. He closed his eyes and drifted with Billie Holiday. She flirted with death, invited it, caressed the lyrics that had been banned for romanticizing suicide. Strangely, "Gloomy Sunday" helped Oliver survive.

The man who wrote it knew his pain. Knew the fear, the hope, the waiting. The loss. People said, "I know how you feel," but they didn't, and even if they did, it didn't matter to Oliver, and it wouldn't matter now to the thousands of people who would wake in the mornings remembering a future they would never have, haunted by the laughter of children who would never be.

He wished for sleep, for a moment of stillness in a world of constant motion. In country after country, troops massed along borders and refugees snaked along cratered roads. Earlier, as he and Harley had run on the beach, the war had seemed far away, a distant backdrop to his investigation into the deaths of the Fleming children. Now Oliver feared what little chance he had to keep his promise to his father would vanish like the ships at Pearl, as possible witnesses and suspects left for the war. Not that his father would understand. A man kept his word, war be damned.

Harley looked up at him, his eyebrows pinched together with concern when Oliver sighed. He rubbed the dog's worry away, easing his own as the smooth fur slid under his fingers. The shepherd stretched and headed for the door. Oliver shrugged on his coat and followed his dog into the night.

Chapter 5

Three days had passed since the surprise attack on Pearl Harbor. People were still in shock. The men at the precinct had been working eighteen-hour shifts, preparing for the follow-up attacks that everyone said weren't coming.

Oliver stepped outside the station and stretched. He noticed a man in overalls and a girl about his niece's age talking to Frank Slater. If the witness to the fire had been killed, Frank would probably know who was behind it; but he sure as hell wasn't talking to Oliver about it, or anything else. His fellow detective had made it his business to make Oliver's life as unpleasant as possible. The men who had seemed interested in learning about fingerprinting lost interest when Frank was around, making Oliver feel like one of those substitute teachers he had tormented when he was a kid.

Oliver stood on the sidewalk and lit a cigarette while he listened to the conversation. The farmer's son, Michael, hadn't been seen since the night of Pearl Harbor. The farmer had called neighbors and relatives, had gone to the houses of Michael's friends, to the cannery where he worked, to the church. No one had seen Michael since he had left his best friend's house.

"Wait," Frank said. "He'll turn up." He took the man aside. "He's probably at a bar or getting laid."

"Getting laid where?" the girl asked.

Frank turned an unattractive color, and the farmer pressed his lips together.

The girl's hands circled her dad's arm and she pulled him toward a truck. The farmer bent toward her and smoothed back her hair, said something to her that Oliver couldn't hear. He looked at his watch and realized he was going to be late. The judge had asked him to dinner—probably wanted a progress report. Again.

Oliver had taken two steps onto his father's porch when Harley woofed. A shape flew out of the dark and leaped onto Oliver's back. Harley spun around, biting at the shoes of the giggling assailant.

"Zoe, I could have hurt you!"

"I got you that time, Uncle Oliver."

"Oh yeah?" He picked up the slender girl and threw her over his shoulder. "Potatoes for sale. Ten cents a peck." He carried her into the dining room, where the housekeeper was setting the table. "Hey, Mrs. Hermit, need some potatoes? They're kind of lumpy."

"No thanks, mister. If they're rotten, you can just dump them out back in the compost heap."

Zoe screamed her protests while Oliver lugged her to the back door. She was almost twelve. He realized it wouldn't be long before she outgrew the game she loved to play with him. Her brother, Theo, ignored them and went to the table. He had never liked the potato game.

After dinner, Oliver followed his father into the study.

The judge looked pleased with himself. "The witness is back."

"How do you know?"

"A friend saw him on Saturday, convinced him the only way to be safe was to tell someone what he knows. He was supposed to come here Sunday night, but with the attack on Pearl Harbor, he probably couldn't make it." The judge reached into a drawer and pulled out a slip of paper. "Someone needs to go see him."

"And who would that be?"

The judge shook his head. "This is serious, Oliver. Your levity is entirely inappropriate."

"Right."

"Here's where he's staying."

"How safe is he?"

The judge shrugged. "Reasonably. He was told to stay hidden. No one else should know where he is."

Oliver looked at the address. Might as well go, and hope to be home early enough to get some sleep. He drove toward Oakland, surprised by the number of newcomers who were already streaming into the Bay Area. When he had first come back, Richmond had been a sleepy little town, but the energy shifted overnight. People were galvanized, in motion. Men enlisted in the military, shipyards sprang up. The entire Pacific coast readied itself for an invasion, worried about the Japanese submarines that prowled up and down the western edge of the country, sinking a ship here, firing on a city there. They didn't do serious damage, but they kept everyone on edge. Immediately after the attack on Pearl Harbor, the Navy had stretched seven miles of metal net across the mouth of the Golden Gate to protect the region from an underwater invasion. The government had been preparing since the thirties for the war they feared would come; they just hadn't expected it to come the way it did. Now almost the entire coast, including Richmond, was a restricted military zone.

Oliver eased to a stop in front of the bungalow where the witness was supposed to be. A peeling picket fence surrounded the yard. Tufts of weedy grass dotted the hard-packed dirt like patches of stubble on a worn-out face. The gate to the yard stood open. Oliver stepped inside. When he brushed through the wild mint that edged the fence, he was reminded of summer afternoons reading with his mother in their garden.

He knocked on the door and waited. The place wasn't big enough to miss hearing someone at the door. He looked through the window and made out an easy chair and a table. Stubbed-out cigarette butts overflowed from an ashtray next to a crumpled Lucky Strike pack. It looked like the man had a serious habit. He'd probably gone to find more smokes.

Oliver walked around the house. The back door was open. Oliver knocked on the jamb and called out, but no one answered. He whistled for Harley, who left the post he was smelling and came to heel. Oliver drew his gun and pushed open the door, holding Harley at the threshold while the dog scanned the room. Then Oliver released him and followed him inside. Harley streaked out of sight, then barked once. When Oliver found him, the dog was sitting by a pool of blood.

Chapter 6

Oliver sat in the Café Avellino, staring at the newspaper. The night before, he had called the Oakland police to report what he had found in the empty house. Eventually two patrolmen showed up and took his report, which would probably gather dust until the corners curled. The cops said there wasn't much to go on, but if a body showed up, they'd let him know.

Harley nudged his knee and looked at the front door. Ah. Zoe's face was pressed against the window. Oliver watched his niece take a deep breath, as if she were steadying herself the way she did before letting an arrow fly toward a target; then she pushed open the door, followed by the girl who had been at the precinct looking for her brother.

From head to toe, Zoe's friend was a mess. Her black hair looked like it had been combed with an eggbeater, one edge of her cardigan hung lower than the other, and her scabbed knees showed under her uniform jumper. Probably last year's uniform, or maybe the year before. One sock had slipped down in the space between her heel and the back of her shoe. No caring mother would have let her out of the house like that. Then the girl looked at Oliver, and he forgot her lack of grooming. He had the feeling there was no mother.

"Uncle Oliver, we need you to help us find Mia's brother, Michael."

"He went missing the night of Pearl Harbor. Almost four days ago." Mia's voice threatened to break.

Oliver stood up and pulled out two chairs, but before he could say anything, Harley poked his head out from under the table. Mia smiled and dropped to the floor to scratch his chest.

"You are so beautiful."

Zoe gave Oliver a hug and whispered, "My dad can't know we're here."

Oliver nodded.

"Sit down. Let's get you girls some breakfast."

When Mia said no, Oliver gestured to the chairs.

"If you want me to listen to you, you'll have to eat with me. Come on."

Oliver signaled to the waitress, but before she could respond, a woman dressed in black came out from behind the counter. Mrs. Forgione, the café's owner.

She asked what the girls would like, then returned with hot chocolate and pastry and listened as they told their story. Oliver asked the usual questions: girlfriends, drinking, had Michael gone missing before, did he owe anyone money, did he have enemies? Mia answered him but occasionally closed her eyes, as if reminding herself to be polite.

"We think the government has him, Mr. Wright."

"Why do you think that? Isn't he a citizen?"

"We all are. Even my dad. But I don't think it matters."

"Uncle Oliver, our music teacher hasn't been to school since we went back after Pearl Harbor. He hated Mussolini. Used to make fun of him and Hitler. Maybe they took him, too."

Mia nodded. "And maybe they took Michael by mistake."

"I want to help you, but I don't know what I can do that you haven't already done, Mia."

Mrs. Forgione brought more coffee for Oliver and sat down.

"I'm sorry about your brother." She patted Mia's hand. "Maybe my nephew can help you, Oliver."

Oliver hadn't said yes, and now he had an assistant. He gave Mrs. Forgione a look.

"I know Michael from church." She smiled at Mia, then gave Oliver a look of her own. "The girls are right. Michael would never leave without telling his family."

"All right. I'll do what I can. Will you find out when I can meet Harry?"

"I'll call him now." Mrs. Forgione disappeared into a back room.

"Harry who?" Zoe sat straight up.

"Harry Buonarotti." Oliver drained his coffee cup. "He's the district attorney, Zoe. Your dad works for him."

The girls stared at each other.

Of course. They were worried about his brother, Peter, finding out.

"Mrs. Forgione and I won't say anything about your being here. Okay?"

They nodded, but didn't seem too sure.

"Honest. It won't get back to your dad, Zoe."

Mrs. Forgione hustled back.

"Harry said he can meet you tomorrow morning. If you can do that, I can tell Mia's father when he comes today to deliver the produce." She looked at the clock. "He should be here soon."

Oliver nodded and pushed back his chair.

"Come on. Harley and I'll drive you truants to school. I'll tell the teacher you're late because of official business, and if she asks you what business, tell her you aren't allowed to talk about it." Maybe he'd ask the school principal about the music teacher, too.

"You better not stay too long at school, or Sister Bernadette will get the truth out of you." When Mia teased him, her face lit up. "They should send her to interrogate German spies."

"I'm tougher than I look." Oliver took her hand. "Stop worrying. Harry and I will find your brother."

Chapter 7

God help him. He'd done it again. Made a promise he might not be able to keep, although he probably had a better chance of keeping this promise than the one his father had wormed out of him. Oliver cut his wheels and pulled on the parking brake. Yawned. Curtains twitched in windows, then women popped out of their front doors like a flock of cuckoos striking the hour and called reluctant children into the houses, urging them with waving arms. People noticed things on this street. Whether they were willing to talk to him was another story.

As he walked down the block to the Aiellos', Oliver caught glimpses of long, narrow back gardens, old fruit trees and gnarled grapevines, a tire swing hanging from an oak tree.

He signaled Harley to stay and took the Aiellos' concrete stairs two at a time. Dried leaves littered the porch. He knocked.

Someone drew a scant inch of curtain aside and peeked through the window. Oliver showed his badge. The curtain fell, and he heard voices inside the house. The latch rubbed as it was turned, and a man hunched inside a handmade sweater looked at him through the barely open door. Oliver looked down at strands of gray hair over a pink scalp.

"Is it about Alfred?" The man glanced up without raising his head. "No. It would be the Army, not the police." He seemed to scold himself.

"I'm sorry if I alarmed you. I'm trying to find Michael Fiori."

The man opened the door and invited Oliver in.

"My wife is resting. Would you like some coffee?"

"No, thank you."

A votive candle burned before a photograph of a smiling man in uniform with his arm around a woman in a print dress. Probably taken when he was home on leave. Oliver nodded toward the photograph.

"Have you heard anything?"

"Nothing official, but the longer it is . . ." He waved a hand in the air. "My wife . . . I don't know." He gestured for Oliver to sit down. "Alfred's our youngest. My wife's friends come, bring food, they pray. She doesn't eat. Can't sleep. I don't know what to do. I wait. Try to ignore the claws tearing at my stomach."

Mr. Aiello twisted his head and looked up at Oliver.

"You know what I'm talking about. That's why you asked." His lips tightened. "Most people look away, pretend we're not there. They don't know what to say. But Michael came as soon as he heard. He and Alfred went to school together. Now Michael's missing, too."

"Did he say anything when he left? Where he was going?"

"We weren't paying that much attention to him—you understand. He said he was going home. I wish I could help his family. It's awful not knowing."

Oliver left the Aiellos' and went door to door. No one had seen anything the night Michael disappeared. The Italians shook their heads, said no, and pushed the door closed, if they opened it at all. They were afraid. Italy had declared war on the United States, and they didn't know yet what that would mean. Ireland remained neutral, exhausted from the first war and unwilling to send men to die helping England in another war with Germany, but the Irish families weren't much help, either. No one knew anything. The night of December 7, everyone had been sitting in the dark by the radio, desperate for information.

"Hey, mister."

Oliver looked behind him.

"Up here."

He scanned second-story windows, then saw movement in an oak tree. Two boys peered down at him from a tree house partially hidden in the leaves. Had to be brothers—they were almost twins, with identical, stick-straight brown hair and freckles.

"Are you looking for the man in the house up the hill?"

"Why? Do you know something about him?"

"What's your dog's name?"

"He's Harley. I'm Oliver."

"I'm Tim. He's Jimmy."

"Jim," the other boy corrected him.

The boys seemed to confer without words and came to a decision.

"If we tell you what we saw, will you promise not to tell our mother?"

"I promise, but why don't you want me to tell her?"

"We were supposed to be in bed, but we couldn't sleep and we couldn't turn on any lights, so we snuck out the window to look for planes."

"Didn't your mother notice you were gone?"

"There are eight of us."

"Got it." Oliver looked down at his shoes to hide his smile. "What did you see?"

"We think two men took him away that night. In a black car."

"Do you know who they were?"

"We think they were G-men."

Oliver tried to get a line of sight to the street in front of the solitary house.

"How could you see what happened?"

"We were up here with our brother's binoculars when the car drove up. We snuck up the hill behind the bushes so we could see if it was spies."

"What did you see?"

"The men went to the door, then they took the old man right off the porch. He didn't even have a coat. They were pulling him down the steps when Jimmy made a noise—"

"Did not."

"Then how did they know where we were?"

"You made the noise."

"Did not."

"Did too!"

"Boys, what happened next?"

"We ran through the backyards to our friend's house and hid there until we thought the car was gone."

"Why did you run?"

"One of the men looked right at us and pulled back his coat. He had a gun."

Chapter 8

The next morning, Oliver stood in the heart of the Café Avellino, looking at lengths of salami and rounds of wax-covered cheese that hung above an enamel counter. He inhaled the smells that surrounded him. Garlic and onions, something roasting. And coffee. Cups of coffee and a plate of cookies sat on a long pine table.

Harry rose and extended his hand to Oliver. He was dark—dark hair, dark eyes, and now dark circles behind his wire-rimmed glasses. Bennie Fiori looked worried-thin, his frame burdened by the weight of the black jacket he wore over a collarless white shirt. His black hair was slicked straight back, the hairs still separated into furrows by the teeth of his comb. He stopped folding and refolding a napkin long enough to grasp Oliver's hand.

"Thank you both for helping us. We've been beside ourselves worrying about Michael."

"Your daughter is very persuasive."

Bennie shook his head, as if wishing things could have been different. "She's had to grow up too fast."

"I found out something when I canvassed the Aiello neighborhood." Oliver filled them in on his conversation with the boys. "Michael could have shown up after the boys left and tried to intervene. The timing fits with when he left the Aiellos' house."

"My son would try to help Mr. Posto, who is my father's friend. But why would men be taking him somewhere? Maybe he was ill."

"I'm afraid that's not what it sounded like to me."

"What does it have to do with Michael? Why wouldn't he call someone, let us know where he is?"

Harry held up a hand as if to slow Bennie down. "The names

of the men being picked up aren't being released, and they're not permitted to communicate with anyone."

"Not even a lawyer?" Oliver found that hard to believe.

"Not even a lawyer." Harry closed his eyes and lowered his head. When he looked at them again, Oliver saw anger and something he couldn't quite identify in the prosecutor's eyes. Shame?

"What we're able to figure out from the few people released is that the detainees are presumed guilty. It's up to them to prove they're innocent—without knowing what they're charged with." Harry's voice was strained.

"Why would they arrest Mr. Posto?" Bennie seemed bewildered.

"Him, specifically, I don't know. A few years ago, the government compiled a list of people thought to be dangerous: Italians, Germans, Japanese, refugees. They started rounding them up the day we were attacked."

"How could anyone think my son was dangerous?"

"It doesn't take much to make the list. Rumor, innuendo, knowing fascist sympathizers. They're going after anyone remotely connected to Italian institutions: the consulate, the Italian newspaper or radio stations. Veterans of the Italian army or navy. All those people are suspect. Even if they're citizens. Even if they're antifascists."

"My son isn't any of those things. He has no politics."

"We don't know that he was picked up, but the timing fits with when he left the Aiellos'. Maybe he was in the wrong place at the wrong time." Oliver thought about chance, how a fraction of a second could change your life.

"At least now we have a starting place to look for him," Harry tried to reassure Bennie.

"A starting place?" Bennie's palms flattened on the table. "What does that mean?"

"They take the detainees to the old Salvation Army building in the city. From there, they go to Immigration or to Fort McDowell on Angel Island."

"I'm going to find him!" Bennie sprang from his chair.

"It won't help if you stir things up." Harry stood and put a hand on the farmer's shoulder. "Please leave it to me and some people I'm working with. If Michael was picked up, finding him is going to be about calling in favors and relying on people who believe we're acting like the countries we're fighting. I have to leave now, get things started. Don't worry. I'll leave messages with Mrs. Forgione to keep you informed." He handed Bennie a card. "You can call me at home."

Bennie rubbed his thumb across the raised lettering and nodded—a reluctant agreement.

"I'll go tell Mia what we know." He shook hands with the men.

Mrs. Forgione picked up a baking pan she had wrapped in a dish towel and followed Bennie to his truck.

When they heard the truck start, Harry turned to Oliver—who knew what Harry was going to say.

"You didn't tell him everything, did you?"

"No. He doesn't need more to worry about."

"What is it, Harry?"

"The detainees are being interrogated none too gently. Those thugs think because a man's on the list he must be guilty of something, even if he's on it because someone lied about him."

Mrs. Forgione came back without the pan. She pressed the palms of her hands together and moved them up and down at the wrist. "I can't believe this is happening. I know Mr. Posto. His poor wife died while he was in prison in Italy for speaking out against the fascists. He barely escaped to come to America. Now this. I can't imagine what he must be going through."

"I'll look for him while I'm looking for Michael."

"Harry?" Oliver hated to burden him further. "I talked to the principal at the girls' school. Their music teacher hasn't been seen since that night."

Harry swore under his breath in Italian, then smiled an apology to his aunt. Hard to mistake swearing for anything else. In any language.

"The government could have targeted him because he taught music at the Italian culture schools until the fascists took them over. He left when they wanted him to teach "*La Giovanezza*," the fascist anthem. Took the job over here."

Oliver suspected Harry had helped the man get the new job, had been quietly helping Italians caught up in the politics of war. He began to wonder how much the Italian community would be affected by the anger and thirst for vengeance that Americans felt toward Japan and the other Axis nations. Whether anyone would be there to save them.

Chapter 9

Almost two weeks had passed since Bennie Fiori had talked with Oliver and Harry at the café. Now he stood with the detective inside the morgue, looking at Doc Pritchard. Not a good place to be on Christmas Eve.

"Mr. Fiori, we don't know if the man we found is your son, but he's the same size and we think about the same age. Are you up to looking at him?"

Bennie frowned. "You're not sure it's him?"

"The body was found in a shallow grave. The face is damaged. I'm sorry."

Bennie sighed, and nodded that he was ready. Dr. Pritchard pulled back the sheet.

The farmer brushed back the hair from the boy's face, then turned away.

"I'm so sorry." Oliver touched his shoulder.

Bennie looked at Oliver, puzzled, then seemed to realized what the men thought. "No, no. It's not Michael."

"How do you know?"

"Do you know how many times I've watched my son sleep, watched him smile at his sister, watched him praying at Mass?" Bennie asked. "Even battered, the face is the wrong shape, the eyes not deep enough, the mouth not wide enough." He took a breath. "Okay. The easy answer is, there is no scar at his hairline from the time he ran into a tree branch. He had a scar here." Bennie pointed. "It's not Michael. But he reminds me of someone."

"We have no reports of a missing person fitting this description."

Bennie looked at Oliver. "One of my customers asked me to keep an eye out for her son. She thought something might have happened to him. I didn't know him well enough to identify him."

"Why didn't she report him to the police?"

"He was hiding. If he was okay, she didn't want anyone looking for him."

"Why was he hiding? What did he do?"

"She didn't tell me, but I think it had something to do with those children who were killed in the fire."

"Let's go see her, Bennie."

They arrived at the woman's house too quickly. Oliver braced himself, but when Bennie's customer saw them at the door, she closed her eyes and crossed herself as if she already knew why they were there.

They had tried to prepare her for what she was about to see at the morgue. Bennie caught her in his arms as she turned away from the gurney. When she had recovered, she said soon after the fire that killed those children, some men had beaten her son and told him he'd better get out of town if he knew what was good for him. She didn't know who the men were. Her son had said it was safer for her not to know. But then he'd decided to come back to see if he could make things right without having to go to the police.

It was late afternoon before Oliver tapped on the door to his father's chambers. He didn't know how to tell him. The judge waved him to a chair in front of his desk.

"What is it, Oliver? What's happened?"

"Judge, I'm afraid the witness is dead."

The color drained from the judge's face. Oliver opened the bottom drawer of his father's desk. Sure enough, there was a bottle and two glasses. He set a drink on the blotter.

"Are you sure?"

Oliver nodded and tried to reassure him. "Those hate groups will disband or go underground now, Judge. They'll turn their hatred and anger into fighting the Japanese. They'll enlist, disappear."

"Not policemen. They'll be exempt from the draft, and the men I suspect won't be hurrying to join up and get themselves killed. They'll stay here and try to turn the war to their own profit."

"You need to give this up. There's nothing you can do now to find out who set the fire. I'm sorry."

"But what about your brother?"

"As much as I hate to say this, the death of the witness will be a good thing for him. If Peter had any other proof, he would have acted by now. This should end Peter's being seen as a threat." Oliver leaned over the desk and touched his father's arm. "I know how much this means to you, so I'll stay until I decide whether to reenlist."

1942

Chapter 10

Cora Slater waved hello to Mrs. Forgione through the café window and smoothed back a few flyaway strands into the twist Frank liked. The second day of January felt more like April, so she had decided to walk to the station and bring him the wallet he had forgotten that morning. It was her fault; she shouldn't have brought up wanting to stay in Pt. Richmond. Maybe if they went for lunch she could smooth things over.

Frank kept asking, *why not leave?* Cora kept asking why he wanted to leave so badly. He had a good job; they lived in a wonderful house, were happy. People said how much he had changed since they'd met. She wished they would stop saying it; what could she say back? She didn't want him to be unhappy, but she couldn't leave, and she couldn't explain what held her there. It would be different if he wanted to move to Berkeley or Oakland, but Colorado?

She walked into the police station, where Harmon greeted her. "Hi, Mrs. Slater. Do you want Frank? Well, I guess you do—why else would you be here?" His ears turned red, and the files he carried slid to the floor.

Cora started to bend down to help pick them up, and Frank caught her by the arm. He shook his head at her. Everything irritated him these days.

"You forgot your wallet, Frank. It's such a beautiful day for a walk, I thought I'd bring it by."

"Thanks. I'm busy right now, but I'll walk you to the corner." Frank held her elbow and steered her toward the door.

"How about lunch? We can talk. Can you leave later?"

"Sure. The Hotel Mac at one." He whispered in her ear. "Maybe we should get a room. Forget lunch."

Cora looked up at him from the corner of her eyes, flirting. Lifted an eyebrow. Frank started to laugh.

"Frank, can I see you for a minute? Hi, Mrs. Slater." One of the firemen had stepped out of the fire station.

Frank looked at Cora.

"Go ahead. I need to stop at the variety store." She kissed him on the cheek. "I'll see you at one."

The firehouse doorway sheltered Frank as he listened to the fireman's tale of woe, and watched Cora walk away. He wasn't kidding about the hotel room. Imagine what the Point would think then. It would be all over town before they got home.

Getting shot was the best thing that had ever happened to him. When he had seen Cora through the haze of his concussion, he'd thought he was seeing a ghost. Or an angel. An angel with skin you could almost see through and pale-blue eyes. Then she had touched him. Cora Lundgren, back in Richmond after all those years. He had drifted in and out of consciousness, wondering what he might have said in his delirium. She'd stayed with him long past her shift, reading to him, putting cold compresses on his forehead. He had responded to her gentleness with a tenderness that surprised him.

"Cora."

Frank's head snapped around when he heard Oliver Wright say his wife's name. Cora turned sideways to greet him. She said something to him, and her hand went to the locket she always wore, a family keepsake. Why did Wright look puzzled? Cora glanced back at Frank, then dropped her hand and turned away. Wright looked after her until she disappeared around the corner. Then he turned and seemed startled to find Frank watching him.

"Frank?" The fireman touched his arm.

Frank shook him off and walked away. He had to walk away. *Is that why she wants to stay in Richmond? Because Wright has come back? Did she bring me my wallet hoping she would see him?* He thought he had settled the score with Mr. Golden Boy, full of his family connections and big-shot education, but nothing seemed to faze him. *He's ruining everything. Again.*

Frank had thought he could handle it, and maybe he could have, if he hadn't just seen them together. For a moment, Frank remembered that Cora still could have married Wright all those years ago, but she hadn't. Maybe she regretted that now.

He didn't think he could stomach having lunch with her while she pined for another man. Let her fucking sit there.

Cora sat in the Hotel Mac, surrounded by the sounds of people talking and enjoying their lunches. She didn't look at the plates of food that passed her; just smelling them was enough to make her mouth water. She sipped at her coffee, wishing she could start without Frank.

The waiter asked if he could bring her something while she waited. No, thank you. She felt the glances of other diners, and her face began to burn. She took a pen and notebook from her handbag and played at making a list. Soon the restaurant grew quiet as it emptied.

Cora's heart sank when she admitted to herself that Frank wasn't coming. Because of Oliver. No matter how much she tried, she could not convince Frank that Oliver meant nothing to her now. She hadn't even known Frank when she'd dated Oliver. So much had happened since then. So much had changed.

She left money on the table for her coffee and gathered her packages. She hesitated in the doorway and hugged herself against the chill. The morning's golden sun was now a cold gray glow behind the fog. She braced herself and stepped into the street, started the long walk home.

That was strange. Oliver stared out the window of the Café Avellino, barely aware of Harley's head on his lap, reminding Oliver he was hungry even if Oliver wasn't. Running into Cora had been less awkward than Oliver had thought it would be, until she had touched the locket she wore. He remembered when he had given it to her years ago, what it had meant.

Why was she still wearing his grandmother's locket?

Chapter 11

Valentine's Day had come and gone, and Michael Fiori still wasn't home. The Army had shipped him to Montana by way of Texas and Tennessee. It shuttled the detainees all over the blasted country as if it had nothing better to do. Oliver's niece had asked him what was taking so long. Oliver leaned back in his desk chair and wondered that himself. Harry had complained that every time he finally found out where Michael was, Michael had just left.

Oliver watched the men leave the station house. Tonight he had volunteered to man the house while the others went to a retirement party for a worn-out beat cop who had spent the last thirty years on the pavement. Oliver had thought he would spend his thirty years in Seattle at his first precinct, a job he missed more and more each day. He closed his eyes, then opened them and shook his head, as if that would dislodge the memory of Seattle that still tortured him after six months of sleepless nights.

He and his longtime partner had been working a crime scene Oliver was not even supposed to be at. He had cleared his cases so he could spend some time with his family at Lake Washington, and then the captain had called. They had what appeared to be a murder, a rare opportunity to show the Seattle homicide department the new methods for processing a scene that Oliver had recently learned. He would be done by the afternoon and could join his family later at the lake.

They worked in their shirtsleeves, ties loosened, talking over the drone of a fan that just moved the heat around. A middle-aged woman in a stained housecoat lay on the floor, part of her face stuck to a whiskey bottle that left raspberry smudges on the slanted linoleum. The husband sniveled in the kitchen, crying over the spilled

Four Roses, over killing his wife, getting caught, who knew why? Maybe he loved her and was sorry. Maybe he was just a maudlin drunk.

Someone cleared his throat. The precinct captain stood in the doorway, holding his cap. He looked at Oliver, who'd delivered bad news often enough himself to see what was coming. Coming toward him. His partner shut up the drunk with a look.

"What is it?" Oliver took a step toward the door.

"Charley's been hurt. Let me drive you to the hospital."

"How bad is it? What happened? Where's Elizabeth?"

The captain shook his head. "I'm sorry."

The words knocked the breath out of Oliver. Everything, everyone in the room disappeared. Except the man in front of him.

"How?"

"They were canoeing in the lake. A powerboat lost control and hit them. It didn't stop. Elizabeth went under. Charley kept diving, looking for her. When the harbor patrol got there, Charley was exhausted, but he dove again. By the time a diver got him out, he was unconscious."

"He would never leave his mother." Oliver felt pain swelling in his chest, filling it, threatening to break him open. Oliver should have been with them. He didn't have to ask the next question.

"They're still searching for her."

They searched while Oliver sat beside his son's bed and willed him to wake up. He told Elizabeth he would never forgive himself for not being there and asked her to send Charley back if that's where he was, still not able to leave her.

The phone rang, pulling Oliver back to the present, to Pt. Richmond. He looked around at the empty desks. Looked like this call was his.

Chapter 12

Night after night, Vincent Marino sat at his kitchen table with a cup of black coffee and watched the trains snake in and out of the Santa Fe railroad yard. Sometimes he fell asleep in the chair, lulled by the movement of the brakemen who uncoupled the cars, or the switchmen who leaned on the tall rods that moved the track junctions. He knew the language of the signals that commanded the locomotives to speed up or slow down. He knew the red arc and splash of sparks when a watchman threw down a cigarette as a train rolled into the yard. He knew where the trains had been and where they were going. Which settled on sidings and which slid through the lines of engineless boxcars straight out to Ferry Point.

Sometimes the phone rang, calling him out to unlock a house for a customer who had lost his keys, or to fit a new lock on a burgled store. When he returned home, he would walk down the hall to his kitchen, put the dollar bills in the tobacco can he kept in the icebox, and light the flame under the metal percolator to reheat the coffee.

Tonight he stood in the shadow of a water tower and looked at his watch. Almost midnight, February 17, 1942. The deadline. He wished Alfeo had done what he had asked. He supposed he couldn't blame him. He wondered if he would have done it for Alfeo. It didn't matter now.

The rain drenched his black suit and the white shirt that chafed at his neck. He ran a finger inside the collar, then touched the breast pocket that sheltered the photo of his mother. He heard the chuffing when the train entered the yard, then the *whup-whup-whup* as it passed the line of still boxcars that hid the approaching engine from his view. He stepped out from behind the water tower, ignored the shouts of a switchman crossing the yard, and lifted his polished shoe over the glistening steel track, careful not to stumble on the uneven rail bed. His right hand had just touched his right shoulder, on the word *Ghost*, when he lifted his head and stared into the window of the cab, into the stricken face of the engineer.

The rain fell, invisible in the darkness until it splattered on the windshield, reminding Oliver of nights in Seattle when he and his partner had ridden together, drinking coffee and talking about nothing much. Maybe if he and Charley hadn't decided to bring Elizabeth home to the family plot, he would still be in Seattle. Only good thing about being in Pt. Richmond was that he was closer to Charley, who went to Stanford, as planned, while Oliver marked time, trying to find a connection that maybe didn't exist.

The tires hissed along the wet street, and the hooded beams glowed on the pavement in front of him, leaving alleys and doorways draped in darkness. He cranked down his window, hoping the chill fog would keep him awake while he drove to what sounded like his second suicide of the night.

He was still trying to recover from what he had just left at the other end of Richmond. A man had jumped, fallen, or been pushed from the roof of an apartment building. It looked like a suicide, but he wouldn't be certain until they had translated the note he had found in the poor guy's pocket. Looked like Italian, that old-fashioned script.

In some ways, he envied the jumper the peace he had found, the ending of pain. For Oliver, the time without pain was in the past, on the other side of an abyss that grew wider each day. His whole working life had been defined by death, but Elizabeth's was the only one to bleach the color from the sky, mute the song of the birds.

Now two people were dead. Both suicides? Did they give any thought to the people left behind, the ones who would have to move through days of grief with no choice but to go on?

A gust of wind sent sparks flying from his cigarette. When he looked down and tried to slap out the embers before they ruined another pair of trousers, the car swerved onto the curb and almost clipped a phone booth. A head appeared in the rearview mirror. Reproachful.

"Sorry. Next time you drive, and I'll curl up in back."

Harley yawned and stuck his nose out Oliver's window. Oliver felt the breeze from the dog's tail and leaned his head against the shepherd's neck. He needed to sleep, but people wouldn't stop dying tonight.

The car bounced over the steel lines that crossed and recrossed the asphalt and stopped outside a small building where a rectangle of light promised warmth and shelter. Harley jumped over the seat and followed Oliver into the rain, threw that black nose into the air, and began casting for something.

A man squatted by a bundle along the railroad tracks. From the back, he looked like a frog about to leap into the pool of the night. He rose and turned toward Oliver. Doc Pritchard. Not long out of training, and not really a coroner, just the poor guy on call. He wiped his round face with delicate fingers.

"Detective Wright. Not a fit night for man or beast, but your dog doesn't seem to mind."

Oliver glanced behind him to see Harley nosing around a water tower.

"What do we have?"

"Suicide."

"You sound pretty sure."

"A switchman saw him walk onto the tracks right in front of the train. Called out to him, but he didn't stop."

"Any chance of an ID?"

"The train threw him off to the side, only ran over his legs."

Oliver lifted his eyebrows at the *only*.

"Yes. Well." Pritchard shook his head. "The impact killed him. His face is bruised but recognizable. The switchman said he thought the poor soul lived in the house next to the yard. He and the engineer are in the office."

"I'll talk to them, see if we can get into the house. Wonder if anyone else lives there, knows why he did it."

"Oh, I found this in his shirt pocket."

Oliver looked at a creased photo of a small woman standing in front of a church, holding a baby in her arms. She looked foreign. Maybe Italian.

Chapter 13

Oliver had fallen asleep while he waited for the Café Avellino to open. He got out of the car and stretched. He rubbed his face and let Harley out for a rather prolonged leg lift on the corner of the building. He could use one of those himself. He watched the shepherd sniffing a lamppost. They'd been together three years now. Oliver still remembered the weight of him in his arms when Oliver had found him bloody and unconscious next to a body. He had searched for a pulse through the soft puppy fur and felt a heartbeat.

"The dog's alive." He looked at the patrol officer.

"Oh yeah?"

"Didn't you even check? What the hell's the matter with you? How about the woman? Did you bother to check if *she* had a pulse?"

Oliver's partner knelt down by the woman. Shook his head.

"What do you want to do?"

"Let's get him to a vet. He looks young, maybe five or six months old. Maybe he'll make it."

He held the dog while a patrol car rushed them to the closest vet. He felt a sense of loss when he handed him over and watched them carry him into surgery. He told Elizabeth about the dog, knowing if the family of the victim didn't want him, she would say they should take him. Charley would love a dog.

Oliver alerted nearby hospitals when the vet called to say he had removed a good-size chunk of flesh and some cloth threads from the dog's teeth. They arrested the woman's brother two days later. He might have gotten away with it, if he hadn't gone to the emergency room for a dog bite.

Charley visited the dog every day until he recovered, and started calling him Harley for reasons only a fifteen-year-old boy might understand. He thought it was hilarious for them to be Charley and Harley. Oliver remembered Elizabeth's surprise when the dog smiled at Charley, who smiled back and threw a ball across the grass.

God, he missed her. But he still had Charley. And Harley.

"Come on, boy. Let's get some breakfast."

When he walked into the café, the regulars were at the table by the fire where they had sat during the wake for Mrs. Forgione's husband. Oliver had been a little envious that Enrico had friends who honored him so zestfully at his death. Enrico's chair had sat empty, the shot glass in front of it full. "Remember, remember," the men had interrupted each other, laughing, talking, hands moving and circling, as if swirling memories up to their friend. Presumably up.

Oliver ordered frittatas for himself and Harley, then made his way to the men's room to wash away some of the gloom of the night. He would eat, then tell the men they had lost another friend.

Harry Buonarotti nodded to Oliver and told the other men not to worry, that Oliver was okay. He was the detective who had helped find Bennie Fiori's son, Michael. Harry looked back at the *Richmond Independent* and continued to translate it for the men who couldn't read English.

> *War makes possible enemies out of people whom we have considered friendly acquaintances for many years. Yet the dangers attendant on having people who would furnish information to the enemy in our midst is too great to allow a relaxation of alertness. Aliens loyal to Mussolini or Hitler are just as dangerous to us right now as the Japanese.*

The men didn't know what to say. The writer compared them to the hateful Japanese, questioned their loyalty.

Mrs. Forgione had refused to put up the government poster that called Italian an enemy language, but the men had stopped speaking the language of their birth in public. They were tongue-tied, their rolling *r*'s and beautiful vowels stuck in their throats. They couldn't find words, English or Italian, for the way the newspaper made them feel.

Harry was concerned because one of the men sitting with them could be arrested if he were caught here in the restricted zone. Like many Italians, Bruno had become an enemy alien overnight, even though he hated Mussolini. And now, because of that dictator, he had to move out of Richmond, where he had lived for forty years. The men who had to leave felt ashamed, lost, as if they had done something wrong that they couldn't make right. For who knew how long, there would be no more mornings at the café. Bruno would go from sitting at the head of his dining room table to being a lodger in his sister's home in Oakland. Sitting every day at her husband's table. Having to be in the house before eight p.m., like a child.

Bennie Fiori pushed through the door of the café with a man who had to be his brother, the sardine fisherman from Monterey. He nodded at Oliver, then joined Harry at the table by the fire.

Bennie introduced his brother. "Jack is going to be staying with me for a while."

Jack looked exhausted. Worse, as if his soul were exhausted.

"How are things in Monterey? What is happening along the coast? With the fishing fleet?" Bruno hadn't let Jack sit down before he had peppered him with questions. Jack looked at Bennie, as if asking what he should say.

"Tell them about last night. It might help." He shrugged. "It can't hurt."

Jack settled in his chair and drank the espresso the waitress had brought him. He nodded a few times, then leaned toward the men, who, in turn, leaned in toward him.

"Last night, we brought our boats to Treasure Island. It was like we were sailing inside a bottle of ink. We were running without lights through the black night, past the dark lighthouses, and then the ocean began to glow. We saw shapes flickering against the shimmering water. The curve of a bow, the reflection off a hull." He shuddered. "We looked like a ghostly funeral procession, sailing through the night from Monterey to San Francisco."

The ever-practical Bruno interrupted Jack's lyrical description of the voyage. "With the war, we need canned fish more than ever. Why did they take your boats?"

"Eh. The Navy knocked on our doors before we even knew if our sons and brothers had survived the attack on Pearl Harbor. They said they needed our boats to help defend the coast. Most of us volunteered to stay with the boats and work with the Navy, but the Navy said no. It didn't need us. Just our boats. What could we do?"

"The government didn't trust you. It took the boats because Italy had declared war on the US," Bruno whispered.

Jack nodded. "It broke my heart to see the schools of sardines glowing in the water. The sardine runs this year have been better than any of us ever could remember. It should have been a year for paying off debts, putting something away for leaner times. Instead the fishing is over and our boats are gone."

"What about your crews?"

"They don't know what will happen next. My friend Carmen insisted on going with me to deliver the boat to the Navy, even though Japanese subs had been seen off the coast. We didn't ask our crews to come. It should be enough to give up the boat you loved, your livelihood, the future of your sons; you shouldn't have to risk the life of your crew delivering her. But some men, like Carmen, showed up anyway."

"What will you do now?" Harry knew fishermen. They were lost on land.

"Without fishing and the canneries, there's nothing left for Italians in Monterey." Jack's smile reminded Harry of mothers watching their sons leave for war. The fisherman seemed to realize how defeated he sounded. He looked toward the window. When he looked back, it was as if he had put his regrets behind him. "I'm too old to join the Navy, so I said good-bye to the *Stella Maris* and came to see if I could learn to catch vegetables."

Bennie put his hand on Jack's shoulder. Harry thought the brothers carried the war's burdens with grace. But this was only the beginning.

Chapter 14

Bruno nudged Harry, interrupting his thoughts about the Fiori brothers, and made that gesture with his chin that meant *Take notice. What do you think?* A stranger was looking in the window of the café.

"Not FBI. I think they travel in pairs, like nuns." Harry tried to lighten the tension at the table. No one felt safe from the agents of the government. The men said only to each other that it was like living in a fascist state—so many people had disappeared in the night, lost their jobs, had to move.

The café's green-and-black-striped awning sheltered Jonah North from the rain. He debated whether to go in. The café looked very Italian. And he wasn't. Italian. But he did like the cosmopolitan feel of the place. If they had cappuccino in there, he'd gladly bear being treated like an outsider. As his boss always said, "What are they going to do? Kill you?"

It was like walking into a kaleidoscope. White-veined black marble on the floor, red marble on the smaller tables, white marble on the counter, and inlaid rugs of different marbles. On top of which sat chairs upholstered in large-flowered patterns.

A group of men looked up at him when they heard the bell on the door, then back at each other. One man nodded. Not an invitation, merely a greeting.

A lone man sat at a table, eating an omelet. He didn't look Italian either. English, probably, with straight blond hair and almost invisible eyebrows. He reminded Jonah of a photograph that had been taken out of the developer too soon. The man looked up, as if he felt Jonah's gaze. His eyes were deep blue, the color of gentians, and reminded Jonah of the deathly flowers of Lawrence's poem. He felt those eyes size him up and memorize him. A cop. He nodded at Jonah, then dropped a piece of bread on the floor. A long brown snout reached out for it. A dog? In a restaurant? None of Jonah's business.

Oliver scarfed down his breakfast, realized he was showing scarcely more manners than his dog. At least he was using his napkin. The stranger who came in looked eastern, in his pleated trousers and jacket with elbow patches. Gray-blue eyes; about five foot ten; medium forehead; ears long, close to the head; long, thin nose; full lips; cleft chin. Filed.

Harley lay under the table and held his tin plate with one paw just in case there were seconds. He licked it every now and then to let Oliver know he wouldn't be averse to a bit more.

Oliver picked up his coffee, walked over to the round table, and sat down when Harry gestured at a chair. Oliver just came out and told them. Their friend was dead.

A man with a handlebar mustache burst out in Italian.

Oliver thought it could be important, or the man could just be asking for another cup of coffee.

Harry calmed him, asked him a question. When the man answered him, the other men made the sign of the cross, muttered, and reassured him.

"What did he say, Harry?"

"Marino offered Alfeo fifty dollars to shoot him last night. Alfeo thought he was being dramatic. He didn't think he was serious."

"No one could have known." Bruno touched Alfeo's shoulder. "Marino couldn't stand the thought of leaving his home, his business. Starting over."

"When was the last time you saw him?"

Sadness clouded Harry's dark eyes. "Last night at the Galileo Club. That's why you're here, isn't it?"

"Harry, you should have been a detective." Oliver's dry tone teased a smile from Harry. "Yes. I found matchbooks from your club in his house. I thought he might be part of your bocce group."

"We didn't play bocce last night, but we were at the club. We held another meeting to explain why only Italians who are citizens can live or work here. We're trying to help people find new places to live, to find new jobs for the fishermen and the cannery workers."

Bruno interrupted. "It isn't easy. Most of them don't speak English, and no one wants an 'enemy alien' working for them or living in their neighborhood. People with Italian names are losing their jobs, even people born here."

"Why did your friend do it? The war won't last forever."

"Eh, no one tells us what will happen after they make us move, or if they're going to send us away, or when we'll come back. *If* we'll come back. They could deport everyone. I can understand why he did it." Bruno hurried to add, "Not that I would do it. I have a family. He didn't."

"Look what's happened to us fishermen. We can't go near the water. Who's a fisherman if he can't fish?" Jack threw a hand up in the air. "What are they going to do for fish, these people? Think the fish are going to jump up on the docks for them?"

"Joe DiMaggio's father can't even go to his son's restaurant because it's on the wharf." Bruno looked at the detective, as if expecting him to share his outrage.

"Oliver, it's hard for the older people to move to a strange place." Harry spoke in an even tone, despite the sadness in his eyes. "In Italy, until recently, each region was like a separate country with its own food, its own language, even different saints. People from one area didn't mix with those of another. Many had been enemies and fought wars over land. When they came here, they stayed in those groups, and now they're terrified of being separated."

"Not to mention most of them couldn't read or write Italian, let alone English. How could they pass the citizenship test? Besides, we—they—were too busy earning a living or raising families to study." Bruno forced a short laugh. "And we thought it didn't matter if we were citizens or not."

"We know better now." Harry's voice grew soft. "My neighbor had to move away. She lost one son at Pearl Harbor, has two more in the army, and now, when she most needs the help of her friends, her church, she is in exile, alone with her grief and her fear."

"No one will be able to give back to these women the hours and days they are spending alone and frightened." Bruno waved away the concern on his friends' faces. "Don't worry about me. I'll be back before you know it." He smiled and raised his cup to them.

"Bravo!" The men returned his salute.

"Listen up!" A voice killed the moment.

Oliver groaned. Frank Slater.

The men looked at Detective Slater. He had never been a friend to them, and now he had the government's blessing to harass them.

The detective pointed at a *sfogliatella*. Mrs. Forgione set the pastry and a cup of coffee on the counter for him, not waiting for him to ask. Or pay. He scanned the café, pausing for a moment when he saw Oliver among the men.

"Listen up." The detective seemed to relish the men's uneasiness. He read from a piece of paper: "'All enemy aliens living on the West Coast—that includes Point Richmond, for those of you not so clear on your geography—must surrender radio transmitters, short-wave radios, cameras, and firearms. Flashlights. All signaling devices and anything written in invisible ink.' Invisible ink—might have a few choice moments with that last one. Come in voluntarily, or we'll search your houses." He smiled. "And you won't like that. Fines and imprisonment if we catch you hiding something." He bit into the pastry. It muffled his next words. "And you won't like that either."

No one spoke. Lots of shrugs and looking at each other and their coffee cups.

Mrs. Forgione broke the silence. "Detective Slater, excuse me, please. I think I have a delivery in the kitchen." A man watched through the glass in the kitchen service door.

Slater banged his cup on the bar.

As he headed out the door, he turned.

"Don't forget to tell your Wop friends."

"I'm sorry." Oliver shook the hands of the men at the table. He wasn't sure what he was apologizing for. Slater? The restrictions? The men's dead friend? He signaled for Harley and walked down the hill toward the station house.

Chapter 15

Chief Cavanaugh's voice rolled out of the meeting room. Oliver slid into a seat near the door.

"Let me repeat. No more blackouts. It has been determined they interfere with the production of ships and planes. Apparently we cause more damage to ourselves driving into things than enemy bombers would cause." The chief looked up, and the men laughed on cue.

He looked back at his notes. "I need teams of men to make sure all the enemy aliens are leaving the restricted zone. The Army is handling the majority of the job, but you know your people: who might hide out, who might have items we need to confiscate. Sergeant Butler will handle that. Slater will take any homicide calls that come in. Wright, I understand you went to two suspicious death scenes last night."

"Yes, sir. I was covering the phones when the calls came in. They appear to be suicides. Italians who killed themselves because they were being forced to relocate."

"No big loss, then."

Oliver didn't know who said it. Could have been any one of them.

The chief smiled at the quip. "From now on, I want you on shipyard crime. Thefts, beatings, drunk-and-disorderlies." He raised a hand as Oliver started to protest. "You've done a great job imparting your *impressive* knowledge about working homicide scenes to the men. Let's give them a chance to see what they can do. Oh, Harmon can help you. I mean Officer Har*mon*, not Har*ley*."

Harmon's face turned red, either because he thought he was being called a dog or because he'd been put with the outsider. Didn't matter which to Oliver. There were times he would need backup, and

Harmon was so new he couldn't have been the Klan informer. Maybe he would be a more willing partner than some of the others, less distrustful of the outsider whom the police commissioner had forced on the chief, who didn't bother to hide his resentment.

"Wright, there was a beating at Moore Dry Dock last night. Get over there; get some statements. Butler has the details. Any other beatings are yours, too."

Oliver ignored the smug looks of some of the other cops and waited for Butler to free up. Barroom brawls and beatings would get Oliver out on the street, where he might be able to find a few informants. Someone might live to regret this.

When Oliver left the room, Slater pulled Cavanaugh aside. "You think that's a good idea? Putting Wright on the beatings?"

Cavanaugh looked down at the hand on his arm until Slater removed it.

"Not that it's any concern of yours, but the commissioner's watching what we do with him. Let me worry about it." He cut off Slater's protest. "You have work to do. Go do it."

Frank knew one of these days, he was going to go too far. He barely hid his contempt for the chief, especially after one of the members of the appointment committee had told Frank *he* should have gotten the chief's job but they had wanted to send him a message. Not even having been shot while saving a fellow officer was enough to overcome his family's reputation. The committee member had shaken his head and told Frank it was a shame, but Frank would always be tarnished by the reputation of his uncle and the rest of the Slater men. If the former chief hadn't been buddies with Frank's family, he wouldn't be on the force at all.

Frank had come to the conclusion that if he wanted a career with some prospects, he'd have to move to a place where no one knew his family. Then that damned Wright came back to Pt. Richmond and Frank had another reason to leave. Now he just had to convince Cora to leave with him. And get to the bottom of that business with the locket.

Chapter 16

Frank's run-in with the chief had left him moody and anxious all day. He got in his car and drove along the bay, ending up where his aimless drives almost always took him. He left the car and walked to the edge of the cliff. He looked down.

Moonlit waves scalloped the sand on Keller's beach, lapped at the rocks where they had found the girl's broken body. For a while, people had shied away from the rocks, had spread their blankets on the other end of the beach, but gradually they had forgotten, moved closer and closer until boys scrambled all over the rocks again, played games and looked for stranded crabs in the pools that had once been red with Phyllis Brennan's blood.

Twenty years later, and Frank still wanted to howl into the night. The silent cry rose from his stomach, pressed on his ribs, and filled the hollow in his throat. He clamped down with his teeth until the bones by his ears ached. He had cursed Phyllis, cursed her for loving him, for making him want to be loved, then cursed her for leaving him alone in the world.

She had been perfect. Well, almost perfect. She was always taking home stray cats and dogs and helping the vet with injured birds. She cried when a sparrow with a damaged throat lifted its head and tried to sing. She said it broke her heart, wondered if the bird knew its song had changed, if it was like her uncle who mourned the music he had lost in the war. She had heard him tell her mother he could never return to the orchestra. The lines on the music score looked like barbed wire, the notes . . . His music was gone.

Frank wanted to shout at her, *Forget about the bird and the dogs and your uncle. Look at me. I'm injured. Take care of me.*

Instead, he comforted her. She never knew he wanted to wring that bird's neck, shut up the invisible uncle who did nothing but hide in the sunroom listening to music. Let the wounded vulture and the stranded turtle and whatever the hell she found next fend for themselves. He wanted to be the one she loved.

And she did love him. Until she met Wright, who broke her heart.

Frank had thought that Cora had healed his wounds, but seeing her and Wright together had brought it all back. He lit a cigarette and looked at the rocks, soft as velvet in the moonlight.

Had Cora married him only because Wright had been long gone from Richmond when she had returned? Frank's last name had meant nothing to her when she nursed him, and by the time he'd left the hospital, she had fallen in love with him.

After they married, he found with her a world so different from the one he had grown up in, a new world where someone looked happy to see him at the end of the day. He avoided the bars where the Slater men hung out and hurried home to Cora. She could tease him into holding a skein of yarn on his hands while she wound it into a ball so she could knit a sweater. For him. He drew the line at going to the yarn store with her, but she brought home samples that she thought would bring out the hazel flecks in his eyes. They sat together and looked at photos of collegiate-looking guys in sweaters, until he finally couldn't take it anymore and just stabbed a finger at one. He loved being with her, loved the way she looked at him as if he could never be anything but good. Sometimes he wished it were true; other times he pretended that it was.

He looked at the slash of moonlight across the bay and wondered if the happiness of the past ten years had been real, or if she had been like him, both of them pretending to be something they weren't.

He wanted to trust her. He had tried for weeks to forget seeing her with Wright, to forget seeing the puzzled look on Wright's face when she touched the locket.

He felt himself drawn to the edge of the cliff. One more step, and it would be over, all of it, but maybe the locket meant nothing. He flicked away the cigarette. Its glowing tip traced Phyllis's path to the rocks below. Frank could almost hear her scream as he turned back to his car.

Death by misadventure. Meant it was an accident, no one was at fault. But he knew that wasn't true. Wright was responsible. Phyllis would be alive if it hadn't been for Wright.

The next morning, Frank took the locket out of Cora's jewelry box. He opened it—nothing inside. He slipped out of the house without waking her and drove into town. Time to see what he could find out, maybe put the whole thing to rest.

He walked down Washington Avenue into the old Dietrich's jewelry store.

"Hey, Shelley," he called to the clerk. "Could you take a look at this for me? I'm trying to trace it. Part of a case I'm working on."

"Let me see what you have, Frank." She took the locket and turned it over. "This isn't something we ever carried." She picked up a loupe. "I think this mark is from Tiffany. Probably a special order."

"Where would someone order something like that?"

"I'd start in the city. Or you could try Powell's in Oakland. Looks like something they might have ordered."

He waved his thanks as the door closed behind him.

There hadn't been much point in hurrying to the car; the traffic on San Pablo Avenue was barely crawling. Frank cursed the people who gawked and gathered and spilled off the sidewalk into the street. He double-parked in front of the jewelry store, ignoring the traffic snarl behind him. He pushed through Powell's door and flashed his badge.

"Good morning, Officer."

"Detective."

"Sorry, Detective. How may I help you?"

"I'm trying to trace this locket. I was told you might have ordered it." Frank dropped the locket on the counter.

The portly jeweler blinked, then spread a black-velvet cloth on the glass, placed the locket on it, and took out his loupe. "I recognize this." He looked at Frank, obviously puzzled. "What are the police doing with it?"

"Who bought it?"

The jeweler looked like he was about to ask another question, but he thought better of it.

"It was a special order from Tiffany. Let me get the book." He pulled a large cloth-bound ledger from under the counter, turned the pages one by one, paused, went forward, then back, running his finger down the lines of tiny handwriting. "Let's see. . . . It was around 1914, for the very first celebration of Mother's Day, I believe."

Frank lit a cigarette. Blew smoke in the jeweler's face. The man coughed, but he didn't hurry his methodical examination of the book. Mother's Day. So maybe it was a family heirloom after all, and had nothing to do with Wright. He felt relieved and a little ashamed at what he had done. He would tell Cora he had taken it to be cleaned as a surprise.

"Ah, yes. Here it is. I thought I recognized the border."

"The border?"

"It's a wreath formed by two interlocking initials: B.R."

"B.R.?"

"Yes. Judge Wright ordered it. Actually, he ordered two. This is the one with his mother-in-law's initials on it. The other had the initials of his wife."

Oliver's father. "When?"

"The order was placed in March 1914."

Frank wanted to smash his fist through the glass counter, or in the face of that smug jeweler, so pleased with himself and his prissy record keeping. He grabbed the locket and started to leave.

"Don't you want to see the special feature?"

"What special feature?"

"If I may . . ." The jeweler held out his palm. "Here." He opened the front. "There's a secret catch."

The jeweler slid a nail under the lip where there seemed to be no space and pressed. The shallow backing opened to reveal a faded blue flower. Frank grabbed the locket, and the brittle petals drifted onto the counter.

"Oh dear, maybe we can put it back together. A forget-me-not, I think." The jeweler pulled a set of tweezers from his vest pocket. "We must be careful. They look to be quite old."

Frank's hand closed over the locket as if he were going to crush it. A forget-me-not. And she hadn't.

"Don't bother."

Chapter 17

Mrs. Forgione dried her hands on her apron and stretched to kiss Harry's cheek.

He folded almost in half so she could reach it. She was worried about how he was taking the news he had gotten the day before, about the death of his friend who had thrown himself in front of a train.

"How are you doing, Harry?"

He waggled his hand, that noncommittal gesture.

"Come. I'll get you some coffee. Have you eaten yet?"

"Yes, Aunt Lucy."

"How about some nice poached eggs?" She had already started toward the kitchen.

"No, no, thank you. I'm here to meet with someone who is having trouble with the new regulations. I'll eat something with him."

"*Bene.* You can help me, too."

Harry tilted his head, asking a question. Lucy had been born here.

"Nothing like that. I just wonder if you can take something home to Paola. Save me carrying it up the hill."

She pointed at a box almost as big as she was. "Guess what it is."

Powdered sugar dusted the black sleeves of her dress.

"Hmm, let me see. Ravioli?"

"No." She pushed his arm.

"Veal cutlets?"

"Harry, a box this big of veal cutlets, I'd have to cook a whole calf. Maybe two."

"I give up."

"*Wans!*" She had gotten up at four, mixed the stiff dough, rolled it out into thin sheets, sliced it, twisted it, fried it, then sprinkled the crunchy cookies with powdered sugar.

"You probably worked all morning on these."

"It was nothing." Lucy poured coffee for them both, took out a platter of *wans*. "What's bothering you, Harry?"

"Paola." He waved a hand. "No, no. Nothing serious. I think she's worried about the way Dom is treating her sister. But she won't complain to me about Isabella and that buffoon she married. I think she's afraid I'll say something to him. Only make things worse."

Lucy shook her head.

"What, Aunt Lucy?"

"I don't like to speak ill of anyone, but I don't like Dom either. I wish he hadn't wormed his way into our family."

"I didn't say I didn't like him."

She smiled. "So *buffoon* is a term of endearment now?"

"Okay. You got me." He took a *wan*, dropping powdered sugar on the kitchen worktable. "Why don't you like him?"

"It's a little bit not fair."

"Go on."

"Our families came from the same town in Italy. Your great-grandfather Vanni wanted his daughter Tomasina to find a good man to marry."

"Grandpa Stefano."

"Eventually. But he had a rival—Dom's grandfather Enzo. A handsome man. He owned a lot of land and sheep, and he charmed your grandmother, but there was something about him Vanni didn't like. He couldn't put his finger on it, so he decided to learn more about him. One morning, before first light, he climbed a hill that overlooked Enzo's farm and sat on the cold ground, watching the scene below him emerge as the day arrived. He climbed that hill morning after morning for six days. He also had your great-uncles, or great-grand-uncles, *come se dice*, poking around and asking questions."

"I assume something happened on the sixth day, and on the seventh day he rested."

"Quit making fun. On the sixth day, he saw Enzo leave his house and close the doors to a barn that had been open since he had started watching the farm. Soon swallows flew at the door, as if to go inside. They must have left the barn while it was too dark for Vanni to see them. A storm of swallows swooped at the door, shrieking and almost battering it in a flurry of wings. Vanni decided to pay the farm a visit.

"He asked offhand why the swallows were so agitated. Enzo couldn't resist the temptation to boast about his cleverness. Every year the swallows came and made nests in the rafters of the buildings. Year after year he destroyed them, but the swallows rebuilt and returned the following year. Finally he came upon the perfect solution. He left the barn doors open and let the swallows sit on the nests. The first morning after the eggs began to hatch, he waited until the foraging birds left the barn to gather insects for their mates and the young. Then he shut the doors."

Harry shook his head.

"Vanni said something to Enzo about the high-pitched cries of the birds inside calling to the frantic birds outside. Enzo said not to worry. It lasted only a couple days before the birds inside starved to death.

"Vanni felt sick—not because some songbirds were going to die; this was a time when the country people ate little birds, not like now, when they're protected." She waggled her hand as if to say *sort of protected*, since they both knew people still ate them. "No, it was the torture of it, the deliberate cruelty of separating the birds who were driven by nature to care for their young and each other. Vanni said the anguished cries of the birds should have made the heavens weep. And this man wanted to marry his daughter."

"What happened next?"

"Vanni couldn't interfere on another man's farm. Opening the doors would only have postponed the inevitable. He told Tomasina what he had seen. The following Sunday, the priest read the banns of marriage for her and your grandfather." She nodded her head emphatically. "So you are a Buonarotti instead of a Criscilla."

"You mean Caputo."

"Criscilla is Dom's father's name. He uses his mother's name now."

"Why?"

Before Lucy could answer, the bell at the back door rang. Dom stood there in his boots and overalls. He always looked as if he needed a shave and a good scrubbing, even when he wasn't carrying a box of meat.

Lucy couldn't understand Isabella's attraction to him. She was a younger version of Harry's wife, both with eyes like picholine olives, black and oval, deeply set above high cheekbones. But now Isabella seemed faded, unsure, always looking to Dom for approval. Perhaps Lucy didn't like Dom because she knew the life Isabella suffered, however she tried to hide it. Dom seemed to be a lot like his grandfather, the torturer of defenseless creatures.

"Mario sent me with your order."

"Thank you, Dom. Just put the box in the refrigerator, please. Help yourself to some coffee."

"Mind if I have a few *wans*?" He dropped the box and stuck his unwashed hand into the cookies.

"Of course not. I'll put the rest in a box for you and Mario."

Chapter 18

Michael Fiori chewed on the pencil and stared at the blue-lined paper. All he had written so far was the date: March 15, 1942. How could he tell his father and Mia everything that had happened since the night of Pearl Harbor? The night his world turned upside down.

Shortly after he had left the Aiellos', he had heard Mr. Posto crying for help. The next thing he knew, he was coming to in the back of a car, trying to figure out where he was, where they were going. Soon the smell of the mudflats had seeped into the car. They were on the Bayshore Highway. The car climbed into the night sky and crawled across the Bay Bridge, feeling its way in the dark. Michael couldn't see the lights of San Francisco. He could have been anywhere in the world. Time was suspended, maybe even gravity. Then he felt the car descending.

When they finally stopped, Michael looked around to tell someone who he was, where he was, but the streets were empty. No one going into a restaurant or hailing a cab. The city had disappeared. Except for glimmers that had escaped the blackout, he could see no streetlights, no traffic signals, no glowing signs or lights in windows—just dark shapes against a deeper darkness.

Mr. Posto huddled beside him in the backseat, trembling. Michael held his hand, patted his knee, tried to calm him. A man in shirtsleeves ran out of the building and spoke to the man driving the car. Then they took off again, and soon Michael and Mr. Posto were herded along a slippery dock and onto a coast guard cutter. The boat rocked under Michael's feet, and he fell onto a seat, almost pulling Mr. Posto over with him.

The sailors didn't answer Michael when he asked where they were going, but another man in handcuffs whispered that he thought they were going to Angel Island. God help them.

Mr. Posto had shaken his head and muttered something.

"Don't worry, Mr. Posto. They'll find out where we are and get us out."

The old man had answered him in Italian, each word distinct, formed as if he could taste it.

"No one will get us out. It is like before. In Italy. When they take you, they can do what they want with you."

Michael had hoped he was wrong, that it was age and fear talking, but for weeks it seemed as if he had been right. Then Michael received a message from Harry Buonarotti saying that he knew where Michael and Mr. Posto were and he was working to get a rehearing for them. Not to give up. Maybe Michael should use a line of his letter and ask his father if he had any news about that, but no, his father would let him know without Michael's asking.

"Michael. *Permesso?*" The captain of the Italian cruise ship that had found itself on the wrong side of the Atlantic when war broke out held a thick wool sweater out to him. "For you."

Michael reached for it, then drew back his hand. "Please give it to Mr. Posto. He needs it more than I do."

"I have given him the extra blankets my American friends sent to me. He is as warm as possible. If you become ill, it will not benefit him. Take it. Please."

When Michael's eyes appeared through the neck of the sweater, the captain gestured toward the cot, asked if he could sit. "Are you writing to a girlfriend?"

Michael waved the blank paper in the air. "I don't seem to be writing to anyone. What can you say in three lines? With no abbreviations? And how do I know what the censor will cut out? It's impossible."

"Whoever you are writing to wants to know you are safe and well. Tell them that. And that you love them." The captain smiled. "Then, in the next letter, tell them about the concert we played on Christmas. And in the next, about the *pasta e fagioli* we are making for dinner. And in the next, who knows? Life here in Bella Vista holds many adventures."

Bella vista: the beautiful view. It *was* beautiful looking out to the

Bitterroot Mountains, purple against the fields of snow. The crews of the Italian cruise ships had renamed Fort Missoula and settled into their barracks, happy not to be fighting a war they didn't believe in. The members of the ship's orchestra were allowed to keep their instruments, and even the captain's little dog was welcomed into the camp.

There were no POWs in this camp, not as there had been in camps they had passed through on their journey here. Michael remembered the German soldiers in one camp who had demanded more butter, more coffee, more everything they could think of. They seemed to know exactly what the Geneva Conventions regarding prisoners of war provided and kept upping their demands, fighting a war of complaints with the Army.

Michael set aside his writing. "I'm worried about Mr. Posto. It's almost as if he doesn't care what happens anymore. He's been like this since they picked us up, and last night he coughed all night. Your ship's doctor said it sounded like bronchitis, but he had nothing to treat him with. I need to get him help."

"Come, Michael. Let us go talk to the commander. He's a good man. Perhaps he will send Signor Posto to the army hospital."

Michael and the captain pushed against the barracks door, almost blocked with the new snow from the night before. Michael took a step and sank to his knees. His pants would be soaked by the time they got back and would never dry in the frigid barracks unless the men had scrounged up more coal for their little iron stove. He hoped the captain could convince the camp commander to help Mr. Posto. Michael didn't know what he would do if his frail friend died. Taking care of Mr. Posto was all that kept him going.

Chapter 19

Had there been a St. Patrick's Day in ancient Rome, Oliver would have thought it was reason enough to beware the Ides of March. The night before, even the decent people had joined the ranks of drunks celebrating until the wee hours.

He had finally gotten to sleep, when the phone rang. *They couldn't need me at the station house. Not yet.* He cleared his throat and answered. Suddenly, Oliver was wide-awake. Charley was calling to invite him to meet his math professor.

Oliver and Harley drove down the peninsula, a trip they had started to make a few times before but had never finished, always turning around before they reached Palo Alto. Being able to see Charley more often had been one of the reasons Oliver had stayed in Richmond, but he tried to let Charley decide when they would meet.

Charley was settling into his life at Stanford. He had come home for Christmas, and they talked every week, mostly about Charley's classes. Oliver had evaded Charley's questions about life in Richmond, not wanting to burden his son with his own loneliness. Besides, he wasn't sure how to be with Charley now that Elizabeth was gone; she had been the bridge between them. Oliver had been so afraid of being like his own father with Charley that he hadn't known how to be anything at all. Elizabeth's advice had been so simple: *Pretend you are Charley, Oliver. Treat him the way you would like to be treated.* But sometimes Oliver just froze—his mind or his heart wouldn't work, and he was not capable of imagining how he would want to be treated. He was never harsh with Charley, but Oliver couldn't quite be the way he wished he could be. Still, somehow, Charley seemed to know that Oliver loved him.

The math professor almost crushed Oliver's hand. He looked like a clerk, with his little mustache and bow tie. Oliver knew the type: an intellectual who would be extra-aggressive on the football field or the basketball court to prove he was really just one of the guys. Because he wasn't, and never would be. He reminded Oliver of his brother, Peter, except the professor glowed with warmth toward Oliver and with affection for Charley.

At the beginning of the school term, the professor had invited Charley to take part in an informal class on cryptology. Turned out Charley had a talent for recognizing number and letter patterns and putting words together. Now he was being asked to become a decoder. Oliver pictured his son parachuting into war zones and being killed before he hit the ground, but before he said anything that would have embarrassed him or, worse, his son, the professor said Charley would be in the navy, stateside, and contributing more than he could with a rifle or a plane. The professor said he shuddered to think of that mind at risk on a battlefield. Oliver thought maybe he should be insulted on behalf of the men he had fought with in the last war, but he made allowances for the guy. He was an egghead.

After lunch, Oliver and Charley walked around the campus, threw sticks for Harley, and caught up until Oliver had to leave. When they got to the car, Charley held out his hand.

"Thanks, Dad. I wasn't sure you'd be okay with this. It'll mean I have to go east."

"I know, Charley, but the professor made it sound like you might win the war single-handedly—without firing a shot. How could you say no?"

Charley smiled, and Oliver saw Elizabeth in his face. He remembered his wife's advice and decided that if he were Charley, he would want his father to be honest with him, not try to protect him.

"Charley, I've been thinking about reenlisting, but if something happened to me . . . after your mother and everything."

Charley's brown eyes glistened. He looked straight into Oliver's eyes, as if trying to make him understand something that might be beyond his grasp.

"Mom's always with me, Dad, and you would be, too, if anything happened to you. I'm not alone. Do it." He looked down at Harley. "What about the big guy?"

"I think he'll go, too."

Oliver held his son. "I'm proud of you, Charley." He felt his eyes fill and might have started blubbering if Harley hadn't woofed and jumped up on them, almost knocking them down as he tried to join in the hug.

Now Harley bounced along beside Oliver as they neared the station house. The dog seemed as happy about having seen Charley as Oliver was. They stopped when they heard a woman berating someone.

"I'm telling you, I want to talk to a detective. A *de-tec-tive*!"

Oliver heard Harmon's sigh and decided to stay by the door and listen to how Harmon handled the woman. Oliver glanced through the window. A girl sat on the chair against the wall, folded in on herself as if she were trying to disappear. Her dusty brown skin was scraped, her crown of braids tarnished, one kinked backward like a dog's leg.

"You can talk to me. I'll take the report and see that someone gets in touch with you," Harmon persisted.

"No, you won't. You'll do just what you did the last time I brought someone in here to report a rape. I got the same runaround, and no one ever talked to me. You think just because these girls are colored, you can ignore what's happening to them? Or do you think these girls can't be raped, that they're asking for it? Well, this time he made a mistake. This time he picked a girl that isn't on the street. A good girl."

"There are no detectives here right now."

"We'll wait."

"Maybe she should see a doctor instead."

"You let us worry about the doctor. Your job isn't to send us to a doctor. Your job is to stop this monster. I'm staying here until we talk to someone."

Oliver had listened long enough. He went into the station to rescue his partner.

The girl drew up her knees when Harley went through the door.

"Here, Harley." Oliver patted his leg, and the dog sat by him. "He won't hurt you."

Whoa. A tall, broad woman spun around and almost stood on Oliver's toes. "You a detective?"

"Yes, ma'am. What can I do for you?"

The woman nodded at the girl on the chair.

Oliver understood. "Come on into the meeting room. We can talk there."

The ugliness of rape sickened him, made him ashamed for his gender, ashamed they couldn't stop this man. Maybe that was why it was so hard to look these women in the face.

The woman helped the girl up and supported her until she slid one hip onto a chair.

"What's your name?" The girl didn't look much older than his niece.

"Becky." The woman stood over him.

"Please sit down."

She glared at him, then sat next to Becky.

"Have you been to a doctor?"

"We're going when we're done here."

"You need to let her answer, ma'am. What's *your* name?"

"Josephine Jessup. I'm Becky's aunt. Everyone calls me Auntie Josephine."

"I need Becky to tell me what happened to her." Oliver smiled at the girl. "Take your time."

"Same thing happened to the other girls." Auntie Josephine looked at him as if he were useless.

"What other girls?"

"Don't you all talk to one another?" She bounded out of her chair, hands on hips. Her bushy eyebrows met over a long nose that broadened at the base. She must have been in her forties, old enough to be the girl's mother.

"Sit down! Please." Oliver looked at her until she sat; then he uncapped his fountain pen and pulled over a pad. "Let's start at the beginning. Assume I know nothing about this." He spoke quickly when he saw those busy lips open to speak again. "I want to help you. Let's get through this so Becky can see a doctor."

Becky and Auntie Josephine told the story in tandem. Becky answered with single words, and her aunt filled in the details. It had still been dark when the girl had left home for school. She had been running late, and even though she wasn't supposed to, she had taken a shortcut through the alley behind Tapper's Inn. It was a pickup spot, but it was early morning and the women had left. A man had grabbed Becky from behind and choked her until she passed out. She couldn't tell if he was tall or short, dark or light. Just strong.

Auntie Josephine tapped the table. "This may sound crazy to you, but these rapes remind us of the ones that happened a long time ago. Must have gone on for fourteen or fifteen years."

"When did those older rapes happen?"

"They started happening a little before the first war. We were scared to go out. The man choked the girl from behind. Whispered things while he was doing it."

"What kinds of things?"

"That he knew you liked it." She lowered her voice. "That he'd be back."

Oliver wondered if she had been a victim.

She wagged a finger in his face, as if she could read his mind.

"Didn't happen to me, but happened to plenty. Back then it happened maybe every six months. But now it's happening closer together. First Sylvie, walking home in the dark after her own birthday party. What a terrible thing for her. On top of being raped, she lost one of her new birthday earrings. She thought maybe the man took it, but what's he gonna do with one earring?"

"Did she go back and look for it?"

"A couple of her friends did. They found a lot of trash, but no earring. Then that sick rapist got Laila, and now Becky. The third girl raped in three weeks. And you people do nothing. Think the prostitutes were asking for it 'cause they, you know, get paid for doing it." Her voice softened. "But Becky was just a girl in the wrong place at the wrong time."

"Let's get her to the hospital." Oliver stilled her protests. "I'll come talk to you, talk to the other women, but first she needs some care."

Becky flinched when Harmon reached out to help her into the

police car. Auntie Josephine rolled her eyes, as if men in general, and Harmon in particular, were completely stupid.

Oliver thought about what Josephine had said. He doubted it was the same man. The First World War had started for the United States in 1917. If the rapes had gone on for fourteen or fifteen years, it meant they had ended sometime in the early thirties. That made for a long time between rapes, unless the man had gotten caught for something else and been in jail or had moved away and come back. More than likely, Auntie Josephine and her friends were just wrong.

Chapter 20

The trap was a work of art. The more she struggled, the more the cords tightened. Harry thought she was dead, but then he saw a tiny movement. The spider had not yet paralyzed her. Harry pulled apart the strands encapsulating the bee in the web, put her on the hive top, and began to ease the bonds away. He attached an end of the silk to a twig and gently unwound the cage that imprisoned the bee. Threads still fettered her translucent wings and the hairlike legs. He hesitated, then decided that trying to free those fragile appendages would do more harm than good.

The warm March day had given the bees a chance to carry out their dead and take some cleansing flights. The bee had probably become entangled in the web while she was patrolling the hive she belonged to. If anyone could help her, it would be her family, her sisters. He offered her the twig. When she grasped it, Harry placed her in the center of the hive opening. Before the golden insect had touched wood, a bee appeared on either side of her and hurried her into the hive between them. They had been waiting for her, alerted by the alarm peeps she had broadcast while she was trapped.

He'd never know what would happen next—whether the bees could finish cleaning her and free her to rejoin the hive. He knew they groomed each other, but he didn't know if they had the ability to unstick the threads. If she had to die, she would be fed and in the company of her family. Not a bad end.

Better to believe what his wife would believe: that the bees would clean her and she would soon be out flying in the sun, walking into the hearts of flowers to gather nectar for her family. At least, that was what Paola would have believed before the war, before their son and his friend Nate Hermit had left college to enlist in the army.

"Harry. You have a visitor." Paola led Oliver into the garden. "You're lucky to catch him, Oliver. He just got back from Washington." Her hand flew to her mouth. "Whoops. Maybe I wasn't supposed to tell anyone that."

Oliver laughed. "I don't think any harm will come from your telling me, Paola."

"Sit down, Oliver. I'll bring you both some wine." She waved a hand behind her at Oliver's protests as she walked back to her house.

"Welcome home, Harry."

Harry gestured to a chair, inviting Oliver to sit with him under the arbor. Winds off the bay jostled the trailing vines of wisteria that sheltered them, creating sinuous shadows on the tablecloth and Harry's white shirt. "It's so good to be home. I kept hearing, 'Washington is a beehive of activity.' I didn't contradict them, but clearly the bureaucrats have never seen bees at work, or they couldn't confuse their own conflict-filled activity with the harmonious ballet of a hive." He gestured toward bees flying in and out of the white boxes.

"May I ask what they wanted of you?"

"They asked me to become a bureaucrat." Harry seemed amused by the idea. "To become one of the confused bees at cross-purposes in the Washington beehive."

Oliver knew Harry was a man used to being in charge, being effective. No wonder he found the idea amusing. "No, no, I can't see that. But you'll want to do something."

"I've talked to Colonel Burton about reenlisting."

"Harry!" Paola set a tray with bread and cheese on the table. She looked upset. "I don't like to be unkind, but aren't you a little old for that?"

Oliver thought she probably couldn't imagine having both her husband and her son at risk.

"Forty-five isn't old. Besides, I'd be part of the Judge Advocate General's Corps, probably stay in the Bay Area. The more Italians there are fighting, working against the war, the sooner it will all end—the backlash against Italians *and* the war."

"I think that's one of the reasons Steve enlisted." Paola turned to Oliver. "Our son. He had never thought of himself as different from his friends, but after Pearl Harbor some of them shunned him and called him names."

Harry reached out for her hand and held it for a moment, there in the soft wind that smelled of the bay and eucalyptus. Then Paola excused herself and went into the house.

Harry poured the wine. "So, what brings you here today, Oliver?"

"It seems neither of us knows when he's had enough of war. I came to tell you that *I* reenlisted. I'm not sure when I'll be leaving, but I wanted you to hear it from me."

"It's not my business, Oliver, but I've wondered why you decided to stay here."

"My father is convinced someone on the police force is connected to the Klan. I promised to see what I could find out."

"I suspected you stayed because of your father, but I'm not sure why he is still concerned about this possible connection."

"He's worried about Peter."

"With good reason. Your brother can be a bit reckless in his exuberant pursuit of the truth."

Oliver thought it was more Peter's exuberant pursuit of his own career that motivated him. Wondered if Harry thought that, too.

Harry slid the knife through the cheese and offered it to Oliver. "Try it. It's mild."

Oliver took the cheese and a large chunk of bread, just in case the cheese wasn't as mild as Harry thought.

"Have you told your father you're leaving?" Harry asked.

"Yes. He's 'disappointed,' but my son gave me his blessing, and that's all that really matters."

The two fathers looked at each other. A crow swooped from the cypress tree on the point and landed on the rocky shore, setting a flurry of gulls into the air above the glittering bay.

"My son, Steve, will be leaving for the war in a few days. You know, you and I were lucky, Oliver. We managed to survive one war almost unchanged. Not like some of the boys we know, who came home so different, it was as if they had been replaced by impostors, not even giving their parents the release of a funeral. I don't want to think about it happening again." Harry shook his head. "I'm meeting my brothers soon to play bocce. Come with me. It's part of a little going-away party for Steve."

Oliver began to refuse, but then he realized he would like to know Harry and his family better. Besides, his easy chair would be waiting for him, and he would still have plenty of time to sit and stare into the night.

"My brothers would like to meet you. You're the detective who helped look for Michael Fiori."

The sound of women laughing floated out to the arbor.

"Paola and her friends are probably swapping stories about the restrictions on Italians. It's all anyone talks about. The restrictions and the war. The community is unsettled by the changes: men without jobs, families separated by citizenship status, unable to visit a father in the hospital or attend a cousin's wedding. They try to make light of the stigma, to talk about the absurd situations the restrictions have created."

"What kind of situations? Those of us outside the Italian community hear little about what is happening day-to-day."

"One of the women who should have been here today can't come into the restricted zone. We don't see so much of her now. She had to move from Richmond, where all she could see from her house was her neighbor's washing. Now she lives in a nonrestricted zone in San Francisco, where she can watch the battleships heading toward the Pacific. It's happening all along the coast. My uncle in Eureka lives in a nonrestricted zone, but he isn't allowed to cross the street to work in his store. So he sits on a kitchen chair at the edge of the restricted zone and yells orders to his son all day. Even the police think it's funny."

"Who's making these rules that don't seem to make sense?"

"Our *friend* General DeWitt."

Harry's voice dripped with bitterness. Oliver realized the prosecutor was taking DeWitt's actions personally.

"The man has the power to intern *all* Italians, not just noncitizens, and the only thing stopping him are the politicians who are afraid of what would happen if he interned the families of the hundreds of thousands of Italians in the armed forces and the defense industry. If not for them, DeWitt would intern me and my family!"

"Like the Japanese."

"Yes. I think they're being punished for Pearl Harbor."

"What, Harry? You don't believe Japanese gardeners are trimming lawns and bushes into directional signals for air attacks?" Oliver was sure Harry would think that was as nonsensical as he did.

"No. And I don't think they're poisoning our vegetable supply, either. What insanity."

Oliver grew serious. "I think it's racial. They look different, have different customs. People think they're inherently untrustworthy. They've lumped Japanese citizens together with the people who attacked us without warning. A completely un-American act."

"Enough of the war. What are you working on now? Any interesting crimes being committed?"

"Interesting, no; disgusting, yes. There have been three rapes in the past three weeks. Yesterday, a young girl reported being raped. I believe the rapist is targeting prostitutes, so she might have been a mistake, or maybe the prostitutes are being too careful for him." Oliver looked at Harry appraisingly. "Harry, if you were a woman who had been raped, would you report it?"

"As a prosecutor, I should say yes, but in fact, my answer is no. What would you do?"

"I walked into my old precinct one night and saw a young woman surrounded by men who questioned her story as she told it. Made her repeat the details of the assault, all the while looking at her as if she had been asking for it." The memory disgusted him.

"Yes, and if the police actually arrested someone, a defense attorney would humiliate the victim on the stand, asking about every sexual encounter she ever had and about her underwear or lack of it." Harry clearly sympathized with the women victimized once again in the courtroom.

"I shouldn't say this to a prosecutor, but if I were a woman who had been raped, I wouldn't tell anyone, but I would hunt down the bastard and kill him."

"Oliver, I think you and I are in agreement, but we shouldn't tell other people how we feel." Harry laughed.

"No. Anyway, the chief put Frank Slater on the rapes. Every weekend, Frank hauls in Negro sailors and tries to get one to confess."

"You have far more experience with serious crime than Frank does. I would have thought you would be investigating."

Oliver simply looked at Harry, then drained his wineglass.

"Ah, yes. It appears you are being treated exactly as I feared you would be."

Oliver shrugged. Soon it would be over.

Harry picked up the glasses and bottle to take into the kitchen. "Come. Let's meet my brothers and forget about war and crime for a while."

Dom watched his brother-in-law get into his car with that detective with the dog. After they disappeared down the street, he got out of his Dodge and crouched along the tall bushes that shielded him from the side of the Buonarottis' house. He had plenty of time before the men got back from their bocce game.

He ducked into the small stone building where Harry extracted the honey from the hives. Part of the house was built into the side of the hill so it could keep oil and wine cool during the summer. The last time he and Isabella had come to her sister's house for dinner, Harry had asked Dom to help him move barrels of *lampante* into the honey shed.

"*Lampante?*" Isabella looked like that stupid RCA dog when she tilted her head and asked the question.

"Yes. A friend sold us some barrels of oil pressed from the olives picked up off the ground. It's not good for cooking, only for lamp oil or starting fires. We'll probably never use it for anything."

"Why would you buy something you weren't going to use?" Dom didn't bother to hide his scorn.

"He's a good friend who needed to sell it," Harry answered, in a tone that warned Dom not to ask any more questions.

They had pushed the barrels of *lampante* behind the barrels of wine, which were now blocking Dom. He set the small package he carried on a table and began to hump the barrels out of the way to clear a path.

"*Maneggia la madonn,*" he swore when he brushed his trousers against the wall. He had to look right for the party. Finally he managed to reach the last *lampante* barrel.

He picked up the package, reluctant to let it go. Just one more look. The cold blue steel shone in the light that filtered through the window. Dom cleaned the gun often, sitting in his kitchen, running the cloth along the six-sided barrel.

He'd been trying to figure out where to hide it for weeks, ever since he'd overheard that Slater in the Café Avellino when he was delivering meat. It had to be in a place where no one would look and where the gun would be protected from rust. He had finally remembered the *lampante* barrels. Perfect.

Dom slid his palm around the crosshatched wooden grip, slipped his finger through the trigger guard, and pulled back the hammer with his thumb. He thought of his father's hand gripping the gun, shooting Austrian soldiers in the First World War until he died at the Battle of Caporetto. All Dom had left of him now was his revolver.

He wrapped long leather bootlaces around the oilcloth package, tied them tightly, and watched the gun sink. He would return for it when the war was over. That bastard Slater wasn't taking his gun. No one was. Not only because it had been his father's, but because of what had happened in New Jersey. Another reason he and Isabella had to move away from the coast. He didn't want anyone looking too carefully at his papers, at who he was.

Chapter 21

If it had been before, in Seattle, Oliver would have waited until one in the morning, when the clubs were swinging and the booze had loosened people's tongues. But in wartime Richmond, it was always one in the morning or eight in the morning, or noon, whatever you needed it to be, whether your shadow lengthened and shortened under the streetlights or hid under your shoe from the sun.

Not just here. Across the bay, streams of soldiers and sailors flowed through the streets, making the most of still being stateside, still being whole and fresh and young. Women crowded the USO, determined to show them a good time. The gaiety and flirting staved off the threat of death, strengthened the pretense that the boys would all come back and the girls would wait.

He parked on a side street and walked up Chesley through the warm April night, making his way through the crowd of young people outside the Club Savoy, where Jimmy McCracklin was playing. Auntie Josephine had agreed to meet him at the Dew Drop Inn and introduce him to some of the girls.

A woman stepped out of a doorway, her hemline at an exceptionally patriotic high.

"Hi, handsome. Got a light?"

She didn't seem like a pro. Probably just working for drinks or some extra cash. Hell, there'd be plenty of men willing to give her whatever she wanted.

"Sure." He flipped open his Zippo and spun the wheel. As the woman bent her head to the flame and cupped his hand in hers, he saw a scowling Auntie Josephine. She gestured with her head for him to get over to where she stood with a caramel-colored woman.

Auntie Josephine stomped her foot. "You down here shopping or to do some work?"

"Maybe she knows something."

"I bet she knows plenty, but it ain't nothing you need to be finding out."

Oliver offered Auntie Josephine's friend his hand.

"I'm Oliver Wright."

She set her gloved hand in his as if she expected him to bow his head to it. A tiny black hat perched on the front of her head, partially hiding her features behind its net scrim. She must have glued that hat to her skull for it not to slide right down off her slicked-back hair. She wore a black silk jacket over a black-and-white print dress. Not your typical two-bit whore.

"Monica."

He didn't know how to ask her if she had been raped.

"Monica's friend was raped." Auntie Josephine had read his hesitation. "You can't talk to her friend, 'cause she's gone out of here. That's the reason Monica came. To tell you what happened."

"Why did she leave?"

The women looked at each other.

"Let's go inside."

Monica led the way into the club, nodded to the bartender, and slid into a booth in the back of the smoky room. Oliver scanned the crowd. Cool, not hostile. He saw all shades of black and brown, no one he would call white.

"We can talk here without any worries. Doesn't matter what the police are saying. We know the man doing this isn't colored."

"How do you know?"

"My friend saw his arm. His shirt slid up for a second. Someone else caught a glimpse of his forehead. Ofay bastard." Monica seemed taken back by her own outburst. "Sorry." She puffed out her cheeks and blew air through her lips and still managed to be alluring.

A waitress set a round of drinks on the table. Looked like whiskey for Oliver and Monica, ginger ale with four cherries for Auntie.

"I'm sorry. She was my best friend, and because of him she's gone off with a man who's beat her before and will do it again."

"She left because of the rapist?"

Auntie Josephine bit a cherry off its stem. "He tells them he knows they liked it, so he'll be back to give them more. She believed he was waiting for her. She was afraid to go out. Couldn't work. Finally, she took off for Detroit with that good-for-nothing, draft-dodging womanizer."

Oliver had read the thin files on the rapes. Whoever had taken statements for the first two rapes hadn't bothered to include any more information than dates and the women's names. It had probably been Frank, who wouldn't want minor details like the color of the guy's arm to deflect suspicion from his favorite Negro scapegoats. Who was this guy? And did he really believe they *liked* it? "Have you told the police this? What you're telling me?"

"We tried, but they don't believe us. Keep saying we're wrong, that it's one of those Negro sailors from Mare Island or Port Chicago. We decided to police things ourselves, watch out for each other. Then he got Becky. We had to try to convince the police again."

"Fat lot of good it did us." Auntie Josephine laid her hand on Oliver's sleeve. "Till you."

Her ring sparkled in the candlelight and reminded him of the missing birthday earring. The more he thought about it, the less he thought it was simply lost.

"Did Becky have any jewelry go missing when she was attacked?"

Auntie Josephine stopped a cherry halfway to her mouth.

"What?"

"She lost one of her favorite barrettes. We thought it came loose in the struggle."

So he might have taken it. "What about the old rapes? Were the women missing jewelry then?"

Monica put her hand to her mouth. "You think he's taking souvenirs? How vile."

"Is there anyone else I can talk to? Anyone who knows anything?"

They gave him a few more names of women who would talk to him and where to find them and told him stories about their friend Zora.

Monica rose. "If Zora phones, I'll ask her if she lost any jewelry that night. See if she'll talk to you."

Oliver got up and held out his hand again.

"How can I get in touch with you if I have more questions?"

Monica looked at him from under her long lashes. She started to answer, when Auntie Josephine butted in.

"You know how to reach me. You need anything, I'll set you up."

Oliver bit his lip, thought Monica might have winked at him through the net. "Okay. Let me see what I can do." *Somehow this is going to have to fall under shipyard crimes.* He nodded to them.

"Oliver?"

He glanced back at Auntie Josephine. "Thank you for coming to our hospital to talk to Becky. Don't think anyone from that station ever walked in there before, 'cept to arrest someone."

"It's my job, Auntie. No need to thank me. Tell Becky I said hello."

He thought about the missing barrette as he turned down the side street away from the noise of the crowds. He heard a shoe scrape on the sidewalk, and a violent shove knocked him into two men who appeared out of nowhere. They grabbed him and pulled him into the alley. He got off a yell before one of them punched him in the stomach and knocked all the air out of him. As he gasped for breath, another blow landed near his kidneys. If that was a bare fist, the bastard had hands of steel. Oliver slammed onto the brick road and managed to snap a kick at the shin of the nearest man. Something gave. One down.

He rolled away from the feet about to stomp him but hit the garbage cans. He rolled back the other way and pushed himself to his knees. A kick to the ribs lifted him off the ground, and he fell sideways. One of the men raised a truncheon above his head. Oliver grabbed a lid and tried to get it between him and the club. If that connected, he was as good as dead. The blow didn't come. Someone ran into the alley, swinging a two-by-four that smashed the man with the truncheon across his ribs and backswung into the face of the other man. Oliver's Good Samaritan stood between him and his attackers, brandishing the length of wood like a bat.

One of the men held out a hand in surrender; the other clutched his side. They grabbed their friend under the arms and dragged him away.

"How badly are you hurt? Do you need an ambulance?" It was the Easterner from the café.

Oliver groaned. "Unfortunately, I think I'm going to live."

"When you're ready to get up, let me know." He could barely get his breath, let alone help Oliver up.

They rested. Oliver tried to breathe without expanding his rib cage.

"How did you know I was the good guy?"

"In the movies, the one getting beat up by three other guys is usually the good guy. Not that I put much stock in what I see in the movies." The man tried to brush off his pants; he still wasn't breathing easy. "I saw you in the Café Avellino. Knew you were a cop." He smiled. "Not that that necessarily makes you one of the good guys, either."

Oliver couldn't argue with that.

"Besides, I saw how you reacted when that asshole Slater came in."

"Yeah." Oliver pulled himself up. "What yard you in? Welder, right?"

"Is that a guess, or you a modern Sherlock Holmes?"

"You have burn marks on your hands, and holes in your clothes. Even Nancy Drew could figure that one out."

"Guess so. But you shouldn't explain. Ruins the effect."

"I'm Oliver Wright."

"Jonah North."

Jonah walked with Oliver to his car, where Harley was barking and trying to squeeze through the wing vent. It took Oliver a few minutes to calm him down. When he had convinced the shepherd the danger was over, he asked Jonah if he could buy him a drink.

"No, thanks. If I get this many burns when I'm sober, I'd probably weld myself to the hull with a beer in me."

Oliver laughed, realizing it had been a long time since he had. And it hurt.

"Want a lift?"

"Nah. My car's not far."

"I haven't told anyone yet, but I'm waiting for orders." Oliver waved a hand, as if to say he knew he was a little older than most new recruits. "If you have some time, I'd like to buy you dinner before I go. It should be sooner rather than later, since I'm not sure how long I'll be here."

"Why not sit it out? Though I think it might be more dangerous for you here than over there." Jonah seemed completely serious to Oliver.

"I'll be more useful there. Harley, too."

"Harley? You're taking the dog?"

"More like he's taking me."

Jonah looked puzzled.

"We're going to the Marine K9 Corps. I'll be teaching in North Carolina until all the dogs and men are trained to work together, and then we'll go wherever they need us."

"I'd like to write a . . . uh, write to you when you go. Would you mind?"

"It would be great. Nothing like news from home when you're far away. Jonah, if you're free, let's meet at the Hotel Mac at seven on Sunday. Does that work?"

"I can make it." Jonah looked at his watch. "I'd better get going. If you're ten minutes late, they treat you like you're part of the Fifth Column."

"Take care, Jonah. Thanks again."

Oliver watched Jonah stride down the street, gathering appreciative glances from the women. He let Harley out of the car and walked slowly with him. From now on, Harley would go with him wherever he went. No more waiting in the car.

Chapter 22

The tiers of candle flames shimmering at the feet of Our Lady of Mercy failed to comfort Lucy Forgione. She knelt at the altar, trying to pray for her sons, but the hatred she felt in her heart consumed her, drove out her faith and her patience. She hated the men who caused the darkening of the pews behind her. Every week another woman appeared at Mass dressed in black, charred by the war.

Waves of sorrow filled the church, yet the women remained faithful. They prayed for the war to end, for the grace to accept God's will, for the souls of the sons they had lost and the protection of the sons they still had. Or thought they had. It was sometimes weeks before they found out the child they had been praying for had already been blown up by a grenade or bayoneted or drowned or burned alive.

They came to the café, where Lucy translated the letters the boys had written them, letters that were now their most valued possessions, perhaps their sons' last words. She wrote back for them, ordinary things to keep the boys connected to the life they had been taken from, to keep them from worrying. Their mothers bit their lips and steeled themselves against their tears, afraid they might blur the words and reveal the truth: everything was not fine.

Lucy leaned on the altar rail and pushed herself to her feet. She had never felt so alone, especially here. As she walked to her pew, she saw Edna Hermit kneeling near the back of the church. She was a hardworking woman. She had been the Wrights' housekeeper since before Zoe was born and still managed to do the Slaters' laundry. Sometimes, when Lucy had been helping with dinner in the Buonarottis' kitchen, she had noticed Edna hanging wash in the Slaters' back garden. Edna's son, Nate, had climbed over the Slaters' fence to play with Harry's children so many times that he had put a gate in the fence that separated his garden from the Slaters'. Lucy had last seen Edna at the train station when Steve and Nate had left for the army.

Before Mrs. Hermit bowed her head, Lucy caught a glimpse of tears, two snail tracks on her mahogany skin. If Lucy felt alone surrounded by people she had known all her life, imagine how that solitary woman must feel. Lucy felt touched by a fleeting grace. There were many ways to pray.

"*Ite missa est.*"

Mrs. Hermit took the priest's dismissal personally and hurried past the women who lingered in the vestibule.

"Excuse me, excuse me."

Not her being called—why would they start talking to her now? Then she heard her name, and the woman who owned the café touched her arm. She was like an elf, barely five feet tall.

"Mrs. Hermit, I'm Lucy Forgione. Steve Buonarotti's great-aunt." She hurried to explain. "We met at the station, seeing the boys off. Nate's a lovely boy. A man now, I guess."

"Yes. I suppose he is. We haven't heard from him in a while." How had that popped out of her mouth?

"You know what the mail is like. Nothing for weeks, then four letters in the same day. But we still worry. That's why I wanted to talk to you. Would you like to join our rosary group? We meet at my house to pray for the boys."

No one seemed to be looking directly at them, but Mrs. Hermit could feel their eyes.

"I don't think your friends would like it."

"Don't worry about them." Lucy brushed the air, as if sweeping away any concern about the others. "Please. Our boys are fighting together; surely we can pray together."

"Together? You have any idea how segregated the army is?" Edna heard words flying out of her mouth as if she were listening to a radio play. "If your son were wounded, God forbid, they'd let him bleed to death before they put a single drop of my son's blood in him. Like it would turn him black. Make him start jumpin' like Bojangles."

The elf looked her in the eye. "I'm so sorry for both of them. And for us. Forgive me."

Before Edna could respond, the woman disappeared, her tiny black shape dissolving in the fog.

Aren't you a fine one, Edna Hermit? Picking on the only one of those women who ever tried to talk to you. And she's half your size. She turned away from the catty little groups mewling about her and headed down the hill toward town.

Was this the right thing to do? Well, the woman had invited Edna to her house, so maybe the invitation extended to the café. If not, Edna wouldn't feel so bad about what had happened in front of the church. She straightened her shoulders and opened the door.

The counter girl glanced at her, then hightailed it to the kitchen. The shrimp came out, drying her hands on her apron. She looked at Edna and waited until Edna spoke.

"You have any of that humble pie?"

"I'm afraid we're sold out."

Edna nodded. "Fine." She turned back to the door, satisfied at receiving the rebuff she had expected. The other woman's voice stopped her.

"I do have some nice crow if you're interested in that."

Edna turned around. "If it's all the same to you, I'd rather have that bun there." She pointed to the case. "Those crow feathers tend to stick in my teeth."

While Lucy was busy pouring their coffee, Edna noticed Detective Slater glance in the window at her. He looked surprised and not that pleased. Thank God he kept going down the hill toward the station house. Edna wandered nonchalantly to the back of the café, and Lucy followed her there. The two women talked about their boys and drank coffee, feeling their way to an accord.

Frank hurried past the café, trying not to jar the pumpkin sitting on his shoulders where his head should be. It was enormous and tender and hurt with each step he took. Water didn't quench his thirst, but he had sense enough not to start the day with the only thing that might ease the feeling of a mouth lined with cotton. Cottonmouth. He felt like one. *Don't tread on me.* Or was that a rattlesnake?

The Stop had been crowded the night before, but after his uncle Sandy had left, no one had challenged Frank's right to be alone in a booth meant for four. He had tried to drink away his disappointment. The guys were supposed to put Wright in the hospital, not end up there themselves. Sandy seemed to trust him again, now that he spent time at the garage and at the bars instead of staying home, but he hadn't cut Frank in on his new sideline yet. Frank figured it had to do with rationing. Everyone knew voluntary gas rationing wouldn't be enough; soon it would be mandatory. Could be some money in that. He gingerly walked down the street, glad he had not given up his real life for a fantasy life with Cora. Anytime he started to miss being with her, he thought about the locket and the lies.

One of the beat cops pulled Frank aside before he made it into the station. The fat slob had grease down the front of his uniform and talked out of the side of his mouth, as if someone were watching them.

"Chief wants to see you, Frank."

Frank shook off the man's hand. "Did you hear that?"

"Hear what?"

"That music." That music that seemed to follow him wherever he went. He hated it—that same strange melody coming out of the fog, from an alley, by his house. Eerie, like a message written in the air.

"Frank?"

"What?" Frank shook his head. A mistake.

"The chief's getting heat about the rapes. A woman's been writing letters to some colored paper back East, saying it's not the Negro sailors."

"Just because we haven't gotten one of them to confess yet doesn't mean we're wrong. We'll find him sooner or later."

It was fun to watch them squirm, see them panic when he wouldn't let them call their outfit to keep from being put on report. Rounding them up served his purposes. The word should be getting out to avoid his town when they had a pass.

"Frank." The slob broke into Frank's thoughts. "The chief's threatening to turn the cases over to Wright if you don't find someone.

He talked to some of the prostitutes last night and told the chief he might have a lead."

Wright. The chief. He was tortured by these upstanding people. One had gotten the job he wanted, and the other . . .

"Where the hell is Slater?"

Frank heard the chief bellowing from his office.

"You better get in there."

Frank balled his fists.

The younger man backed out of reach and hurried toward the street.

"Where have you been?"

The chief glared at Frank when he stuck his head in his office.

"Spent most of the night looking for a girl who had been raped but didn't report it. I guess we aren't looking too good out there. That's my fault, Chief. I know it is." *What an ass—Cavanaugh always falls for a little groveling.*

"Well, Wright's out there doing your job for you. He turned up someone who seems to know something."

"What's her name?" Frank leaned against the wall.

"She calls herself Zora now. Not her real name. Her friend said no matter what she called herself, he'd know her, because sooner or later she'd say, 'Why was I born beautiful, instead of rich?' Gave him the idea it was a joke because she wasn't exactly beautiful."

"I think I know who he's talking about. Used to call herself something else. Chief, it's my case. Tell Wright to stick to those beatings."

"I'm the one who tells people what to do. Not you."

"Sorry, I didn't mean it like that. I'm dead on my feet."

"Find out who's doing this, or I'm putting Wright on it. The last thing we need is a colored newspaper snooping around."

Chapter 23

For the past two weeks, Mrs. Forgione's new friend had been coming to the café every day. Jonah looked up from his writing when he heard Mrs. Forgione ask Mrs. Hermit what grits were.

"Why are you asking about grits?" Edna's lips rolled in as if to keep herself from smiling.

"Two women asked me if the café served grits." Lucy leaned forward over her coffee. "They were wearing dresses that looked like flour sacks with sleeves, much too thin for the weather. Seemed very backward. They must really want grits if they were willing to ask about them. Truthfully, I didn't understand their accent. But they seemed so lost."

"You don't know grits? I should make you some. It's cornmeal cooked into a cereal, with lard in it."

"Lard?" Lucy shuddered. "Maybe I should offer polenta in the morning. It sounds like grits. Without the lard. I wonder why they don't make it themselves."

"Lots of those places where these new people live don't have any kitchens. Lots don't even have bathrooms. Lots are just lots." Edna looked thoughtful. "If you wanted polenta and I gave you grits, would you be happy?" She answered herself. "No. Why not give them what they want?"

"I'm too old to start cooking things I never heard of. Especially underseasoned, overcooked American food."

"I'll do it." Edna looked as if she had surprised herself. "I could make breakfast for these folks. But you need to think about it. You might be starting something you don't like in the end. These people just keep coming and coming. The ones from the South are ruining things for the rest of us. White people can only take so many of us at a time."

Lucy set down her cup and stared at her friend.

"Don't give me that look! White businesses used to let us shop—not try any clothes on, but we could buy things. Now they won't let us in. Won't cash our checks. We can't even get buried in the damned cemetery anymore."

Lucy pursed her lips. She looked as if she were converting a recipe by thirds in her head. "The café is named after the town my father came from—Avellino. He told me stories of his journey to England and then America, and how he felt when he was tired and hungry and the restaurants and boardinghouses had signs that said 'No Dogs, No Dagos.' But I love the café the way it is. I don't want my longtime customers to feel like strangers here."

For a moment, as he listened, Jonah felt good. Nothing would change.

Then Lucy went on as if she had read his mind. "But the world is changing whether people want it to or not. So we'll fix up the storeroom, scrape the paint off the windows and door, make another side to the café, with another entrance. If we don't like what happens, we'll close it down. I don't think this side of the café is what the new people want. I think my real friends will stand by me and the heck with the rest of them." Lucy set down her cup and smiled. "I think Papa would approve."

Edna opened her pocketbook, took out a notepad and pencil, and licked the tip. "We're going to need some supplies, starting with lard."

Jonah picked up his cup to cover his smile. The friendship between the two women intrigued him. After eavesdropping on them these past few weeks, he had decided they were sisters under the skin—well, obviously *under* the skin. Now they were teaming up to change the café. *His* café.

Chapter 24

In the two weeks since Oliver had been attacked in the alley, he and Harmon had been working dull cases that amounted to a kind of adult babysitting, breaking up brawls and arresting people still holding the knife they had used in the fight. He felt like a garbage man instead of a detective. Then a fitter had been found beaten to death. Could have been because of his race, or the labor unions, or both.

It had taken time, but he had developed some trust with a few workers, colored and white, and gradually his network of informants had grown. Harmon was smart and willing to learn and had become almost a friend when Oliver had stepped between him and the blowtorch a woman welder pulled when they tried to arrest her for beating on her husband and his lady friend.

Oliver would rather go through that again than sit through dinner with his father and his brother, but after her archery meet, Zoe had begged him to come celebrate with them.

After dinner, Oliver walked down the hall, looking for his brother so he could leave, pick up Harmon, head back to the streets, and try to get a lead on this newest beating. It was technically a homicide, but it was definitely a shipyard crime, so Oliver had pressed the chief until he had reluctantly let Oliver keep the case.

"All right. I'll meet you wherever you say." Peter put the receiver in the cradle.

"Who was that?"

"It's nothing that concerns you."

"Sounded like someone wants to tell you something."

"Let it go. It's got nothing to do with you."

"If it concerns the shipyard beatings, it has a lot to do with me." Oliver watched his brother—no reaction. "It's about the Fleming children's deaths, isn't it? Peter, you can't go. You're a prosecutor, not a cop. Lawyers don't know how to deal with thugs, not until we've done the dirty work and they're handcuffed to the table."

Peter gave him the cold look, the one that reminded Oliver of their father.

"Think I can't meet someone and talk to him without you around?"

Damn. Why did he forget everything he knew about handling people when it came to his brother?

"Let's go together."

"He said to come alone or he wouldn't talk."

"He doesn't have to know I'm there." Oliver played the only card he had. "Think about Jennie and the kids. What if something happened to you?"

"I forgot you're supposed to be a hotshot at interrogation. Is that your gift? Knowing the other person's weak spot?" He nodded toward the door. "Let's go out on the porch. I don't want anyone to hear us."

Oliver followed Peter outside, lit a cigarette, and waited for his brother to start talking.

"I don't know who it was. He said no one was supposed to die."

"When are you meeting him?"

"There's nothing definite yet."

"I heard you say you'd meet him."

"I said there's nothing definite yet. He's going to call back."

"Peter, I'm not nine years old anymore. I've sat in on more interrogations than you have and sure as hell can tell when someone's lying to me. Especially you."

"Stay out of it, Oliver. This isn't your fight anymore. You left, remember? And you're leaving again."

"I'm not exactly going on a pleasure cruise."

"If it weren't the war, you would have found another reason to leave."

"You don't need me here."

"That's right. We don't need you. Our father asked you to do one thing for him, the one thing you're actually supposed to be good at, and you let him down."

He turned back toward the house.

"Peter, you've managed to change the subject again. We were talking about *your* family. About the risks *you're* taking."

Peter hesitated in the doorway.

"For what, Peter? Becoming a judge?"

Oliver watched through the window as Peter walked into their father's study. All of it suited him, suited them both—the Tiffany lamp on the desk, the rows of legal books on the floor-to-ceiling shelves, the chess game set up on the table in front of the French doors. Judge Wright sat in a leather wingback chair, a glass of amber liquid at his hand.

"Your brother's stubborn, Oliver. He'll never understand."

Jennie's voice came out of the dark. She walked up the porch steps.

"Peter can't see that the judge was one kind of father to him and an entirely different kind to you. I guess that happens to a lot of children—their parents playing favorites, giving all their love to one child, probably without even knowing they're doing it."

Oliver remembered his father's disappointment in him. For as long as he could remember, he had wondered why. Why his father didn't look at him the way he looked at Peter. He had been given a chance to change that, and he had decided to leave. What if the judge was right? What was Peter getting involved in?

Oliver lit another cigarette, drew on it.

"It doesn't matter anymore, Jennie. His life is here, with you. Mine will be where Charley is. After the war."

"I love having you back. So do Zoe and Theo. Well, I think Theo does. He's invited you into his studio, so he must be happy you're here." Jennie sat on the wooden porch swing. "You know, we've named you as their guardian in our will."

"Don't do that! Oh, God. I didn't mean that the way it sounded. I mean you don't *have* to do that. It wouldn't hurt my feelings if you chose someone else, someone married, better suited to take care of children." Peter must have thought that was droll. Finally tying Oliver to the family, from beyond the grave. Oliver was willing to help out but not to be the one responsible, not forever.

"They're not really children anymore. Peter and I don't know anyone we would rather see help them become adults. For all his anger about your leaving, Peter loves you, respects you. Look how fine a man Charley is."

Oliver stared into the darkness. He always credited Elizabeth for Charley.

"What about your sister? She has children."

"It's Theo. He's never going to grow out of whatever it is that—God, I don't want to say *is wrong with him*—makes him different. Wonderful, but different. For some reason, he's closer to you than to anyone else, except me and Zoe."

Oliver caved. He would do it for Jennie, for Theo. For his niece, whom he adored. Besides, it would probably never happen.

"Peter's a lucky man."

Oliver could hear the smile in Jennie's voice.

"I tell him that all the time."

Chapter 25

Oliver and Harley climbed almost four hundred feet to the top of Nicholl Nob, just over the tunnel that ran to Garrard Boulevard. Oliver looked toward the Pacific, where, almost six months to the day after the attack on Pearl Harbor, the US Navy had defeated the Japanese navy in the battle for the Midway Atoll, Japan's worst naval defeat in 350 years. The tide of the war in the Pacific had turned, and now the Allies would begin a relentless battle to take back the Pacific islands on their way to invading Japan.

While Harley explored the trails, Oliver listened to the songs of the red-winged blackbirds that swayed on the tops of rushes in the marsh below, their epaulets flashing red in the June sunshine. His orders had finally come through, and he was leaving the next day for Camp Lejeune, North Carolina. He had made peace with not knowing when Michael Fiori would be home from Montana; Harry wouldn't give up until the boy was back safely. It still bothered Oliver that he hadn't been able to connect the Klan to what had happened to the Fleming children, but Peter and his father would be safe as long as Peter didn't uncover new information about the fire. No, it was time for Oliver to leave, and he had come to say good-bye to Pt. Richmond, the bay, and the Golden Gate.

The trail he had played on as a child was blocked with olive-drab logs pointed at the sky like gun emplacements. Before enemy planes could get this close to the refinery and the shipyards, they would have to evade the ring of forts and camouflaged artillery that protected the headlands. Oliver had sat in the dining room at the Top of the Mark the night before, surrounded by white linens and candlelight, and listened to the thunder of the guns practicing while searchlights swept the entrance to the bay.

Soon he could be hearing artillery fire aimed at him. And Harley. At least they would be together. He didn't think he could have sent Harley to the Corps without him, but people all over the country had volunteered their family dogs to help win the war.

The shepherd loped out of the brush, tongue hanging out one side of his mouth in that goofy smile that made him look like a puppy again.

"Let's go see Mrs. Forgione and get you some water." They raced down the hill, Harley leaping in the air and spinning in circles.

Tonight, dinner with the family; tomorrow, active duty in the Marines. Oliver rubbed Harley's head.

"You and me, boy, off to who knows what. Let's go the café and finish saying our good-byes."

"Oliver, Oliver!" Mrs. Forgione stood in front of the café, beckoning him to hurry. "Thank God! You have to help the dog. I called Harry. He should be here soon. But they took the dog!"

"Calm down. Tell me what's happened. What dog?"

"Harmonica Man's dog, Emma."

"Who took her?"

"Paul Butler. Frank Slater made him take her to the pound."

"Why?"

"He said the dog attacked him when he arrested Harmonica Man, but she didn't. Mrs. Hermit and I saw it. The dog growled, but she didn't bite him. She tried to get between them, that's all."

"He arrested Roan?" *He must be frantic, locked up and without his dog.*

"Frank accused him of being an illegal alien and asked for his papers, and when Roan tried to walk away, Frank grabbed him and they started to tussle, and then the dog got in the middle."

"Where's Roan?"

"*Madonna mia!* At the police station. I called Harry to come help him. You need to help the dog. They're going to put her to sleep. I think if Mrs. Hermit and I hadn't gotten in the way, Frank would have shot her right there."

"Don't worry, I'll get the dog. But first I have to see Roan."

Harley started to get up, tongue still hanging out the side of his mouth. Oliver motioned him back down.

"Could Harley have some water? Please. I'll come back for him." He signaled the dog to stay.

When he ran down the slope beside the fire station to the back door of the jail, Oliver heard yelling and swearing and high-pitched keening. He pulled open the door and stopped.

A flurry of brightly colored rags and ribbons engulfed Frank. Bells jingled as Harmonica Man tried to free himself from the police holding him down.

"Stop! Just stop! Roan, stop struggling! I have Emma."

"E-m-m-m-m-ma?"

"Yes. I have her. Calm down."

"Stay out of this, Wright! I thought you were g-g-g-gone!" Frank mocked Roan and swung around on Oliver.

"I'm not gone yet, and I'll be back."

Frank stepped into Oliver's space. "Maybe you'll be back and maybe you won't. But *if* you come back, make sure you're in one piece. There's no room on the force for cripples."

For a moment, Frank's words stunned Oliver, but then he shook them off. "Why in God's name did you arrest Roan?"

"For all I know, he's an illegal alien. He doesn't have any papers. He roams around the Point, spying on people, sitting on the hills, watching the bay, playing that damned harmonica. It would be the perfect cover for a spy."

"You know he's not an enemy alien, and he's not a vagrant." Oliver wasn't sure how long Roan had lived in Pt. Richmond, but when Oliver had come home to visit his mother, he had caught glimpses of Roan walking the hills. "He lives in Mrs. Dunn's boardinghouse. You know that. What the hell is wrong with you?"

"Doesn't matter. He resisted arrest. He's staying here." Frank became conciliatory. "Why don't you come to the back and fill out a report on his background, and we'll see what's what?"

Roan started wailing again, and Oliver realized Frank was trying to delay him."Don't worry, Roan. And don't resist. I've got her!" Oliver took off and ran into Harry at the door.

"I'm going for the dog. Tell him that Emma is safe."

Oliver hoped what he said was true. Frank had tried to delay him.

They weren't going to wait to kill the dog. He ran up the hill to get Harley, then jumped in the car and sped past the Indian statue to the veterinarian's office. When they arrived, Oliver flung open the car door and ran inside. He waved off the secretary and cautiously poked his head into the treatment room, where Andrew was looking into a dog's ear.

"Sorry to interrupt, Andrew, but it's an emergency."

"What is it?"

"Emma's at the pound, about to be put down!"

"Emma?" Andrew looked puzzled.

"Harmonica Man's dog, Emma!"

"But why?"

"I'll explain on the way. Just come."

"God, she must be terrified. She and Harmonica Man are never apart. Let me get some supplies."

"Hurry up! We could be too late."

Oliver glanced at the vet. *Wonder if Roan cares what they call him.* "Harmonica Man. His name is Roan."

Paul Butler turned around when the car squealed to a stop in front of the pound. He hooked his thumbs on his gun belt and smiled when Oliver and Andrew jumped out of the car.

"No point in working up a sweat—she's already in the chamber. Wanna watch?"

Oliver pushed Butler aside and ran behind Andrew to the gas chamber.

"I've tried to convince the pound to stop gassing the animals, but they argued dollars and cents and wouldn't listen." The vet shook his head. "You don't ever want to see what happens inside them."

"Too late for that, Doc." Oliver could never forget what he had witnessed one day in Seattle when he had gone to interview an animal control officer about a burglary. The dogs had been thrust into the chamber on long poles with a noose at the end. The panicked animals had scrambled to get out again. They whimpered and howled until the gas had begun to work and they collapsed on the floor. Perhaps the worst part for Oliver was having been told that sometimes when the animal control officer opened the refrigerator door to put in freshly gassed dogs, a tail wagged among the pile of bodies. Then they were burned.

Oliver watched Andrew, white-faced with fury, grab the chamber operator by the arm.

"Shut off the gas and open the door!"

"I can't open the door. The gas will escape."

"Get out." Andrew shoved the man toward the door, then shut off the gas himself and grabbed the door latch. "Oliver, when I open this door, hold your breath and help me carry Emma. We'll have to get outside ASAP."

"Got it."

Emma's orange-and-white paws twitched on the metal floor. Andrew took in a deep breath. Then he dove into the chamber, grasped Emma's shoulders, and pulled her through the opening.

Oliver caught her back end as it slid by and helped Andrew rush her outside.

They laid the limp dog out on the ground by the car. "We've got you, girl." Emma's eyelids flickered when she heard Andrew's voice.

"She needs oxygen. She's drowsy but responsive. Get my bag, please." Andrew checked her gums and lips.

"The oxygen should stop any damage to her heart and brain." He fit one end of a tube to a bottle and the other end to a metal funnel. "I don't know if this will work. Hold the bottle while I press the funnel against her face."

Oliver held the green-and-black bottle with one hand and stroked Emma with the other. "What is this?"

"A bailout bottle. I have a college buddy in the Army Air Forces who's working to develop a better system for pilots who ditch. He brought me a couple bottles to see if I could figure out a way to rig them up with canine gas masks. Unfortunately for Emma, I've been too busy to work on it."

Andrew checked Emma's eyes and tried to take her pulse while holding the funnel tight. "The bottle holds about eight to ten minutes of oxygen. The tricky part is that there's no regulator, but with all the play in the funnel, I'm sure she's not getting too much at once. If anything, it will be too little."

The men soothed the dog and waited. Harley lay nearby, his head on his paws, watching. Soon Oliver heard a *thump, thump, thump.* For a second, he didn't realize it was Emma's tail striking the packed earth.

"Oh, good girl, Emma."

She tried to raise her head.

"Let's get her back to the office. She needs fluids. We want to make sure she doesn't have any long-term effects from this."

Harley gave Emma a sniff and hopped in the front seat. Andrew sat in the back, stroking Emma's head.

"What kind of dog is she?" Oliver asked.

"I can't figure her out." Andrew said. Oliver watched him in the rearview mirror. He shook his head. "She could be a golden retriever crossed with a bull terrier; or an Australian shepherd crossed with a corgi or terrier; or maybe boxer, collie, and something else short. Hard to say."

"Maybe Harley knows."

"Wouldn't doubt it."

The shepherd, who sat square on the front seat as if he were the navigator, looked over his shoulder when Emma whimpered.

"My father is also a vet. When I opened my practice, he gave me a plaque to hang in my office." Andrew stroked the golden dog's head. "On it were engraved the words of St. Francis of Assisi that I had read time and time again in my father's clinic: 'If you have men who will exclude any of God's creatures from the shelter of compassion and pity, you will have men who will deal likewise with their fellow men.'"

Oliver thought about war, about gratuitous cruelty.

"That Slater has a lot to answer for."

Chapter 26

It was almost closing time when Oliver finally made it to the Café Avellino.

"Oliver, what happened? How are they?" Edna Hermit called to him from behind the counter.

"Andrew thinks Emma will be as good as new. After Harry got Roan out of jail, he took him over to Andrew's office to wait for us. I guess Paul Butler went back to the station and told everyone Andrew and I were at the pound. Everything is good. Charges dropped, Emma safe. She was woo-woo-wooing to Roan when she wasn't licking his tears. Harry had a time keeping Roan under control until he knew Emma was safe."

"Too bad Harry wasn't there when Frank was waving that gun in Mrs. Forgione's face. I'd like to have seen what Harry would have done then!" Harry would have taken Frank down a peg or two. Edna smiled at the thought.

Mrs. Forgione asked Oliver what he would like to eat, then started making his sandwich. "That Frank. He was a mean one, but he seemed to change after he married Cora. Now I don't know. Seems he's back to hating anyone who's happy." Mrs. Forgione layered ham, fontina, roasted peppers, and caramelized onions on Oliver's ciabatta. A squirt of olive oil and a dash of vinegar finished it off. "I think he can't stand how much Harmonica Man and Emma love each other. As if he has to smash the love." She handed Oliver his sandwich over the counter.

"What did you think of Frank? When he was a boy?" Oliver leaned on the marble top.

"He was hard to figure out. Sometimes he seemed anxious to please, could be a real charmer. Other times he looked right through you. I've seen him throw mud on a girl's new dress or knock a bird's nest out of a tree. As if he had to spoil what other people had. Maybe because he had precious little himself." Mrs. Forgione shook her head. "Let's hope whatever has brought back that anger goes away soon."

Edna muttered to herself, "I think I'm looking at what brought back that anger, and he's going away tomorrow."

"What did you say, Mrs. Hermit?"

Ouch. She hadn't meant to say that out loud. "I said I hear you're going away tomorrow. I wish you well, Oliver."

Edna didn't think it would matter how far away he went now. Probably would've been better if he hadn't come back. Probably would've been better if Cora hadn't come back to Richmond after her mother died, but she had thought of Dr. Chalmers and his wife as a second family. The doctor had understood when Cora had told him that she and Edna were more than just friends, and he had been as upset as Edna was when Cora took up with Frank. Edna still didn't like him. Something off about that man.

"Penny for your thoughts, Edna." Mrs. Forgione started to chop the greens.

"Just thinking about Cora and Frank, how he seemed to be a different person there for a while."

"He had a hard life. I often wondered what might have happened if Phyllis Brennan hadn't died. Cora's probably the first person to be kind to him since then."

"Phyllis Brennan?"

"A local girl he'd been sweet on since high school."

"What happened?"

"They found her on Keller's beach. No one ever knew what happened. There was a rumor she might have been pregnant, but I would have been surprised if that were true."

Edna thought about pregnant young girls. Not an easy life for anyone.

"Was there anyone for Frank after her?"

"A parade of blondes, but no one for long."

"He surely charmed Cora." Frank had seemed to make her happy. But now, when Edna went to do the laundry that gave them an excuse to be together, Cora was different. It was as if a light had gone out in her. Again. She had been a shining girl, but what had happened that last month in nursing school had changed her. Edna would be there if Cora needed her. What they shared tied them together for life, Frank be damned.

Oliver sipped his cappuccino and bit into the warm sandwich. Sometimes he felt like a barbarian when he ate in the café. Most of the men cut their sandwiches with a knife and fork, missing the feeling of warm bread in their hands, of biting through the layers, of wiping juice off their chins. The Italians tried to blend in because of the war, but they had no idea how many things made them stand out as "not American."

He took a little package out of his pocket and opened it again. The bundle looked like Roan: red and yellow ribbons woven together to make a little scrap of cloth, much like the streamers of cloth Roan decorated himself and Emma with. You could barely see his face through the strips of fabric and feathers he had sewn into his cap.

He wandered with Emma up and down the hills of the Point, pushing his bicycle or fussing with the bundles he had lashed to it. He had a room, so why did he carry so much stuff with him? Maybe he was afraid someone would take his strips of cloth. Some were from Guatemala, some from Peru and Mexico. Roan would explain the embroidery and say where things were from, but he wouldn't tell how he got them. Sometimes you heard the plaintive harmonica before you saw them: three dots on a hillside, Emma out in front, leading the way, her magnificent feathered tail like a drum major's baton, Roan pushing the bicycle, all three festooned like Christmas trees.

The cloth in Oliver's hand contained a small tin heart, concave on one side and convex on the other. He thought it was called a *milagro*.

Roan had still looked shaken when he'd handed the bundle to Oliver. Then he raised his head and looked Oliver directly in the eyes, and Oliver saw him, saw into him. Something passed between them in that moment. Something beyond two people, beyond ordinary life, as if their souls had become one, on a plane of pure being. It passed and Oliver was left looking back into Roan's eyes, at deep intelligence and pain, at earnestness. He dropped his own eyes, overwhelmed by the beauty of the other man's unguarded emotion. *He saves people from seeing this, with his camouflage of color and pattern, with his lowered gaze and odyssey through the hills. He's just Harmonica Man, labeled and dismissed.*

"Thank you." Roan stumbled over the words. Partly not used to talking and partly not able to, Oliver thought.

"You're welcome, Roan."

Roan hesitated, opened his mouth, and struggled to form the words he wanted to say. Oliver struggled, too—to keep his mouth shut and not try to guess what Roan wanted to tell him. Finally, he heard, "Will you be Em-Em-Em-ma's . . ." Roan stopped, defeated. "Will you t-t-t-take care of her if anything happens t-t-t-to me?"

It was more likely something would happen to Oliver than to Roan, but, given the events of the day, maybe Roan just needed reassurance.

"I'd be proud to be Emma's guardian. And I'll tell Theo and Zoe that if you and Emma ever need anything, they're to help you. Go to them, or Mrs. Forgione. She'll know what to do."

Roan tapped his chest twice to thank Oliver, then gestured to him with those fingers, as if he were making Oliver a promise.

Oliver rubbed the little silver heart, wondering where Roan had gotten it and what it meant to him. He slipped it into his pocket. *Every warrior needs a talisman.*

Chapter 27

Jonah sat outside the Café Avellino, enjoying the warm, dusty smell of autumn.

He felt guilty sitting in the sun, having a cappuccino. He always felt guilty when he wrote to Oliver.

Dear Oliver,
Mrs. Forgione says hello. Yes, I am once again at the café, indulging myself. I won't tell you what I am having. You can probably guess.

It's hard to believe you've been gone four months. Especially since I thought you would have won the war by now. We've had our own little war here. Someone decided Pt. Richmond would be a good place to open a Negro USO. Even found an empty building they thought would be perfect. But the good citizens did not agree. Guess who won?

Despite my shortcomings and tendency toward self-immolation, I'm head of a welding crew now. I'm lucky to have easygoing folks who just want to get the job done. The women make pretty good welders and fit into some of the smaller spaces. Sometimes there's tension when a couple guys decide they both like the same girl, but if they weren't fighting over that, they'd be fighting over something else.

How is that handsome Harley doing? Making friends? My landlady just took in a stray. Don't know where she came from, but I suggested we not let her go out and bring the rest of the street dogs home with her. Mrs. Standish is calling her Minnie Marie. Don't ask. I don't know why.

I ran into a friend of yours—Auntie Josephine. She says hello. Wanted you to know nothing has changed. I told her there wasn't much you could do about it from North Carolina. She just snorted. But I think she likes you.

As you can see, I'm running out of room. Keep safe, Oliver.
Your friend,
Jonah

Wonder what he's doing right now. I should have told him a woman named Monica asked after him, too. Next time.

Jonah looked down the street toward the police station. The Indian statue had collapsed, its pieces used for scrap in the war effort. A golden glow touched the tops of the eucalyptus trees, and they bent in the wind as the sky flared red, then orange, and the sun slid behind the hills.

Chapter 28

They had been on the road since daybreak and had just made the turn to go back to base. The soldiers moved as one to the rhythm of the count, boots slapping on tarmac, beating out a song of their own. Nate Hermit's face glistened with sweat. Another scorcher. October in Texas, and ten miles to go, with the heat radiating up through the soles of their feet, full packs digging into their shoulders. Minus the weight of the carbines they'd had to turn in shortly after they'd been issued. The men had given the rifles back reluctantly, complaining to each other.

"How we supposed to kill those Krauts if they don't let us practice?"

"Expect we need to get good at throwing them potatoes we're always peeling. Closest thing we're going to have to hand grenades."

The men had made uneasy jokes about it, but the fact remained they weren't being taught much of anything about fighting. Rumor was, the town had complained to the base commander about arming Negroes.

God knows why the military would send us where we aren't wanted. Why make it so fucking hard on everyone? Nate had been wondering that since his feet had hit the Texas dust and he and Steve Buonarotti had been separated again. Right now he tried not to think, wanted to just enjoy being outside, even in this god-awful heat. It felt good to be moving. Moving instead of digging a latrine or washing dishes. He ached to run, to play ball or swim in the bay. To feel the heat fade away at the end of a day instead of laying heavy on him, leaving no room for sleep or dreams.

Sweat ran down his back. Soon, he hoped, they would take a break. He had tossed and turned the night before, thinking about what had happened in the PX that day. The colored soldiers had gone pin-drop quiet when Steve and two of their friends from Richmond came in and sat down with Nate. He heard a rumbling around him. The men in his unit started to push back their chairs, but Nate waved them back to their seats, got up, and hugged Steve and the other men. *Fuck the Army if they think they can keep us segregated just because we're in this Lone Star hellhole.* If he couldn't go to their canteen, they damn well would come to his.

He had barely gotten them a soda from the cooler, when the door banged against the tar-paper wall. *How the hell did that mean-assed corporal find out so fast?* He flew into the canteen, flanked by two MPs with their hands on their service weapons. He yanked Steve off his chair and ordered him and the other white soldiers out. When they balked, an MP drew his sidearm and motioned to the door.

"This canteen is off-limits to you nigger-lovers. Got it?"

Steve turned back to the corporal, his fists balled.

"Mind what you're about to do, Bone-a-rotten. I might not be able to do more than put you in the stockade for disobeying an order, but these 'people' don't have powerful relations to help them."

He flicked his head at the colored men frozen in place.

The corporal walked around Steve, smacking his baton into his palm. "You're almost dark enough to pass as one of them. Want me to transfer you? Want to eat with them, sleep with them, do their work?"

Steve threw a glance at Nate, didn't answer.

"No, I didn't think so. Hypocrite."

Nate didn't blame Steve for not jumping at the chance to be a second-class citizen, but he thought Steve might be blaming himself.

Nate almost bumped into the guy in front of him when the whole unit stopped without Sarge's barking out the order. The men broke rank and moved up to see what was going on. Sarge didn't react; he seemed to be keeping an eye on their white lieutenant.

Four police cars blocked the road. State troopers stood outside the cars, holding pump-action rifles. The lieutenant faced off with one of them. If the lieutenant hadn't been white, they probably would have shot him.

"We don't allow Nee-groes to march on our roads."

"We are the United States Army! We can march where we damn well please!"

"Not in Texas."

"Move those cars. We're going through." The lieutenant ordered the men to fall in and signaled the sergeant to advance. The men obeyed, shooting looks at one another. The lieutenant was new—decent, but not someone who inspired confidence. The sergeant walked down the ranks, telling his men to keep cool.

Nate heard the noise of the cops' rifles chambering a round; the *ka-chunk* made the hairs on the back of his neck stand up.

"Off our road." The trooper took another step toward the lieutenant. "Get these fuckin' niggers off our road."

Four more men with shotguns got out of the police cars.

The lieutenant looked to the side of the road. A ditch filled with dirty brown water and weeds ran between it and a thicket of brambles and thistles.

"There's no place to go."

"Way I see it, that's not our problem." The trooper gave them that superior smile only those Southern rednecks could do.

The lieutenant seemed to be about to argue. Nate wondered what would happen if the police fired or if the soldiers jumped them. *Not going to turn out good for anybody.* The lieutenant seemed to come to the same conclusion. He nodded to the sergeant, who ordered the men into the ditch.

Nate climbed a foot or so down the bank and sank up to his knees in the muddy water. *Jesus Christ.* How long were they going to have to slog through this? They must be eight miles from base.

The police fanned out along the road, threatening stragglers with their rifles. It looked as if some of the soldiers were about to go at it with them, take their chances, when one of the rifles boomed and water erupted in front of the first man.

"Cottonmouth." The trooper smiled a cold smile. "You're welcome."

Nate almost flew out of the ditch. Another guy grabbed his arm. "Easy, brother. Don't give them the satisfaction. Be patient." He spoke calming words, but his voice shook with anger.

The men started forward, and the cars followed. Along the way, a pickup carrying men with guns and a Confederate flag joined the procession. Cars coming the other way honked and yelled at them. Some even turned around to join the line of cars and trucks that followed the troopers. Nate thought it was a fucking humiliating circus parade, with them as the performing animals. And then Sarge began to sing "Oh! What a Time." The song moved back through the line of men, connecting them to one another and to other men who had endured and survived. Nate clapped, that clap that came from your whole body, even if you were walking in a ditch. The men could have been at their Sunday service, voices blending together in that harmony that lifted your soul, brought you back to who you were, separate from the white devils who tormented you. Eventually, the ditch dried up and the going got a little easier on their legs. Even so, it was a long way home, and they sweated every step, not sure what the growing crowd might do.

Chapter 29

Columbus Day. Harry should have been happy that Italians were no longer considered enemies, that they were even allowed to fish again. Of course, the Navy still had their boats, which meant some crews would have to sign on with non-Italian owners whose boats the Navy hadn't asked for.

Bennie Fiori's brother had decided to stay on land, helping Bennie supply vegetables to the community. Harry had seen the Fioris after Mass, when Michael had stopped to thank him for his help in bringing him home. The boy was too thin, too quiet. While Paola talked to Michael and Mia, Bennie told Harry that Michael blamed himself for Mr. Posto's death. He had died of pneumonia in the cold of Montana, even after Michael had gotten him into the hospital. Harry wondered if the man had simply given up, died of a broken heart.

While Michael healed, he would help his father work some land in El Cerrito. People thought Bennie had bought the land and house for a song when its owner and his family had been taken away. Some people admired Bennie for his shrewdness, and some criticized him for taking advantage. But Bennie had told Harry he didn't care what people thought, as long as they didn't figure out he was taking care of the property until the Japanese were released. If people knew it still belonged to the Japanese family, they would destroy it, the way they had destroyed the florist's greenhouses.

Maybe Harry couldn't get excited about Italians' not being classified as enemies anymore because the war had done nothing to change people's prejudices. He had no illusions about the reason for changing the status of Italians. The Democrats needed Italian votes in the upcoming election to stay in office, to maintain control of Congress in a country seething with unrest over labor disputes and racial discrimination.

Racial discrimination. The reason he hadn't slept much since Steve had called two nights ago, his voice raw with hurt and anger. Harry had no answer to his son's questions about what had happened to him and Nate. Steve would never ask for special treatment for himself, but he begged his father to get his friend out of the South.

While Harry's staff car sped across the Bay Bridge, he thought about having seen Steve and Nate off at the train station the day they'd left for the army. Mrs. Hermit and Paola had put on brave smiles, glanced at each other when Anna Maria kissed Nate on the cheek and told him she would write to him. It startled Harry: first his son going off to war, and now his little girl growing up—neither of which was supposed to have happened yet. He ignored the insidious voice that kept reminding him of that kiss, whispering, *What if you bring him back and they want to be together? What will you do then?*

The car bypassed Treasure Island, one of the busiest naval headquarters in the country, and made its way to the Presidio. Harry breathed in the smell of the bay and eucalyptus and relaxed. The Fourth Army support battalions sprawled across the former Spanish garrison, but when Harry entered its forested hills and tile-roofed buildings, he felt as if he were traveling to another century.

While he waited outside Colonel Burton's office, Harry thought about his conversations with his contacts on local draft boards and with white officers who were working with new recruits. None denied the mistreatment of the Negro soldiers, although some still thought the troops needed to be segregated.

He hoped his old friend Miles Burton had not become too "army" and would okay Harry's plan. If he did, Harry could help Nate without having to confront the whole issue of institutionalized discrimination.

Would he be as concerned about a man he didn't know, who hadn't grown up with his son and sat at his table? Maybe not, but if his plan worked, it would help other Negro servicemen, too. One step at a time.

Finally, he was ushered into the office.

The colonel finished signing the paper under his hand and looked up at Harry."The uniform suits you, Harry. I think you should have stayed in with me."

"I don't think so, sir."

"At ease, Captain." Colonel Burton waved Harry to a chair. "What did you want to see me about?"

"Are you aware that the Army Air Forces are training colored pilots at the Tuskegee base and the Navy is enlisting colored men to serve as more than messmen?"

"Yes. What does that have to do with us?"

"There's a movement to achieve at least the appearance of equality in those forces. I think we could do something similar and get out in front of the administration."

The colonel looked interested. "What do you have in mind?"

"Negro assistants. Train them as MPs and attach them to JAG offices. They can do investigative work under the supervision of white officers. It would help promote the appearance of fairness in our investigations where colored personnel are involved."

"Interesting. How would you select them?"

"We'd consider standard intelligence-test scores. We already have data on most of the men, and we'd take the best. We could start with a few good soldiers as a trial, get some good press, and if it didn't work as planned, we would return them to their units."

The colonel smiled. "I assume you have someone in mind."

No fool, the colonel.

"I do. A man who has been friends with my son for years. They went to Berkeley together. He intended to go to law school one day. Good family. Quiet. Nice manners. Very acceptable." God forgive him. He couldn't believe he was talking that way about Nate. Next thing you knew, he'd be showing the colonel Nate's teeth.

"How many in all?"

"I'd like to start with twelve. I can oversee a training program, and then we can decide where they might be most useful. If it's successful, we can add more men."

Harry watched the colonel consider the idea. He was known for his decisiveness, which could work against you sometimes. But he also liked to be thought of as a maverick.

"Do it. Keep me posted. And good luck. I think you're going to need it."

1943

Chapter 30

It had been a year, four months, and a bit over two weeks since Oliver had started his work at Camp Lejeune. But who was counting? He sat in the October heat against the trunk of a poplar tree, aware of how they had been used throughout the South. Whenever he looked at them, he heard Billie Holiday's haunting indictment of white America. "Strange Fruit," indeed.

Harley dug down to cooler earth and stretched out, panting, while Oliver unfolded a letter from Jonah.

As I write this, Oliver, the wind sweeps across a blackened hill, swirling bitter ashes down on the Point, the street, this letter.

The town is up in arms. Everyone says it's just like the fire that killed two children before the war. You must remember. They were trapped when a cross burning set this same meadow on fire and spread around the hill. Sammy and Ellie Fleming. Don't know if you knew the family.

No one can believe the stupid bastards who burned the cross then were willing to take the chance of burning one again. They had to have known it was too windy and too dry, but they went ahead anyway, so intent on intimidating an uppity minister that they didn't care who else got hurt.

It was more than a coincidence that they picked the spot where the minister had started to hold sunrise services. The same minister who was renting a house in a white neighborhood.

Apparently, he mistook tolerance for acceptance. Tolerance—an ugly word, don't you think? The inherent judgment and superiority oozing from the syllables.

Everyone thinks they know who did it, but no one can prove it. Just like before, the likely suspects were all conveniently playing cards together and the police can't shake their stories. Wish you were here to get to the bottom of this. (Now I sound like Auntie Josephine.)

Everyone says it's the Klan again and that the Slaters and the Butlers must be involved because their families have been longtime Klan members. Have to wonder. That kind of hatred can run deep in families. Slater is investigating, along with his pal Butler. Talk about the fox and the henhouse.

If they leave it up to Slater, he'll find a way to blame it on the Negro servicemen.

Take care, Oliver.

Your friend,
Jonah

Oliver looked up at the flag hanging limply in the still heat. *The Klan again. Wonder why they picked the hill instead of the house the minister wanted to rent. Something feels off about the whole thing. Peter will see this as another chance to find out whether the Klan was involved in the Fleming deaths. No point in writing to him, trying to get him to be careful.*

Maybe Harry will be able to talk some sense into him.

Chapter 31

Drops of rain silvered the window behind Harry's desk. He had swiveled toward it to compose himself. He knew running back and forth between his JAG duties and the district attorney's office was wearing down the little patience he had. It had taken a year, but the training program for the Negro MPs was established and now Nate Hermit was an MP assigned to him.

The two days he was spending at the district attorney's office were barely enough to keep up with the avalanche of cases caused by the increased population of Richmond. He had been letting most of the work fall on the shoulders of his staff and realized he needed to appoint someone as acting district attorney for the rest of the war. In all fairness, that person should be the man sitting on the other side of his desk. Peter Wright. Harry turned away from the window and leaned toward his eager assistant.

"You're not a one-man band, Peter. You have to keep me informed about what you're doing."

"I didn't want word leaking out about my investigation."

"If you didn't need my approval to give this informant immunity, you probably wouldn't be telling even me this much!" Harry breathed on his glasses, rubbed them with a handkerchief. "Tell me everything."

"There's not much to tell. A few days ago I got a call at home from a man who said he had been there that night in 1941, that it was an accident—not the cross burning, but setting the meadow on fire—and he had proof of who else had been there."

"What kind of proof?"

"He said there were photographs."

"Of whom?"

"He wouldn't say." Peter leaned forward in his chair. "They do photograph these things. I once saw a postcard of a crowd of people smiling and pointing at a man they had lynched. There were even children there."

Harry swallowed in disgust. He had seen similar things. He thought the people in the crowd had to be less than human, the product of decades of denying the suffering of slaves, of thinking of Negroes as property. But then he realized the photos he had seen were taken in Indiana. Not a slave state. He couldn't think about what it meant to enjoy the torture of another human being. To celebrate it, to want a souvenir of it. He cleared his throat.

"When will he give you this proof?"

"This weekend, after he has the agreement. We're meeting somewhere outside Richmond—he doesn't want to take the chance of being seen talking to me. He hinted there was more to it than we've thought."

"Is he saying there was more to it than merely intimidating the professor?"

"He hinted that there was. Said he had proof of what was behind it."

Harry considered the man before him. Peter seemed to quiver with energy. It was exhausting trying to keep a rein on this bright, ambitious man who wanted to become a judge like his father. This could be the breakthrough case that did it for Peter.

"Why would this person risk his life informing? Isn't he afraid of reprisals? And what does he think will happen if his *friends* decide to inform on him?" Harry asked.

"He doesn't want to testify. I'll talk to him, but he seemed pretty sure he could survive this as long as he wasn't indicted."

"How can we make a case without his testimony?"

"He says we'll have all the proof we need without it."

"Has it occurred to you that the people involved in this might have heard more about your progress in the investigation than I have? You haven't stopped nosing around, asking questions. Maybe they think you might be getting close, and this is a trap." He raised his hand to stop Peter's protest. "Think about it. How did he know to call you, not me or someone else in the department? Or the police. And why two years later?"

Peter hesitated. "I think he called me once before, after that beating on Cutting Boulevard where the Negro shipyard worker died, but then he didn't call back. He must know me. Besides, I think the more recent hill fire might have something to do with why he's coming forward now."

"Perhaps. But no one was hurt this time." Harry thought for a moment. "Maybe he'll change his mind again."

"I don't think so. He choked up when he talked about the Fleming kids. Mentioned their names, as if he knew them."

Harry waved a secretary away from the door to his office, but she opened it and poked her head in.

"We're busy here. Whatever you have can wait."

"But—"

"Out! I'll speak to you later about this."

The blond woman hesitated, took a moment to apologize, and closed the door.

Peter slipped the grant of immunity forms into his briefcase. "Where were we?"

"Wondering why the informant called you."

"Maybe he knows me, knows I've been investigating. He needn't have a sinister reason."

"Don't be naive. The men who did this have a lot to lose. They were tolerated, maybe even admired, but the whole city would still like to see them punished for killing those children. I don't need to tell you to be careful."

"Yes, boss." Peter grabbed his briefcase and headed out the door.

Harry shook his head. *He thinks he's invincible.*

Chapter 32

Peter should have sent someone to pick up the car. Friday was busy enough without adding errands. How had Sandy been awarded the contracts for the city's business? Something else to look into.

Near the back of the garage, Peter saw a man who seemed to be arguing with himself. He was large; the white apron strings digging into his back reminded Peter of the strings around a pork roast. An arm in a blue sleeve waved a paper that semaphored in and out behind the larger man. Must be Sandy Slater back there.

The larger man moved. Sandy hesitated when he saw Peter. "Mr. Wright."

The other man teetered like a top as he spun around. Sandy muttered something, and the man nodded to Peter and left. Peter tried to place him as he watched him leave the garage.

"Mr. Wright. Didn't see you there. What can I do for you?"

"Who was that, Sandy?"

"George, the butcher."

"I know him from somewhere. Not the shops."

"He's very civic minded." Sandy said it as if it were a bad thing. "Probably seen him in the newspaper. I think he's taking a run at city council or something."

"Right." Peter was still distracted by the scene. "I came to pick up the car you're servicing for us. Someone from the office dropped it off."

Sandy wiped his hands on a greasy cloth. His reddish hair stood up in a wave off his forehead, and he had a round sort of nose. He looked like the character in Zoe's French book. The one with the little white dog.

"The person who brought it in said it had stalled a few times. It might be the timing. Haven't had a chance to get to it yet. I thought you didn't need it till Monday."

"I need it this weekend."

"You know we do everything we can to keep the city cars in tip-top shape." Sandy looked at the neon Harley-Davidson clock on the wall and sighed. "It's late, and I wanted to leave early tonight, but I'll drop everything and make sure it's ready. Let's say an hour, hour and a half."

"I don't want to put you out." Peter's tone was pitched to remind Sandy who the customer was.

"No. No. It's fine. It's better to be sure she's ready for the road. Are you going far?" Sandy seemed to want to mollify him.

"Just a district meeting in Sacramento."

"How you planning on going?"

"Not much choice, really. I'll probably go straight up the Lincoln Highway."

"Well, take it easy. There've been some heavy rains around Davis. Least that's what I've been hearing."

"I have some work to do." Peter tapped his briefcase. "I'll be at the Baltic if you need me. If not, see you at five."

On his way to the Baltic, Peter passed the Café Avellino. He didn't understand what Oliver had seen in the gaudy Italian place. Jennie had dragged Peter to Enrico's wake. Seeing the men laughing and speaking to each other in Italian had disgusted him. All he could think of were the mobs that had grown in strength during Prohibition and the violent way they dealt with law enforcement.

How had Buonarotti become the district attorney? It wasn't a position traditionally filled by someone with an *i* at the end of his name. He must be connected to some of the old Italian families with money. Before the war, they had been growing powerful. That was part of the reason they hadn't been interned like the Japanese. The mayors of New York City and San Francisco were both Italian, although Mayor Rossi's political career was probably over. He hadn't been a fascist sympathizer after all, but the mud his enemies had thrown still stuck to him.

The Baltic smelled like beer and cigarette smoke. Peter considered the row of single-malt whiskeys behind the mahogany bar and settled on a Macallan. He slid into a booth, his back to the wall, and faced the window that looked out on Park Place. He sipped his drink and tried to concentrate on reading the pleadings written by newer members of the staff. Paperwork had piled up while he pressed the police and informants about the fire on the hill. It was so damned frustrating. No one would talk. As outraged as the community had been two years ago, the Klan's long memory and reputation for vengeance chilled everyone. Most people thought Sandy Slater and his nephew Frank had something to do with it. Some had even seen a group of men in the back of Sandy's truck coming from the hill. Still, it was a case of everyone's being sure they knew who had done it but having no proof. Until now.

He looked at the paperwork for Mr. X's immunity. He would fill it in when he met with the informant the next morning, hopefully to get names for indictments. After he and Jennie returned from Sacramento, he'd submit them to the grand jury.

He wanted those bastards. This wasn't a case of breaking windows or beating up some shipyard worker. As much as people had been willing to look the other way where the Klan was concerned, this time Peter was sure he could get a conviction.

Curious to see how credible this guy is. And why he's willing to betray the Klan.

No matter what Peter had promised the informant, if he didn't come through with enough evidence to convict, Peter would make sure he testified. More than one way to skin a cat.

The next morning, Peter wished he had stayed in bed. Four o'clock was an ungodly hour to meet anyone. He stood in the drizzle behind an all-night diner in Berkeley—the informant's choice. Vagrants slept on soggy newspapers that tore when the men stirred in their sleep. Dreaming of what? The past? Their mistakes? Maybe their next drink?

Peter skirted the iridescent puddles and unidentified patches between him and the back door of the diner. The men didn't seem to go far from their beds to relieve themselves. He clenched a gloved hand over his nose and mouth and picked his way to a half-open door. Something dark skittered into the shadows between the garbage bins. Glass clinked.

He nudged the door open with a corner of his briefcase and stepped onto checkerboard tiles that stretched down a narrow hallway. The air smelled of bleach and some kind of disinfectant. He took a few tentative steps, then steeled himself and moved toward the door at the end of the hall. He was halfway there when he felt pressure against his back.

Chapter 33

"Oh dear. Are you all right? I'm so sorry. My fault. I didn't know anyone was here. Let me wipe that off." A woman who looked like she hadn't gotten enough to eat growing up, or since, pulled out a gray rag and dabbed at Peter's shoes. She had backed up out of an office with her mop handle sticking out of the bucket.

"You stupid woman!" Peter had almost fainted when he'd felt the mop handle between his shoulder blades. "It's fine. Just stop. It's fine."

He waved her off and continued down the hallway.

A man motioned to Peter from a doorway.

Peter held out his hand. "I'm Peter. What's your name?"

The man looked at Peter's hand, then reached for it as if he knew touching it would mean no going back. He pumped it once and let go.

"I need to know your name."

"Regis. Regis Simmons."

Regis had one of those squared-off heads, the chin as wide as the forehead, blunt. He looked to be in his late twenties, maybe early thirties.

"Good. Let's sit down, Regis."

"You want something to drink?"

"No, no. I'm fine. You picked this place, so I assume it's safe."

The guy nodded once. Nodded again as if reassuring himself.

"Why don't you tell me what happened, Regis? Take your time. I'm going to take some notes so I keep it all straight. Okay? Let's start with the fire in 1941."

"Look, no one was supposed to get hurt. That's why we burned the cross on the hill instead of in the neighborhood." It was more a plea than a statement.

"Why did you burn the cross at all?"

"To put that uppity colored teacher in his place. He thought he could buy a house in a white neighborhood. We had to do something. They said the war would bring more and more of them in, and if we didn't show them we meant business, we'd be overrun with them, like rats." Regis said the words as if they disgusted him. "Anyway, we never meant for anyone to get killed, not then and not—"

"Not . . . ?"

"Nothing. Just a fight that got out of hand. Most of the men involved are in the service now."

"But not all of them."

"No." Regis looked down at his hands.

Regis could be talking about the death of the Negro shipyard worker that Oliver had been investigating.

"Did you call me after that fight? And then not show up?"

Regis nodded. "I don't want to talk about that right now."

"Okay. Tell me about the fire in 1941. What happened?"

"The hill was so dry. We cleared an area, but the winds kicked up instead of dying down like they should've. I told him! I told him we should wait, that the wind could carry that fire anywhere. But he said it was too late to wait. They had just found out someone was going to sell to that teacher, and if we didn't move soon, no telling what would happen."

"But you tried to stop it. That says a lot about you. About your character. You were in with the wrong crowd. It can happen to anyone."

The man looked away, then back. "It might be hard for you to understand, but when I was first invited to join the group, I thought it was about being American, about fighting for what you believed in."

"And something happened to change what you thought?"

"The night we got back from the fire, I heard the leader talking on the phone. It sounded as if he had been paid to set the fire, but then I thought I must have misunderstood. And then I forgot about it."

"But now?"

"I think we were being used. For someone else to make money. Now I'm sure of it."

Peter started to ask why Regis was sure, but the man went on talking.

"I just feel so bad about Sammy and Ellie. And Joe. We thought he was finally getting over it, and then this last fire just stirred everything up again. He goes to that meadow every day and just sits. Maude can't get him to do anything. He won't eat, can't sleep." He muffled a sob. "It would have been better if he had died in the fire!"

"You know them? You know the Flemings?"

"Maude's my sister." Tears ran down Regis's face. "I had to go to their funeral. Help carry their little coffins. Hold my sister's hand while she cursed God and asked how someone could do that to her babies. Now she wants Joe to live with me for a while if he'll go. Until they move. She can't bear living by those woods anymore."

"Where are they moving?" Peter wondered where in the world they could go to escape the memory of the fire.

"Up north. Maybe Sebastopol. As soon as they can find a place."

Peter would have to keep track of the Flemings. He would need them if this case went to trial.

"Tell me, who else was at the fire?"

"First you have to promise me my name won't get out."

"We can protect you from anyone. Even the Klan."

"You can't protect me from my sister hating me if she ever finds out I was there at the cross burning. If I tell you, you *have* to keep me out of it."

"Why tell me at all if you're so worried?"

Regis looked up, his eyes still haunted by what he had done. He didn't have to explain.

"One of them might tell the police that you were there. I can't save you from that."

"I know. I'm willing to take that chance. Besides, I'm only giving you some of them. That way I won't be the only one who isn't picked up. They won't tell on each other. If you get the leader, that should break them up here and send a warning."

"Why didn't you send an anonymous letter naming names?"

"It wouldn't have been enough. You already suspect some of them, and you haven't been able to do anything. But I have proof. You can use it to shut them down."

"What kind of proof?"

"Negatives. Some of them are so arrogant, they pose for photos of their heroic deeds without their hoods."

"Some?"

"Some of us are a little smarter than that."

Chapter 34

The man in the truck peed in the jam jar, screwed the lid on, and set it on the floor. Where the fuck was that district attorney? He shook his thermos and threw it on the seat. Empty. He shook it again, hoped he hadn't broken the damn thing. He'd been sitting above the Wright house since five in the morning. Maybe he had it wrong and Peter Wright wasn't meeting the squealer first thing.

What the fuck? He watched Wright turn the corner and pull up to his house. He had missed him. Goddamn it. Wright must have met the squealer already. Why else would he be out so early? He watched as the wife and kids went down to the car. Unless he had stopped somewhere on the way home, whatever he'd gotten from the guy who had turned on them had to be in the car. Maybe Wright had stopped at the office. Easy enough to check there. He'd wait to see if Wright went inside the house, then try to figure out what to do.

As soon as Peter pulled up to the house, Theo ran down to say goodbye, stopping a good foot away from his dad's window. Peter thanked his son for the drawing he had found in his briefcase that morning, a portrait of Brio, their marmalade cat, crouched at the edge of the grass, waiting for his prey. Theo just nodded, but Peter detected the faintest smile.

He heard Edna Hermit shoo Jennie out the door, telling her to go. Everything would be fine. But Peter wasn't sure about leaving now. He wished he could cancel the trip to Sacramento, see Harry, and set the case in motion, but he had disappointed Jennie so many times, and once this case began, he would have no time for her at all. Too bad his father was in Los Angeles at a conference. He could hardly wait to tell the judge who had been involved in the fire and that Peter had gotten evidence that would tie those people and the Klan to the Fleming deaths. Something Oliver hadn't been able to do.

He drummed his fingers on the steering wheel. He should call Harry and tell him what Regis Simmons had said, but Harry either would want Peter to go in to the office or would assign the case to someone else. It was cancel the trip to Sacramento or wait until Monday. Maybe he'd cover all his bases and call Harry from the hotel tomorrow. If he timed it right, Harry would be at church and Peter could leave a message. No one was going anywhere before Monday. It could wait.

Peter watched Jennie kiss Zoe good-bye. He debated whether he should go in and change his shoes. They weren't wet now, just a little spotted. He yawned. It was fine. He wanted to get to the hotel and take a nap.

Chapter 35

The tires sizzled along the wet pavement as they headed home, vacation behind them. Peter had managed to forget about work for almost a day, and he and Jennie had been reminded of what life had been like before they had gotten caught up in working and raising a family. He glanced over at her. She had rolled down her window and closed her eyes. He saw her chest rise as she breathed in the smell of eucalyptus trees. The pungent scent reminded him of their being children together—the boys swinging on a towrope from the tree branches while the girls gathered the dimpled nuts and strung them on cords. Peter remembered Jennie tumbling off their cardboard toboggan as they slid down the Point's golden hills on slicked-down grasses as slippery as ice. The fun had lasted barely a week before the firemen had found out what they were doing and come to burn the dry hillside.

He heard his name and realized Jennie was asking him something: what he wanted to do for Thanksgiving. He began to answer her, but lights came up behind them, high off the road, like lights on a truck.

The guy flashed his beams, but there was no place for Peter to go. The truck tapped his bumper, and the car lurched, began to slide out on the slick pavement. Peter tried to slow the car as they came into a curve, but the truck hit them again and pushed them along the road. Jennie braced herself. The truck dropped back, and Peter struggled to control the fishtailing car. He straightened out as they headed into another curve. The truck sped up and rammed them, this time sending them off the road into the trees. Peter heard Jennie screaming while he fought to steer a car that was airborne. And then the crash, the rolling, the sound of glass breaking. Then nothing.

Maybe he shouldn't have left the briefcase in the wrecked car. He had gone through it, and had taken out a list of names and a grant of immunity. *Well, well.* He wasn't that surprised. He didn't find anything else that might tie them to the cross burning. Shoulda burned it in front of the house, but the man paying the freight didn't want to risk the surrounding houses that he owned. He had paid a bonus for those kids' deaths. Might need something extra for this, too.

That blonde married to Butler's cousin had something coming to her. Maybe a sawbuck so she could buy herself something nice. She'd sniffed out what was going on in the prosecutor's office. Closed-door meetings, a glimpse of a grant of immunity form, and Peter Wright looking happy as a pig in shit. He was sure Wright hadn't taken anything to the office after he met the informant. The secretaries would have been called in if they were getting ready to file indictments. Whatever Wright found out was no threat to them now. There wasn't any proof, and soon there'd be no squealer.

He glanced back at the hole through the woods. *Looks like an accident.* The board on the truck's bumper hadn't left any paint on the car, and any dents would look like they came when the car crashed through the trees and rolled. No, leaving the briefcase was the smart move. Made it seem more like an accident. He'd wiped it down pretty good before throwing it in the backseat. The blood was all in the front, where Wright had taken the steering column in the chest. Red splattered the roof and the dash. The woman's door was wide open. He took a quick look around but couldn't see her. Must have flown pretty far. She'd been in the suicide seat.

Chapter 36

The shipyard glowed at night. Sometimes when the lights on the cranes blinked against the black sky, Jonah felt a yearning for something just out of reach. Fog floated over from the water and muted the noises of men and women working fast and hard to finish another ship, to draw the end of the war closer for themselves and the men fighting it. He thought his crew transcended their fear and fatigue the way combat units must do. Helping each other, encouraging newcomers, never giving in. They had to win. Anything less was unthinkable. The black-marketeers and people profiting from the war didn't matter to his crew, who worked as if the war were theirs to win single-handedly. They were good people.

Jonah spotted Regis Simmons squeaking in under the whistle. Regis had transferred to Jonah's crew and had begun to seek him out at break time. Regis was a good welder, but the week before he had seemed to be in a trance. His tacks had had to be chipped off, and he had lifted his hood absently and gotten a flash burn to his eyes. Physically he was fine, but whatever had him so distracted was putting other people at risk. Jonah had told him to take a few days off.

"Hey, Regis. How you doing? How was the weekend off?"

"Good." Regis's smile seemed forced.

"Be careful today. I don't want you or anyone else hurt." Jonah patted him on the shoulder, dragged his own lines across the platform, and set to work.

Regis had come in to work as usual, even though he could barely concentrate. Something would happen soon, but until it did, he couldn't afford to draw attention to himself. He had spent his time off in Marin, making sure he didn't run into any of the men he had informed on. Once they were arrested, it would seem normal for the ones who weren't indicted to keep their distance from one another.

Regis tried to pull himself together, to act as if everything was normal. He took a deep breath. *Focus. Do your job.* He lowered his hood and tried to lose himself in his work. When he set down his torch, someone tapped him on the shoulder. His heart lurched.

"Break time."

One of the welders nodded toward the pier where the crew usually gathered. Regis took off his hood and waited a moment for his heart to quit racing. He grabbed his lunch box and started to follow but stopped when he saw a flanger reading a newspaper in a pool of light.

ACCIDENT CLAIMS LOCAL DA.

Regis asked if he could look at the front page. He scanned the article. The pier began to move under his feet. How could they have known? *Was* it an accident? What did it mean?

Regis dropped his lunch box and looked around for Jonah. He hurried to the inner hull, where Jonah would be checking the work. Regis tripped over a wrench, and Jonah turned toward the clanging. Regis opened his mouth, but no words came out.

"What is it? Is someone hurt?" Jonah started to move toward the exit.

"No. No. I just. Oh, God."

"What?"

"I'm in some trouble I don't think I'm going to get out of."

"What can I do?"

Regis hesitated. What if he did make it out of this? He'd be a fool to confess and then wish he hadn't.

Chapter 37

Harley inched closer and closer to Oliver along the belly of the plane, until he lay across Oliver's thighs, pinning him to the floor. When Oliver's hand found the shepherd's ruff and tightened into a fist, the dog closed his eyes and pressed even closer against Oliver's body, as if he were trying to absorb his man's pain.

Oliver's eyes were closed, too; his jaw clenched. He wanted to bury his face in the dog's fur and release the grief and anger that had been growing in him since the chaplain had walked onto the obstacle course looking for him.

Not again. Not that look of sadness and regret. *Not Charley. Please, God, not Charley.* To his shame, Oliver had felt a moment of relief when the chaplain said it was about Peter. His brother had been in an accident.

Now Oliver was on his way home—home to another funeral and more grieving children.

It had been a week since Peter's funeral. Later that day, Oliver would be going back to Camp Lejeune, and Edna wasn't sure how they'd manage without him.

"Dinner's ready. Go wash up. That fried chicken's gonna get soggy waiting on you."

She had made Oliver's favorite food, hoping he would do more than push it around on his plate and drop pieces to Harley when he thought no one was looking.

"Get Theo from his studio, please." Didn't have to remind the boy to wash up. He scrubbed like a surgeon.

She set the mashed potatoes and gravy on the table, happy to see Zoe smiling again. Edna had thought her heart would break holding that girl while she sobbed after the accident. Thank goodness Oliver had come home and pulled it all together. Zoe clung to him, and he seemed to know how to talk to her, to listen. Hard to tell with Theo, but he seemed to fret less. He'd sit stroking Harley's fur until Edna thought he'd rub the dog bald like a favorite teddy bear. When one of the assistant DAs had brought Peter's briefcase by after the inquest, Theo had grabbed it and run to his studio. Now he carried it everywhere he went. At first they had tried to take it away from him, but Oliver had told them to let the boy have it. If it gave Theo some comfort, what harm could it do?

Edna wished she could comfort Oliver. When he wasn't playing with Zoe or Theo, she saw him looking into the distance, saw his face darkened by passing shadows of grief. She wished she could forget the look on Judge Wright's face when Oliver had dropped his duffel bag and reached out for him. The judge had turned away as if he couldn't stand the sight of his surviving son.

They still didn't know how it had happened. Jennie couldn't remember anything, not even how she had made it to the road, where some hunters had found her dazed and cradling her arm. She had begged them to help her husband, but there had been nothing they could do. At night Oliver sat with her on the porch after the children were asleep and held her while she cried.

Oliver knocked on Harry's door, then turned and watched the bark of the trees turn copper in the golden light. A layer of fog crept under the maroon clouds that streaked the pale-pink sky, and within seconds a purple-gray wash muted the colors and the sun disappeared.

Oliver turned back when he heard the door open.

"Harry." Oliver nodded.

"Come in. I'm glad you're here." Harry had grown thin. His cheeks were sunken, and the lines between his nose and mouth had deepened.

Oliver refused coffee and food with a shake of his head. He hadn't been hungry since the chaplain had told him of his brother's death.

All Oliver had thought since was that he shouldn't have enlisted—he should have stayed, been there. Even the regret felt familiar. He wasn't where he should have been, and now someone he cared about was dead because of it.

"Tell me how this happened." Oliver didn't have to elaborate. Harry would know Oliver had come only to find out everything he could about his brother's death.

Harry motioned him to a chair by the fireplace and sat facing him. "Peter was supposed to meet an informant that weekend, someone who said he had photographs of the '41 cross burning. I tried to warn him, but you know what he was like." Harry held up a hand. "I'm not saying it was his fault; I'm just trying to tell you how it was."

Oliver nodded his understanding. "*Did* Peter meet someone? Wouldn't he have called you?" Even as he asked the question, Oliver realized his brother might have kept it to himself for his own reasons.

"I expected him to, but . . . Oliver, he wanted to run the case. I think he wanted to wait until Monday to make sure I didn't put someone else on it." Harry leaned back, shook his head as if he would never understand it. "Jennie said he met someone that Saturday morning. He told her they had to make the most of their trip because once he came home, he would be working day and night. He called here Sunday morning and left a message that he'd call when he got home."

"Did Jennie know whom he had met?"

"No. Peter would never tell her the name of an informant."

"Even if they were run off the road?"

"I think it would've been the last thing on his mind when he was struggling with the car, and afterward. Well . . ."

Harry described the scene. How he and Doc Pritchard had noticed crushed stems leading to the center of a stand of giant ferns. It looked as if Jennie had been thrown from the car and landed among them. The fronds had cushioned her fall and saved her from more serious injury. If she hadn't crawled out of them, no one would have thought of looking for her there. He had made sure everyone in Richmond knew she didn't remember anything. Just in case.

"But you think it wasn't an accident, don't you, Harry? You think somehow the people who set the fire knew about the informer. But how? Who else knew?"

"Nobody knew. At least from our end."

"Who was the informant? Maybe he could tell you who else might have known."

Oliver knew he was telling Harry things the prosecutor would already have thought of, but he was so angry, he couldn't help himself.

Harry ran a hand through his hair. "The day after Peter's death made headlines in the paper, Maude Fleming found the body of her brother hanging in his garage. Regis Simmons. He hadn't come to take his nephew Joe, the surviving boy, to the movies. I think he might have been the informer."

"Hanging. Was it a suicide?"

"That's how the police treated it. By the time Doc Pritchard got there, the body had been cut down, the rope was removed from his neck, and people had been in and out of the garage. Frank Slater said they did it to spare Maude."

Slater again. Perhaps he *had* thought it was a suicide. Oliver wished he knew which side Frank was on.

Harry shook his head. "Like your brother's death, it was too coincidental. If Simmons was the informer, I wish he'd have come to me. Peter's death must have terrified him." He raised his finger. "One odd thing: Doc Pritchard said the piece of rope left hanging from the beam was braided—like a dock line or anchor line. It would have been more painful than a thicker, softer line, but if you're going to kill yourself . . ."

"And?"

"Later, Doc asked Maude if her brother sailed. She said he was afraid of the water. I know that's not dispositive, but it gives us more reason to question his death. And your brother's."

For a few moments, the men sat quietly, each lost in his own thoughts. Then Harry seemed to rouse himself,

"Let me get you a drink, Oliver."

Oliver stood. "Thanks, Harry, but I need to get to the airfield for my flight back to camp."

Oliver wanted out of there—out of that house and out of Richmond, back to the war, where at least he knew who the enemy was. But when the war was over, he'd find out what had really happened to his brother.

1944

Chapter 38

The war seemed to be reversing the natural order of things. American soldiers were in Italy, fighting to liberate the country from the fascists and the Nazis, and Italian soldiers were in America, collecting garbage and working in the fields. Harry was an attorney—he had no illusions about life being fair or justice existing in the world. But there had to be limits to unfairness. He had tried to explain that to Paola when she'd asked if he would mind having two Italian prisoners of war to dinner on New Year's Day.

Harry had said they were *prisoners* of the country, not guests, and they could well have killed American soldiers. Soldiers like their own son. He empathized with the angry parents of American boys who were dying overseas while the Italians they had captured were safe, dancing and drinking wine in the States, walking the streets of San Francisco in surplus army uniforms. Except for the plastic buttons and ITALY patches on their shoulders and caps, they could have been American soldiers home on leave. The POWs helped with the manpower shortage, but working shouldn't entitle them to extra privileges. It should be privilege enough that they were not sitting idle behind barbed wire.

But they're Dom's sons, Paola explained. Her sister had begged her to invite them to dinner so they could see Dom.

When did he get sons? Harry asked, and how did Dom know his sons were POWs?

Paola said Dom's friend delivered supplies on Angel Island and knew as soon as he looked at Cesare that he had to be Dom's son.

Paola explained that when Dom's wife died, he had left the boys in Italy with their grandmother. He had come to America to work and planned to send for them.

Apparently, that hadn't happened. Harry ducked his head and looked up at Paola.

No. No, she didn't know why, but he ended up in California, and married Isabella, and, well . . . She had run out of steam.

Why couldn't they go to Dom and Isabella's house? he had asked, only to be told they couldn't make the trip and be back in time for curfew.

Paola had put her hand on his arm, reminded him it could be their son, God forbid, who was a prisoner. What would Harry want for him?

Harry had embraced her, grateful once again for her beautiful soul, the soul that asked for the best in all of them.

Fine, he had said. Fine.

Harry had been unable to say no to Paola, and now two Italian POWs were at his table. The older one, Tomaso, had started dinner crouched over his plate, but Harry had noticed the boy watching Harry's family eat and then finish the meal sitting up straight.

"That was pretty good. Almost as good as my mother used to make." Dom tipped the dining room chair onto its back legs and rubbed his stomach.

"Would that be the boys' grandmother who is still in Italy? In the middle of a war? I see how you value her." Most of the evening's conversation had been in Italian, for the benefit of Cesare and Tomaso, but now Harry spoke to Dom in English.

Paola rose to clear the table, giving Harry a *be nice* look as she turned her back to Dom, but Harry knew if she weren't so fond of her mother's dining chairs, she would wish Dom would fall over, hit his head, and forget he had ever known them.

Dom blustered about how he had worked and worked so he could send for the boys and their grandmother, and then the war had broken out.

Harry and his father exchanged a look but said nothing. Dom didn't seem to notice.

Dom led the boys to the table under the arbor.

"Why didn't you send for us and Grandmother *before* the war? Who knows what is happening to her now? And why did you tell us not to tell anyone we were seeing you?" Tomaso spoke to his father in English. He had understood Harry's question.

"So, your English is pretty good. Think you're smart." Dom nodded toward Cesare and switched to Italian. "It's a long story, but I couldn't come back to Italy for you."

"Oh, the new wife doesn't have anything to do with that?"

Dom's eyes grew hard. Tomaso wasn't sure what Dom was about to say when Cesare broke in: "I want to hear what happened."

"When I left Italy, I ended up on the East Coast. Some *paisani* had a business there. I started to work for them."

"Doing what?"

"It was Prohibition." Dom smiled, as if to say, *What do you think we did?* "We brought liquor in from Canada. Things were bad for Italians. The Americans looked at us like we were no better than animals. When Sacco and Vanzetti were arrested, things got even worse. People hated us, attacked us. We decided to fight back." He broke off a branch of rosemary, stripped the needles. "One day we were ambushed. I got knocked down, and another man grabbed my gun. It went off by accident. He hit a policeman who had come around the corner." Dom shrugged, implying, *These things happen.*

"Oh my God." Cesare's eyes shone.

"I had to leave New Jersey. I grabbed the gun, because it was the only thing I still had of my father's, and ran. I ran as far away as I could, all the way to the Pacific Ocean."

Tomaso could see his brother believed every word. When the boys had left for the war, their grandmother had reminded Tomaso to take care of his brother, something he had been doing his whole life. But how was he supposed to protect Cesare from his need to believe this man they hardly knew?

"Do you still have the gun?"

"It's in a safe place." Dom's eyes flicked to the side.

"But why can't we tell that we saw you?" Cesare looked puzzled.

"Because Nic Criscilla disappeared. My friends let it get around that I was dead. No one can know I'm alive." Dom stabbed his finger at them.

"But if it was an accident, no one would blame you."

Dom looked at Cesare as if couldn't believe how stupid the boy was. "Of course they'd blame me. You think they'd believe a dirty dago?"

"Fine, Papa. We will not tell anyone we saw you." Cesare gave his father a hug. Tomaso held back. Only when Dom threw an arm out for him did he reluctantly accept the embrace.

Tomaso glanced at the house. "It was good of Uncle Harry to invite us."

Dom spat on the path. "It's easy for him. He's always had everything handed to him. Not like me."

"I think Tomaso likes Cousin Anna Maria," Cesare teased.

"She's not our blood cousin." Tomaso pretended to poke at his brother, who danced away.

Dom took a crumpled piece of paper from his pants. "You have to leave soon. You can call me at this number." He handed the paper to Tomaso. "But remember—no one can know I'm here."

Harry gazed into the winter garden and watched Dom talking to his boys, Italian soldiers safe under the bare wisteria vines. Did they know how fortunate they were to be here instead of in Italy? Mrs. Forgione's son, Nicky, was there, in Naples, not far from the village of her father. He had written of the destruction the Allies found when they landed. In retaliation for Italy's surrendering, the Germans had nearly destroyed Naples before the starving Napolitanos had managed to drive them out.

No one in Italy was safe from the vengeance of the fascists and the Germans. Civilians in the north were savagely murdered for suspected resistance or for harboring escaped prisoners of war trying to join the Allies in the south. The country, the people, were being destroyed.

Harry turned away from the window to find his father watching him. "Harry, come have coffee by the fire." Angelo sighed. "I feel so old. I don't know how many wars a man can be asked to live through."

Harry saw him swallow hard. "Papa."

Angelo waved his concern away. "I'm not going to cry, Harry. If I started now, I don't think I could stop until the war was over." He shook his head. "The pity of it all. They're destroying the countryside where your grandfather was born. Once again, the blameless will suffer: the children, the dumb animals. They will destroy what gives life to the body and spirit, gives shelter for the living. Again the fields will be scarred and the trees bare, the olive groves splintered and the orchards turned to charcoal. When the fighting ends, the women and old men will harvest only bones and mines. The want and hunger will continue for years. I wonder where the people will find the strength to survive."

Chapter 39

The men at the Café Avellino listened as Harry read the newspaper. They had felt the blast that had rocked the Bay Area the night before and had listened to sirens wailing through the hot July darkness. No one knew where the fire trucks and police cars had been going. Some people thought they were being bombed, then they heard a call had gone out for doctors and first-aid workers to go to Port Chicago, the naval munitions port on Suisun Bay, thirty miles northeast of Richmond. Sleepy neighbors had gone out on porches to ask if the base had been attacked. Then news began to trickle in from drivers who were bringing in wounded men for treatment. There had been an explosion.

Harry summarized the article. "They say over three hundred men died in the explosion, including some two hundred Negro munitions workers." He cleared his throat. "The men were almost vaporized. Bombs they had been loading into a Victory ship exploded and set off almost five thousand tons of high explosives and ammunition in a ship docked next to it.

"'Residents of Martinez saw a great sheet of white fire that flashed across the sky.' Did any of you see a flash? No. 'They saw it as far away as St. Helena. . . . A moment later, two explosions rolled them from their beds.' Martinez is five miles away from the docks.

"'When rescuers came, they could not find the pier, or the locomotive, or the railroad tracks. An explosion equivalent to five kilotons of TNT propelled house-size pieces of the ships more than three thousand feet in the air and created a twenty- to thirty-foot tidal wave. Farmers are finding five-inch shells two miles away. The coast guard is warning all mariners in the bay to look out for munitions that might be floating in the water.

"'Many civilians were injured by flying glass and debris. They were taken to the Richmond hospital and the one in Oakland so the more seriously injured could be treated closer to the blast.' Let's see, they're saying it was worse than the earthquake of 1906. It knocked the needle off the seismograph at the University of California." Harry blinked. "Sailors were up all night picking up the pieces of their comrades."

Lucy and Edna came into the café. They looked as if they had been crying.

Harry walked over to the women. "Aunt Lucy, Mrs. Hermit, come. What is it?"

Edna shook her head and went into the kitchen.

"Her nephew," Lucy said. "He was one of the men at Port Chicago. They haven't been able to find out anything. He hasn't called."

"The Army and Navy took over communications. The phone lines and the roads have been jammed." Harry told her what he had read in the paper. "Do they know if he was working last night?"

"No. No one knows anything. We went to a Mass for their safety. What else can we do?"

"Let me try to find out what's happening. I'll phone you later, Aunt Lucy."

Lucy went into the back to take off her hat and put on her apron. She hoped work would help, but it got harder and harder to keep going. The war ground everyone down. It had been more than two years since Midway, since the tide of the war in the Pacific was supposed to be turning. Since they were supposed to be gaining ground in Europe. But it just went on and on. People jumped when the phone rang. They peeked around curtains to watch the Western Union car travel through the streets; they were relieved when it passed their houses, but then felt ashamed, knowing the bad news would stop somewhere. The longer the war went on, the more chances there were that her boys would die. That was what ate at her—the fear and the waiting.

Chapter 40

"Die, Marine, die!"

The words drifted through the dark July night. They came from nowhere and everywhere in the lulls between artillery fire. Harley's ears swiveled forward—listening but not alerting. The Japanese were out there on the rain-soaked plateau, so close even Oliver could smell them.

Oliver pulled his poncho around Harley, more to comfort himself than to keep the shepherd dry. Daylight had almost faded by the time the marines had blasted and burned their way through the enemy cave defenses, and now, exhausted, the men made do with what they had: they deepened depressions created by their own shelling and hunkered down.

Something was brewing. The Japanese had been laying down intense artillery and mortar fire along the marines' lines, making it impossible to hear enemy movement or judge its strength. More than a thousand Americans had died taking the hill, and what was left of Oliver's division had to hold a front of some five miles on the Fonte Hill above Asan Beach, Guam. It was more a series of strong points than a frontline. While the marines had been capturing the ridge, the reserve Japanese had gathered and planned their counterattack, one huge offensive meant to break through the line and sweep the marines back to the sea.

The marines were quiet. During breaks in the artillery fire, they could hear the enemy clinking bottles, laughing and singing. Any movement or sound from the marines' line drew gunfire from the Japanese. Around midnight, Oliver heard the gunfire become more regular, as if the enemy had begun to fire along the line, looking for weak spots where there were no marines to return their fire.

Oliver remembered the advice of a Pacific-seasoned gunny: "A lot of the Japs speak English. Don't shout your names to one another; one of them will shout the same name later, and the marine who sticks his head up will lose it. If they scream to get you to shoot, don't. If you do, they'll know where your automatic weapons are. Don't take the bait. And stay loose if you face a banzai charge; don't fire till you see their buckteeth!"

Buckteeth? What had happened to him? He used to hate those propaganda depictions of the Japanese as a race of nearsighted, bucktoothed devils. Now it was the Japanese he hated. The truth was, they were extraordinary fighters who showed no mercy to civilians or prisoners, to anyone in their way. The stories of Japanese atrocities traveled through the Allied forces. The unwritten rule in the Pacific had been to take no prisoners, even before the Allied soldiers had found out what had happened on the India–Burma border. Two dogs on patrol had led their handlers to a clearing where seven heads stuck out of the ground, talking to one another: Americans, buried by the Japanese in neck-high foxholes, peed on, hit with rifle butts, and abandoned to die.

Quit thinking and stay loose. Oliver wished his men could do what they always did: joke and tease to keep each other going, to hide their fear. He could feel their nerves strung tighter in the silence of waiting, in the heaviness of the black night. Fighting was easier than anticipating. There was too much time to think.

He waited, the men waited, while the Japanese built up the courage to die taking back the island. Oliver closed his eyes and scratched the base of Harley's ears. They had landed on Guam on July 21. Just four days ago. Four days that seemed like four weeks.

He and his men had watched offshore from their transport as US bombs and artillery lit up the island that had been taking a pounding for more than three weeks. Someone joked that it should have sunk by now under the sheer weight of the artillery piling up on it. Hundreds of Corsairs and Hellcats dropped bombs and napalm, then rolled over and strafed the beach and the surrounding cliffs. Red tracer bullets and small fires sparked on the beach; the hill behind it exploded in bursts as shells from the battleships' sixteen-inch guns jammed home. Earlier, the Japanese planes that had been in the area had been destroyed. From the ship, it looked like the enemy was being annihilated. Should have been a piece of cake.

But when the men waded ashore in hip-deep water, their dogs swimming beside them, they emerged on a beach circled on three sides like an amphitheater. Machine-gun bullets and mortar shells came down at them from all sides. Amphibious landing craft disappeared in sprays of water and blood. The Japanese were still being bombed and strafed, but their defenses were so cleverly and securely placed that the American planes and ships couldn't reach them.

Oliver urged his men through a blood field of the dead and dying, herded them across the sand and coral to the scant safety at the base of the cliff. The noise did not stop, all of it carrying the sound of death. The dogs' training held. They followed their handlers without question, unflinching as artillery shells exploded around them and mortars burst, sending showers of sand and chunks of bodies through the air. The men ran through the screams of the falling and fallen, dragged wounded comrades as they went, left the dead for later.

There was no background movie score to romanticize the killing, no triumphant crescendo of strings to signal victory—just a relentless battering of the senses, the smell of blood, the stench of urine, the whimpers of grown men knowing they would not see their mothers again. At the base of the cliff, they regrouped, Oliver yelling, "Dig in! Dig in!" to marines who needed no urging and dug frantically, looking for cover for themselves and their dogs.

Oliver scuttled along the line of men, counting them off, steeling himself for losses. Miraculously, every soul—man and dog—had made it.

Sergeant Hirsch ran to him in a crouch.

"Don't look now, Lieutenant, but I think we're surrounded."

"Like shooting fish in a barrel." Thank God "Hershey" had made it. Oliver would be lost without his friend's combat experience and good sense.

"The fuckin' Japs knew where we would have to land. They built themselves some concrete bunkers and registered each damned gun to chew up as many of us as they could."

"We need these islands to get to Japan, Sarge. They knew we'd be back."

"Yeah, they're not stupid. Just evil sons of bitches!"

"Did everyone in your group make it?"

"Adams has his ticket home. He got hit in the leg, but his dog's fine."

While the sergeant rambled on as comfortably as if they had been chatting over coffee in the mess, Oliver pulled out a map. Their orders were to go to the command post. He studied it, then handed it to Hershey.

"What do you think?"

"What do I think? I think this is a map of some other fuckin' island! Shit, this don't look nothin' like where we are."

"Here I thought it was just me." Oliver scanned the beach. They needed to move.

"What else we got, Lieutenant?"

Oliver took out the recon photos. They both looked at their position, trying to make sense of where they were.

"Come on, Sarge, let's get our people off this beach."

Hershey and Oliver scouted the area around the command post. Glints on the hills above them confirmed that the Japanese were doing what the marines would have done: watch the enemy below and wait to see where they dug in for the night. The Japanese counterattacks would come at nightfall, as the drone of the American planes that had been covering the landing faded away, using the last light to make their way back to their carriers.

The next day, and the next, and the next, marines fought for the hills where Japanese mortar and machine guns punished them and kept them pinned to the beach. Their orders had been as old as warfare itself: take the high ground and hold it. The marines climbed the slopes and limestone cliffs with rifles slung on their backs, defenseless, searching for a handhold, a foothold, perhaps a clump of grass to grab on to, while Japanese soldiers emerged from holes dug into the cliff, picked off a soldier, then disappeared. Men with nowhere to hide clung to the side of the cliff and watched hand grenades roll toward them, but they kept climbing. Machine-gun fire tore up whole companies in the struggle to take the hill.

The dogs were of no use in that kind of fighting. Oliver and Harley and the other dog teams spent the days taking point on patrols through the deep saw grass. They searched for enemy soldiers who had survived the bombardment and had hidden in holes behind clumps of brush and grass, waiting to take out the exposed marine patrols.

Harley worked off-leash in front of Oliver. The heat punished the dogs, and the humidity and mosquitoes drained the men, bringing with them the threat of malaria and dengue fever. Patrols passed Japanese soldiers propped against trees, their bodies swelling in the jungle heat until they burst. The dogs ignored the corpses, but the stench clung to the men and followed them for days. As the bombardment wore on, parts of bodies hung from trees; the ditches filled with bloated corpses writhing with maggots. A rotten miasma filled the marines' mouths and noses. And then more flies emerged. And more mosquitoes.

The night brought no relief. The dogs lay in the dirt at the edge of foxholes, on guard, protecting the sleeping marines. All the men slept easier with the dogs nearby, especially after the night Max nudged his handler and pointed his nose toward a tree at the edge of the camp. At first light, a marine sharpshooter blasted the Jap sniper out of the tree before he got off a shot.

Die, Marine.

Oliver closed his eyes and felt inside his shirt for the letter from Theo that had caught up with him before they'd left Guadalcanal. More drawings than words. Since he'd shipped out, Oliver had found himself touched by any news from home. Jonah's letters informed and amused him; he read and reread them. But when he saw a letter from Charley or Jennie or the kids, he could barely swallow the welling of emotion that filled his body. He would turn away and hold his breath to keep the tears from spilling.

Harley stirred under Oliver's hand, rose, and pointed his nose toward Mt. Tenjo. Oliver keyed his handset: "Alert down the line. They're coming."

Orange flares stained the sky, silhouetting clumps of grass and dead bodies. Hundreds of Japs screaming, "Banzai!" flickered in the orange light and charged the ragged line with rifles and hand grenades. A marine alerted the battleships, and they lit up the plateau with bursts of white star shells. Oliver told Harley to stay. He thought of his fellow marines, ready to die for one another and for the families they had left behind.

He shouldered his rifle. "There are already too many fucking dead marines. It's your turn."

Tuesday
October 24, 1944

Chapter 41

Lucy wiped the counter and glanced at the door of the café once again, willing her friend Edna to rush in wearing that smile that made you feel like it was good to be alive, the smile that had been absent for the past six weeks while the trial of the Negro munitions workers from Port Chicago dragged on. Now the trial had ended and the naval court was deliberating. Soon the men would hear the verdict.

Edna's nephew was one of the men on trial. A pass to Oakland had saved his life, but he had come back to find most of the men in his unit dead or missing. For days, he and the rest of the munitions workers had shoveled up pieces of their friends' flesh and put them into baskets. When they had been asked if they would load explosives at a newly built pier in Vallejo, he and the other men had said no.

They were plain scared. Nothing had changed to make them think the work would be any safer than it had been before the explosion. They had always been told that the munitions weren't armed and couldn't explode. Until they did.

The men asked for other duty. Asked to be sent into combat, where at least they would have a fighting chance. But instead, when they resisted loading the ships, they were arrested. The Navy characterized their disobeying the order as mutiny, a charge that carried more severe penalties than insubordination. To many, it seemed like a heavy-handed attempt to frighten the troops and quash any protests against the way the Negro servicemen were used.

Although Lucy should have been in the kitchen, she couldn't bear to be back there when she expected Edna to walk in any minute, so she stayed out front and stacked and restacked the boxes of nougat candy she gave to her customers. She glanced at the door. Edna stood there, her face ashen.

Lucy's hand went to her heart. "No."

"Guilty." Edna shook her head. "They were all found guilty. It only took the judges eighty minutes to decide. Eighty minutes after six weeks of witnesses testifying. He could get five to fifteen years' hard labor, with a dishonorable discharge."

The news traveled to Angel Island, where Negro troops waiting to ship out for the Pacific were stunned and angry, though not surprised. Perhaps nothing would have happened that night if an Italian POW hadn't bragged that he had tickets to a Lena Horne concert.

Wednesday
October 25, 1944

Chapter 42

Oliver opened his eyes and shivered. It was the same fucking dream. In it he dug a grave. When he finished, he stood up and wiped his forehead. All around him, fields of graves marked with helmets dangling on rifles stretched as far as he could see.

The doctors had told him all he needed was time to recuperate, to put it behind him. He told himself it was just a dream—had been telling himself over and over, morning after morning.

He was back in Pt. Richmond, but Guam was only as far away as the next night's sleep. It wasn't the memory of fighting, of being wounded, that tortured him. It was walking away from the endless graves, from the rifles stuck bayonet-down in freshly turned dirt. His men had buried too many friends, friends who had died beside them, sometimes quickly, sometimes so slowly they had begged their buddies to finish them off. Then the living had moved on—on to more killing. The war allowed no time to mourn, to grieve, to honor the death of a man they might have loved as deeply as they would ever love anyone again. They moved on, they fought, they buried more men, they moved on—and no one could see that they were drowning in unshed tears.

Oliver had hidden his face when the hospital plane taxied down the runway. The medics expected him to be grateful that he was leaving the fighting, but grief filled his heart and his mind. He was leaving behind friends willing to sacrifice their own lives for each other and for their dogs. It was why they fought. Forget the pretty speeches about preserving democracy and freedom—they died for each other, killing and being killed to end the fucking killing.

Back in Richmond after weeks in the naval hospital, Oliver fought sleep until he was exhausted. Some nights he found peace in the blues clubs, where he stayed late into the night after the crowd left and the musicians played for each other, for themselves, driving deeper and deeper into a world of their own making. The plaintive tones of the sax, the indescribable sadness of the clarinet, comforted him, took him to another country. No, not another country—a place with no countries, a place with no lines to defend or hills to take. No graves to dig. He loved the music, but it had been more the sound of the voices that had drawn him into the dark club that first afternoon.

They were the voices of salvation, the first tones he heard as he regained consciousness on the bloody ground. Slow and deep, conversational, soothing his dog."Easy. You be awright, fella. Lemme help you. Tha's a boy. Good dog." The sound of a man knowing how to talk to animals.

"His name's Harley." Oliver couldn't believe Harley was still alive enough to try to guard them. "How bad is he?"

"I's not a vet, but it look like that bullet done gone through his neck. They's a lot of blood, but if he gonna die from it, he be dead by now."

Oliver faded away and woke up in the field hospital. He remembered surviving the first two waves of banzai attacks, and then nothing until that voice.

"Hey. How you doing?" Hershey stood by his cot, holding a canteen of water.

"Where's Harley?"

"At the vet hospital. I'll bring him by later. He's going to be fine."

"What happened?"

"You were shot in the knee. Still have your leg, but you're leaving for Hawaii later; your days on patrol are over." Hershey tried to lighten the mood. "Seems I won't have to keep saving your ass. Leave me time to end this blasted war, now I don't have to babysit you."

Oliver swiped at his chin where the water had dribbled down. "Harley needs to go home with me."

Hershey sucked his teeth. "I don't think they're going to allow him on the plane."

"We need to figure something out, Hersh. He never enlisted. He still belongs to me, not the Marines. He is a marine, but he doesn't belong to them."

"After what you two did last night, I think we should be able to wrangle something."

"What we did?"

"You don't remember? Holy shit!"

Oliver shook his head and winced. "Please, just tell me."

"In one of the breaks between banzai attacks, Harley alerted behind us. We crept out in the dark and saw some Japs sneakin' along the gully that runs toward the field hospital."

"And then?"

"We called to warn the field hospital, then picked up some men and headed down after the Japs, but when we tried to cross a gap between the gullies, we started taking machine-gun fire. Figgered there was a nest behind a clump of saw grass above us. We were pinned down. Couldn't get to the field hospital. So you and Harley flanked the nest, came down behind them, and took out the machine gun."

"Is that when I got shot?"

"No. You caught up to us, and we tore down the hill to the medic tents that were under fire from the Japs. You should have seen it. Well, you did see it, I guess. The warning we called in gave the hospital time for the docs and the walking wounded to drag and carry the worse hurt down to the beaches. Cooks, medics, the docs, mechanics, marines with head bandages and crutches, half undressed and armed just with the rifles they came in with, held off those Japs until we showed up."

"I remember someone talking to Harley. Helping him."

"That was Luther, a cook from the colored mess unit. He told me what happened after you and I got separated. He saw you get shot in the leg and fall. A Jap was about to finish you with his bayonet, but Harley broke cover and flew at his throat. You know the dogs aren't supposed to do that, don't you?" Hershey winked. "You grabbed your weapon and shot at another Jap, who was aiming at Harley. You missed, and he shot at you, but you distracted the bastard aiming at Harley long enough for Luther to cold-cock him. With a friggin' fryin' pan. Harley got hit somehow while he was guarding you in the middle of the fight."

"And I missed the whole damn thing."

"The docs say it'll come back to you bit by bit. The second bullet just grazed your head, but you probably have a concussion."

"And Luther?"

"Back to mess duty." Hershey looked hard at Oliver. "You might not want this next part getting around, specially if you're planning on taking Harley home with you. Luther's not talking about it. But you oughta know."

"What part?"

"Harley killed that bastard who charged you. Tore out his throat."

Oliver turned his head away. "He *is* a marine."

"Damn straight!"

Oliver wondered if the shepherd ever dreamed about Guam. They'd had no trouble getting him on the plane after word had spread that he was the dog who'd caught the enemy sneaking down to the field hospital. Now Harley was resting his head on Oliver's rumpled bed, snuffling at him to get up and let him out.

"They were going after the halt and the lame, Harley. What kind of people are they?" Oliver sucked in his breath as he hobbled over to the door. "Talk about the halt and the lame."

Oliver and Harley waited for the chief to hang up the phone. He seemed frazzled, overwhelmed with trying to keep peace in a boomtown. When he had become chief, Richmond had been a sleepy backwater with a police force adequate for its twenty-five thousand people. The war industry had changed all that. Even though the city had the money, it had not been able to recruit the additional policemen it needed for a population of more than one hundred thousand. The war effort was winding down, and the shipyard had started to let people go, but not many folks seemed to be leaving town. Richmond might not have treated them too kindly, and they might not have jobs anymore, but people had more opportunities for a good life there than in the places they had left.

"Have a seat, Oliver. It's good to have you back." The chief motioned to a chair.

"Thank you, sir." Oliver sat with one leg outstretched, hoping to appear casual.

"I asked you to come in because the Army needs help with a sensitive investigation. A death on Angel Island. The colored troops heard about the verdict in the Port Chicago trial last night and took it out on the Italian POWs. The MPs thought they had things under control, but this morning they found the body of an Italian POW. JAG wants an experienced homicide detective to oversee the investigation. Someone who will be able to work with the military but be as impartial as possible. Because of the verdicts in the mutiny trial, this whole investigation will be scrutinized for any kind of discrimination. Harry Buonarotti knows we're understaffed and suggested I ask you. He'll provide you with an assistant." Oliver could see the chief assessing him. "If you need more time to recover from your wounds, you don't have to do this. You *are* still on medical leave."

"I'm fine, sir. When do I start?"

"Now. Do you need a driver? With your leg."

"I can manage, sir. It's just an annoyance."

"Right." The chief looked skeptical. "I see you have a weapon."

"Yes, sir." Oliver touched the holster on his hip.

"Take these. You might need them." The chief pushed cuffs, their key, a badge, and a Richmond Police Department ID across the desk. "You need to get to the coast guard ferry ASAP for transport to the island. An MP corporal will meet you. Here's an envelope from Captain Buonarotti. He'll speak to you after you've had a chance to see what's happening there."

"Chief, if the Marines release me, I'd like to come back here."

The chief looked away. "Let's see how things go on Angel Island. See if your leg holds up."

Chapter 43

When the last of his men had boarded the ferry to take them back to Angel Island, Luca Respighi walked on behind them. The Italian POWs huddled together in the shelter of the upper deck and began a game of *morra*, trying to keep their voices low as they called out numbers, betting the small wages they earned from emptying garbage cans in Oakland.

Luca stood at the rail, feeling the sunshine on his face and the vibration of the ferry engines beneath his feet. They were early coming back today; the fog crouched out in the Pacific, not yet ready to obliterate everything more than a few yards away. In this light, the ocher hills edging the bay were the hills of Sicily; even the water gleamed like golden silk behind them. If he closed his eyes, he could almost pretend he was crossing the Strait of Messina. Almost. The shrill sound of the gulls and the smell of fish and salt were the same, but not this piercing cold that blew in from the Pacific.

Still, it was infinitely better than the heat of the African desert where he and his men had surrendered. Or been captured. He wasn't sure what to call it. The British, the French, and the Americans had surrounded them. The men were hungry and dehydrated, sunburned and exhausted, plagued by lice, and, more to the point, had no ammunition left to fight with. Leaflets from the Americans fluttered down on them, advising them to retreat. They did, until they could go nowhere but into the sea. Luca concealed his men from the British and French and waited for an American patrol to reach them. Then they surrendered.

Luca had waited for the Americans because they were said to treat their prisoners well, but he had begun to think he had made a mistake when the prisoners were packed into a boxcar like sardines.

For ten days, the men suffered inside the car as the desert sun baked them and the night air chilled them. They had no food and little water and could lie down to sleep only if other men lay down under them. They had dug a hole in the floor of the car to use as a latrine, but soon every breath carried the taste of air filled with the stench of bodies and illness.

But when the train finally stopped, an American soldier marched the dazed prisoners to barracks where they were given soap and water and clean clothes. They ate canned chicken and were even given cigarettes. Luca could do nothing for the prisoners of the French, who were thrown into an unshaded wire enclosure where Moroccan guards kicked and abused them.

The voices of children penetrated Luca's thoughts of the desert. Several women with young children clustered around the aft deck, throwing bread to the seagulls that strafed the wake of the ferry. Must be families of the officers on the island going for some special event. His mind wandered to what might have happened the night before. It must be over, or they wouldn't have allowed families to visit today.

As he walked back to check on the men, he saw a dog sitting beside a marine who had sallow skin and the pinched look of someone ill or in pain. He reached down often to touch the dog, as if to reassure it, or perhaps to reassure himself. Not Luca's favorite breed. Too many memories of the way the dogs menaced the villagers, frothing and straining at their leashes while the German soldiers smiled.

The dog tensed and looked past Luca, who turned to see what had captured its attention. A red object bobbed in the wake of the ferry. It took the POW a moment to realize that a little girl who had been playing on the deck had fallen overboard. The dog flew past him and barked at the water.

"*Madonna mia!*" Luca tore off his coat and boots and dove over the rail, leaving the shepherd barking behind him.

"Stop, or I'll shoot!"

A soldier raised his pistol and searched the water for Luca.

"Stop!"

Luca broke the surface ten feet away from the ferry. The soldier fired at the bobbing head, then aimed again. A cane struck his arm.

"Stand down, soldier!" Oliver stumbled against him, then righted himself with the cane. "Can't you see what's happening?"

"Oh, I get it." The guard smiled and lowered the gun. "Why waste the ammo? That dago won't last ten minutes out there."

Something flew past their heads once, then again. An MP threw a third life preserver into the bay. Harley trembled at the rail and barked sharply at Oliver. The dog flew into the air and over the side as soon as Oliver's hand began the signal to go.

The MP saluted. "My people don't much take after Johnny Weissmuller, but we do have a talent for throwing. Corporal Nate Hermit, sir."

Their hasty introductions were subsumed in shouts and cries.

"Man overboard! Come about, come about!"

The ferry shuddered as the engines slammed into reverse. Above the vessel's groans, a woman shrieked. Soldiers and prisoners rushed to her side.

Another group of POWs spotted a motorized skiff lashed to the rail and raced toward it. Nate took off after them, reaching the boat as it swung out and back against the side of the ferry, the POWs straining to lower it and the weight of two of their compatriots. Oliver watched Nate launch himself into the skiff, knock down one of the POWs, and almost wrench the lines free.

"Sorry. If I don't come with you, that cracker with the pistol will sink you before you can help that little girl—and your captain." He righted himself and looked toward the water. Oliver heard him mutter, "Then again, he would just as happily sink me, too."

The POWs looked for a moment as if they were going to pitch the MP out of the skiff, then shrugged and focused on the men on deck, who gestured and shouted, directing the boat to the swimmer.

Luca hit the water hard. It didn't yield to his body as the soft, warm water of his home did. He surfaced, gasping from the impact and the shock of the cold. His trousers weighed him down. He swam, lifted one arm after the other, kicked, pulled, and pushed himself toward the place he thought the child might be. He had gone into the water almost immediately after she had fallen; he must be close to her. But he did not know these waters and could only hope the current would not take her away from him faster than he could follow. The frigid water numbed his skin; he dove, forcing open his stinging eyes. The sun lit a path that glowed just under the chop. He surfaced and lined up on the spot where he thought she had gone in and dove again. *Eccola*—there was her red coat, billowing like a scarlet jellyfish, trapped air suspending it below the surface of the water. He pushed and kicked himself toward the form, his body growing heavier and heavier. He didn't think about what he would do when he reached the red coat, but he wasn't giving up before he got there. He grabbed the coat and pushed for the surface, broke through the water, and pulled the cold air into his lungs.

He rested on his back, holding the child on his chest. Something bumped him from behind. As the word *shark* formed in his brain, he saw a white flash to his left. He spun and saw not an underbelly, but a life preserver bobbing and dipping. He reached toward it, slapped it, but it slid out from under his numb hand. He didn't have the strength to chase it around the bay. And then it came back to him gripped by the shepherd, just head and rudder-like tail above the water as it struggled toward him. The dog nudged the ring tight against Luca, who held the limp girl in the crook of his arm. He tipped the ring on an edge toward him and tried to flip it over the girl. It slipped away, and the dog pushed it back. Again. And again. And then it happened. Luca wedged her inside the canvas circle as best he could. She was safe now, as safe as he could make her until help came. But she was cold, too, and so tiny. He tried to think how long they had been in the bay, even as he began to drift to sun-warmed waters.

The waves of the bay of his home rocked him gently, and he listened to the sounds of the fishermen returning to shore.

Chapter 44

The army doctor turned away from the POW captain and nodded to Oliver.

"If he doesn't get pneumonia, he should be fine. If he begins to cough or run a fever, I'll need to see him right away."

Oliver sat beside the bed and willed Respighi to wake up. He had ordinary, even features, a deep bow in the center of the upper lip, a forehead that might have been high even before the baldness. In the movies, it could be the face of a hero or a villain.

Oliver heard someone enter the room and turned to see Nate, who had cleaned up after helping the POWs get Luca, the girl, and Harley out of the water.

"You don't remember me, sir? Nate Hermit?"

Oliver smiled. "Sure I do. You're Edna Hermit's son. I haven't seen you for how long?"

"Last time I saw you, I was probably twelve or thirteen. A lot has changed since then." Nate stopped speaking and nodded at the bed.

Oliver turned around. The captain had the eyes of a leading man. The man who always got the girl. They were dark, concerned.

"The little girl, is she alive?"

"She's fine. Thanks to you."

"Not me. *I* did not get her out of the water."

"True, your men did, but only after you risked your own neck to save her."

"Was there a dog?"

Oliver smiled. "Yes, you weren't hallucinating. That was Harley, my dog. He likes to help out when he can."

"Well, thank him for me."

"You can thank him yourself, and Corporal Hermit here, who

threw in the life preservers and probably saved your men from being shot by that idiot guard."

"Thank you."

Oliver and Nate looked at each other. Oliver plunged ahead.

"I don't know how much you know about what has been happening on the island."

"I know something happened, but we left this morning before we learned anything."

"An Italian POW was found dead. Carlo Fusco. Did you know him?"

"I know of him. I have as little as possible to do with the Fascisti. Your government was supposed to have sent them to another camp by now. All they do is cause trouble, harass my men." He rubbed his head. "Is this an interrogation?"

"Good Lord, no. I do need to know where you were last night, but we're here to ask for your help."

"What kind of help?"

"We need someone we can trust to translate for us. I think your men will feel more comfortable talking with you than with an American translator. After what you did today, well, you captured our attention."

"Tell me more about what happened."

"There was a fight last night. The colored soldiers had heard about the verdict in the Port Chicago Mutiny trial, and later that night, some of them attacked one of the POW barracks. We need to know what happened to Fusco. It looks as if the Negro soldiers are going to be blamed for his death—"

"As usual."

Oliver ignored Nate's interruption. "If they did it, that's one thing, but if they didn't, we would like to find out who did."

"And you want me to help you perhaps incriminate one of my own men."

"Perhaps. But only if he's guilty."

The captain smiled, as if he knew Oliver had taken the measure of him. "*Bene.* I will be happy to help. But I think I will need some clothes." His arms went out to his sides, and he shrugged, as if to say, *I can't go like this.*

Chapter 45

"May I?" Luca gestured toward the pole where the body had been found.

Oliver nodded and walked beside him. "The commander said it stopped raining last night sometime after two a.m." He motioned to Nate to keep up.

Luca canted his head, looked at the ground from different angles. "You say he was beaten, then hanged?"

"That's what the men who found him thought."

"There is no blood on the ground. And it is not very disturbed."

"Yes, I noticed that." Oliver decided to see if the POW came to the same conclusion he had. "What does that tell you?"

"That they hanged a dead man. The beating did not occur at this spot."

"They hanged him to make it look like we did it." Nate thrust his chin forward, narrowed his deep-set hazel eyes. "The colored troops waiting to ship out."

Luca looked confused.

"It's what happened at Fort Lawton. Your people got away with murder there, and my people got blamed. As usual. Worked once—why not try it again?"

"You're saying whoever did this figured we wouldn't look any further than the rioting soldiers." Oliver considered the idea.

"I do not know what happened at Fort Lawton." Luca's tone was matter of fact. "We heard only about the death of one of us. It was understandable that a soldier could have killed him. There have been other incidents between the POWs and the soldiers."

"The Negro soldiers," Nate said.

"Yes. There is much hostility. I cannot blame you for that. Your government treats us prisoners better than it treats you—something my men and I do not comprehend."

Luca squatted on the ground by the pole. Nate ignored him and spoke to Oliver, who had grasped the pole and bent forward as far as he could. "Can you tell how many different boot prints there are, Lieutenant?"

"Do I look like an Indian scout, *kemosabe*?" Oliver tried to lessen the tension between his helpers.

Luca tilted his head and glanced up at Oliver, who waved the captain's unspoken question away. Luca rose to his feet. "There is not a great deal here to examine. There should be more disturbance, signs of a struggle."

"Even if you find prints, it doesn't help us much." Nate pointed at Luca's boots. "You POWs wear government issue. The boots could belong to you, us, anyone on the island."

Luca wandered toward the incline that bordered the exercise area. "Look here." Some distance away from the pole, there was a clear imprint of a boot that was not government issue. "This looks like the boot a fisherman would wear. The toe is rounded, the heel not well defined. The outline is soft."

"It had to have been made after the rain stopped early this morning, or it would have been washed away." Nate pointed to the print. "This proves the soldiers didn't do it."

"Until we know when Fusco died, this boot print only tells us that after the rain stopped, someone might have been on the island who didn't belong here." Oliver was beginning to wonder if Nate had been the right choice for this job.

Oliver stretched his back and shifted his weight. "Let's cast it, Nate. And take a few photos, in case the MPs missed it earlier. Better hurry, before it gets dark. Then you go talk to some of the men who were not involved in the fighting last night. Try to get us a direction for further questioning: who was missing from the barracks, who might have started it, whether anyone had trouble with Fusco. Whether anyone was outside after the rain stopped. Luca and I will go talk to the POWs. Then we'll meet and decide our next step."

Oliver and Luca walked toward the barracks where the Italian Service

Unit POWs were housed. They had been separated from the fascist POWs, who refused to work for the enemy.

"Captain, do you think one of the fascists could have done this because the Army is cracking down on them?"

"It is possible. It will be difficult to get them to talk to us. Some of the soldiers mislabeled as Fascisti would like to join us, but they are afraid of the true Fascisti, who believe the rest of us are traitors."

Oliver knew what he would think of any American POWs who worked to help the Japanese win their war, whether the United States had surrendered or not. "Why *are* you helping us win the war? I know Italy is on our side now, but still. It wasn't that long ago that we were killing each other."

Luca stopped and looked across the bay. He began to explain twenty years of Italian history. "Since 1922, Italians have fought the rise of fascism. Mussolini and his thugs retaliated with imprisonment, torture, beatings, and murder. They killed or exiled those opposed to fascism, even hunted them down in France and Switzerland to kill them. When Mussolini invaded Ethiopia, there were still a large number of anti-Fascisti, but they had been silenced by threats and violence. The Church had already been bought off by the Lateran Accords, which made the Vatican a separate state in exchange for its agreement not to interfere with Mussolini. The people who had accepted the Fascisti had thought they were dedicated to unifying the country, to repairing the damage done in the First World War, and that they were better than the communists, who were gaining power. Gradually, even they began to see that the goal of fascism was to completely dominate the people, but by then Mussolini controlled the press and the military and had abolished all the trade unions and other political parties."

"You're saying, in effect, that he had become the dictator of a country that opposed him."

"Yes, eventually. Except for the core group of Fascisti, who were running the government and the military. If you wanted to work anywhere, you had to join the Fascist Party, but it was on paper only. The people were still socialists or communists, who I know you Americans think are as bad as Nazis. Mussolini's alliance with Germany, our traditional enemy, alarmed many people. What a mistake that was—soon he was shining Hitler's boots. Since the armistice with the United States in '43, there has been civil war in Italy. Italians are now fighting to liberate the country from the Fascisti *and* the Germans."

Luca started walking again. "To answer your question, we are weary of war and death. We simply want to go home, find our families, rebuild our country. Again. We do what we have to do to end this war." Luca turned to face Oliver. "We wish your country would send us home now, so we can help fight, help liberate Italy from the Germans and Fascisti. We are your allies now."

"You know why we can't do that. How can we tell which of you would fight with us and which of you would help the Germans?" Oliver moved forward. "Have you done this before? Investigated crimes in Italy?"

"Why do you ask?"

"Have you?"

"We could go on answering each other's questions with more questions all day, so I will capitulate and answer you. I have a close friend who is a detective in Sicily. Sometimes he asked me to accompany him to crime scenes, consult on interesting cases."

"What did you do . . . before the war?"

"I was a psychiatrist—hence my ability not to answer questions. I suppose I still am—I listen to people and help them to face their fears."

"And your greatest fear?"

"During wartime? What we all fear: first, death, for ourselves and the people we love, but, in the end, the most destructive thing of all: becoming like the enemy."

Chapter 46

Becoming like the enemy. Luca wondered when the shifting of sides would end and he could be sure who the enemy was. The American soldiers resented them; the Fascisti hated them. Perhaps he would find a friend, an ally, in this lieutenant, who seemed like a fair man. He had not reprimanded the angry corporal for his near insolence but had remained patient with him, even though Luca could see the lieutenant was in considerable pain, which he tried to hide. Luca would go cautiously. Perhaps by helping his captors, he could gain an advantage for his men. Besides, the idea of assisting with the investigation intrigued him.

He looked around the barracks. Some men read books from the YMCA; others played cards or wrote letters. One man held on to a towel tied to a pole and leaned back, waving one hand in the air to invisible music. He was probably practicing for the dance the men had arranged in San Francisco with money they had earned from their work.

When the men had been asked to join the Service Units, to fill in for American men off at war, many had leaped at the chance to escape boredom and leave the base. Then the beatings had started. The doctor in the infirmary must have thought the POWs were accident prone, as they showed up one after the other with black eyes and bruises. Eventually the Army had figured out that the Fascisti punished anyone who volunteered for the units, and had put the volunteers in separate barracks. But the Army could not do anything to stop the Fascisti still in Italy from retaliating against the volunteers' families.

Three things kept POWs from volunteering: fear of the Fascisti, loyalty to Italy, and fear of being sent as support personnel to the Pacific front, with its heat and mosquitoes and artillery. When the carrot of privileges had not worked, the United States had threatened to send the men to camps where they would not be so comfortable, the camps where the Fascisti were going. The men had been caught between Scylla and Charybdis, and most had decided to volunteer. Now they went on picnics and suppers with American Italians who sought them out, invited them to church activities, and welcomed them like family. In many cases they were related, if not by blood, then by village.

Luca gestured toward Oliver and talked to his men. A few of the men exchanged looks, shrugs, seemed to come to a decision. One of them spoke up. In Italian. Luca listened, then turned to Oliver.

"Carlo Fusco was not well liked. The men say a number of people wanted him dead."

"Who in particular?"

"He and one of the colored soldiers had a fight. Larry Kimballs."

"What was it about?"

"Fusco had to pass the colored barracks on his way to his job in the kitchen. He came upon a group of soldiers looking at a photo of a young woman and made a rude gesture—like he wanted to, *ehhhh* . . ." Luca trailed off. Oliver understood. "It was a photo of Kimballs's sister. He hit Fusco, who hit him back, and then an MP came by and broke it up."

"Did he report it?"

"No. The MP was Negro. Both men could walk away. Nobody wanted the trouble." Luca took off his cap and rubbed his head.

"What?"

"The men try to settle things among themselves. We have heard a Negro soldier put on report for fighting can be punished severely. That only makes things worse for everyone."

"Maybe Kimballs decided to even the score later."

"Maybe."

"What else did they say?"

"They said to talk to the Fascisti. Fusco had some trouble with one of them."

"He seems to have had a lot of trouble."

"There are a couple of men in with the Fascisti who would like to join our units, but they are afraid of reprisals. Also, they heard the Army is sending them to a segregation camp in Texas that is supposed to be an unpleasant place."

"So?"

"They would know more about Fusco. I think we could get them to talk to us if we could protect them."

Oliver was getting tired of not being able to ask questions himself, and of not understanding what people were saying. He could have been at the opera. High drama, hands in the air, arms out to the side, interruptions, shrugs, walking away. He thought the Service Unit POWs were required to take English classes. They didn't seem to have done this group much good.

Luca took the men aside to promise that the people who talked to them would be kept separate from the Fascisti.

Finally, Luca and one of the prisoners walked over to Oliver.

"Giugi speaks a little English. He will talk to us. But he wants us to take his friend, also."

"Agreed." Oliver motioned for the man to sit. "So, Giugi, what do you have to tell us?"

"Fusco, he not a good man. Always say know America. Live here before. Before the war."

"What? Did he say where?"

Giugi gestured over his shoulder. "East. Maybe New York? New Jersey?"

"Did he say when?"

"Sacco *e* Vanzetti time."

Oliver looked at Luca and said, "1929 or so. But if he lived in the US, how did he end up in the Italian army?"

Luca shrugged. "He must have gone back to Italy at some point. What else did he say, Giugi?"

Giugi looked at Luca. "Money." He rubbed his thumb and finger together. "He get lotsa money soon."

"How?"

Giugi rattled on in Italian to Luca; then Luca translated for Oliver: "He says Fusco always had a scheme going. Even when they were fighting in Italy, he knew how to get things, to make money. Must have been a genius if he could find money in Italy during the war. He also says Fusco was looking for someone to help him."

Chapter 47

Fusco's effects were little different from what Oliver and Luca would have found in any Italian POW's barracks bag: socks, handkerchief, underwear, garrison cap and field hat, pants, all secondhand US Army issue.

Oliver shook the canteen—nothing inside. Luca carefully set aside a rosary with black beads and told Oliver that carrying it could be more a sign of superstition than one of devotion, maybe a reminder of the mother or girlfriend who had held it in her hands.

Oliver unwrapped a piece of waterproof cloth and found a few photos. An old woman standing before a pump in a village, the forbidding face of an older man, and a photo taken at a beach. He picked up the beach photo. A beautiful woman knelt on the sand in front of an art deco building. "I know that building. That's Atlantic City."

"*Dov'è?* Where is it?"

"New Jersey. I think we've got us a clue, Luca. Fusco could have been a tourist, but maybe he lived there, and if he did, he sounds like the kind of guy the police might have had dealings with. Let's get to a phone." Oliver thought for a moment. "We'll start with Newark. They have a large Italian population."

Oliver called the Newark Police Department and asked if anyone there might remember a Carlo Fusco from about the time of the Sacco-Vanzetti trial.

"I'm pretty new here, but I can pass on the information. Sergeant Doran will be back from vacation tomorrow. He might know. Been here longer than God."

"What time should I call?"

"He'll be in by seven, but you might want to wait until after roll call and morning briefing. Say, nine."

"That'll make it six our time. Thanks for your help." Oliver put down the phone. "Luca, if it's okay with you, I'd like the commander here to assign you to me. You can stay at my house. It will be easier than having you on the island."

"Fine, Lieutenant. I am at your service. Allow me to pack some items and inform my sergeant."

"I'll be back in an hour. I want to see what Nate has dug up and ask about this Larry Kimballs."

Night had fallen by the time Oliver stepped through the door to the colored barracks. Nate called the men to attention; some rose a little slowly from their bunks. One man took his time closing his footlocker before turning to face Oliver. It was nothing Oliver could call them on, but it was there: a lack of respect tinged with suspicion.

Nate motioned him aside with an angry flick of his head.

"I was on my way to find you. They've already made up their minds. They took one of the men to lockup. Larry Kimballs."

"Why?"

"The men told me one of the white cooks said he saw Kimballs outside last night. A lieutenant who's had it in for Kimballs got the okay to lock him up. No one has seen him since they took him away."

"There was a fight between a Larry Kimballs and the victim."

"The men told me about it. Said Fusco made an obscene gesture when he saw a photo of Kimballs's sister. The men were already angry about the Italian POWs holding dances and going to parties while they're stuck here without passes."

"Why don't they have passes?"

"For the same reason *none* of the colored units get passes the way the white units do."

"And what reason is that?"

"Because!"

"Because?"

"Because that's the way the army is. Sir."

This was not going well.

"Look, Nate, we need to find out what happened so these men aren't blamed for something they didn't do. And you don't have to add *again*. Let's do our job."

Nate nodded, tight-lipped.

"We need the men to cooperate. I promise you nothing will happen to them."

Nate shut his eyes.

"Yes, sir."

Oliver looked at the men destined for the horror of the Pacific. He thought of the Negro marines who had defended the US ammunition stores throughout the night of the banzai attack, beating off wave after wave of Japanese trying to destroy it. And then there was Luther.

"I'm a homicide detective on medical leave from the Marines. I was where you're going. My dog, too." He tried to look as many of the soldiers in the eye as he could. "I don't want you to be blamed for something if you didn't do it. I want to help, but I can't do that on my own." There was silence. "Anyone want to tell me what started things?"

One of the men spoke up. "We were already piss . . . annoyed with the POWs. Then Stagno wouldn't shut up about him and some other POWs going to see Lena Horne. It was the last straw. A few of the guys decided to teach them a lesson. So they wouldn't be so comfortable sitting at the concert."

There were some smiles at that.

"They waited until midnight, got some sticks, and snuck up to the Italian barracks. They were gonna beat on them, not kill them. Just wanted to let off some steam."

"You know, some of them dagos could have been the ones that killed our friends in Africa. They'll be here, sittin' in the catbird seat, while we're getting killed in the Pacific." This from a man with a swollen eye.

"One of them Larry Kimballs?"

"*Sheeit*, no. Kimballs don't like fighting."

"I heard he got into it with Fusco."

"He punched him for being rude about his sister. You would've too, sir. But then it was over."

"Where was Kimballs when all this was going on?" Oliver turned to another man, who had been watching the exchange and didn't look as if he had been involved in a fight.

"Here, patching up people as they came back in. He never left the barracks. We tried to tell that lieutenant who came and took him away, but he didn't want to hear it. Thinks we're lying to help him. We were up most of the night, what with people going to the infirmary and being yelled at by the brass for starting the fight. I don't think anyone was out of barracks after it stopped raining."

"MPs will be coming in to get statements from each of you. In writing. They're going to ask you to put down what you know, where you were, who can vouch for where you and other people in your barracks were." He held up his hand to stop the mumbling. "I'm not asking you to rat on anyone. We just need a timetable. I don't think this murder had anything to do with you, but we need your statements to prove that. You may have noticed something that didn't mean anything to you at the time but now does."

Oliver waved toward the door, and Harley leaped down the wooden steps, wagging his tail, no worse for his adventure in the bay.

The corporal turned at the bottom of the stairs. "Well? Do you think they did it?"

"It's early days, Nate, but no, I'm inclined to believe they didn't. I have to call Captain Buonarotti and have him get Kimballs back to his barracks. And we need to talk to the cook who said he saw Kimballs outside. Where was the cook, and what was he doing out there? He could be lying, or he could be mistaken. I'd like to know which."

"The men are worried that if Kimballs is charged, they will be, too, and after the Port Chicago verdict, they don't think they'll get a fair shake. If colored soldiers get blamed again, there will be riots that make what happened in Detroit last year look like a Sunday-school picnic. Sir."

Chapter 48

The muted sounds of "Moonlight Serenade" filled the kitchen. Jonah watched Mrs. Standish as she hummed along, her back to the door.

"Excuse me, ma'am." Mrs. Standish looked up from the biscuit dough struggling under her rolling pin. Strands of gray hair escaped her hairnet and stuck to her flushed cheeks.

"Breakfast'll be ready in half an hour, Jonah. In the meantime, there's coffee and some cinnamon buns on the table."

"Thank you." Jonah poured himself some coffee. "I ate breakfast this morning. I can't believe you make breakfast for every shift. Why do you do it?"

"You workers are helping to bring my boy home. It's why I opened my house to strangers. Besides, it's easier to work than to lie awake at night worrying about him."

Jonah thought about the mothers all over the country worrying about their boys, and about his own mother, who was gone now.

"Did you see anyone outside my room today, ma'am?"

"Is there something wrong?"

"No, no. Someone left me a message. Just wondered if you had seen anyone."

"I've been in this kitchen since six a.m.; haven't been upstairs all day. I'll ask Patty if she saw anyone. She's gone now."

"Well, thanks anyway."

Jonah sat in his room and flipped through his notebook, hoping for a clue about who might have left the note under his door.

Come to the brickyard at 1:00 a.m. I have answers to the questions you've been asking. I can't be seen with you. Come alone.

Come alone. Who in the hell did he have to take with him? He thought of Oliver and wondered how his leg was. He didn't think the marine was up to a meeting at the brickyard.

Maybe Jonah was getting close to something. Negro servicemen weren't raping these women. The sailors were just convenient scapegoats, like the letter to the *Courier* had said. It had to be someone local, as Zora claimed. Monica's friend had come back from Detroit angry with men in general and dead set on getting the rapist. She wanted to check with another one of the victims, someone who thought she knew who he might be. Jonah thought the guy should be praying that the police got him before Zora did.

Someone had noticed him asking questions. Good guy or bad? Jonah thought he had been subtle, joining conversations at lunch with the hands on the welding crew or after work at the Double R Restaurant. Maybe someone had figured out what he was doing. Could have seen him at the deeds office. Just in case he got in trouble, he had better call in. Do something with his notes.

As usual, the Double R was fit to bursting with noise and people, like everywhere you went these days. Guys in hard hats clustered together by trades: the welders, the electricians, the crane men. A group of Pullman porters seemed to be celebrating a birthday. There were white groups and colored groups; no mixed groups, even though the Double R was one of the few places in Richmond open to everyone.

Jonah slid onto an empty stool at the counter. Still warm. Nothing was unused long enough to cool down. There was no day. No night. Even the movie theaters were open twenty-four hours. Gave people some place to sleep until they found a room. He didn't see Ralph. He was pretty sure the ex-boxer had figured out his secret, and wondered if he had shared it with his wife. Probably not. Ralph seemed like a man who could keep a confidence.

"Ralph around?"

"Nope. Said he needed a night off. He'll be in tomorrow morning."

He ordered the chili and cornbread, set his cap on the stool, hoped no one took either one of them, and walked over to the pay phone.

"Leonard, it's me."

"Jonah! What's up?" His editor sounded happy to hear his voice.

"I got a note to meet someone tonight."

"Who? Why? Where?"

"Writing the story already?"

"No, you ass. Wondering if this is something you should do."

"It could be from someone who was at the fire that killed those children, or someone with information about the rapes."

"Or someone who wants to stop what you're doing."

"It feels a little hinky, but how will I find out anything if I don't take a chance?"

"Depends how big a chance you're taking."

"I think I can handle it, but, just to be on the safe side, I've sent you my notes." He looked around to see if anyone might be listening and tucked the receiver under his chin. "I've been researching at the courthouse. I think I'm close to finding out who was behind the cross burning and why it wasn't burned in front of the house the professor was buying."

"Do you have proof?"

"Not yet. I'm still tracing ownership of the houses in the neighborhood, the same neighborhood where the minister was going to rent a house. I've been asking around—some Negroes are renting in parts of Richmond without any trouble, but not in this lily-white part."

"Any progress on who burned the crosses? Individuals, not the group."

"My source in the police department said they found used flashbulbs near the road where the first cross was burned. That confirms what the welder told me about negatives of the cross burning and a meeting of local men." Jonah tried to keep his voice low.

"Your source in the police department? You can't trust anyone there."

Jonah pictured Leonard holding the candlestick phone, pacing back and forth as far as the cord would stretch. "I don't think he's one of them; he was the partner of the homicide detective who joined the Marines."

"That means nothing. Do *not* do this. I'll call my contact at the

Justice Department, see if we can get more information before you go ahead."

Jonah was gratified. Leonard rarely put anything before a story.

"I know what I'm doing. Look, I gotta go; someone is waiting for the phone. You have this number if you get anything from your contact. If not, I'll talk to you tomorrow. Same time, same station."

He hung up, grateful for the woman who quickly picked up the phone and jiggled the hook for the operator. If Leonard tried to call back, he'd get a busy signal.

Jonah shivered in the wind coming off the bay. Part chill, part uneasiness. He felt as if he were a million miles from anyone who cared about him. He parked at the gate and walked toward the brickyard. Spooky place. He could see the lights of the city across the bay, glimmers of brightness in the black. He longed for the warmth of a bar, the jujube traffic lights blinking in the hours that belonged to the nighthawks. This space devoid of human energy was not for him. No moon, no streetlights, just fathomless darkness. He was an idiot for coming here.

He turned around and ran back toward his car, shining his flashlight on the uneven ground. Something rustled. A barrel rolled in front of him. He jumped over it and brought up the flashlight. A white hood. So, he was right. The flashlight bobbed as he ran; black and white flickered like a magic lantern show. More of them. They circled him. A torch flared, and the night became timeless. It could have been any place, any time, in America.

"Hey, snoop."

"Were you looking for us?"

Jonah turned slowly, trying to find a way out, to make his mind work through the fear. He struggled for the words his heart told him wouldn't help. Might as well go out proud.

"And I guess I found you." Jonah tried for nonchalance. "Didn't take much to smoke you out. And I didn't come alone. The cops will be here soon."

Laughter surrounded him, and a nightstick flashed in the light of the flames.

"This'll teach you to mind your own business!"

The beating didn't take long. Six against one. Jonah felt them going through his pockets, his clothes, taking his wallet and money. One of the men swore and said he was going to search Jonah's car.

They dragged his semiconscious body up the hill and tied him to a fence. They stretched his arms out and twisted the barbed-wire strands around them.

"See how long it takes him to get out of that!"

"Goddamn it." One of them had pricked himself. "Hurts like a bitch!"

Jonah slumped forward, his feet twisted on the ground. He groaned, tried to speak. The one who had pricked his finger turned back.

"Want some more, asshole?"

Jonah screamed when the billy club slammed through his shins.

His legs seemed separate from him, but he could feel searing pain when he tried to move. *Shins. Arms. Pain everywhere. Chest. Head. Don't push. Don't push.* Last time Jonah had tried to push himself to stand, he must have passed out. His breath came hard, as if something were pressing on his chest. His head lolled forward. The night fog left the bay, climbed the hill, and swirled around him.

Jonah drifted off the fence, rode the currents into the sky, into the cold clouds. So different from home's sweltering nights. It was summer, frogs calling, a mockingbird pretending to be a screen door squeaking. The last lazy summer, long before the war. He and his mama were talking on the wooden porch swing, the chains catching and sticking on each backward arc. *Click, thunk, click, thunk.* She brushed back the hair from his forehead, tried to smile. He could see what she was thinking—as if he were in her mind.

Please, God, make him stay. That was what she thought, but she said, "I can't say I fault you, Jonah. There's little for you here, where folks know your kin. I'm just afraid of what lies ahead if you do this way. How hard it'll be." But she knew he was used to hard, to taking chances. He was the daredevil, the first one in the river in the spring when petals from the serviceberry still eddied against the banks.

"I don't see I have a choice, Mama. If I leave, I can send money home. There's no work here I want to do."

She could see his mind was made up—see it in the set of his chin, the only way he resembled the man who had fathered him. *Don't waste your breath. And don't make it harder for him.* She could feel his power. Part ambition, part smarts, lots of parts of anger. Who knew what would happen to him if he stayed? He wasn't going to be a man who stepped off the sidewalk for long. Still, her heart ached to keep him with her. She cleared her throat, letting him know a story was coming.

"When I was a girl, my daddy worked for a man with lots of land and animals and a big pond. He decided to raise geese for people to eat, so he got himself a dozen babies. Now, he didn't want them to fly off. He had to make a choice: he could clip their wings every now and again, or he could pinion them, cut off the last part of the wing, here." She laid her fingers across her wrist. "If he clipped them, he'd have to keep doing it, or they'd be able to fly one day, but if he pinioned them, they'd never fly again. So he picked what was easy. He cut off their wings at the wrist."

"He took away their God-given gift of flying?"

She had watched Jonah leap from sheds and wagons, willing himself airborne since he was a child. She knew he longed to fly, to rise in circles, feel wind rushing past as he dove from a tree.

"He wasn't a God-fearing man. The geese pretty much grew up just swimming on the pond and waddling on the banks. Then, one Sunday when the family was away, I heard a ruckus. A goose landed on the pond. The others beat the water and called in a way I'd never heard before. I stopped behind a bush to watch, though I don't think they would have noticed me, they were so worked up. I counted the geese, wondering if there were more visitors, but there were only twelve geese. While I was looking on the shore for a thirteenth goose, the one causing the commotion ran across the water and took flight again, circling the pond and calling to the other geese. They ran across the water, like him, and beat their wings frantically, but they were water bound, couldn't lift their bodies into the air. It tore at my heart.

"The one who could fly landed again, and the other geese surrounded him. I realized then that there was no visiting goose; the goose that could fly was one of the original flock. Somehow his wing had healed from the cutting, or maybe it wasn't cut off all the way. I don't know. But he could have flown away and didn't. He tried to join the flock again, but they attacked him. I think he woke up some deep memory in them—some ancient longing they carried from the centuries of geese they came from. They drove him from the water and wouldn't let him back at first, but after a bit they settled down, and maybe they aren't the brightest of birds, 'cause they seemed to forget they were upset with him."

"What happened to him?"

"He stayed with the others, even though he could have left. I counted the geese every day, and there were always twelve. They were almost ready for market, and a few weeks later they carted them off. The goose who could fly must have gotten away before they rounded them up, because the next day, I heard honking and ran down to the pond to see one goose circling and calling, and then he flew off."

"It must have been him. It's not natural for a goose to be by itself."

"No, Jonah, it's not."

"Mama, I understand what you're saying. I do. But I have to try."

The fog seemed silver now, summer far away. Jonah tugged at his arm to free it from the wire, but the barbs dug deeper. He tried to stand.

Thursday
October 26, 1944

Chapter 49

Theo Wright pedaled through the fog, his knees poking outward on either side of his sister's bike. Zoe couldn't ride a boy's bike, so when her tire had worn past more patching, he had put one of his tires on her bike. He had raised the seat as high as it would go, but she still teased him that he resembled an ungainly grasshopper.

The leather briefcase that had belonged to his father thumped against his back when he stood up to pump. It held his sketchbook and pencils he needed for his job. And other things. Theo liked getting up early to go to work, cherished the quiet on the edge of darkness, as it both washed from charcoal to a shell-like pink morning and deepened from periwinkle into indigo night. He felt most at home on the edge of day, the edge of night, the mystical, chimerical time. This morning he planned to sketch at the ferry building, to capture the intensity of the workers as they teemed off the boat. Tomorrow he'd focus on the buses that took the workers to the shipyards.

Dried grasses showed a hint of muddy gold as the sky lightened. He slowed, unwilling to overtake the barely visible figure at the top of the hill. He stopped and balanced, one foot on the ground, but the figure didn't move on. He coasted a few feet closer, then sped up when he realized it was the back of a discarded scarecrow that had caught on the barbed-wire fence. It was oddly beautiful. Even a bundle of clothes was sublime in the right light. He memorized the vision as he approached it. It would make a beautiful charcoal sketch. He glanced back as he passed it, and lost his balance.

Theo could see the shape of an ear and the profile of a nose on the head that hung toward the ground. It wasn't a scarecrow. He dropped the bike and took a tentative step toward the fence. Something seemed familiar, something that caught the thin morning light. A row of mother-of-pearl buttons glowed against the torn shirt. It was Ralph's friend Jonah.

What should he do? Did he have to tell? Talk to strangers? He stumbled around in a circle, rubbing his forehead. Then the wind riffled the grass, and something shiny caught the light. Theo entered that special space where all that existed was the possibility of art. He skirted a boot that lay on its side and picked up the object that had caught his eye. When he turned back, it was as if he were seeing the body for the first time.

What should he do? He could go home. He should have stayed home. He wanted to go home to Zoe.

Zoe. What would she tell him to do? He sighed and got on the bike and headed to the ferry building.

"He called me so I would call the police." Ralph tried to shield Theo from Frank Slater's sight. Theo huddled in his jacket, his back toward them. Ralph had arrived to see the boy wrench himself from the detective's grip. "He's not comfortable with strangers."

Slater pushed Ralph aside. "Hey, kid. Hey!" Theo did not respond. Frank grabbed him by the shoulder and whipped him around. Theo flinched and pulled back.

"Did you see anyone? Did you touch the body? Pick up anything from the ground? Give me that briefcase."

Theo shook his head and clutched the briefcase, his eyes cast down.

"Look at me, damn it! I asked if you touched the body."

Ralph forced himself to unclench his fists and breathe. He silently urged Oliver Wright to hurry.

"Theo, you all right?" Oliver slammed the car door behind him and started to jog up the hill, then slowed, the brace on his knee making running on a slope impossible. Harley raced to the boy and leaned against him while Luca ran to the body, then shook his head at Oliver.

A man turned around. He looked relieved to see Theo's uncle.

"Are you Ralph?"

The man nodded and smiled at Oliver. The right side of his face was scarred, the chestnut skin puckered around the eye.

"Thank you for calling the station. I know Theo thought I was away and he didn't want to talk to someone he didn't know, but why did he call you?"

"He thought he recognized him"—Ralph nodded toward the fence—"and thought I knew him, and thought . . . I really don't know why." Ralph faltered. "Theo comes to my restaurant. He's comfortable with me."

"How could he know who it was?"

"Said he recognized the buttons on his shirt."

"Buttons." Oliver looked at the sky, as if the key to understanding his nephew might be there. Then a car door slammed, and Oliver turned to see Doc Pritchard starting to climb to the body.

Oliver struggled up the hill to his nephew. "Theo, what were you doing out here at this hour?"

The boy shrugged.

Ralph spoke for Theo. "He was on his way to Ferry Point to catch the workers coming from the city."

"Ralph, are you sure it's your friend?" Oliver kept an eye on Frank when he spoke to Ralph.

"I'm afraid so." He cleared his throat and said it again, almost to himself.

"What's his name?"

"Jonah. Jonah North."

Oliver felt it in his gut. Another good man gone. He watched Doc Pritchard examine Jonah, then direct the men removing the body from the fence.

"We'll need you to go to the hospital and formally identify the body. Any next of kin we need to notify?"

"I don't think so." Ralph hesitated.

Frank got in Ralph's face. "What do you mean, you don't think so?"

"Nothing. I didn't know him that well."

Oliver was sure Ralph had been about to tell them something before Frank bullied him—his solitary interviewing skill. What was

Frank doing here, anyway? He hadn't been at the station when the call came in, yet he'd been at the scene when Oliver arrived.

Oliver turned to Ralph. "May I ask a favor? Would you mind taking Theo and his bike home? I can't leave yet, and I think he's a little shaken."

"I'll take him." Frank reached to snatch the briefcase from the distracted boy's hand, then jerked back when Harley moved between them, his ears forward and his eyes fixed on Frank. "Hey, Wright, call off the dog. I'll just throw the briefcase and bike in my car. I'm going back to town anyway."

Theo huddled over the briefcase and shook his head.

"My nephew is leaving. He's too upset to talk to you now. Besides, he's already told you he didn't see anything." Frank wasn't having another shot at Theo. "What are you doing here, anyway?"

"What are *you* doing here? You're not on the force anymore, and even if you were, *I* investigate homicides, remember?"

Oliver hadn't seen Frank since the day he had tried to kill Roan's dog. Anger rose in Oliver, and he turned away.

"Will you take Theo, Ralph?"

Frank shoved his hands into his pockets. "Easy to see what happened. We all knew one a them 'teach the new guy a lesson' beatings was gonna end up this way sooner or later. Probably some Okie didn't know his place, or maybe he was messing with somebody's girl."

"Let's wait for the autopsy before we start jumping to conclusions. We need some men to comb this area before the winds pick up, see what they can find."

"I'm just saying. Mix those Southern rednecks and those uppity Nee-groes with the liquor that caps every shipyard shift, and all it takes is some skirt in an overall to set them all off." Frank chuckled at his own joke. "A skirt in an overall."

Oliver turned to Luca, who seemed interested in the conversation.

"Do you mind if I follow up on a few things here while we're waiting for Newark to get back to us? I'd like to pick up Nate and talk to Ralph Robinson about Jonah before we go back to the island."

"Hey, Wright, it's not your case. Butt out. You're not a detective anymore. Probably never will be again. Too bad, that." The good-old-boy humor had disappeared. Frank smiled.

Chapter 50

Frank watched the briefcase slipping away. When Sandy had shaken him awake at the Stop that morning, he hadn't understood what the hell his uncle was talking about.

"Wake up. We have a problem." He told Frank what had happened in the night.Jesus Christ. Frank was trying to keep what they were doing under wraps, and Sandy was running around beating people left and right.

"I'm done helping you. Uncle or no uncle. You're going to get us all thrown in jail. If I hadn't gotten rid of the rope at the Simmons hanging, you'd be looking at a murder inquiry. That Pritchard notices everything. And now this."

"This guy was alive when we left him. Get over there. Be the big hero and rescue him. My source at the courthouse said he was taking notes from the property ledger. Search him for something small. A key to a locker or something. Maybe he stashed them before he went to the brickyard. I didn't check his boots. We know he has notes, and they're not in his car or in his room."

"Sandy, I'm done. Send someone else."

"Anyone else would seem suspicious. But you're a cop. No one would question you."

"No."

Sandy leaned back. "You'll help me, or I'll make sure everyone knows how close you and your mother were." His eyes narrowed, and one corner of his mouth turned up. "Get my drift?"

Frank couldn't think. He was fifteen years old again.

"Oh yeah, she told me. She and I were pretty 'close,' too. Her way of taking care of family. Can't say I blame you for running away from that sick bitch."

Sandy patted Frank on the cheek and left.

Frank cringed, hating the memory of those times with his mother. After his dad had run off, she had rarely come home. Then, one day, she barged into the bathroom, noticed her little boy was a man, and coaxed him into bed. He knew it was wrong, that people wouldn't understand, but he felt special, as if he mattered to her. There was no question he pleased her. They were a family.

When she didn't come home one night, he'd made the rounds of her old haunts, first furious, then sick with worry. She waltzed in three days later as if she had never been gone. He shoved her when she wouldn't tell him where she had been. A shadow flickered across her face, just a shadow—something sad. Then she laughed. Said she had been with a man, a real man. Not a crybaby mama's boy.

Frank grabbed some clothes and started sleeping in the back of the Stop, where Pappy the bartender made up a bed for him. Frank stayed away from girls at school after that. He didn't need to be nice to them. He got what he wanted from the women who hung out at the bar. Didn't even have to pay them. Hell, some of them paid *him*.

He had thought all women were the same, and then he'd met Phyllis and everything had changed. He'd still have her if she hadn't met Wright. He'd started following them and had watched them laugh and talk. He'd hardly been able to stop himself from bashing in Wright's pasty face.

Twenty years later, and he still wanted to bash in Wright's face. Almost had when he took that briefcase.

Sandy was sure the guy on the fence had dug up something about the fire that had killed those kids. Damn kids. People acted like it was the end of the world because some kids got killed. And now *this* kid was getting in the way. If the evidence wasn't on the body, and it wasn't on the ground, the kid had to have picked it up. Probably put it in his fucking briefcase. One way or another, that briefcase was going to be Frank's.

Chapter 51

Bailey Pritchard had become a doctor to heal people. Treating a man shattered by a car crash or mangled by machinery energized him, kept him working eighteen-hour days, but seeing this body made him want to lie down and say no, not because the man was dead, but because someone had chosen to beat another human being to death.

Although, now that he had examined the body more closely, something about his conclusion bothered him. The face was battered, but there was no blow sufficient to have caused death on its own. Bruising occurred only when blood was pumping, and the swollen and bruised condition of the torso and extremities signified that some time had elapsed between the beating and death. Possible exsanguination? Then there should have been more blood at the scene. Of course, the ground could have soaked it up. Although there was a lot of rock on that hillside. He was dithering.

He reached for the telephone.

"Nigel, it's Bailey Pritchard. How are you?"

"I'm quite well, Bailey. Thank you. I assume you have a reason for ringing, beyond your concern for my health."

Caustic as ever. "I wonder if you have time to consult on an autopsy. There's something here I can't put my finger on."

"Normally, I would be quite pleased to assist you, but, as you surely must know, it is all we can do to manage the burdensome volume of patients here. The situation is quite untenable, yet we keep on keeping on."

"I wouldn't ask, but I think you might want to see this."

"Well, if nothing else pops up, I could plead an emergency and avoid the certain boredom of the staff meeting. I should be able to come around close to ten. I'm intrigued by a corpse that requested a second opinion."

Bailey wasn't quite sure how to respond to that.

"That *was* a witticism, Bailey."

"I knew that . . . I think. Around ten, then."

Chapter 52

Luca looked out the window as they sped up Cutting Boulevard to Eighth Street. Harley leaned into him, eyes closed, almost in a trance, while Luca scratched behind those impressive ears. When they had left the station, Nate had jumped in the front seat. Apparently, an American corporal outranked an Italian captain and a K9 hero.

There were people everywhere. They had pitched tents in empty lots and built shacks out of cardboard. Long johns and a flowered dress fluttered on a line strung between two cars. Every now and then, a pot of flowers brightened the front of a garage. He saw two boys in pajamas in the doorway of what seemed to be a chicken coop. *Madonna. Hope they cleaned it before they allowed them to sleep there.* There were young ones everywhere, but he didn't see many adults supervising them.

"Oliver, don't the children go to school?"

"The schools are operating in two shifts. During school hours, half the kids are running wild, and the rest of the time, they all are. The schools are overwhelmed. There aren't enough teachers, some of the kids have never been to school, and even with double shifts, each class has twice as many pupils as it had before the war. My nephew and niece go to a Catholic school, and even that's overcrowded."

"You're Catholic?"

"No." Oliver shifted into third. "Their mother is. Anyway, all these kids running around with no supervision are making it even harder to keep some kind of order. This must have been what it was like during the California gold rush, but without all the children."

They pulled up in front of Ralph's Restaurant. It filled a triangle, its front door at the narrow end. It was rounded on the corners and faced with white tile. A neon sign curved from the roof almost to the top of the door; pink, yellow, and blue neon stripes bordered the vertical letters that spelled out JASPER's. A small painted sign in the window read RALPH'S RESTAURANT. Oliver knocked and saw Ralph slide off a stool.

The room widened toward the back, taking the shape of the block it spearheaded. Metal menu and napkin holders dotted the linoleum-topped counter on the right side of the room.

Nate walked along the cork-faced walls, looking at the sketches thumb-tacked at precise intervals. All the same size paper. All signed with a blocky *TW*.

"These sketches are alive; you can feel who these people are, not just what they look like." Nate gestured to the men.

They walked over to the wall. In one drawing, you could almost hear the laughter from the full-faced man whose head was thrown back. In another, a colored woman ate up a letter with her eyes and her heart.

Ralph saw the pride in Oliver's face.

"Yes, your nephew is quite talented. He comes in the afternoon and sketches the customers. All they have to do is admire one, and he gives it away. He's so shy, he leaves them by the register for me to give people when they pay their bill."

Ralph thought about the quiet boy and wondered how he was doing after what he had seen that morning. Reminded, he went behind the counter and pulled out Theo's briefcase.

"Oliver, are you going to see Theo today? We got his bike out, and he forgot his briefcase in my car. Looked like he was waving goodbye, but he must have been trying to get me to stop."

Oliver ran his hand along the top of the briefcase.

"I'll take it to him. Thanks, Ralph." Oliver introduced Nate and Luca. "We're working together on another case, but I wanted to talk to you before we go back to Angel Island. Find out what you know about Jonah."

"Sure. How about some coffee, something to drink?"

"We're good," Oliver responded, without consulting the others.

Ralph saw Luca roll his eyes, and he smiled at the POW.

Oliver opened a notebook. "When did you meet Jonah?"

"He started coming in here around the beginning of the war. We hit it off, used to talk sometimes when the restaurant was slow." *And when most of the white folks were gone.* "He was a welder at the Kaiser shipyards. Learned how to weld at the ferryboat college. He rode back and forth to the city until he got it. He used to come in with some of the other welders." Ralph got quiet.

"What is it?" Oliver asked.

"Well, he seemed educated. Better educated than most of the tradesmen who come in. But, you know, you can't make too much of that. The money is good, and maybe he just needed a job that paid well."

"Educated how?"

"Well-spoken. He liked to talk about books. And poetry. He gave me a book of poems by that Englishman who wrote the novel that was banned—*Lady* something." Ralph frowned, then gave up trying to remember. "Anyway, that's what we mostly talked about."

"What else did you talk about?"

"He asked a lot of questions. I was never sure what he really wanted to know. Kind of indirect, if you know what I mean."

"He must have given you some idea."

Ralph hesitated but then decided to tell Oliver everything he knew. "He seemed to be nosing around about the rapes. Asked me if I thought the Negro servicemen were doing them."

"Did you?"

"No, and not just because of my color."

"Then why?"

"Look, I don't want any trouble with the police. Right now I've a mind to trust you because of your nephew, but what I tell you can't get back to the real police."

Ralph noticed Oliver's reaction.

"Sorry, the active police. You know what I mean."

"Why not?"

He scrunched his battered eyebrows together and looked at Oliver like the detective might be a bit slow.

"Seriously, Ralph. I want to know."

"Take a good look at me, Lieutenant. Slater will probably be watching me now, just for being there this morning. I don't want to be picked up every time I get in my car."

Nate nodded. "It's open season on us, sir. Go down to the jail on Friday nights and see who's in the cells—cops are picking Negro workers up as soon as they cash their checks. If they pay the cops, they can go on their way. If not, they spend the weekend behind bars and get labeled drunk and disorderly."

Oliver's face got a little red. "I won't say anything to anyone else. Just tell us what you know."

"Some of the older folks say it's an old rapist returning. That the rapes are like something that happened once before."

"How are they alike?"

"The women were grabbed from behind, choked unconscious, didn't see the person. And he whispered he'd be back. The prostitutes that hang out by Tapper's Inn and the Savoy can't talk about anything else. They're scared. Figure one day he's going to go too far and someone's going to die. Long time ago, one of the girls started to come around, and he choked her again. They said he doesn't seem to care if they live or die. And I gotta tell you what I told Jonah: the girls say it isn't Negro sailors doing it. No matter what the police think."

"Didn't the one who started to come around see him?"

"She was slumped over a pile of boxes. He was behind her."

"So Jonah seemed to be investigating on his own?"

"Yeah. He asked me how he could talk to some of the working girls. I told him, the normal way. But then he wanted to know did I know anyone who would talk to him, especially someone who hung out by the Pink Kitchen, where the last rape was. I set him up with a woman I know, Auntie Josephine. She knew a couple of the girls who had been raped."

Oliver smiled.

"What's so funny, Lieutenant?" Nate was on guard again.

"Nothing. Just that I know Auntie Josephine."

Ralph cracked a grin. "Ain't she just something?"

"So Jonah was interested in the rapes."

"That's not all he was interested in." Ralph gestured toward a black device on the wall. "He used the pay phone over there. Said he couldn't make calls at his rooming house."

"And?"

"You can hear people's phone conversations in my office. Something with the heating ducts. Let me show you. You go in my office, and I'll pretend to talk on the phone."

The investigators did as he asked. They could hear Ralph clearly as he pretended to talk to a supplier.

"Interesting. So, what did you hear Jonah say?"

Ralph started erasing the blackboard where the daily menu additions were listed. He banged down the eraser, causing a chalk-dust explosion.

"You might think this sounds crazy, but those of us who live here don't think it's anyone's fantasy."

"For God's sake, Ralph, will you just tell us!"

"He was talking about the Klan."

"Doing the rapes?" Oliver sounded incredulous. "That makes no sense."

"No, not the rapes. The beatings. And he seemed to have uncovered proof of some connection between the Klan and the hill fire." There, he'd said it. "I know about you through Theo, and I'm trusting you with this. There is no one else on the police force I would tell." *Especially that Slater.*

"Proof? What kind of proof?" The lines between Oliver's eyes deepened. "The whole town thought the Klan started the fire that killed the Fleming children, but there could have been other reasons Negro shipyard workers were beaten—"

Nate interrupted. "Besides, Jonah was white."

"Didn't matter what color you were if you were a newcomer." Ralph wrote on the board, his back to the men. "Besides, I don't think so." He turned around.

"You don't think so, what?" Oliver's voice sounded a bit testy. He leaned against the counter and extended his left leg.

"I don't think he was white. I think he was passing."

Nate chimed in. "Wouldn't be the first person to jump the color barrier that way. And don't look so skeptical, Lieutenant. Hard to believe, but some Negroes are whiter than you." Nate almost managed to hide his smile.

"So how do you know that someone is passing?"

"Can't explain it. Little things. And they're more relaxed with us when there are no white people around."

"But he didn't come out and say it." Oliver was finding it hard to believe the fair-skinned man wasn't white.

"He didn't have to."

"If you could tell, then so could other people. Why wouldn't someone have exposed him?"

Nate and Ralph shared a look. "Anybody making it on the other side, we just leave them be. My cousin passes. Has a dark wife and a mixture of kids. They live in the Negro section of town. He drives his car and parks by the bus line, gets on with the white passengers, and goes to his job."

"He never has friends from work come to his house?" Oliver asked.

"He works white, lives colored. His worlds don't mix. He's lucky he's able to stay with his own people outside of work. Other folks go all white. Must be a lonely kind of life."

"So you think Jonah did it for a better job?"

"Not exactly, Lieutenant."

"Ralph, this is like pulling teeth."

"I think he was undercover. I think he was a reporter for a colored newspaper."

"Why do you think that?" Nate seemed intrigued by the idea.

"One day he was waiting for a call and asked me if I would take a message. Said he had told the other person to leave it with only me. It was from the *Pittsburgh Courier*."

"Which is what?"

"A Negro newspaper."

"I never heard of it."

"Pittsburgh, Pennsylvania, not California."

"That doesn't make him colored."

Nate and Ralph shared that look again. Whites didn't know jack about the colored world. Nate took up the explaining.

"It's not likely a white man would be working for a colored paper. Even if he wanted to, they wouldn't want him. But a colored man who could mix with whites, work with them, live with them, he could find out a lot colored reporters couldn't begin to get near and go places they couldn't go."

"So you're saying there may be more to his killing than the normal animosity between the locals and the newcomers—something to do with his investigating, maybe even something to do with his being Negro." Oliver pulled himself up on a stool.

"My guess is, no one white knew Jonah was colored."

"Maybe not. I sure didn't." Oliver shrugged. "But why do you think the Klan has anything to do with the other beatings?"

"Just talk. Some of the old-timers remember when it was happening to Mexican workers. Down in LA, they lynched the ones who wouldn't toe the line, but here they were beaten and hung by their clothes on poles or fences. The Klan let it be known it was them doing it."

"So why aren't they advertising now?"

"They are. I've heard people say they're wearing their robes for the beatings and hanging people on the fences like before, like Jonah. But people are afraid to say more. If we know, someone in your department has to know. Someone who's been here awhile."

"They could think it was a coincidence."

"Maybe," Ralph said, not willing to get into it with Oliver. Nate shook his head, as if exasperated.

"Did anyone die before?" Luca asked.

"No. But some were never the same. Mostly they disappeared with their families. The rest of the Mexicans fell in line. Chinese, too."

Oliver looked at his watch. "We need to get going. Anything else, Ralph?" He turned to go. "Oh—do you know where he lived?"

"Mrs. Standish's place. On Nevin."

Ralph watched the three men walk out to the car. He thought about Theo. "Wait up. Maybe you want to see this."

The trio turned around. Ralph went back into the restaurant and came out with a piece of paper.

"Theo gave me the sketch," Ralph said. "I asked him not to do any more of Jonah, but I couldn't quite throw it away."

Theo had drawn a three-quarters profile of a white man looking pleased about something. There was nothing remarkable about his even features and wavy hair, except that in the sketch a dark-skinned man with Jonah's light eyes looked back at him from a mirror.

Chapter 53

If Jonah had found evidence linking the Klan to the Fleming children's deaths, Oliver might finally be able to find out who had killed his brother. Would that help his father? Peter's death had made him a tremulous old man. He sat in his study, poring over scrapbooks of Peter's triumphs or gazing out the window, no longer joining his friends for cribbage. He mourned Peter's death as if it had happened yesterday.

When Oliver reached the car, he handed the keys to Nate.

"Nate, you drive. Let's check Jonah's room to see if he left any notes that might tell us whether Ralph is right about him. Then we'll go to the station, call the *Pittsburgh Courier*, and see if Newark has called us. We'll grab something to eat, talk to the coroner, and go back to the island. Captain Buonarotti said he had Kimballs released. We need to talk to him."

"'Grab something to eat.' It sounds so American." Luca smiled.

"I suppose so. But maybe I'll surprise you."

Nate seemed annoyed at the banter. "I think Ralph knows what he's talking about."

"Do you know of this newspaper?"

"I never paid any attention to it until they banned it from our base."

"Banned it?"

"Yes, sir. Banned it and other Negro newspapers. Sometimes we managed to smuggle a copy in, but if we got caught, we paid for it. Same with certain authors—Langston Hughes, for one."

"Sounds like the fascists were running your base," Luca said.

"We should let the paper know about him if he was working for them," Nate suggested. "You know, there was a column called 'A Thorn in Their Side' that often talked about things affecting Negroes in the Richmond defense industry."

"Who wrote it?"

"John A. Thorn." Nate seemed to hesitate and then reached a hand into his shirt pocket. "Here. I carry this around. Not sure why. It's by him."

Oliver unfolded the newspaper cutting. "It's an anagram. Jonah North, John A. Thorn—they're the same letters."

Luca leaned forward. "Could you read it out loud?"

Oliver scanned it. "Nate?"

"Sure."

Oliver cleared his throat and tried not to think about the man who had helped him in the alley, been his friend. He read:

Detrimental to Morale
By John A. Thorn

You would think the gates of heaven had opened after the Selective Training and Service Act of 1940 passed. Negro men clamored to enlist in record numbers, wanting to do their part and escape their dead-end lives. They believed they would be treated like everyone else—trained and sent overseas to fight the Nazis.

What they didn't know was that the act also gave the War Department final authority to implement it, and the fix was in. The War Department announced it would not intermingle colored and white enlisted personnel. To do so, in its words, would be "detrimental to morale and the preparation for national defense."

The military can convince men to jump from aircraft, dive in submarines, and land on enemy-held beaches, but they want us to believe they are incapable of convincing those same men to sit down to eat with a Negro, share a row in a theater, or crap in the same latrine.

No matter where they go, Jim Crow rules. Even though they are on federal territory, base commanders bow to "local customs" and will not admit colored men into white training courses or schools. What the Negro soldiers want to do is fight, not cook and clean for white soldiers.

At Pearl Harbor, Dorrie Miller, a messman, carried several wounded sailors to safety, then grabbed an antiaircraft gun—one he had not been trained to fire—and downed Japanese aircraft. He was the first Negro to receive the Navy Cross.

Despite segregation and discrimination, our men are willing to sacrifice their lives in this war. You would think the government would want these men—all able-bodied men—overseas fighting. But then, they don't think of us as men, do they?

For the second time in an hour, Oliver felt ashamed. He thought about an investigation into the death of a Negro journalist and the kind of furor that would cause. Some sort of racial incident might be unavoidable, but maybe they shouldn't be avoiding anything. Maybe the country needed to face what it was doing to the Negroes. Then he thought about what the country was doing to the Japanese. Not the same thing.

When they pulled up at Mrs. Standish's place, Oliver saw the blue star in the window. She had someone in the war.

The men waded through a sea of dogs in the front yard. Looked like she hadn't taken Jonah's advice about not attracting all the strays in Richmond. Mrs. Standish seemed a bit taken aback at their group. Oliver explained why they were there as the dogs flocked around them. An English mastiff seemed drawn to Nate, who danced away from ropes of saliva hanging from the dog's jowls.

"Howard, come here." Mrs. Standish lifted a cloth from the porch railing and wiped the dog's mouth. "Better come in quick. Won't be long before that sweet face needs wiping off again."

She led them into the kitchen, where pies were cooling on the counter. "I'm not sure if this means anything, but yesterday Jonah asked me if I had seen anyone by his room."

"Why did he ask that?"

"He said someone left him a message but didn't sign it."

"Did you see anyone?"

"No, but later I remembered seeing a police car driving away from the back garden."

"Did you see who was in it?"

"No. I'm sorry. That poor boy. I'll miss him. He had such lovely manners."

She pulled keys out of her apron pocket with her thumb and index finger. "Here's my master key. You can go up on your own, I hope. I need to get these biscuits in the oven. It's the third door on the left."

Oliver watched as Luca closed his eyes and inhaled the scent of warm apples that filled the kitchen.

"You go first." Oliver gave Luca a little nudge to bring him back to reality.

Nate and Luca floated up the stairs while Oliver thudded after them one step at a time, climbing with his good leg and swinging the other out and up to meet it. He moved as fast as he could, but when he reached the door, the other men were inside the room.

"It wasn't locked. I think it's been forced." Nate examined the latch.

Someone had dumped the dresser drawers on the floor, slashed the mattress, torn the carpet from the floor and the blind from the window, and thrown the knobs from the bedposts against the wall.

Nate looked around at the chaos. "This wasn't a robbery."

"No, I think someone was searching for something." Oliver leaned on the wall. "Someone who either didn't care if Jonah found out or knew he wasn't coming back. Maybe the note he found lured him to the brickyard. Someone thought he had something that could hurt them."

"Perhaps the same thing we search for, and I do not think they found it."

"Why do you say that, Luca?"

"The mattress. Why slash the mattress? It has the feeling of someone angry, frustrated."

"Same thing with this broken picture?" Nate picked up a framed Currier & Ives print.

Luca waggled a hand. "No, I think he broke that to see if something might have been concealed between the print and the backing. So, something thin—paper, perhaps."

"If Jonah was John Thorn, then he must have had notes, articles, things he was writing. Maybe a typewriter. Where is it all? It wouldn't be behind a picture frame." Oliver looked around at the mess.

The men searched through the piles, not expecting to find anything.

Nate gave up and sat on the windowsill. "They must have taken his papers but were still looking for something else. But what?"

"Perhaps they did not find anything here. Perhaps Jonah suspected something and hid his notes elsewhere before he went out that night. Perhaps the men searched for a key." Luca opened a hand and tilted his head.

"Let's go break the news to Mrs. Standish. She's going to find it difficult to replace all these things. And expensive." Oliver waved them on.

As the men drove up MacDonald Avenue, Luca watched all colors of men and women bustling in the street. The stores seemed to be filled with merchandise, even during a war. Signs in some of the windows said NO NEGROES, NO MEXICANS, NO DOGS. *Wonder how they feel about Italians.*

The land of equal opportunity had never been invaded, never been bombed, never seen the beauty of its cities reduced to ashes, never seen its young men lined up to be machine-gunned as punishment for an act of resistance. They had no idea, these people, how fortunate they were. He could only imagine the devastation in his country. If the Badoglio government had made peace at once with the Allies after removing Mussolini, it might have prevented the Germans from occupying all of central and northern Italy, cut short the killing and bombing as the Allies fought their way north from Naples. He thought about his mother, his sister. When would the war end?

The three musketeers, as Oliver was beginning to think of them, walked into the police station. Frank Slater pushed past them out the front door. They heard him greeting another policeman.

"Hey, Butler, I have the beginning of a joke for you. A cripple, a dago, and a jungle bunny walk into a police station . . ."

"You're right, Frank. Got to be a good joke there."

Oliver gripped Nate's arm. "Ignore him. He'd love to get you for something. We have work to do."

Oliver sat down, finally, and picked up the phone to call New Jersey. This time, Sergeant Doran answered.

"Did you get my message about Carlo Fusco?"

"Aye, what's he done now?"

"So you *do* know of him."

"He was in a lot of trouble here in '29 or '30. What's he done out there?"

"I'm afraid he's gotten himself killed."

"Well, now, still making trouble for the police one way or another."

"What can you tell me about him?"

"He ran with a bad crowd. We suspected them of bringing in booze from Canada, which wouldn't have made them much different from a bunch of the other Eye-ties here, but then some of them killed an off-duty officer from this precinct."

"I'm sorry. What happened?"

"It was right around all the furor about Sacco and Vanzetti. There were demonstrations, bomb threats, all kind of anarchist shite going on. Fusco's friends decided to rob a bank. We were shorthanded; our men were being sent all over the city to try to keep a lid on things. Later we wondered if some of the calls had been diversions to keep us spread thin. Anyway, poor Saunders was on his way to see the doctor and happened on the robbers leaving the bank. He drew his gun and tried to stop them, and one of them shot him."

"Was it Fusco who shot him?"

"No. The bullet didn't kill Saunders outright; he was able to tell us who shot him. One of the gang we had picked up before. But we never got him. Word was, the gang killed him and buried him in a field somewhere. A load of rubbish! They would have dumped him on our doorstep to stop the rousting we gave them. Fusco might have been at the robbery. He disappeared, too. I heard he ran back to Italy with a load of cash. Guess he hadn't counted on another war."

Oliver was disappointed. He had hoped for something to shift suspicion from the Negro troops.

Doran went on. "The shooter was a man called Nic Criscilla. We suspected him in a number of beatings. He was tight with Fusco."

"Well, thanks for your help. I'll see what more I can find out about him here."

"Good riddance to the bastard. Saunders was a good man." Doran hung up.

"Looks like a dead end." Oliver recounted the conversation to Luca and Nate.

"Perhaps not." Luca seemed reluctant to speak. "There are two brothers in my unit who are named Criscilla. It is not a common name. There might be a connection there."

"Let's get back to the island."

"Let's eat first, Nate."

Nate looked at his watch. "Okay if I catch up with you later, Lieutenant?"

"Sure. We'll see you at the morgue in about an hour." Oliver started toward the café. "Luca, I think I have a treat for you."

Chapter 54

When he saw the elaborate copper-and-brass espresso machine on the counter, Luca kissed his bunched fingers. He greeted Mrs. Forgione with a small bow, and they conversed in Italian. Oliver walked into the second room and checked it out. Four soldiers sat at a table, downing biscuits and gravy. They were probably billeted at the St. James Hotel up the street. He stood behind three boys hunched toward each other and talking in whispers. One of the boys looked up toward Oliver and signaled the other boys to stop talking. Suddenly, eating their burgers appeared to require as much concentration as walking a tightrope.

When Oliver turned around, Luca held a small cup in his hands, breathing in the aroma.

"You can drink it. I'll make you another." Mrs. Forgione gestured toward the machine.

"It makes me both happy and sad." Luca said.

Mrs. Forgione patted his hand.

Enough commiserating. Oliver was hungry and they needed to get going, but first he had to ask her about the boys in the other room.

She waved a hand to dismiss his worry. "I've heard them talking. They're building traps for the Japanese. They and some other boys. They call themselves the Home Guard and keep watch on the hills, dig bunkers, signal each other with flags, that kind of thing. They're too young to fight, thank God, but they want to do their part. They're harmless."

"Let's hope so." Oliver thought about how much trouble adolescent boys could get into, then let it go. Not his problem, and he had enough to keep him busy. "Mrs. Forgione? Will you sit with us a moment?"

She perched on the edge of a chair and looked at Oliver expectantly.

"I have some bad news about one of your customers, Jonah North." Oliver told her Jonah had been killed but did not tell her how.

She crossed herself. "He was such a sweet man." She lifted her glasses and dabbed her eyes with her handkerchief. "When someone wrote 'No Shipyard Trash' on the café window after we opened the American side, Jonah helped clean it off." She rose from the chair. "He was the kind of man a mother would be proud of."

Oliver watched her walk to the niche by the cash register. She lit a candle in front of Saint Lucy, her patron saint, who smiled serenely while offering her gouged-out eyes on a golden plate. Catholics seemed to take mayhem and dismemberment in stride. Pretty bloody history.

"Have you determined cause of death?"

Oliver set his cap on a stack of medical books and tried to hike a haunch up on the coroner's desk. He cursed his leg and settled for leaning. Locking and unlocking the brace that held his leg upright just drew attention to something he was trying to pretend didn't exist. Doc Pritchard motioned to a tall man in a white coat. "My colleague, Dr. Carter."

Oliver introduced Luca and asked about cause of death again. Carter answered.

"We're listing the cause of death as hypovolemic shock with cardiac arrest and hypoxia from compromise of the lungs."

As Oliver began to speak, Luca interjected: "He was crucified."

"Crucified?" Oliver thought of crucifixion only in a religious context. "Hanging on the fence? That was a crucifixion?"

"When the arms are extended, the muscles we use to breathe are stretched and exhaling is no longer automatic. One must push the air out of the lungs with the diaphragm. Try it—it requires more effort than you might think." Carter motioned to Oliver and Luca, who both did as he asked.

Oliver frowned. "You couldn't do that for long."

"No. Also, only a small amount of air can be inhaled. That puts stress on the heart. Eventually, it gives out. In this case, it would have given out even sooner. It was not in good shape."

Carter picked up an enamel basin and showed Jonah's heart to Oliver. "Probably the reason he wasn't in the service."

Oliver remembered Jonah trying to catch his breath in the alley. He drew back and shooed the basin away. Carter set the basin on a tray, smiling at Oliver's reaction. "In fact, the men who did this may not have intended to kill him."

"Why do you say that?"

"It appears someone smashed a long, rounded object across his shins while he was hanging on the fence. Perhaps they were ignorant of the effect of such a blow." Carter removed his glasses and rubbed the bridge of his nose. "Unlike the Roman soldiers who broke the legs of the two thieves to bring on their deaths."

Oliver thought of Jonah hanging on the fence through the night. "How long? How long would it have taken him to die?"

Luca made the sign of the cross.

Pritchard sighed. "It depends. If the crucifracture occurred at the same time he was hung on the fence, he would have died within minutes, at the very most an hour. Without his legs being broken, much longer. An excruciating death. No macabre pun intended."

"Time of death?"

"We think between midnight and four a.m."

Not long before Theo arrived.

"So, the beating could have taken place anytime between ten p.m. and two a.m."

"Approximately."

Nate burst through the door then. "Sorry to interrupt. The coast guard cutter's waiting for us. The base commander's worried about more trouble, so they're taking extra guards to the island. We need to hurry."

Chapter 55

At one time, Angel Island had been called the Ellis Island of the West, because of the Chinese and Japanese immigrants who had languished there while waiting to enter the United States. Later, it had been a peaceful refuge for Oliver and his friends, who had boated out to picnic on the sandy beaches. Now it housed Fort McDowell and rang with the sounds of cadence being called. It was the last stop for hundreds of thousands of men waiting to ship out for the Pacific.

The coast guard boat nudged the edge of the pier.

"Thanks for the lift. We're going to need a ride back." Oliver balanced against Harley as they stepped onto the dock.

"Sure." The seaman looped a line around a dock cleat. "We'll be in the area. Last night one of the men in the auxiliary coast guard thought he saw a boat in the shadows near the shore. On the Richmond side. We need to check it out, but the station will patch you through."

When the three men entered the POW barracks, Cesare sat hunched over a table, gluing toothpicks along the strut of an airplane wing. He looked frail, not much more than a toothpick himself. His long fingers held the plane delicately. His face, too, was long and thin, and his collar stood out inches from his neck. Oliver could hardly imagine him lifting Fusco to hang him on the post, but there was the brother. Maybe together they could have done it.

Cesare looked up at the men and dropped the plane. It shattered.

Luca touched the boy's shoulder. "Cesare, if you want me to speak to you in Italian, I will, but Lieutenant Wright would like to ask you some questions and hear what you have to say. *Bene?*"

Cesare nodded.

Oliver motioned to Nate to stand on the other side of the table, while Oliver pulled up a chair and sat heavily. "First, tell me where you were last night."

"Here. In the *baracca*."

"Did you leave at all?"

"No."

"What about when the American soldiers were attacking the barracks?"

"We hear noise outside, but no go out."

Oliver looked to Luca for confirmation, but the captain turned up his palms and shrugged. "I sleep in another area."

"And your brother? Where was he?"

"Here, with me."

"Where is he now?"

"Work. In kitchen."

"What about your father?"

"My father gone long time ago."

Oliver acted as if they already knew Nic Criscilla was Cesare's father. "Nic Criscilla. A thief and a murderer."

"*No!*" Cesare seemed to catch himself.

"No? He's a murderer, and you and your brother are, too."

"No. Not us. Not him."

"How do you know?" Oliver nodded at Luca to pick up the question.

Luca seemed to pursue it reluctantly. He asked first in English, then in Italian.

Oliver interrupted. "We know you have seen him."

Cesare shook his head no.

"You have seen your father the murderer."

A torrent of Italian spilled out of the boy. Luca translated: "He said his father didn't do it. It was an accident."

"Didn't do what, Cesare?"

Cesare slumped. "Kill policeman."

"Did Fusco know? Did he try to blackmail you?" Luca continued.

Cesare rattled off in Italian.

Luca translated again: "Fusco heard them talking about their father. They told Fusco they heard from him through a friend but he left here in '42, after the restrictions against Italians, because he was afraid he might be picked up. They said they did not know where he was now."

"Do you believe him?"

Luca shrugged.

"Have you seen your father?"

"*No, no.* Never."

"*Ti calma.*" Luca put a hand on Cesare's shoulder.

Nate had been pacing while the men questioned the boy. Now he banged his fist on the table, making the toothpicks jump. "Who cares about Nic Criscilla and a shooting in New Jersey? What about Fusco? We need to clear the colored soldiers."

"Nate, it's only day two in our investigation. Calm down."

"You think those soldiers are feeling calm while they're waiting to be blamed for something they didn't do—again?"

"Trust me. I know what I'm doing."

"Yes, sir." Nate looked like he had to bite his tongue to keep quiet.

"Let's find out if the Criscillas have been off the island visiting anyone." Oliver looked around for Harley, who had his nose pressed against a crack in the floorboards.

"Harley, let's go."

Harley snorted and padded after the men.

Tomaso Criscilla had seen the coast guard cutter land and had watched the dog and the three men walk along the path to the POW barracks. He waited until they were inside, then crawled under the building to listen. He had been worried that the investigators might connect Fusco to them ever since his body had been found. His brother, Cesare, was sweet but a bit slow. God knew what they would get out of him.

When the dog's dark nose blocked the crack in the floor, snuffling and sniffing the air under the house, Tomaso froze. Now he moved. Once that detective found out the boys had been to Uncle Harry's, they'd find Dom. That damned Fusco. He had started this, and now they were stuck in it. Tomaso should have done what Fusco had wanted. He smoothed out the paper with the phone number of his father's friend. Maybe the girl in the PX would let him use her phone again. He had to warn his father.

Tomaso hated boats, all kinds of boats, yet here he was in one, huddled under a stinking tarp. He flinched at every smack against the waves, then groaned, realizing that once he had warned his father, he would have to get back in the boat.

The boat slowed. He felt Mario, his father's friend, jump over the side and pull it close to shore.

"Come on. Before someone sees us."

Tomaso peeked out from under the tarp. It was almost dark now. The boat was still a few feet from land. He would get wet. He shook his head.

"*Maneggia!*" Mario pulled the boat farther in.

"Tomaso, what's happening?" Dom appeared from behind one of those tall gray plants with flowers like blue torches.

"I overheard the police asking Cesare questions. Carlo Fusco was killed yesterday, or the day before. They want to know who did it."

"Carlo Fusco. It's been years since I heard that name. But why are they talking to Cesare?"

"Because they said Fusco was in a gang with a man called Criscilla. So they are questioning us." Tomaso thought about what he had heard. His father might not have been so innocent. "They're going to find out we were at Uncle Harry's, and they'll know your new name. I came to tell you to leave now before they find you and send you to New Jersey."

"I can't go without my father's gun."

"Leave it. It connects you to a crime. If they find it, so what, as long as you're gone."

"I can't. We're not far from Harry's house. I can climb the hill, get the gun, and leave without anyone seeing me. It'll only take a few minutes. And then you and I will go away."

"Me?"

"Yes. You're a fugitive now, too."

"No, I'm not. I'm going back to the island and pretend I don't know what's going on."

"We'll talk later. For now, stay here with Mario."

Dom motioned for Mario to get him a net from the boat. Dom reached for it across the water and dropped it into the bay. He shook his head and waited for the fisherman to retrieve it. "Hurry up! I need to get to Harry's before the police do."

Chapter 56

The deep red and mahogany leaves of Chinese pistache trees shaded the entry to the Buonarottis' house. The men walked under an archway of bougainvillea onto a path nearly obscured by rampant herbs. The scent of thyme and rosemary enveloped them. Oliver thought they smelled ready for the oven by the time they got to the porch. He rang the doorbell.

"Oliver, how good to see you. And you, Nate." Harry turned to Luca. "You must be Captain Respighi. I heard you were helping with the investigation. And of what you did on the ferry. It's an honor to welcome you into my home."

"Harry." Oliver took off his cap. "We're here as part of the investigation on the island."

Harry seemed a bit puzzled but invited them in. Oliver didn't believe Harry could have known about Nic Criscilla; the DA was such a straight arrow.

"We are about to eat. Join us."

Luca looked like he was going to swoon from the smells coming from the kitchen. Oliver smiled in spite of himself.

"Thanks, Harry. We don't have much time."

"You have time for a bite. We can talk while we eat."

Luca needed no persuading, but Nate turned toward the door. "If you all are going to sit down, I'd like to run up the hill and see Mrs. Slater for a minute. Can I take the car, Lieutenant?"

"Sure, be back in half an hour or so."

"Yes, sir."

Before Nate could leave, Steve Buonarotti ran down the stairs, excited to see his old friend. Oliver and Luca followed Harry into the dining room. They were pulling out chairs at the table, when they heard raised voices from the hall. Then the front door slammed. The other men waited for a moment, then resumed their conversation, although Harry seemed distracted by what had taken place in the hallway.

Oliver was reluctant to ask about Harry's relative, so he stalled by telling him about finding Jonah. He repeated what Ralph had told them about the Klan.

"The Klan." Harry looked disgusted. "There have been many such beatings. The group was active and widely accepted in California. The *Richmond Independent* once carried an editorial defending its right to exist, saying the paper didn't exactly approve of the Klan's 'invasion of homes' and 'infliction of cruelties,' but that it was just like any other secret society and every 'freeborn American citizen' had the right to join."

Harry stopped talking when Paola and her sister, Isabella, brought in manicotti stuffed with ricotta and homemade sausage, lettuce dressed with olive oil and vinegar, and chicken roasted with potatoes and rosemary. Luca listened and ate, happily sampling course after course. Oliver drank coffee and wondered where in the world Luca was putting it all.

Harry continued, "During the thirties, the Klan began to merge with groups like the Silver Shirts, a fascist-inspired organization, and targeted all non-Aryans. Once the war began, we saw less activity. Many Klan members are probably overseas, fighting another enemy. I imagine some of the men who were involved in the cross burning that took the Fleming children are in the armed forces now."

"I've explained that to my father—but he thinks I should still have been able to find them."

Luca looked puzzled at the reference to Oliver's father. Harry passed the bread to him and explained. "Before the war, two children died when a cross was burned in a meadow. Oliver's father convinced him to stay here and try to find out whether someone on the police force had been involved. Then the war broke out, and after Oliver reenlisted, his brother, an assistant district attorney, was called by a man who said he had information about the fire. Unfortunately, Peter died in a car accident the same weekend he was supposed to have met with his source."

Luca put down his knife and fork. "Did you think his death was not an accident?"

"We considered it."

Harry stopped speaking, as if something had just occurred to him. He left the table and came back with a piece of paper.

"I missed it because it wasn't there. I'm sorry, Oliver. I should have realized this sooner."

"What? What did you miss?"

"This is the inventory of Peter's briefcase. There's something missing that should have been on it: a copy of the grant of immunity, with the informant's name. It wasn't there."

"Maybe they didn't meet."

"That's what I thought, too. But then there should have been *two* blank copies. They aren't on the list of items from Peter's office at home, either. No. Someone had to have taken them from the briefcase." Harry did not meet Oliver's eyes.

Oliver knew it wouldn't have made any difference if Harry had realized this sooner. He touched Harry's arm.

"Don't be hard on yourself. Think about it. We already knew."

"Yes, I suppose we did."

Oliver wanted to change the subject. "Harry, we're here about the death on Angel Island. Things are heating up there and we need to find out who killed the Italian POW." He took a deep breath, hating to bring bad news to this man. "You had two POWs visit you, Cesare and Tomaso Criscilla."

"Yes. They're the stepsons of my sister-in-law, Isabella. She asked if she and her husband could meet with the boys here."

"Why here?"

"They live too far out for the boys to have gotten back to Angel Island by their curfew."

"And your brother-in-law's name?"

"Dom Caputo."

"How are they Isabella's stepsons?"

"They're Dom's boys."

"But they have a different last name."

"He used to be called Criscilla, but when he came here, he said, they used his mother's name instead of his father's."

"They?"

"Immigration." Harry shrugged a shoulder, as if to indicate Immigration was responsible for many such things.

"Could his first name have been Nic?"
"Nic, Dom—they are both short for Dominic."
"Do you know where we can find him?"
"First tell me what's going on."
"I'm afraid he's wanted for questioning in a murder in New Jersey."

Chapter 57

Nate slammed the door of the house that had been like a second home to him. He could bear his bitterness toward Steve and Anna Maria as long as he didn't think about what they all had shared. The memories of them riding their bikes down Tewksbury hill or fishing for perch off the pier only made him miss a life that he could no longer dream about, a life that didn't exist anymore. Maybe it never had.

The road made a sharp hairpin turn, and he was in front of Cora's house, just above the Buonarottis'. She came to the door in her gardening apron.

"Nate! Look at you." She brushed her hands on her apron and hugged him. "Come in, come in. Let me wash my hands. I was just making some herb pots to take to the church bazaar."

Cora hadn't changed. If she had any gray hairs, they were invisible in the spun gold of her hair, hair like an angel's on top of a Christmas tree. The love on her face eased his heart. If only they could go back to before the war. Before he learned to sort people by color, saw first that Cora was white and only second that she seemed overjoyed to see him. He had avoided her since Texas. So why was he here now, running to her like a kid with a scraped knee?

"I've meant to come by," he started to explain.

"I understand. I know it's been hard for you."

"Hard? You think you know how hard it's been for me?" He saw the surprise and hurt on her face and turned to leave. He had to get out of there before he poisoned everything, before he said something he could never take back. "This was a mistake. I need to go."

"Nate, please. Come sit down." She took his hand and led him into the kitchen.

He sat at his old place at the table, she at hers.

"Talk to me, Nate."

He poured out his anger at not having been trained to fight. He told her how he and other soldiers had written letters to the Negro newspapers, to Mrs. Roosevelt, to the NAACP, to their churches. What it was like to have found out that the world believed Negroes were tarnished by an indelible stain, a stain that marked them as inferior, that penetrated to the soul, to the heart of being, and could never be removed.

He told Cora that once he had understood that, it had stopped him from answering Anna Maria's letters, letters that reminded him of a time when he thought anything was possible. She had written letter after letter—at mail call he had hoped for them, but for some reason, as much as he wanted to, he couldn't write back. Her last letter had said if he didn't answer, she would stop writing.

Nate showed Cora a photograph he had kept hidden when he was in the South.

"When was that taken?"

"Our last summer at Keller's beach."

Nate saw something flicker in Cora's eyes.

"What, Cora?"

She smiled wistfully. "Nothing. Just the memory of being young and in love at Keller's beach. A long time ago."

Nate looked at the photo. Anna Maria stood between Nate and Steve, arms linked through theirs, laughing, her dark hair hidden inside a sun hat. It had been one of those perfect summer days, wind off the bay, the smell of jasmine all around them. Anna Maria had taken his hand as they'd waded into the water, then dropped it. It was if electricity had flowed between them. After that, they had begun to see each other in a new way.

Now Nate felt an emptiness, a resignation. He carefully tore the photo into pieces. "It's over. She means nothing to me."

Cora stood and held him. Tried to comfort him.

"Oh, my poor Nate. Know that you are loved."

Nate turned away and wiped his face. He thought he saw Frank's reflection in the darkened window. "I better go now. I'm sorry."

When he turned around, no one was there.

Chapter 58

Clumps of blackberry bushes and wild fennel shielded Dom as he scrambled up the hill to Harry's house. He had known the time would come when his past would catch up with him. Without the war, maybe things would have worked out. But at least now he had his boys, and he could go back to Italy and make a life with them when the war was over. It was better than nothing.

Dom crawled alongside the bushes that bordered Harry's yard and crept into the honey house, stumbling over the fishing net he had taken from the boat. The wind picked up, and the clouds sailed across the sky, revealing the moon. It shone through the door, lighting the inside of the honey house. Dom wrestled the barrels in front of the *lampante* oil to the side. He had just gotten the lid off the barrel when the honey house went dark.

"Who's there? What are you doing?"

Dom swung around, the heavy net in his hand, and lashed out at the shape in the doorway. He didn't hit him that hard, but the person was knocked off balance into the stone wall of the house and fell to the ground. Dom swore. He had to retrieve the gun and get out of there. As he turned back to the barrel, he heard yelling. Someone was out there. He dropped the net, jumped over the body, and fled down the hill.

Frank had seen Wright's car parked in front of his house and had come in through a side door, expecting to catch Cora with Wright. Instead he found her with that Hermit boy. He hid in the shadowy hallway and watched the tender scene in the kitchen: Hermit swearing he didn't love the other girl, Cora picking up the pieces of the photo. She held them, then dropped them in the wastebasket. When he heard her feet on the wooden stairway, he slipped into the kitchen and picked the pieces out of the basket, dumped them on the table, and fit them together. Hermit with a white girl. Of course. The Buonarotti girl. And Cora there to comfort him. The older woman and the younger man.

He had suspected there was something between them. Cora was always touching Nate when she thought no one was looking. No wonder she suffered that Hermit woman around the place all the time. It gave her access to the boy. She was no better than the rest of them. He had seen her with Wright, and now with this one, and who knew how many others there had been? He stuffed the photo pieces into his pocket. He'd throw them in her face. Let her know he was nobody's fool.

He looked out the window into the back garden, biding his time until she came down to give him his supper, and saw someone going into the honey house. He sneaked out onto the dark porch to see what was happening and tripped over Cora's damned clay pots. He yelled when he crashed into the garden tools propped against the porch railing.

He looked down the hill as a figure ran from the honey house and headed for the bushes. Frank sprinted to the gate that opened into the Buonarottis' yard and saw a body lying across the threshold. Ah, the young master of the Buonarotti house, apple of his father's eye. Hurt. Frank went through the gate and quickly scattered the photo scraps around Steve's body. Felt the pulse. Not dead—too bad. His boot drew blood on Steve's cheek. He stomped his chest and enjoyed the sound of a bone cracking. He raised his boot again but lost his balance on the loose gravel. He heard voices, and light spilled across the path. Frank ducked around the back of the honey house and tried to control his breathing.

Chapter 59

When Nate went back to the Buonarottis' to wait for Oliver and Luca, Paola grabbed his arm and took him into the kitchen. She scolded him as if he were a child again, and told him he was the one who had changed, the one who had hurt his friends; they had never cared about the color of his skin and didn't care now. The only thing they cared about was his letting it come between him and them. She shooed him out the kitchen door in search of Steve, who had gone the back way to Cora's house to try to reason with his angry friend.

Nate climbed the path, wondering if Paola was right. Shadows of branches waving in the wind obscured, then revealed, the garden. The smell of crushed tomato vines reminded him of the times he and Steve had sweated in the sun, picking bushels of pear-shaped Principessa Borgheses for Paola and Anna Maria to put up in Mason jars. The house had smelled like tomatoes, and only tomatoes, for days while the women sweltered in the kitchen, trying to can enough thick sauce to last until next year's harvest. He remembered how he and Steve had chased Anna Maria with bits of the sticky honeycomb they had pulled from the honey extractor. He glanced toward the honey house and saw a form on the ground. It looked like Steve. Nate ran to him and knelt down to feel for a pulse. Someone grabbed him from behind. He shouted for help as he struggled to get free.

"Now I've got you."

Nate heard a familiar voice and then felt a blow to his head.

"What's going on out there?" Harry and Luca ran up the path, with Oliver trailing behind. Paola had been working by the open kitchen door and had called Harry when she'd heard Nate cry out.

Frank spun around to face the men. "I heard a fight and ran down to see what I could do."

"Oh my God, it's Steve. And Nate." Harry turned to Frank. "What happened? Who did this?"

"Harry." Oliver gestured toward the kitchen, where Paola stood in the doorway, and Harry ran back to head Paola off and flick on the outside lights. Harley trotted to the bushes alongside the garden, then followed a scent back to the honey house, where Oliver was helping Nate to his feet.

Frank pointed at Nate. "I caught this one kicking him. Easy to see what happened."

Nate started to come around. He raised his hand to the back of his head. "My head." He looked at Frank. "Why did you hit me?"

"Paola's calling an ambulance." Harry had run back up the hill and hovered over the boys. "How bad is it?"

Luca knelt beside Steve, pulled a small flashlight out of his pocket, and tried to examine him. "His pulse is weak."

"I'm taking this one in." Frank started pulling Nate away.

"The hell you are. Get your hands off him." Oliver faced Frank down. "This is an Army matter. Did you touch anything?"

"Of course not."

"You're involved, Frank. You need to leave. Someone will talk to you later." Oliver turned to Nate. "Can you walk?"

"I'm fine. Take care of Steve."

Luca pressed the clean part of his napkin against the cut on Steve's cheek. Oliver saw him flick the flashlight at the feet surrounding him, glance up at Frank, then turn back to his patient.

Frank swore and stomped up the path and through his gate. Oliver heard Frank's gruff voice and looked up the hill to see Cora break away from Frank and run down the path.

"Nate, Nate! What happened?" She reached out a hand to him and saw Steve on the ground. "Nate. What did you do?"

"How could you think . . ." Nate turned to Harry. "I need to sit down."

"Nate, I'm sorry. I know you would never hurt Steve. That's not what I thought." She reached out for him again.

"Of course not, Mrs. Slater." Nate walked toward the house, leaning on Harry.

Cora looked down at Steve, her brow wrinkled. "But how did . . ."

"You need to leave, Cora; this is no place for you." Oliver pointed back toward her gate.

She turned away and walked back to her house, slowing as she looked back at the body.

"Oliver, we need a paper *sachetta* for the photo fragments. And someone to search for footprints here and around the grounds." Luca seemed to have taken charge of the crime scene.

"I'll ask in the house."

He limped back with a paper bag and kitchen tongs and carefully placed the photo scraps in the bag. "What are you thinking?"

"Perhaps we can get fingerprints from them. Find out who tore them up."

"We'll need prints from Steve and Nate."

The ambulance attendants lifted Steve onto a stretcher and carried him away.

Luca pointed to the ground. "That is curious, no?"

"What is?"

"There are no scraps where the boy lay. It looks as if they were sprinkled around him when he was already on the ground."

"If the photo had been torn up in the heat of the moment, you would expect them to be under him, too."

Raised voices came from the house. Harry threatened to commandeer the ambulance and drive it himself if they didn't put Nate in with Steve and take them to the same hospital for the same care. Oliver thought the whole hillside must have heard Harry bellow, "Forget it, I'm coming with you. Both these men are soldiers! Keep it up, and you'll be wishing you still had your deferments!"

The ambulance wailed away, and Luca and Oliver turned back to the scene.

"What do you think happened, Luca?"

"You know how it seems."

"Yes, as if they had a fight and Nate came out the winner—until Frank showed up." Oliver looked up at the Slaters' house. "Convenient, Frank being here."

"I am not inclined to believe his account of events."

Oliver started to protest, then stopped. *Let Luca talk.* Maybe he needed to hear what someone objective had to say about Frank Slater.

"Tell me why."

"One"—Luca made a fist with the thumb standing up—"there is something cruel about him. I have known men like him. They enjoy causing pain. Usually to someone they have power over." Luca raised a finger. "To make him a suspect, we have two: his interest this morning in the briefcase of Theo."

"Wait a minute. What does that have to do with Steve?"

"I do not know. Not yet. But I think if we open our eyes, we will see something that is there in front of us."

As if taking his own advice, Luca walked into the honey house. "Oliver, why would there be a fishing net in a house for honey?"

"Good question." Oliver felt the net. "It's still wet. Maybe Steve surprised whoever brought it in here." Oliver looked around the little building. "What's in here that someone would want?"

"And why would you need a fishing net to get it?"

"Because it's in one of these barrels."

"*Guarda.* This lid is pushed aside a little." He slid the lid off the barrel, then gestured to Oliver as if to offer him the honors.

Oliver shook his head, and Luca tested the oil by bringing a drop to his tongue. "Pah!" He wrinkled his nose. "It is *lampante.* A fishing net might well improve the taste." He removed his jacket, rolled up his shirtsleeve, and dipped the net into the oil. Something clunked. He caught it and eased it along the side of the barrel.

"*Eccola.*" The net contained an oilcloth bundle tied with laces.

Oliver took out a pocketknife and cut through the shoelaces, preserving their knots. He folded back the oilcloth to reveal an unusual gun.

"This gun does not bring back good memories." Luca gestured toward it. "It is the revolver most of us were issued in the last war. In Italy."

"And who do we know who is from Italy?"

"In addition to me and a large number of Italian prisoners—who, I must add, no longer have weapons—perhaps the father of Cesare and Tomaso. We must inquire whether he knew this oil was here and would probably never be used."

When Harley and the men were back in the car with the photo scraps, gun, and fishing net, Luca raised a thumb and two fingers.

"And three: there is the blood on his boot. Brand-new boots, I think."

Oliver was confused for a moment. "Oh, you're still talking about Frank. But he was there, at the scene."

"The blood was on the toe, not the bottom. He was standing over Corporal Hermit outside the little building. The blood did not come from him or the ground around Steve. No. When I put the light on it, it was bright red and wet." Luca held up the bag. "It would be interesting, would it not, to see whose fingerprints are on the photo?"

Oliver glanced at the bag. "I'm not convinced that Frank would do something like this. I agree he's not a good man, and no friend of mine, but what would he have to gain? He cuts corners and can be rough on people, but hurt Steve? And why lie about Nate?"

Luca shrugged. Oliver's defense of Frank did not seem to bother him. "What if Nate interrupted the beating? Perhaps Frank was afraid Nate had seen something. And is Frank not one of those Klan people? You say they hate Negro people."

"I don't think Frank is a Klansman. I've been away, and I didn't know him at all when we were younger, but I think he tried to distance himself from his family, tried to make a life on the right side of the law. I don't like him, and I didn't like how he handled Theo, but from what I've heard, he was a good detective. He probably would have gotten the chief's job if it hadn't been for his family's reputation."

"Oliver, it is possible that the disappointment of not being promoted because of something he had no control over pushed him to the side of his family."

"You mean he decided being one of the good guys hadn't gotten him anywhere? Maybe." Oliver had seen what Frank had tried to do to Roan and Emma.

"A pity we cannot compare his prints to the photo."

"Ah, but we can. The chief had me take all the officers' prints for elimination purposes. Tomorrow we'll see what the photo scraps tell us. But now let's go bring Theo his briefcase. He's probably lost without it." He shifted in his seat to ease the pain in his leg. "We can sleep there, and tomorrow we'll go see my friend Rob Cowrie about the gun."

"What about Nate and Steve? Maybe they can tell us something."

"I guess we can swing by the hospital now." It would be a while yet before he could put his aching leg up.

"Bene."

Friday
October 27, 1944

Chapter 60

Theo fell on his briefcase as if he had been parted from it for a year instead of a day and ran outside to his studio, leaving his half-eaten toast on the kitchen table. Luca watched the briefcase reunion, noting the lack of contact between Theo and Oliver. Only the briefcase mattered. He thought of the sketches on the wall in Ralph Robinson's restaurant. The Wrights must know of Theo's condition. Had they tried to help him? Not that help would be easy.

Before the war, Luca had met an Austrian pediatrician, rather an awkward man, who planned to publish his study of a condition he called Asperger's syndrome. Theo exhibited two of the symptoms Dr. Asperger had described: a deep, well-developed talent, and social awkwardness. Granted, Luca had observed Theo only in rather unusual circumstances, but that the boy had not sought comfort from his uncle after finding Jonah's body seemed significant to Luca.

"Theo has not been himself since his father died." It was as if Oliver had read Luca's mind. "He's always been extremely shy, but he's become more withdrawn. The briefcase belonged to Peter. After it was examined, we let Theo have it. It seemed to comfort him. That and Harley."

"Does he have friends he can talk to?"

"Not really." Oliver poured another cup of coffee, offering more to Luca, who declined. "He mainly talks to Zoe, his sister. And his mother."

"What is in the briefcase?"

"Everything that means anything to Theo: paper, pencils, his sketchbooks, all the bits and pieces he picks up along the way to put into his art. He notices every scrap that he can use for art but can completely miss a parade going by. I'll ask him if he would like to show you some of his creations. He's usually willing to do that. Not that it matters if you like them or not. As long as he's satisfied with them, that's enough for him."

"It appeared to me that Frank Slater showed too much interest in the briefcase. *What could it have to do with anything?* I thought. Now that you say it is where Theo puts things that interest him, it occurs to me that Frank was trying to find out if Theo had picked up something from the place Jonah died."

"If someone sent Frank there, it would explain how he knew about Jonah."

"We make many assumptions, Oliver."

"Let's talk to Theo and take a look in the briefcase, if he'll allow that." Oliver rubbed his eyes. "I had a hard time falling asleep last night, trying to decide if I believed Frank could deliberately kill someone. I still—"

"Uncle Oliver, the phone is for you." Zoe stood in the doorway.

"Hello, I'm Zoe." She held out her hand. "You must be Captain Respighi. Can I get you something? I thought I might make waffles. Have you ever had them? I got some butter and two eggs from Mrs. Forgione's cousin. That should be enough for all of us, and there's still maple syrup from the tin Uncle Oliver brought us back from New England. Do you know New England? I wonder if it's like old England. Someday I'd like to see it. Well, both, really—old England and New England. And Sherwood Forest. Do you think they have maple—"

Oliver came back into the room. "Zoe! Take a breath." He smiled at her. "I'm sorry, honey, but we can't stay for waffles."

"Thank you for the offer of waffles. Perhaps another time, *bella*."

"*Bella?* What does that mean?"

"That you are a beautiful and enchanting young woman. *Arriverderla.*"

Zoe was momentarily silenced. Oliver quickly kissed her and told her to keep an eye on her brother.

"Uncle Oliver! Wait! Did you bring Theo's briefcase, or does that Detective Slater have it? I can't spend another day with Theo fretting about it."

"Slater?"

"Yes, he came here yesterday." Her face clouded. "He didn't believe

Theo didn't have the briefcase. We told him Mr. Robinson drove off with it after they got his bike out of the car."

Oliver frowned. "If anyone comes here, including Detective Slater, tell whoever it is you can't open the door unless *I* am here. Do you understand?"

"Yes. But I have archery practice today."

"Fine, but please tell your mother that Theo should work in the house today. I'm leaving Harley here with you."

After he heard his name, Harley's eyebrows started moving up and down like a seesaw as his eyes tracked back and forth between Zoe and Oliver.

"Sorry, fella. You need to take care of Theo and Zoe."

Oliver and Luca waved good-bye to Zoe and hurried to the car.

"You are disturbed. Who was that on the phone?"

"Harmon. He thought I would want to know that Ralph Robinson's restaurant was broken into last night."

"You think it was Slater in search of the briefcase?"

"Yes, or maybe someone thought Jonah had given his notes to Ralph. Also, there was an attempted rape last night. A woman named Zora. She's in a coma. They think she isn't going to make it." Oliver remembered what the women had said about the rapes. "Tell me something. Women are saying the rapes now are the same as rapes from ten or twelve years ago. I wonder if maybe someone moved away and came back, something like that. What do you think?"

"It is possible, certainly. I have read also of rape sometimes being caused by a stressor."

"A stressor?"

"Perhaps the man doing this is acting out his anger against another woman or women—his mother, his wife, someone who controlled or hurt him. If the stress diminished, he might be under less pressure to act out. If it started again, so might he. But it would be unlikely that he would be quiet for ten or twelve years. That kind of personality would probably be more volatile." Luca waggled a hand. "Perhaps it is a combination of things. The man could have been acting out, left, and then returned. If you ever have a suspect, you could find out if he has lived elsewhere and if similar rapes were committed when he was there."

"Harmon also said Dr. Carter was trying to get hold of me. He's finished the autopsy on Fusco."

"Why did an Army doctor not do it?"

"They wanted an independent autopsy—no hint of collusion or cover-up allowed. A high-powered attorney from the NAACP is in town, making waves about the Port Chicago verdict. Thurgood Marshall, I think his name is. The Army is not going to do anything that might let him get his foot in the door on this one."

"So. What is our plan?"

"First, let's stop by the hospital and see Dr. Carter; maybe Steve will be able to talk to us this morning. All we accomplished at the hospital last night was stopping Nate from leaving. Then we need to take the gun to Rob Cowrie. And we still haven't dusted for fingerprints on the photo scraps."

"We also might want to see Mrs. Forgione this morning."

"I can't think of any reason we'd need to see her." Oliver tried to keep a straight face.

"*Allora*, she is related to the Buonarottis and perhaps can tell us if the father of Dom was an officer in the Italian army."

"Why do we need to know that?"

"Because the gun we found has a fixed trigger guard. The model enlisted men were given had a collapsible trigger guard." Luca smiled innocently, as if that were the only reason to go to the Café Avellino. "I believe we will have difficulty obtaining records of the First World War from the Italian government."

"Yes, and while we're there, you just might find time for an espresso."

"And perhaps a pastry."

Chapter 61

They found Dr. Carter in the morgue.

"Ah, Lieutenant Wright."

"Oliver, please."

"Yes." Carter cleared his throat. "I have something to show you."

"On Fusco's body?"

"Not exactly *on*." Carter smiled.

Oliver thought the Brit needed to go to the Pacific. See if he thought that was funny.

"The cause of Fusco's death is drowning."

"Drowning? Not asphyxia?" Luca asked.

"Drowning. An assisted drowning. He is bruised on his back and arms, as if he were held facedown in shallow water. I found sand in the mouth and throat passages and water in his lungs. I also found something unusual *in* his body that might interest you." Something rattled in the metal pan he produced.

Oliver picked it up. "It's a button from a field tunic."

"It was in his stomach? He ate it?" Luca looked at it.

"It's metal." Carter smiled. "Had to be hard to swallow,"

Oliver didn't think it was the time for feeble jokes.

"Then it's from one of the soldiers. Our uniforms have plastic buttons." Luca pointed at his jacket. "You must admire Fusco. He provided us a clue. The men said he was shrewd."

"I think a surprise inspection is in order, Luca."

"I also have something to show you on the Buonarotti boy. Follow me."

Carter paused at the door to a stairwell, then continued down the hall to an elevator. Oliver realized Carter was making a concession for his leg and felt the heat rise in his face. Luca glanced at him and fell in step with Carter, as if to give Oliver a moment to collect himself.

The men entered a room where four beds were crammed into space for two.

"All the hospitals are filled to overflowing, even with the shipyard injuries going to the Kaiser facilities." Carter walked over to the bed by the wall. "Hello, Steve. How are you feeling today?"

"Ready to go home, sir."

"No, not quite yet. May I show Lieutenant Wright your bruise?"

"Sure."

The doctor lifted the gown that covered Steve's taped ribs and rolled the boy a bit onto his side.

"The bandage obscures part of the bruise, but observe this pattern here."

Luca and Oliver took turns at the bedside, examining the bruise.

"Thank you, Steve. I'll be back to see you tomorrow morning."

"Before we go, I'd like to ask him a few questions."

"Certainly, Lieutenant."

"Did you see who hit you last night?"

"No." Steve paused, as if trying to remember what had happened. "I was on my way to see Nate at Mrs. Slater's. I'd hoped she could help smooth things over between us, but I heard someone in the honey house and went to see who it was. Next thing I knew, something came out and hit me in the head. Then I don't remember anything, except when I started to come to, I heard someone near me, and then someone kicked me. I don't remember anything else."

"Could you tell if it was the same person?"

"I don't think it was. I thought the first one stepped over me and left."

"Did you fight with Nate at the honey house?"

"No. We argued at my house, then he went to Cora's."

"Could he have been the one who kicked you?"

"I didn't see who did it. But I told Detective Slater I don't believe Nate would have done that." Steve began to get agitated. "He kept saying I was wrong."

Carter motioned for Oliver and Luca to leave.

Oliver spoke over his shoulder as he left the room. "If you remember anything else, don't tell anyone but me. Not even Detective Slater."

In the corridor, Oliver asked Carter why he had wanted them to see the bruising.

"It reminded me of the bruising I saw on Jonah North's body. He had been stomped by a boot with the same tread pattern in about the same place."

"That's pretty thin," Oliver said.

"The bruise has a defined pattern within the sole area. Quite distinctive. Dr. Pritchard has photos of the bruises on North's body. When we compare them with photos of the bruise on Steve's body, I believe we will find them to be almost identical. The bruising suggests a link between the two beatings." He seemed to consider what he was about to say. "I think this bruise is a bit larger, but then, I could be mistaken."

Right. Carter would think he was mistaken when pigs could fly.

Luca raised his leg and showed the men the bottom of his boot. "Nate would be wearing boots like mine. The tread pattern does not resemble the pattern of the bruise."

"Yes, it is quite different," the doctor concluded.

"*Dottore*, have you mentioned this information about the bruise to anyone else?"

"Not directly, but that rather arrogant detective chanced to come in when I was photographing it."

Chapter 62

A thin line of silver shone between the black of the bay and the deep gray of the sky. Cora sat on her back porch, gazing out toward the water, willing the silver line to widen, willing an end to this endless night. When she had returned to the house after seeing Steve on the ground, she had heard Frank slamming out the front door. She had pretended to be asleep when he came back, and as soon as he'd begun snoring, she had gotten up and gone downstairs, first trying to sleep on the sofa, then finally making coffee and sitting in the dark on the porch.

She kept asking herself the same questions. Were those photo scraps the ones she had thrown in the wastebasket? If they were, what were they doing around Steve? Did Nate come back in and take them, then fight with Steve about them? Could he have hurt Steve? He had been so angry the day before.

Voices floated up from the road. Women on their way to catch their ride to the cannery or the tank plant. They walked past every morning, speaking in soft tones, mindful of their sleeping neighbors. Cora envied them their sense of purpose, even more their friendships. Sometimes she caught bits of sentences: "And then he . . ." or "all white orchids . . ." or "not since March . . ." She wanted to know what he had done, or what the white orchids were for. She wanted to laugh softly with them and complain about their manager, to eat sandwiches from a lunch pail and drink lukewarm coffee.

She had heard them talking about the newspapers and letters they put in the tanks when they were ready to go overseas. A surprise for the men. Cora had waited for them one morning while Frank was sleeping and asked if she could do something for the boys. Now she knit socks to put in the tanks. Frank didn't approve, but she had enough free time to make them when he wasn't around, and she saved a bit here and there from the grocery money to buy her supplies. She knit wishes for good luck and safety into them and imagined one of the boys pulling them onto his blistered feet and feeling good that someone back home cared about him.

Her days were so empty. Dr. Chalmers had impressed upon her the need for a woman to have something of her own, but Frank had nagged and cajoled her until she had quit nursing. He'd said that maybe if she stopped, she would get pregnant.

She had known it wouldn't make a difference, and it hadn't, but it never seemed like the right time to ask him about going back to work. She had brought it up when the war began and nurses were in short supply. At first it had seemed as if he would say yes, but a few weeks later, he had told her not to bother trying. No one would want a nurse who had quit and then hadn't cared enough to keep up her training.

Her hand went to her chest, to touch her locket. For a moment, she had forgotten it was gone. Frank must have taken it. How else could it have gotten out of her jewelry box? The locket had something to do with the way he'd changed, but he couldn't have known who had given it to her or why she wore it. She had waited for days for him to explode, to accuse her. The blow-up had never come, but he had treated her as if she were a stranger, as if he had never loved her. She had been too afraid to ask if he had taken the locket, but maybe she should have.

It had been her touchstone, the gift Oliver had given her when he had asked her to wait for him—on their last day together. She had taken it off when she went on her nursing shift, but she knew it was there in her pocket, reminding her of him. Funny, the locket reminded her only of his loving her, of the good part of the day. Not about what happened later. Not about her ignoring his letters and refusing to see him. Now that she was older, she suspected she might have underestimated him. But he had been young, too. She'd never know.

Maybe she would walk to the café. Edna might be there, and Cora could find out how Nate and Steve were. Then she decided against it. If Frank woke up while she was gone, he would be angry. Besides, she needed to talk to him. It was time for some answers.

Chapter 63

"Fusco was drowned." Luca pursed his lips. "Where could he have been drowned? And why?"

Oliver braked for a short man in a cowboy hat that had to be fifty gallons if it was a quart. "It appears there was a fight, maybe near the bay. He was killed on an island, after all."

"But it is unlikely that he would have been down by the water. We are not permitted to go there."

"I don't think breaking a minor rule would have meant much to Fusco." The clutch slipped, and the car stalled out; Oliver ignored the horns behind him.

"We must determine why Fusco would have been there. To meet someone?"

"I would have thought the island was off-limits to any kind of boat traffic, Luca. The bay's heavily guarded."

"I understand the defenses are against submarines and big ships—against threats from outside the bay. I know the fishermen of my village would be able to evade detection around islands in our waters. Perhaps it is the same here."

Oliver remembered how he and his friends had sailed and rowed in the bay. All the caves and hidden beaches they had found. And they had been kids just fooling around. Imagine what the fishermen must know about the shores and the currents. Something else to check. That and civilian suppliers to the island.

The DeSoto crossed San Pablo Avenue and headed up the hill. It climbed through Albany and wended its way to Wild Cat Canyon

Road, where a pack of beagles ran to the fence and bayed at the car through the cloud of dust it left in its wake. It rocked to a stop at a dead end overlooking a deep canyon.

"How beautiful!" Once more, Luca longed for home as he watched the grasses that shimmered and changed color in the wind blowing through the cleft. He heard a creek somewhere beyond the oaks that marked the end of the road. *To sit here in the evening with a glass of wine.* He was becoming attached to this place.

"Luca," Oliver called from the porch of a yellow house.

A large man pushed open the door, grabbed Oliver, and lifted him. First time Luca had seen an American man hug another man. But there was the lifting—the show of strength, not really an embrace.

"Hey, Oliver, it's good to see you. I heard you'd been wounded in the Pacific. You look great! Wait till the wife sees you. Where's Harley?" The man nudged Oliver aside so he could see behind him.

"He was wounded, too, but he's fine now. Saved my life. Him and a cook armed with a skillet. But it's a long story for another day, Rob." Oliver gestured toward Luca. "This is Captain Luca Respighi, of the Italian army. We need your help with a gun we found in a barrel of olive oil."

Rob's eyes lit up when Oliver said *gun*. "Storing it there was smart. Would probably keep it from rusting. Let's take a look."

He led the way down several steps to a room whose walls were lined with guns, many of which Luca did not recognize.

Rob walked to a workbench with a vise grip and various bottles of cleaners and solvents. "Let's see what you have."

Oliver set the oilcloth bundle on the table, and Rob unfolded it.

"A Bodero. Designed in the 1870s and used until 1912 by the Italian military, and sometimes the police. It was replaced by the Glissenti, but many soldiers still kept the Bodero. This one was designed for an officer. You see the trigger guard? The enlisted men's guns didn't have one. The trigger folded up into the gun."

"Would this kind of gun leave marks that could tell us if a bullet was fired from it? We think it might have been used to kill a police officer in New Jersey."

While Rob launched into a well-rehearsed lecture about rifling and lands and grooves, Luca wandered around the room, thinking about men's fascination with guns. Before the war, he had thought little of the rifle kept on his family's farm. It was like any other tool with a purpose necessary to the safety of chickens and other animals. He had used it to hunt wild boar with his father. He remembered the shots ringing out in December, and then the wonderful food the animal provided. Wild-boar sausage, *pappardelle* with mushroom and wild-boar sauce . . .

"Luca!" Oliver interrupted Luca's musings.

"What?"

"I can only imagine what you're daydreaming about, but I would bet it has something to do with food."

"Forgive me. I did get distracted there for a moment." He gave a tiny bow with his head. "What were you saying, Signor Cowrie?"

"That if the New Jersey police recovered the bullet, there's a good chance you'll be able to identify it." He started rummaging in a box. "Let me shuffle through my ammunition for the kind of bullet designed for this gun."

"I believe it takes .422-diameter bullets," Luca volunteered.

"Have you used one of these guns?"

"In the First World War."

Rob broke the gun and checked that the barrel was not obstructed. "Whoever your bad guy is, he cared for this gun."

Rob loaded it, pulled back the hammer, and fired into a tank of water. The bullets slowed quickly in the liquid and sank.

"Did you have to do that? Pull back the hammer to fire it?" Oliver seemed intrigued.

"Not very efficient, is it? Although it is safe. It would be almost impossible to fire it accidentally." Rob used a rod to push out the spent cartridges. "My sympathies to you, Luca, if this is the weapon you were supposed to win a war with. Having to poke the cartridges out before you could reload surely would encourage you to finish things with the first six shots."

Oliver and Luca did not get back to Pt. Richmond until the late afternoon. Luca hoped they were going to eat. Now it was a matter not simply of desiring an espresso but of requiring sustenance. If the Newark police still had the bullet that had killed the police officer,

Oliver would send the bullets Signor Cowrie had prepared to New Jersey. It would not help them solve Fusco's murder, but it might help the Newark police convict Nic Criscilla.

"*Buon giorno, signora.*" Luca smelled peppers and onions frying. "How are you today?"

"*Bene,* Captain." Mrs. Forgione glanced at the door. "Are you on your own?"

"Lieutenant Wright will be here shortly."

"While you're waiting, would you like to come into the kitchen?"

"Certainly! I have missed the whole music of cooking." He spoke of the sizzle of oil in a pan, the *thunk* of a knife through onions, the *clunk-clunk-clunk* of a spoon against a pot to cleanse it after stirring, the wet *slap* of fish on a board. His hands rose above his head, made circles in the air. And then the smells: rosemary, garlic, sage, oregano.

Mrs. Forgione led him into the kitchen. "Tell me, who do you think is responsible for hurting Steve?"

Luca tasted a bit of salami. "Oliver and I do not think it was Nate."

"Neither do I."

"Steve does not remember much. We think he was knocked out almost by accident when he surprised someone—probably Dom—in the honey house, and then someone, a different person, kicked him while he was on the ground." Luca tried a spoonful of *pasta e fagioli*. "*Bellissima!*"

"Who do you think kicked him?"

"Between us, I think it was Frank Slater, but we do not know why he would want to hurt Steve."

"Who knows with some people? Frank enjoys causing pain."

Luca bit into a breadstick. "What happened to create such animosity between him and Oliver?"

"A girl. A long time ago."

"No, it seems like something more recent."

"There's also Cora, Frank's wife. She and Oliver were sweethearts for a short time. Again, a long time ago."

Luca waited, convinced there had to be more.

Mrs. Forgione changed the subject. "I heard about the torn-up photo of Harry's children and Nate."

"Who told you about it?" Luca was certain Oliver had kept that a secret.

"Mrs. Hermit heard about it from Cora."

"How did she know about it?"

"I don't know. Maybe Frank told her."

Luca momentarily forgot about the breadstick. How did Slater know who was in the photo? Luca and Oliver had not known until they had fit the pieces together. And if Slater could not have told his wife, how did she know? She might have seen the scraps around the body, but how did she know who was in the photo?

"Luca, we need to eat and get going." Oliver beckoned to Luca from the door to the dining room. "But first, Mrs. Forgione, could you sit with us for a moment while we're eating?"

"Of course. Would you like some *cannelloni* for your lunch? And spinach with garlic? It's ready to eat, and you seem to be in a rush."

"Sure." Oliver didn't consult Luca, who nodded his agreement to Mrs. Forgione. He and Oliver found a table near the fire.

"What did you find out? Do they still have the bullet?"

"Yes. It's in evidence at the station. Sergeant Doran said that they noted what an odd caliber it was at the time of the shooting."

"And now?"

"As far as we know, this gun has nothing to do with our case, but we'll hold on to it until we wrap up Fusco's murder. Then the gun will be evidence in the policeman's murder in New Jersey."

Mrs. Forgione sat down after she'd finished serving them.

"*Mangia!* It will get cold."

"Mrs. Forgione, we need to find out if anyone in Dom's family was an officer in World War I." Oliver unfolded his napkin.

"His father was an officer. May he rest in peace."

"We need to find Dom. And Tomaso. The commander left a message at the precinct that Tomaso's gone missing. I think he left the island to warn Dom, who then went to Harry's to retrieve his father's gun. It was probably Dom in the honey house." He looked at Luca. "No matter what happens now, Tomaso will be out of the Service Units."

"What if he helps us? If he is returned to the regular POW camp with the Fascisti, he will be badly treated."

"I don't know, Luca. Let's see how this plays out."

"I feel sorry for those boys, having a father like Dom." Mrs. Forgione thought for a moment. "Let me talk to some people. We're a small community—someone will know where they are. Excuse me."

Oliver lowered his voice. "Harmon found many smudged prints along the edges of the photo scraps. Makes sense. Most people try to avoid marking the subject of the photo. But he did find several partial prints in the center. They could have been made by someone who touched each piece while reassembling the photo. He took Steve's prints at the hospital. They weren't a match, but the boy told Harmon that Anna Maria probably sent the photo to Nate. Harmon will take her prints later."

Luca raised a finger. "Mrs. Forgione knew the photo scraps were of Nate and the Buonarotti children."

"What?"

"Yes, she heard it from Edna, who heard it from Cora. Perhaps the prints are those of Cora. How did she know what that photo was? She was not close enough to see last night."

"Interesting. Harmon was able to identify two of the prints. Guess whose?"

"Frank Slater."

"Yes. We need to talk to him. He didn't come in to the station today. The chief said he was probably out late, interviewing the prostitutes about the rapes."

Luca drained his cup. "What now?"

"Now we pay a visit to Frank. Interrupt his beauty sleep."

Chapter 64

Tomaso crept out the back door and walked down to the bay, hoping to clear his head. The night before, Dom had returned to the boat breathless and without the gun. He had ignored Mario's questions and sent him away, while Tomaso had pleaded to be allowed to go back to the island. Dom had stalked off, leaving him no choice but to follow. Dom insisted they lie low until he figured out what to do tomorrow. That was today, but so far Tomaso was the only one awake, the rest still sleeping off the drink of the night before.

He looked out over the water to see if he could find a familiar landmark. How could he convince Dom to leave him in peace? As hard as it had been, he and Cesare had been better off when they were orphans. He wished he had a father like Captain Respighi or Uncle Harry, though now that he had met Anna Maria, he was happy they weren't related.

Dom was going to ruin that, too. Late in the night, a man had shown up at the house and grabbed Dom by the shirt. Tomaso had thought he was going to punch Dom; that hadn't bothered Tomaso at all. The man said Steve had been badly beaten and that Dom had made trouble for all of them. Of course, Dom said he hadn't done it. Said he hadn't known it was Steve. Then said he had only scared Steve with the net and the boy had fallen against the wall and been knocked out. Tomaso didn't believe him. Dom had lied about sending for them, about New Jersey, and now he was probably lying about this, too. But what could Tomaso do? Maybe he could get to Captain Respighi and tell him what had happened. Maybe he could fix this.

"Tomaso, didn't I tell you not to leave the house? Someone could see you. Turn us in." Dom stumbled down the hill barefoot, holding up his beltless pants with one hand.

"No one is out here. Just a fishing boat. What do they care about a man sitting on the beach?"

"Let's go inside. We have to make plans."

"The only plan I'm interested in is how to get back to the island."

"You are so stupid!" Dom swatted Tomaso's head. "What do you think is going to happen if you go back? You'll go to jail, that's what. And they'll blame you for things you didn't do. Like me."

Chapter 65

As they passed the Richmond Natatorium, Luca asked Oliver what it was.

"It's a swimming pool."

"It is beautiful, and looks to be quite large."

"Someone drilling for oil or gas found an artesian well instead. Eventually he donated the land to the city. The birth of the Plunge."

"Can anyone swim there?"

"By *anyone*, do you mean you? You haven't had enough swimming to last you for a while?"

"I used to swim every day at my home. In the sea. Not like your bay. No, it was warm and soft, embracing. Like the arms of a lover."

"Do you have one? A lover, a wife, a girlfriend? Children?"

"No. And you?"

"I have a son. Charley. He's in the service." Oliver told Luca about the boat, what had happened to Elizabeth.

"I'm sorry."

Oliver looked over at him. "You know, Charley told me his mother is always with him."

Luca smiled and nodded his head.

"What? You think it's true?"

"I know my father is watching out for me. He was the one I asked for help when we were in the desert. I do not know about 'true,' but I know I believe it. And that is sufficient." He was silent for a moment. "Perhaps one day you, too, will believe such a thing is possible."

Oliver thought that was unlikely.

They rode through the tunnel out into the sunlight again. Oliver turned right at Western Avenue and drove up the hill.

"There was someone once. I met her at university, but we drifted apart when I went on to study medicine. She did not want to wait that long to get married, have a family, and I did not want to give up my dream of becoming a psychiatrist. Since then, life." Luca shrugged his shoulders, as if to say, *You know how it is*.

Oliver saw Luca watching the Buonarottis' house as they passed it. Probably thinking about food again, although he had also seemed somewhat taken by Paola's sister, Isabella, who had gone to pieces when they'd told her why they had come for Dom. The old damsel-in-distress attraction—seemed even psychiatrists weren't immune to it.

Oliver parked in front of the Slaters'. Time collapsed when he saw the arch of pink roses climbing the trellis, and he was back on Cora Lundgren's front porch in Santa Cruz, twenty years earlier. He still didn't understand what had happened. He had dropped Cora off at nursing school after he had asked her to wait for him, then hurried to the train that took him east to school. She had written for a month or so, and then her letters had stopped. His mother had told him to go after her if he loved her, to swallow his pride.

He had rung the bell and waited in a cloud of pink roses. The canes waved as the breeze lifted them and swirled a peppery fragrance around him. The woman who opened the door looked so much like Cora, he couldn't speak. Mrs. Lundgren's eyes filled with tears. Cora didn't want to see him. She was sorry. She opened her mouth as if to say something else, then shook her head and closed the door. He had almost knocked again. Now he wondered what would have happened if he had.

Through the trellis, he saw a tall, thin woman ringing the Slaters' bell. She turned, her hand on her chest, when she heard the car doors slam.

He told her who they were. When he asked if something was wrong, she told them Cora wasn't answering the door.

"Maybe she's gone out."

"No. I'm sure she's home. I saw her earlier, and she asked me to come over and help her with a project for the church around four o'clock. This isn't like her."

Oliver glanced up and down the street. He didn't see Frank's car. He tried the door. It was locked.

Luca walked toward the back of the house. Oliver heard him yell, "Oliver, come! Quickly."

The captain teetered on a garbage can, shielding his eyes from the glare so he could see through the window. "I see her feet on the floor. I think she has fallen."

Oliver smashed the glass in the kitchen door with the butt of his gun, reached in, and undid the lock. He blocked the neighbor at the door and asked her to go home and call for an ambulance. She nodded and hurried to her house.

"Cora!" Oliver knelt beside her.

"Let me." Luca felt for the pulse in her neck. "She has been beaten. Choked, too, I think. And her clothing is disturbed." He pulled her dress down to cover her.

"Was she . . ."

"It appears so. Who would have done this?"

"The rapist? Do you think he did this to get back at the police?" Even as he said it, Oliver didn't think it made sense. Why would the rapist care about the policeman's wife? Especially since the policeman didn't seem to have a clue who he was? How had he gotten in? The kitchen door was locked with a turn bolt, but the front door might have locked automatically when it closed. They would have to check that, and the windows. Maybe Cora had let the assailant in.

Cora groaned. "Frank."

She was calling for Frank.

"Please."

"Cora, who did this? Did you see him?"

"Frank."

"We'll find Frank for you, but tell us who did this."

"Stop him. Nate."

Cora passed out again. Oliver fumed while he waited for the ambulance. He wanted to kill Nate. He had trusted him. Liked him. He tried to remember whether Nate had been back for all the rapes. But Auntie Josephine had said the man wasn't Negro. Besides, he was too young. Maybe this had nothing to do with the other rapes.

After the ambulance left with Cora and the neighbor, Oliver sent Luca to Harry's.

"We still need to find Dom and Tomaso. Paola can help you reach Harry. Explain to him what's happened. Ask him to call the station and tell them to try to find Frank. He needs to know that his wife has been hurt. If any word comes through about Dom, Harry can help you. Ask him to get Harmon to go with you. But be careful. Dom has killed once—don't underestimate him."

Mrs. Forgione hung up the phone at the café. Just as she'd thought. Dom couldn't stay hidden in their little community. One of her friends had seen Tomaso and Dom from his fishing boat and had asked around until he had found out they were staying with Maurizio, Mario's cousin, but were going to be moving somewhere to wait for a car to take them inland. She would tell Nate when he came back from the doctor.

She called Harry's house, hoping Oliver was still at the Slaters' and that Paola might go there and ask Oliver to call her. A busy signal. Probably Anna Maria talking to her friends. While she waited to try again, she heard a familiar voice in the café. She peeked around the door. It was Maurizio. He flirted with the girl at the counter while she made sandwiches for him. Mrs. Forgione motioned for Mrs. Hermit to come to the back.

"He's the one hiding Dom and Tomaso. We need to get help, tell someone he's here." She tried calling Harry's again. Still busy. She wished Nate were there.

They heard the bell over the door ring. Maurizio was leaving, walking away from the café. They watched him cross the street and get into a green coupe. They ducked when Dom looked out the passenger window.

"Come on. We have to follow them."

"How?"

Mrs. Forgione spied the chicken man's truck idling in the alley next to the café.

She grabbed Mrs. Hermit by the arm and hurried her toward the truck. "Can you drive?"

"I drove the truck on the farm when I was young."

"Then get in, and let's go."

"Mrs. Forgione!"

"He hurt Steve. And Nate got blamed."

Mrs. Hermit needed no more urging. Lucy struggled to pull herself into the truck, and Edna jumped into the driver's seat. She pressed the clutch and ground through the gears until she found first. They hopped through the alley and turned left in the direction in which they had seen the green coupe go.

When they saw it, it was several cars ahead of them, stopped by the wigwag at the railroad crossing. A long freight train lumbered out to the bay.

Mrs. Hermit had the driving fundamentals down, but no practice. Lucy had to give her credit—she stalled only the first time she stopped. The women had rolled down the windows and could hear the cackling of the chickens behind them. Soon they were crawling up MacDonald.

"I think I'm getting the hang of it!"

Mrs. Forgione's feet didn't touch the floor. She bounced in her seat, grabbed at the dash, the door, anything to keep her balance. When they stopped at a light, a man grabbed a crate of chickens and hightailed it. She wagged her hand in the air.

"*Madonna.* Now I owe the chicken man for a crate of chickens."

"And that highway robber didn't give you any coupons for them, either!"

Lucy started to laugh, perhaps a bit hysterically, as what they were doing began to sink in, and Edna joined her.

"We stole a truck and we don't know how many chickens."

"We didn't steal them, Mrs. Hermit. We're taking them for a ride."

Traffic began to clear. Soon they were only two cars behind. Lucy caught a glimpse of another man in the back seat of the car. Probably Tomaso.

"Dom knows you, Mrs. Forgione. Get down on the floor."

Slimy produce and God knows what else littered the floor. "I'm not going down there." Mrs. Forgione snatched a bandanna from the rearview mirror and tied it over her head. She would wash her hair when she got home. "He knows you, too."

"He won't recognize me." Mrs. Hermit winked at her passenger. "We all look alike."

The coupe began climbing into the hills. Mrs. Hermit struggled to hang back without stalling the truck. The car pulled onto a dirt lot. Mrs. Forgione turned her back to the window as they passed the men and drove around the bend. The truck began to stutter.

"What are you doing?"

"It's not me. I think the truck is running out of gas."

With that, the truck stopped. Mrs. Hermit tried the ignition; it ground but wouldn't start.

"We need a phone." She jumped out of the truck and gave Mrs. Forgione a hand down.

Lucy looked into the back of the truck. "I think the chickens are cold and want to go to sleep."

The women found a tarp in the truck and pulled it over the crates. Mrs. Forgione hopped up and down to reach her side. She hushed the chickens. "Shh. Go to sleep. You should be happy you went for a ride in the fresh air. You could be in someone's oven."

"What now?"

"We have to call Harry. Tell him where Dom is."

The Grand Canyon Chateau sat like a dowager aunt on the hill above them.

"The chateau."

"I think they're closed for remodeling."

"Let's hope their phone is still in order." Mrs. Forgione smoothed down her dress. "You stay and watch in case another car comes. I'll go find the phone inside."

"I should come with you."

"No. Keep watch. If a car comes, you can get its license number."

Mrs. Forgione climbed the road to the chateau, respectable now after its rowdy past as a speakeasy. The doors were locked. She walked around the building and tried the windows. One slid upward when she pushed. Luckily, the bottom sill was only a foot above the porch floor. She crossed herself, hiked up her skirt, and climbed through the opening.

Chapter 66

Cora lay in the ambulance, her eyes shut against the world. Her throat hurt, the way it had once before, and she began to sink into that deep, quiet place far from pain, far from men who hurt her. She had counted on Frank's iron core to protect her from shadows and dark rooms. She had never imagined he could turn his coldness toward her, but she had shivered when he'd said her name.

"Cora."

She was in the kitchen, her back to him. Water leaped from the glass she held.

"Frank. I made stew. You must be starving."

Her hand shook as she set the food on the table. He shoveled in the stew while looking up at her. She turned away to wipe the counter.

"Sit down."

"Just let me finish—"

"Pretend I'm your darkie boyfriend. You sat with him yesterday. Held his hand."

Cora's bone-deep tiredness undid her. She just didn't care anymore. Didn't care if he yelled, if he hit her, if he called her names. She was tired of trying to please him—and she was angry. Edna had told her the blow to Nate's head had threatened his eyesight. Even if Frank thought Nate had fought with Steve, hitting Nate with his gun was unforgivable. She scraped the chair on the floor, then sat and faced him.

He waved his spoon at her, and sauce from the stew splattered on her dress. "Don't try to deny it. I saw you."

Cora wondered what he had seen and heard that could have made him this angry.

"You saw me trying to console a boy I've known for years."

"He's a man." Frank stared at her. "As you well know."

"I'm like an aunt to him. He was telling me about the service." *And how it made him realize how limited his future would be.* Cora fussed with the salt and pepper shakers that had belonged to her mother. Feeling the cool glass against her palms, she remembered the desolation that had filled her soul when she had found herself without a future, at least the future she had imagined.

"What about the white girl? Did he tell you about her?"

"They were children together. It was puppy love. He's not interested in her anymore." She could not have Frank making trouble for Nate over a white girl.

"No, he showed you that when he tore up the photo. He's only interested in you now. You're like a bitch in heat. They can smell it on you."

Cora barely registered the insult. He knew about the photo. "*You* put the photo scraps by Steve's body. You hurt Steve and tried to blame Nate."

"And why not? Why shouldn't your colored lover get what's coming to him?"

"For God's sake, Frank. He's a boy!"

"Quit saying that!" Frank leaped up and pulled her off the chair. His fingers dug into her forearm, and she sank to her knees.

"I saw you with him. Comforting him. Hugging him. Touching that black skin."

Cora's mouth twisted with loathing. For his bullying, his jealousy. Frank must have seen it. He slapped her, then grabbed her hair and pulled her head back so he could look into her eyes.

"Did he touch you?" He grabbed her throat. "Were you in my bed with him? Did you beg him for more?"

Tears flowed down Cora's cheeks.

"Oh, am I hurting you? Well, you deserve to be hurt, the way you hurt me. Lying about Wright, and now about Nate, who deserves even worse. Coming into my house, eating my food, touching my wife." Frank released Cora. He took his gun and started for the door. "There'll be no one to rescue him today."

"Frank, stop! Stop!" Cora felt the words rasping against her throat.

The backhanded blow knocked her head against the cupboard. She fell to the floor and grabbed his leg.

"Frank, you can't. Please. Please leave him alone."

Frank kept moving toward the door, dragging her behind him. Cora begged him to listen, to stop.

She had to stop him.

"I'm his mother, Frank. I'm his mother!" Oh God. What had she done? "Do you think I would make love to my own son, that he would make love to me? Do you think we're sick?"

Frank froze. Then he turned back to her and grabbed her face, half lifting her off the floor.

"His mother?" Frank squeezed. "He's a nigger. He's that Hermit woman's son, you lying bitch!"

"I gave him to her to raise." She fell to the floor when he pushed her away. "He's why I didn't want to leave Richmond. I wanted to tell you, but I couldn't."

"So you've been lying to me all this time. And Edna, too? Just shows how good a liar you are." Frank stalked back and forth, then turned to her and bellowed, "So, are you lying now, or just been lying as long as I've known you?" He squatted back down, his face inches from hers. "Who's the father? That nothing Edna married?"

"No."

"So who? Tell me." He grabbed her throat. "He's not your son. You're saying that to protect your lover!"

"I was raped. I got pregnant. The rapist must have been Negro." She had wanted no part of that baby. All she remembered of having him was pain and darkness, almost dying in her bed. For a long time she wished she had. She didn't care that the midwife said she would be barren. *Barren*—a good word for her. Edna and her husband took the baby and raised him as their own. Cora lay in bed for weeks, not caring about anything, too depressed even to miss Oliver.

"So, you want me to believe that you were raped and Nate is your son because the man who raped you was Negro."

Cora was exhausted. "Yes."

Her nose dripped blood onto her dress. She looked up at a cold smile.

"Cora, I don't think you understand."

"What?"

"I *know* you're lying. Maybe you had a colored baby, but it wasn't because you were raped."

"I *was* raped. At nursing school."

"But that's not when you got pregnant."

"My God, Frank. It was. Why won't you believe me?"

"Because the man who raped you wasn't colored."

Cora froze, terrified of something she didn't want to hear.

"How . . ."

He yanked her off the floor and threw her over the table. "Remember this, Cora?" He wrapped his arm around her throat and tore at her clothes. "I was sorry about what I did to you. But not anymore. This time I want you to know it's me." She groaned. "*Now* do you understand how I know you're lying? And this time, I won't be back."

Cora didn't struggle. She drifted in and out of consciousness while Frank used her. When he finished, he increased the pressure on her throat and the pain ended.

Chapter 67

Pappy hung a hand-lettered sign in the window of the Stop: CLOSED DUE TO DEATH OF OWNER.

As he turned away, he saw Frank Slater hurrying toward the bar. Strange that he should show up today of all days. Pappy unlocked the door.

"Frank, come on in. I was just fiddlin' in here. Thinking about Roy. Be good to have some company."

"Did you hear that?"

"Hear what?" Pappy's brow creased.

"That damned music. I hear it all the time."

"I don't hear anything, Frank, but my ears aren't that good anymore. Come on in."

A half-full bottle of Jameson sat on the bar. Pappy filled another glass.

"To Roy." Pappy lifted his glass. Frank hesitated, then followed suit.

"What'll happen now that Roy's dead?" Frank nudged his glass over for a refill. "You still be the manager here?"

"Yep. The new owner doesn't want to change anything." No one needed to know who the new owner was. "So, how you doing, Frank? Haven't seen you for a while."

"Been busy. Working on a few things."

Pappy waited, but Frank didn't say more. Years of bartending at the Spot had fine-tuned Pappy's ability to read the men who came in to celebrate their joys or drown their sorrows. Frank was quiet; of course, there was no one else there to stimulate his arrogance, but *reflective* was not a word Pappy normally associated with Frank.

The bartender busied himself wiping bottles, polishing glasses, and sipping whiskey.

Frank cleared his throat. "You knew my mother, didn't you?"

"Sure. She came in here a lot when Frank Senior was away."

Pappy glanced at Frank's reflection in the mirror behind the bar. Sure was taking his time getting to what he wanted to say.

"He hated me. Sometimes I wondered if he was really my father. Maybe I was adopted."

Pappy turned around and smiled. "I saw your mother pregnant, Frank. You weren't adopted."

"Then maybe Frank Senior wasn't my father. Was there any talk at the time?"

"Let's not talk trash about your mother."

"So there's some trash to tell." Frank seemed gratified. "Just asking if someone else could have been my father."

"Your mom got around. Frank Senior was gone a lot, and when he was here, he wasn't good to her . . . and she liked a good time."

"So maybe he wasn't my father."

"Maybe not."

"Any idea who was?"

Pappy polished the glasses, playing for time. He had wanted to tell Frank for a long time. Maybe now. But Frank seemed in a strange mood. Instinct and need battled inside Pappy.

"I take that as a yes," Frank said.

Pappy leaned on the bar toward him.

"Look, Frank, maybe you're better off not knowing some things."

Frank grabbed him by the collar, hurting him. "Tell me, you black bastard!"

So that was how it felt to be on the receiving end of Frank's rage. "You want to know? She was spending a lot of time with Roy Lane before you were born."

"Roy Lane was white."

Pappy watched Frank smile with relief. Pappy hesitated for a moment. *Does Frank suspect? But why? What the hell. Today's not the day for lies.*

"Yep. He was as white as you are." He leaned both hands against the bar. "And as black as I am."

Frank's smile disappeared. "What are you saying?"

"I'm saying Roy was my son."

"Your son?" Frank's glass stopped halfway to his mouth.

"And that makes you my grandson."

"Your grandson? That can't be!"

"It is."

"Why didn't you say?"

"Because I figured you would rather be a white orphan than a black bastard."

The weight of telling Frank settled over the old man like a shroud. Roy had told Pappy he was sure he was Frank's father. Of course, it had been an accident; Roy never would have risked having a baby. Might have been awkward if he'd turned out dark. But now Pappy thought maybe it would have been better if Frank had looked more like Pappy and less like Roy.

"Chances are, you never would have found out and life would have been easier for you—like it was for Roy—if people thought you were white. I told him to tell you when you were old enough to understand, but he wouldn't do it."

"I *am* white!"

Pappy pressed his lips together.

"Did my mother know that Roy was colored?"

"Of course not. Think she'd let a Negro touch her?"

"Who else thinks that Roy was my father? Or that he was colored?"

"Frank Senior probably knew he wasn't your father, but I don't think he cared who was at that point. No one knew Roy was colored. Some might have suspected he was your father. He and your mother were quite an item. She wanted to marry him, but he wasn't the marrying kind."

Pappy wondered what was going on in Frank's mind. "What made you ask? Why now?"

Frank's answer was slow in coming. He tilted his head sideways at Pappy, as if what he was about to say amused him. "My loving wife said I spawned a black bastard of my own."

"You have a child?" Pappy didn't know what to make of Frank's expression.

"He's a black bastard!"

Pappy winced. "Still a child."

"Not to me, old man."

Pappy watched calculation and anger harden Frank's dark eyes.

"This is between us, Pappy. No one ever hears it. Understand?"

"Doesn't it matter to you that I'm your kin? Why do you think I watched out for you when you were young? Why Roy let you sleep here?"

Frank put the whiskey bottle to his lips. Drained it. Slow. Considering. Then he shattered it on the bar and thrust it at Pappy's face.

"You are nothing to me. Don't ever forget that."

Pappy flinched at the jagged shards pointed at his eyes. As Frank walked away, Pappy called after him. "You might want to know what Roy died of."

Frank faltered for a second. "What's it to me, old man?" The door banged shut behind him.

Pappy lifted a chair off a table and sat down. What had he done? He had thought with Roy gone, he could tell Frank. Burying Roy today must have made him stupid. He had made a mistake looking for kin in that boy. He had thought Roy's son might want to know he was loved, that he was connected to someone by blood, but maybe it was too late for Frank. Pappy wiped his hand down his face. He'd have to tell Frank sometime. He needed to know sickle cell was hereditary. But not today.

Chapter 68

As Oliver raced away from the Slaters' house, his headlights lit up the dried stalks of wild licorice that lined the railroad tracks along Garrard Boulevard. When he was a kid, he had made whistles from their hollow stems. A couple of lifetimes ago. Oliver tried to slow his breathing, to calm down. Did he believe Nate could have hurt Cora? To get back at Frank? Maybe Nate had been in love with Cora and she had rejected him. Too many questions. None of it made any sense to him.

He slid to a stop in Carlton's parking lot. The neon treble clef sputtered and flickered, repeating itself against the black window. The first time Oliver had walked into the club, he had felt as out of place as a cotton ball in a coalscuttle, but over time he had begun to blend in. Sort of. Nate hung out there, too, often lingering at the bar long after most of the other patrons had left to catch the last bus home. It was worth a look.

The band was on break. Louis Carlton watched Oliver through a cloud of smoke and noise as he wended his way to the bar. Louis tipped the spouted whiskey bottle over tall glasses. The colors swirled, dark ribbons in lighter pools.

"Louis, have you seen Corporal Hermit?"

Louis asked a couple of people, then turned to Oliver. "Nah, no one's seen him. It's a little early for him. For you, too, come to that."

"If you see him, will you call the station?"

"Maybe. Is he in trouble?"

"I just need to talk to him about our investigation."

"Sure, Lieutenant. I'll let you know." Like hell he would. His mama hadn't raised no fool, and he surely could tell when a white man was lying to him.

After Frank left the Stop, he headed home, ready to discover his poor dead wife, only to see an ambulance pulling away from his house. He parked farther up the hill so he could watch what was happening. Oliver said something to that dago prisoner, then got in his car and tore away. Frank waited until the POW walked behind the house, then followed Oliver. He hung back, headlamps off.

How had they found her so fast? He had been gone less than an hour. He had made sure she had no friends, so he knew no one would have just stopped by. Had she told Wright what had happened? The ambulance had used its siren, so she must still be alive. Fuck.

Frank slowed down when Oliver stopped at Carlton's. He sure as hell wouldn't think Frank would step foot in that jigaboo joint. Maybe he was looking for the Hermit kid. He sat in his car and waited to see who would come out of the club. It reminded him of waiting for Cora twenty years ago.

He had hidden in the shadows cast by the bay trees and watched her walk across the courtyard to a row of small buildings. She looked like a bride, carrying the bouquet of wildflowers she and Wright had picked that day. Frank had seen them earlier, not far from Keller's beach and had watched Wright court her, turn on the Wright charm. Her hair caught on a branch, and when she loosened it to roll it up again, Wright stopped her, gathered the golden strands, and buried his face in them. She closed her eyes and tilted back her head. He kissed her throat, then her mouth. Frank followed them to the nursing school and watched the girl hurry to the hospital for her shift. He waited outside, catching glimpses of her through the windows. He was in no hurry.

It was dark when she finally came out, waving good-bye to a few other students, who headed off in another direction. She took off her nurse's cap, and that spun-gold hair tumbled to her shoulders. He thought about burying himself in her hair. He felt the heat in his face and the shiver through his body when he thought about taking her, taking Wright's woman. The campus was still, as if the students were waiting for the last possible moment to return from break. Still and dark.

When she opened the door to her room, he slammed into her from behind, his hand on her mouth, his forearm against her throat. He kicked the door shut and shoved her across the bed. She struggled and twisted, and he increased the pressure on her throat until she went limp in his arms. "Just like in the movies, Cora."

He thought it would be simple: ruin her for Wright and be done with it. Instead she was like a drug. He pulled a pillow slip over her head so she couldn't see him if she woke up. He wanted to stay with her all night, take her again and again, but someone laughed outside the building, and he suddenly realized a group of people was outside. He slid her window up and tumbled out onto the grass, his fly still unbuttoned. He still wanted her. Had promised her he'd be back.

Frank could almost feel it again: the excitement, the power Cora had unleashed in him. He had tried to find it again, that first exhilarating thrill. It hadn't felt the same with the throwaway women, but he knew there'd be little police time wasted on them. He kept looking for a special one. And then Cora appeared like a gift when he was wounded, and she was his—until Wright came back.

Oliver limped away from the club. Where else might Nate be? Maybe someone at the station had heard something. He walked along the embankment edge, trying to ease the stiffness and pain in his leg before he drove back. The band started up again, and the music got louder, then softer, as the door opened and closed. He wondered how Cora was. Maybe he should've gone with her instead of running off half-cocked after Nate. But she had asked for Frank. Her husband. Not Oliver's place to go. But he could find the bastard who had hurt her.

He heard a sound behind him and tried to swivel, but his leg didn't know how to do that anymore. The revolver aimed at his head missed and hit his shoulder as he fell. Frank Slater loomed over him, trying to do to Oliver what he had done to Nate. A lucky swing of Oliver's cane caught Frank on the wrist, and the gun fell from his hand. As he bent to grab it, Oliver jabbed at his eye with the tip of the cane. Frank held on to the cane, and as he tried to wrest it from Oliver's hand, Oliver kicked him in the stomach. Frank fell and they grappled, neither getting the purchase he needed to gain an advantage. Then they rolled off the embankment onto the rocks and sand below.

Chapter 69

Luca waited at the Buonarottis' for news of Oliver or Cora. Harry had just walked through the door when the phone rang. He nodded at Luca to answer.

"Buonarotti residence."

"We found Dom." Lucy sounded triumphant. "Is Oliver there?"

Luca hesitated. What to tell her? "Cora Slater was attacked today." He heard a gasp. "She will be fine. Do not worry."

"Is Oliver with her?"

"No. He is looking for Corporal Hermit. We think he did it."

"How could you think that? Nate would never hurt her. Besides, he was at the café all day. He should have been in bed, but he came down to the café to patch a wall."

"Why did Oliver and I not see him when we were there?"

"Oliver had told Nate to stay in the hospital, so when he heard you, he thought it would be smart to stay out of sight."

"He was there all day?"

"He left at four thirty to go see the doctor, and then he was going back to the café to finish up. He's probably there now."

Luca agreed with Mrs. Forgione's view of Nate. The young man was angry, but Luca sensed he was a gentle man at heart. "If Nate did not hurt Cora, who did?"

"What did she say?"

Luca thought back to Cora's words, something for which his training suited him. "I am an idiot! We asked her who had hurt her, and she answered 'Frank'. We thought she was asking for him. We did not realize she was answering our question. I must find Oliver."

"First someone needs to come here before Dom escapes. We can't stop him by ourselves."

"Stop him? Where are you?"

"At the Grand Canyon Chateau. Mrs. Hermit and I are watching him."

"*Aspetta*. Wait. Wait."

Harry clenched his jaw when Luca told him what his aunt was doing. He spoke in a calm, measured voice, but Luca felt the receiver shake by his ear as he listened in.

"Aunt Lucy, you need to get away from there. We think Dom has killed once. He's not going to hesitate to hurt you if you get in his way."

"Harry, we can't leave."

"Yes, you can."

"No, we can't. The truck won't start. We think it ran out of gas."

"What truck?"

"The chicken man's truck."

"Is he there, too?"

"No." Silence. "We borrowed it."

"Oh my God, Aunt Lucy. We'll sort that out later. Right now, you need to hide. We'll be there as soon as we can. If Dom leaves, don't try to stop him."

"If another car comes for him, we'll get its license number."

"No! Just stay hidden."

Luca grabbed Nate from the cafe and ran to the police station where Harry stood only inches from Harmon. The prosecutor gripped Harmon's upper arms and stared into his eyes.

"The most important thing is to keep the women safe. If you have to put the women in danger to capture Dom, let Dom go. You only succeed if the women are unharmed. Do you understand?"

"Yes, sir. Save the women." Harmon pulled his gun and spun the cylinder.

Harry raised his eyes to the ceiling, then turned to Luca. "I know *you* understand. Make sure to keep them safe. I would come myself, but I should return home in case Oliver calls. He needs to know you believe Frank may be the one who hurt Cora. Good luck."

While the police car crawled up MacDonald Avenue, Luca told

Nate what he and Oliver had found at the Slaters. The boy seemed torn between saving his mother and going to Cora. A rainbow of lights glowed through the fog that swirled among the groups of servicemen and defense workers who crowded the street. Shoe-shine boys called out for customers at the entrances to dark alleys, where a customer could slip in unnoticed if he wanted to pay a little more for a special polishing.

Harmon cut over to Nevin, trying to make some time and get away from a loudspeaker truck advertising women wrestlers and other exotic acts at the carnival in South Richmond. The sounds faded as the car traveled the side streets, winding its way through quieter neighborhoods where the distance between houses lengthened and scarecrows waved empty arms over victory gardens. Soon the car ascended out of the fog and raced to the Grand Canyon Chateau, somewhere at the back of beyond.

"Pull over by the chicken truck." Luca pointed ahead.

Nate's mom and Harry's aunt popped out from behind some bushes. The men shook their heads and shooed them back under cover.

"They're in that little building. We think there were only three men in the car we followed. No one else has gone in," Lucy whispered.

"Mrs. Forgione, Mrs. Hermit, you both have been splendid. *Brava!* Now you have to stay out of the way. If anything happened to either of you, Harry would never forgive us." Luca guided them into the shadows.

Grasses rustled as the men crept along the back of an old, abandoned building. Harmon put an ear to the door of the shack, then reluctantly agreed that it made more sense for Luca to eavesdrop, since he spoke Italian—a suggestion Luca had made earlier but Harmon had ignored. Luca listened and then waved the other men to the side.

"They wait for a car to take Dom and Tomaso to Reno. Tomaso does not want to go, but Dom says he has no choice. There are only three voices. What do you want to do?"

"We should probably take them before their friends show up.

Especially if you think the boy doesn't want to be part of it." Harmon seemed confident.

"What if they're armed?" Nate asked.

"You have a gun; I have a gun. Let's go in, weapons drawn, and maybe we'll be able to avoid any shooting."

Luca shook his head. Harmon's logic escaped him. Shooting seemed much more likely if weapons were brandished.

"On the count of three, I'll hit the door and you two follow."

"Try the door first." Luca shrugged, as if to say he could be wrong. "It is an old shed. Perhaps it does not have a lock inside."

"Right." Harmon pressed the latch and burst into the building, followed by Nate and Luca. He shouted, "Police!" and leveled his weapon at the men. The two older ones sat at a table, cards fanned out in front of them. One of them slipped a hand below the enamel top.

"Hands where I can see them." Harmon waved his gun.

Tomaso sprang from a cot, yelling, "Dom, no!" and knocked down one of the seated men. Dom's shot went right though the eye of Betty Grable, who had been flirting with them over her shoulder, and left her dangling from a thumbtack.

Nate grabbed the gun and yanked Dom to his feet. They cuffed the older men and asked Tomaso if he would cooperate. He had fallen all over himself and his father in his desire to help, so they believed him when he said yes. He had knocked the pistol from Dom's hand as he aimed at Luca, the only one without a gun.

Chapter 70

Oliver came to slumped against a rough surface that stank of petroleum and iodine. When he raised his head, the skin on his face scraped against a thousand sharp edges. It felt like the side of a grater, a grater with razor-thin ridges that sliced his hands when he grasped the piling he straddled. Handcuffs dug into his wrists.

A match flared.

"Feel like a last smoke, Wright? Can't offer you a last meal or a blindfold. Just a cigarette."

"This isn't funny. Get me out of here."

"Wasn't meant to be funny. Not to you, anyway."

"Take these off, Frank."

Frank stood above the waterline. Oliver's lap was wet now, the water like ice. He tried to pull himself up.

"Let me go, you bastard."

"Yell all you want. No one's going to hear you over the music and the water. You're under a pier!"

"For God's sake, Frank. Why are you doing this? Why aren't you with Cora?"

"Cora. Is she all you can think about? Even now, when you're about to drown? I should shoot you, but I'll enjoy knowing you're sitting here in the cold with the water rising around you, struggling to free yourself, thinking about how if you hadn't taken the only person I wanted, then thrown her away, you might not be drowning in the darkness. Alone."

"What are you talking about?"

"What am I talking about? I'm talking about Phyllis. Remember Phyllis? Oh, probably not. She didn't mean anything to you, did she?"

"She was lovely. What happened to her was a tragedy."

"*What happened to her?* Like you had nothing to do with it." Frank stepped toward Oliver and raised the gun.

"I *didn't* have anything to do with it."

"You threw her away like so much trash when you met Cora."

"We dated. Phyllis knew it was nothing serious." *Jesus, we're arguing like teenagers.*

"It was serious for her. She's dead because of you. It wasn't enough that I loved her." Frank's voice softened, sounded wistful. "She didn't see me, didn't look at me the way she looked at you, the man of her dreams. I wasn't good enough, even after you threw her away."

"Frank—"

"Shut up!" He kicked Oliver in his knee. "So I took something from you."

Oliver slumped against the pilings and fought through the nausea. "You killed Peter?"

"No. That wasn't me. Sandy took care of that."

"Then what are you talking about?"

"Cora.

"Cora? You didn't take her from me. That was over long before you met her."

"Really? Then why did she keep your locket? The Wright family heirloom. You should ask Cora sometime why she left Richmond. Oh, right—you won't be able to, because you'll be dead, being eaten by crabs, while I get what Theo took from the stiff on the fence. Maybe I'll have a little fun with Zoe while I'm there. She's fruit ripe for the plucking. Think she kind of fancies me."

Oliver struggled against the piling. "I'll kill you."

"And how are you going to do that? It's over for you, Wright."

Frank raised the gun.

Chapter 71

Harmon siphoned gas into the chicken truck and got it started. Figuring out how to get all the vehicles, the women, and the prisoners back to the Point was like the problem of the fox, the goose, the grain, and the rowboat. Finally, Luca decided Harmon should take Dom and his friend to jail in the police car, Nate should drive Tomaso back in the green coupe, and Luca would take the women home in the truck, then join Nate.

After they had secured the truck and the coupe behind the police station, they took Tomaso to Nate's car. Nate drove while Luca sat in the back to question Tomaso. As soon as the doors shut, Tomaso began talking. "Can you help me, Captain Respighi?"

"I will do what I can. Perhaps the fact that you kept your father from shooting me will persuade the army to let you stay with the Service Units. But now, tell us what you know about Carlo Fusco. Did he know about your father?"

"Yes. I noticed him staring at Cesare now and then. As if he knew him, but he never said anything. Once I met Dom, I understood."

"Cesare does look like him. I imagine Fusco saw the resemblance, especially if he knew Dom when they were both young."

"One day, after Cesare and I had been to Uncle Harry's, Fusco heard us talking about our father. We convinced him we didn't know where he was, but Fusco said if I didn't help him, he would tell the police that Dom was wanted in New Jersey."

"Did you help him?"

"I was going to, and then I thought, *Let him tell*. Dom ran away once; he could do it again."

"And then?"

"It worked for a while. Then he told me someone in the mess was stealing food from the fascist POWs and the buyer was coming to the island that night—the night before they found his body."

"Why would the people stealing food talk in front of Fusco?"

"He pretended not to speak English. The Americans got used to him being around and ignored him."

"How were they planning to transport the food off the island?"

"He said one of the supply boats was in on it. They smuggled things back and forth all the time, but that night a smaller boat was bringing someone to inspect the meat."

"So, what happened that night?"

"Fusco said he was going to get proof of what they were doing. No one would believe him without it."

"Do you think Fusco wanted to blackmail them?"

"Who knows, with him?" Tomaso paused, considering the idea. "I think he was truly angry about them taking the food from the Fascisti. He was one of them. Thought they were the true patriots. He wanted me to go down to a little cove where they were meeting. He wanted a witness. He said the Army would believe me more than him because I had switched loyalties to the Americans." Tomaso looked away.

"But you didn't go?"

"No. I wanted to be able to go to Uncle Harry's, and I wasn't going to risk my privileges for Fusco and the fascists."

"Do you know where the people taking the food were meeting? They were taking a big risk—the island is a military installation."

"There's a cove people use when the island is fogged in."

"Did Fusco tell you who else was involved?"

"Not a name, no, but there was a cook—a fat cook. Fusco said the cook was getting fat while the prisoners starved."

Nate said, "That could be a figure of speech. Getting fat can mean making money."

"Maybe, but I don't think so." Tomaso sounded tired and confused.

Luca almost felt sorry for him. "Let us get you settled, and then we will try to locate Oliver."

Wisps of music floated from the blues club, a rich contralto that glided through the black night, caressed the body that leaned away, then back, swaying with the movement of the tide. A wave splashed into its open mouth, and rivulets snaked into its lungs. Oliver coughed, tried to get his breath. He dragged his torso out of the water and slumped against the piling. The singer's words teased at him.

"Skylark." He would like to soar away. From the pain. No, she didn't say pain. Pain. His head hurt, his leg was ice and fire, but he wasn't dead. He thought about Charley. He had to get out of this. Why had Frank only hit him with the gun? He could have shot Oliver and gotten it over with. Maybe he had been afraid someone would come to investigate the sound of a shot. Or maybe he planned to come back after Oliver had drowned and take off the cuffs. Make it look like an accident. Or maybe he enjoyed the power of leaving Oliver incapable of protecting Zoe and Theo.

Well, the hell with that. Oliver hugged the mussels and tried to inch his way up the piling. He bent his left leg and pushed, but he couldn't get high enough to drag the braced leg up. *Trigonometry.* He was a triangle. Or was that geometry? The water reached his waist. How much time had gone by? He heard a car door close, laughter, people heading toward the warmth of the club. He yelled, but the laughter disappeared into the swell of the music as the door opened.

At full tide, the water would rise at least as high as the mussels that clung to the piling, and they were over his head. If he could stand, maybe his head would be above water at full tide. He strained to see the tidemark on the piling, but it was too dark. He bent his good leg and pushed, but he couldn't drag his other leg up. It wouldn't bend, and he couldn't reach the brace to unlock it.

Think, Oliver. Try something else. He rolled onto his bad hip and dug his heel into the mud and sand, then bent his good leg and pushed, rolling farther onto his bad leg, using the piling like a pivot point. He swung about a foot above the water before he slid down again. That would work, but first he needed to rest. Maybe as the water rose it would support him.

He leaned against the piling and closed his eyes, listened to the clanging of a buoy out in the bay. He loved the sound of the buoys, the deep song of the lighthouse. Seagulls had rested on the swaying markers as Oliver and his friends sailed by. *Ding, ding. Ding, ding.* He wondered where it was. You could hear the bells long before you could see the buoys. Sound traveled far on water. That meant something. Should mean something. But what?

It meant he needed to make a noise, but yelling had proved futile, and he was tired. Very tired. He reached above his head, about to pull himself up again, and the handcuffs clinked against each other. He raised his hands and hit the cuffs together. If he hit them just so, the ringing echoed and traveled along the water. *Dot dot dot dash dash dash dot dot dot.* If he could keep it up, maybe someone coming out of the club would hear him. Maybe the coast guard, if they were still hunting for the boat they had told him about the day before. *Dot dot dot dash dash dash dot dot dot.* Wartime. Everyone knew the Morse code distress signal.

Oliver rested his head against the piling and continued his monotonous song, soon mixing up the dots and dashes.

An empty rowboat floated along the length of the pier. The boat had arms that pushed it along the pilings. Oliver closed his eyes. His brain must have shut down from the cold. He felt a bump and raised his head. *The Japs.* They had finally gotten him.

A hand went over his mouth. "Be quiet, Oliver. I'm going to get you out of here."

They do speak English well. And he knows my name.

"Do you have a key to these cuffs?"

Oliver nodded. "Hope so."

"Where?"

"Pants. Right-hand pocket."

The figure tied off the boat and slid over the side into the water. When he had unlocked the cuffs, he pulled Oliver away from the piling and helped him to his feet, still under the cover of the pier. Oliver staggered. He was close to hypothermia, maybe even past it. He shook in the cold air, from the chill, from shock—he didn't know which. He looked at the man supporting him.

"You really are Japanese." Oliver shook his head. "I must be hallucinating; you're all gone."

"Not quite. Besides, I'm American. Not that it makes any difference." The man smiled.

Oliver wondered why the man wasn't angry, why he would help someone whose country had imprisoned his people.

"They haven't found you?"

"No. And don't worry. I'm not a spy. I'd have enlisted, but the government would never have allowed my father to stay at home with people who would care for him. He's not well; he wouldn't have survived in the camps." He repositioned his shoulder under Oliver's arm. "I could've been fighting in Europe against the Germans or breaking Japanese codes in the Pacific. You must know this."

Oliver shuffled his feet through the sand and rocks, trying to help his rescuer, who breathed heavily under Oliver's weight.

"How did you get yourself in this predicament?"

"It's too complicated, and I'm too tired." Oliver could barely talk through the shivering. "How did you find me?"

"Your SOS. But someone else may have heard it, so we need to hurry—I have to get back to my father."

"If they see you, they'll probably shoot you. Were you the boat they saw Wednesday night?"

"Yes. I was pretty sure they saw me moving in and out of the fog, so I hid and made my way back to my father. Usually I don't go out, but the person who brings us food and medicine didn't show. I stayed in last night, waiting for him. If he can't come to us, he's supposed to leave supplies for me at a prearranged spot, so I went out tonight and picked them up. I was heading back when I heard you."

"Wait. How did you know my name?"

"We have a mutual friend. Besides, when you came home, you were a bit of a local hero."

"Can I do something for you?" Oliver looked down at his pitiful condition. "Not now, of course, but later?"

"The person who helps us knows you. He told me you helped him once. If we ever need you, he'll let you know. Actually, there *is* something you can do. I can't ask anyone else."

"Name it."

"Will you try to find out if something has happened to him? To Roan?"

"Roan? Why . . . Oh. All right. But how will I reach you?"

"I'll be here a week from today at two in the morning if it's foggy. If not, I'll come on the next night that is. If Roan shows up within the week, he'll let you know you needn't come." The man took a deep breath. "Are you ready? I need to get you up the embankment before the moon breaks through again."

"What's your name?"

"Just Tom."

Oliver leaned on Just Tom, who supported him while pushing and pulling him up the slope. Oliver swayed on the walkway, looking for his cane. If he fell, he wouldn't be able to get up again. It might be easier to crawl to the club anyway. Car lights swept across him, barely catching Just Tom's back as he disappeared over the rocks.

Chapter 72

Louis Carlton took one look at Oliver and hustled him into the bathroom. Oliver tried to thank the customer who had taken him to the back of the club without asking any questions.

"We need to warm you up. I don't think a hot shower can hurt, and it'll help with the stink. You're covered in that damned oil from the refinery." Louis turned on the taps and waited for the water to get hot. "I'll dig up some clothes for you."

"I need to call someone."

"Hurry up and get in there. You're not going to do anyone any good if you pass out. You need some help?"

Oliver had taken all the help he could stand for one night. "I can manage."

He struggled out of his clothes and held on to the wall with one hand while he washed with the other. The brace chafed like hell, but he left it on. A little more water wasn't going to hurt it.

He was leaving the shower when Louis returned with some athletic clothes.

Oliver couldn't imagine the dapper man sweating, not with his marceled hair and the uptown look he cultivated.

"Here. They belong to one of the waiters; he's training to be a boxer."

"I need to call someone."

"You said that before." Louis pushed the phone over to Oliver. "You might want to take that brace off. Wet like that, it's gonna rub you raw."

"I need to be able to walk, so it stays."

"Wait." Louis rummaged in a desk drawer. "Take off the brace and wrap this around your leg before you put it back on." *This* was a cashmere scarf. "I had plans for that. Cute little number comes in here on Tuesdays." He winked.

Oliver did as he was told. The soft warmth felt good, but soon the brace's wet padding would soak through it.

Oliver called Jennie, willing the damned dial to go around faster. A busy signal. *Get off the phone!* He was afraid to call the operator to break into the conversation—not until he knew what was going on.

He called Harry, wondering for a moment why he wasn't calling the station. Harry picked up on the second ring.

Before Oliver could explain what he needed, Harry told him Nate had not hurt Cora—that he had an alibi.

If Oliver had trusted Nate instead of tearing off after him, he probably wouldn't have ended up handcuffed to a piling. He told Harry what Frank had done, and that he might be going after Zoe and Theo. Oliver noticed Louis hanging on every word.

"Were there any witnesses? Did anyone see?"

Oliver frowned. "Do you think Frank would try to kill me in front of a crowd?"

"So it would be your word against his."

"Harry, do you think I made this up?"

"Oliver, I believe you. I'm just thinking what to do next. For now, Frank needs to believe you're dead. Give me a moment."

Oliver needed to move. He needed to get to Theo and Zoe.

"Harry!"

"I'm here. My brothers are here. I'll go with them to Zoe and Theo and figure out a reason why on the way. If we run into Frank, I'll pretend to know nothing. In the meantime, come to my house. No, that won't work—Frank could see you from his house. Go to my Aunt Lucy's. I'll meet you there, and we'll figure out what to do about your failure to die. I must go, Oliver. I'll see you at my aunt's house."

"Harry, he has a gun. Be careful." Oliver realized he didn't have his gun. Did Frank have it? Or was it in the bay?

"Don't worry."

By now Oliver was more than ready to leave, but Louis seemed to have other ideas.

"Drink this." He held out a mug. "It's soup." He put a gun on the desk. "You might need this. It's registered, and I have a permit, Mr.

Policeman." Louis walked to a closet and pulled out a crutch. "I ain't sayin' you need it, but you might want it."

Oliver glared at him. The guy was like a damned magician pulling things out of a hat.

"A customer left it. Said he could walk out on his own steam." He waved the crutch. "And he did."

"Oh, all right." Oliver pulled himself up, leaned on the crutch. "Look, Louis, do you think you could keep it quiet that I was here? Until I work some things out?"

"Sure. The guy that brought you in won't talk, and I don't think anyone noticed you coming in the back. Just take care, Oliver. That Slater is one mean son of a bitch."

"What do you know about him?"

"Come back when this is over. See how it shakes out."

"I have another favor to ask."

"Go on."

"Can you drive me somewhere? On the QT. I need to leave my car here. The keys are in it—someone will pick it up."

"Let's go."

Oliver was quiet as they drove to Mrs. Forgione's house. Harry and his brothers should be with Zoe and Theo by now. Frank seemed to be spiraling out of control. What did Theo have that Frank wanted so badly? And how did Frank intend to get it without implicating himself in something? *Remember, he has to think you're dead. So far, he's free. And he'll want to stay that way.*

What a beautiful night. The clouds boiled in the sky, raced along the horizon. Bits of moonlight peeked through and dappled the darkness in front of him. Frank floated up the hill, window rolled down, one elbow on the doorframe, feeling like a teenager out for a cruise. Cora had lied. That Nate wasn't his. Maybe wasn't even hers. Couldn't be. Or maybe *she* was colored and Pappy was wrong. Who said Roy was Frank's father? He might have to do something about Pappy, stop him from telling his filthy lies.

He went into the house. Cora was gone, but he felt her presence in the shadows of lies that filled the room. Frank missed her, even though she might not be dead. He missed his idea of them together, her sheltering against him on the deck of the ferry to Sausalito. They had driven for hours to the lighthouse at Point Reyes, laughing as they climbed down the hill, hoping to catch sight of the whales on their migration up the coast. Cora had huddled against him, and he had wrapped her inside his jacket. She hadn't been able to find a thing to eat on the restaurant's game-filled menu. What is the difference between eating a rabbit and eating a lamb? he had asked her. She'd said now she didn't want to eat lamb, either. But she had insisted they stay and had charmed the chef into making her a plate from the side dishes.

Charmed the chef the way she charmed everyone. A charming little liar.

He changed his clothes, stuffed the wet shirt and pants into the laundry basket, and remembered the Hermit woman. What was he going to do about her? And his laundry?

He was hungry again. He walked through the blood and mess on the floor and filled one of those colorful bowls with stew. While he ate it cold, standing at the sink, he saw the headlights of a car swing out of the Buonarottis' driveway and move down the hill. He belched. Time to call the station and report what he had found at his house. Time to cry about his wife.

Chapter 73

Louis and Oliver stood on Mrs. Forgione's porch, both trying to pretend Louis wasn't holding Oliver upright.

"Come in, come in."

"I can't stay, ma'am. Just making a delivery." Oliver tried to thank him, but the man just waved and skipped down the stairs.

"Oliver. Come, sit down."

He refused the arm she offered.

"Sit down. I'll bring you some coffee." She shook her head at him and went to the kitchen.

"How is Cora? Do you know?"

"The doctor thinks she'll be fine. She gave me a message for you. She said to tell you Frank knows about the locket and to take care of Nate."

Take care of Nate how? Oliver picked up his cup and drank, then realized he had been drinking a lot, and that the bathroom was probably upstairs.

"Do you have any idea where Luca and Nate are?" He kept forgetting Luca was his prisoner. He should know where the man was.

"We—they—found Dom and Tomaso. Dom is in jail, and Luca and Nate are taking Tomaso back to Angel Island tomorrow. They're staying overnight at the coast guard station. If you want to wash your hands, there's a bathroom through that hall. We put it in when Enrico broke his leg. But when you come back, I want to hear what happened."

Oliver returned to an ice pack and an adamant Mrs. Forgione. How to tell her how hopeless and angry he had felt, trapped in the cold, terrified about what Frank might have been doing to Zoe and Theo? And Jennie, who had been through enough. Imagining Charley hearing that his father was dead.

"Sitting here, warm and dry, I find it hard to believe what happened tonight. Except for the pain in my leg—and my head."

"Harry said we're pretending you're missing?"

"I'm not sure whether that's the best thing to do. I'd like to talk to Luca about it."

"I'll call the coast guard station."

Luca was examining Oliver when Harry arrived, assuring Oliver that everyone at the Wrights' house was fine and he had left his brother on guard. Oliver refused to go to the hospital. What would be the point? he asked. I'm already dead. Then he recounted what Frank had done. The others brought Oliver up to date, and Mrs. Forgione pretended to lock her lips with a key.

Harry shook his head at Oliver's questioning look. "Don't ask."

"What do we do now? I can't be dead forever." Oliver shifted the ice bag on his knee.

"Although that is customary." Luca looked up from the brace he was blotting with a towel.

"What do we do about Frank Slater? He tried to kill Oliver, hit me with a gun, and probably was the one who beat Steve." Nate seemed bewildered. "We need to stop him before he hurts anyone else."

"I think he already *has* hurt someone else—Cora." Luca looked around at the men. "Oliver, think back to what we asked her."

"It was a lifetime ago, Luca. How can I remember?"

"I remember it clearly. You said, 'Who did this to you?' And Cora answered, 'Frank.'" He raised a hand to stop Oliver's protest. "You assumed she was asking for Frank. But she was answering your question."

"Then why did she say 'Nate'?"

"You said, 'We'll find Frank for you, but tell us who did this.' And she answered, 'Stop him'—pause. 'Nate.' I think she was afraid for Nate and asking us to stop Frank."

"That makes some sense of what Mrs. Forgione said: that Cora wanted me to take care of Nate. Why was she afraid for you, Nate?"

Nate got up, turned away toward the window. "I think Frank was listening when I was talking to Cora yesterday, while you were at the

Buonarottis'. He may have misunderstood. My mother told me how jealous he was, that it might be better if I stopped going over to visit Cora. Even before the war. I'll kill him if he's the one who hurt her and Steve."

"Everyone needs to calm down." The pencil Harry had been taking notes with snapped in two. "Why do you think Frank is the one who hurt Steve?"

Luca spoke up. "Nate probably interrupted him kicking Steve—I saw the blood on Frank's boot. Dom told us that he swung the fishing net at Steve and knocked him down, but then Dom heard a noise and ran down the hill. I believe Frank saw Steve on the ground and, for a reason I do not know, kicked him. When Frank heard Nate leaving Paola's kitchen, he hid, and then seized the opportunity to hit Nate and try to frame him."

"And there's the print on the photo scrap when he said he hadn't touched them," Oliver added. "The torn-up photo of Nate, Steve, and Anna Maria that was strewn around Steve."

"But *I* tore up the photo when I was talking to Cora. I left the scraps in her kitchen," Nate said.

"Another reason to believe that Frank was the one who hurt Steve. He had access to the photo scraps and scattered them around Steve so it appeared you had done it," Luca said.

"But I would have explained. Steve would have said it wasn't me."

"He does say it wasn't you, Nate, because he doesn't believe you would hurt him. But he didn't see who did it." Oliver shook his head.

"I would have said I'd left the photo scraps at Cora's."

"I think something was going to happen to you when you tried to escape from Frank."

"But—"

"He was dead set on taking you away."

"But Cora would have said . . ." Nate gazed at the wall as if a sad movie played on it.

"What is it?" Luca asked.

"When she saw the scraps on Steve's body, she asked me what I had done. So maybe she wouldn't have said I couldn't have done it." Nate scuffed his boot on the floor.

"Nate, it was reasonable for her to wonder. You might have gone back for them. And you were angry." Luca tried to console him. "But it might explain what happened between Cora and Frank. If Frank heard Cora and Nate talking and then saw the photo, he could have leaped to the wrong conclusion."

"Which was what?" Harry asked.

"That Nate had given up Anna Maria for Cora."

"That's crazy." Nate was incensed.

"Yes. But regard his other actions. Not those of a healthy mind, surely."

"If he beat and raped Cora, how could he get away with that?" Nate stumbled over the words.

"She's his wife. It's not a crime to rape your wife, no matter how despicable it is, or to beat her. He won't feel threatened by that." Harry raised his hands, palms forward in front of him, as if to say, *Don't blame me—I'm just stating the facts.*

Luca interrupted. "But handcuffing Oliver to the pier? It was insane. Which brings me to something I have been wondering: Why does he hate you so much?" He turned to Oliver, who looked at the floor, then raised his eyes to Luca.

"He blames me for a girl's death."

"Phyllis Brennan." Mrs. Forgione looked up from her rosary. "Frank adored her. And she adored you. But then you broke it off, and she was devastated. The whole Point knew." She tilted her head to the side. "I'm sorry, Oliver."

"I met Cora. I didn't think about how Phyllis would take it."

"What happened to Phyllis?" Luca asked.

"Her body was found near Keller's beach. Everyone assumed she had fallen, or jumped. It was kinder to believe she fell."

"Or maybe she was pushed."

"Nate!" Mrs. Forgione spoke as if Nate were twelve years old.

"An interesting idea, Nate. Frank is pathologically jealous. If she rejected him, perhaps he snapped. Perhaps that was the catalyst to all the rest." Luca seemed interested in the theory.

"When we were by the bay, Frank said it wasn't enough for Phyllis that he loved her. He also said I took something away from him, so he took something away from me." The men looked puzzled. "Cora."

"But she married Frank years after it was over between you two. That doesn't make sense, Oliver," Mrs. Forgione the historian chided him.

"He said to ask her why she went away, and then he laughed, because of course I couldn't, since I would be dead."

"But what happened to make him act against you now?" Harry wondered.

"I don't know. Wait—Mrs. Forgione, you said Cora wanted me to know Frank knows about the locket. Maybe that's it. Under the pier, Frank asked me why she kept it. Called it the Wright family heirloom, so he must have found out it came from me. Maybe that's what did it." Oliver explained what the locket meant, then shook his head, which made it hurt.

But it was Harry who said, "I'm getting a headache. The past, the present . . . what about the future? What are we going to do?"

"What has Cora said?" Oliver looked at Mrs. Forgione.

"She said Nate didn't do it, but she doesn't know who did. She said the man was white, then started laughing and crying and the nurse had to give her a sedative. Shock, I guess. Anyway, no one believes it was the rapist, because he doesn't go into houses. He's hurt all those women on the street."

"There's still the question of Theo and the briefcase. Frank told me under the pier that Theo took something from Jonah and he was going to get it back."

"My head hurts more now." Harry stood up. "I think we need to sleep. Luca and Nate can come home with me."

When the men protested, Harry held up his hands. "*Basta!* We're too tired to think. Oliver almost died; Nate not only plastered a wall but apprehended, with Luca, a man wanted for murder in New Jersey; and I have comforted a wife and daughter who are distraught about Steve, a sister-in-law who has discovered she married a murderer—or maybe not married, since his papers were forged, another legal mess—all after spending the day dealing with the results of the court martial. Plus, I have to settle up with the chicken man. We need sleep. We can meet again in the morning."

"The chicken man?"

"We'll tell you tomorrow, Oliver."

Saturday
October 28, 1944

Chapter 74

The smell of coffee convinced Oliver to try to sit on the edge of the bed. He hurt everywhere. His leg hurt so badly as he limped to the bathroom that he almost wished he had let the navy surgeon cut it off. Maybe it would still come to that.

The face in the bathroom mirror was a mess. The bruise on his temple almost eclipsed the dark circles under his eyes, and his face and arms were crosshatched by small cuts. He washed up, ignoring the stinging as best he could, and struggled into the uniform Harry had brought him the night before. He limped into the kitchen.

"*Buon giorno!*" Luca greeted Oliver with his usual good cheer. "Mrs. Forgione had to go to the café." He yawned.

"Luca stayed up with Paola and Isabella last night. Regular hen party." Nate ribbed Luca.

"After years of being only with men, I was delighted to listen to them talk. Isabella was furious, then sad, then furious again." He rubbed his bald head. "I hid my delight; it would not have been well received, but to be with women overcome with emotion was exhilarating. It reminded me of home, my sister and her friends lamenting betrayals or rejoicing together."

"You think of Isabella as a sister, then?" Nate glanced at Harry.

Oliver smelled bread burning. "Luca, the toast."

Harry seemed grateful for a change of subject. "Something nagged at me, Oliver, after you told me about Jonah North's death. As if the name should have meant something to me, and last night I remembered that I had heard it in connection with Regis Simmons's suicide."

"In what way?" Oliver asked.

"Regis was a welder on Jonah's crew."

"So they knew each other."

"More than that, they were said to be friends."

"So if Regis was the informer, perhaps he confided in Jonah when he found out my brother was dead."

"Exactly. And that means Jonah's death may be tied to your brother's death. I'm authorizing you to investigate it and the death of the Fleming children for my office."

"Frank told me under the pier that he didn't have anything to do with Peter's death. That Sandy engineered that." Oliver grimaced when he moved.

"Did you believe him?" Luca looked skeptical.

"Why would he lie to a dead man?" Oliver smiled. "The problem will be getting Frank to tell anyone else that Sandy did it."

Nate had been growing visibly restive. Oliver knew he wanted them to focus on clearing the Negro troops. "Luca, what have you learned about Fusco's death?"

"It appears it had nothing to do with the Negro soldiers. They seem to be accounted for when Fusco died." He handed Oliver the toast. "Tomaso told us last night that Fusco had planned to go down to the cove to spy on black-marketeers. It is reasonable to believe he died there. It would have made no sense for the Negro soldiers to take him down to the cove, drown him, then carry him back up that hill to hang him when they could have left him there."

Luca glanced at Nate, who nodded and said, "They wouldn't have drawn attention to themselves by imitating what happened at Fort Lawton, but someone trying to frame the Negro soldiers would have."

"Makes sense."

"Luca and I could go to Angel Island and continue the investigation there. If that is still what you want us to do." Nate was raring to go. "We'll take Tomaso back to the island, talk to Cesare again, now that we know what went on, and try to figure out what Fusco discovered that got him killed."

"That reminds me." Oliver told Nate and Harry about Carter's having found a metal button in Fusco's stomach. "I think a surprise inspection is in order. Someone is missing a button."

Harry signaled that he would arrange that.

"We also need to find out what Frank thinks Theo has. Then we will have more information, possibly, and what we learn might help us understand what has been going on." Luca looked at Oliver, who asked, "And what about me? Am I alive or dead?"

"Let's act as if nothing has happened," Harry said. "I'll take a statement from you, and we'll hold on to it in case we need it. We don't want to give anyone any reason to impede your investigation into Fusco's and Jonah's deaths. Frank will be the only one surprised that you're not dead; perhaps it'll throw him and he'll make a mistake. In the meantime, I've had someone pick up your car."

"Thanks, Harry. We never did talk to the *Pittsburgh Courier* after we saw Ralph. They might be able to clear some of this up."

"Oliver, let me do that. I think you should go see Zoe and Theo and try to find out what Frank is after—if you can find their house." Harry nodded toward the window.

A dense gray cloud had descended on the Point.

Chapter 75

The thick mist camouflaged Roan and the golden dog Emma, smudged their outlines into the trees above the Wrights' house. Roan fretted, tying and retying strips and ribbons on Emma's collar.

Roan had watched out for the boy and his sister since Oliver had left for the war. He was back, but Roan liked the children, liked being part of their goodness. They reminded him of a time he cherished, when he had lived with his sister and her girl.

He hovered over Theo like a guardian angel, protective but invisible. Theo hadn't noticed Roan following him on his morning excursions, hadn't realized Roan was there when Theo found the body on the fence. Roan almost had gone to Theo when the boy started spinning, but then Theo had stopped and picked up something from the ground and ridden off.

Roan had been transfixed by the sight of Jonah's body. He hid in the weeds and stood vigil with it as the morning light limned the whitecaps the wind licked off the bay. Roan knew death, had walked among acres of it in the fields of France. As he sat on the hill, the barbed wire became the barricades of his war, and he saw the bodies of his fellow soldiers dangling from them in the yellow haze that rolled across the ground. He was lost in the whistling of shells, struggling to reach the wounded, when an angry voice scattered his battlefield memories. Roan had looked toward the road and seen Frank Slater yelling at Theo, who had returned. He was trying to turn around and pedal away, but Frank held the handlebars of the bike and grabbed for Theo's briefcase.

Roan knew how to help the boy. He crouched in the fog and played the tune that drove the detective crazy, the haunting aria his niece had sung the last night Roan had seen her alive. She had left the house but had run back in to take him outside. She sang an aria from their favorite opera and pointed to the sky, filled with a cascade of falling stars. *E lucevan le stelle*—and the stars were shimmering.

They had listened to the aria often after Roan had returned from the First World War. He had known why Phyllis sang it, why she played the record. She had sensed his despair, his desire to end the memories that tormented him. When she had been sad after Oliver left her, she and Roan had listened to it together. Phyllis said Tosca threw herself to her death not for love, but to avoid her punishment, and that the aria belonged to the doomed artist who did not want to leave the world: "And never before have I loved life like this!" the tenor sang. *That is our anthem, Uncle Roan. No matter what happens.* Their anthem, and Roan's ironic promise to Frank. Roan knew his niece hadn't killed herself.

Roan realized that remembering the morning Theo had found the body must have made him shake, because Emma was licking at his face, bringing him back to her, to the present. She didn't like it when he shook. Roan soothed her, crooned to her, and they settled down together in the fog to wait. After Frank had tried to take the boy's briefcase, Roan had cached supplies for his friend Tom, then returned to watch the children. Someone had to protect them. Roan knew Frank would come for Theo.

Not quite day. Not quite night. Frank felt the same way. Not quite anything. He missed Cora. Even though she wasn't dead.

When he had shown up at the hospital the night before, she had flinched and reached for the button to call the nurse. He put a finger to his lips, sat down on her bed, and told her what she was going to say. If she said anything else, her precious Nate would suffer for it. Cora nodded.

At least Wright's gone. Both Wrights. The Slaters against the Wrights, and the Slaters won. Who would have guessed?

All he had to do now was get what that weird kid had taken from the man on the fence. The dead guy had been sniffing around property records, copying names and drawing diagrams. Sandy insisted there were notes or papers that revealed too much about the death of those kids. Frank had figured out that Sandy had been paid to burn that cross. The Klan had warned him before about profiting from what they did. Maybe Frank would let the Klan know that little fact. They had been furious about those kids' deaths. Imagine what they would do if they found out Sandy had made money from it. He'd be lucky if all they did was kill him.

Now that Frank knew why the cross had been burned, all he had to do was find out who would have paid to protect that neighborhood. The answer had to be in the briefcase, and when he knew who to put the squeeze on, he'd have the money he needed to start over in Colorado.

Frank eased out of the car, careful not to slam the door. The dense fog covered him as he sneaked to the back of the Wrights' property. First he would look in the kid's studio. If the briefcase wasn't there, he'd go to the house. It looked like there was a light on in the studio. Was that moron already inside working? It didn't matter to Frank if the boy was there or not. One more Wright hitting the dust didn't bother him any.

The fog muffled the sound of his stalking. *Easy going.* Until he tripped over something stretched across the path and all hell broke loose. Damn kids and their war games.

Frank waited to see if anyone in the house had heard the tin cans. He started to creep forward, and then he heard the music. Eerie, as if it were dissolving in the mist. Frank hesitated. A dog started to bark and Frank turned toward the sound. Bells jangled around him, and snatches of color glowed through the fog. Of course. It was the freak and his dog, and this time Wright wasn't there to save them.

"I know what you did. I know and I'm going to tell." Roan was singing in a whisper. Singing and not stuttering. What the hell? Frank didn't answer. He took cover in the brush and crept toward the barking. One good blow with the gun would crush the dog's skull.

Roan darted across his path. Frank lunged and came away with a strip of cloth. He forgot the dog and chased the flying ribbons. He was going to be rid of this nuisance for good. The fog separated, and Frank could see Roan running exactly where he wanted him. Frank had almost reached him when Roan suddenly leaped into the air. Frank stopped and watched Roan stumble at the edge of the tiger pit. He had dislodged some of the grass stalks and palm fronds that camouflaged the hole and revealed the sharp points of stakes that stuck up from the ground. It was ingenious. The kids must have gotten the idea from Tarzan movies. Too bad they didn't work that hard at something useful. Then again, this was turning out to be pretty handy.

Frank laughed. Roan scrambled over the edge of the pit and lay on the ground. "Get up, idiot. Do you think I didn't know what those kids were doing and every place they dug one of their enemy-catchers? Think you could trap me?" He raised his gun. "Shut that dog up, or I'll shoot it."

Roan whistled and Emma stopped barking, but her whimpers filtered through the fog.

Frank walked around the edge of the pit. "I said get up. You're going to have an accident."

Chapter 76

Nate and Luca stood in the bow of the cutter on the way to the island. Nate was less excited about wrapping up the Fusco murder than he had thought he would be. He couldn't figure out what Cora and his mom had been whispering about when he'd walked into Cora's hospital room. He had heard her say, "He's his father, Edna. What are we going to do?" Still, he wouldn't have thought anything of it if they hadn't both looked so guilty when they saw him in the doorway.

Luca interrupted Nate's thoughts. "Tomaso looks green. I think his numerous trips in a boat might be punishment enough for his misdeeds."

Nate smiled. "I can understand his wanting to warn his father. Maybe Harry can do something to help him. He helped me."

"Helped you? In what way?"

Nate wasn't sure where to begin.

"I didn't understand what it meant to be Negro in America until the Army sent me to Texas for basic training." He looked at Luca. "I think it was a lot easier for the men who had grown up in the South. The rest of us never knew when we were about to do something wrong." Nate struggled for an example. "Like using a pay phone on the street, or sitting on a bench in a park. It was impossible. No matter where we were, a bigot was watching. The fear was probably the worst part. Knowing that any one of those hate-filled people could destroy us for any reason, real or imagined."

"Did the other soldiers, the white ones, defend you?"

"Not where I was. Steve came to our canteen, but the white officers dragged him out."

"It is like that in Italy. The darker you are, the farther south you come from, the more you are looked down on. I am from Sicily. It is hard to go much farther south." Luca hurried to add, "I know it is not the same as what you experienced, but the feeling is, the frustration, the hurt. The anger."

"They called us troublemakers. We only wanted what the white soldiers had—a bus ride to town, a seat in the PX. Guess they figured if we didn't have a bus, we couldn't invade the town."

"Why are you smiling?"

"We used to sit in that leaky canteen and figure we were those white folks' worst nightmare. Last thing they wanted to see was strong young men, educated, confident, ready to die. They must have realized one day we might decide we could fight for freedom here. I think we scared the hell out of them. Anyway, Steve called his father, and Harry managed to get me out of there. Maybe you can convince him to help Tomaso."

The boat slowed. An MP waited for them on the dock.

"Would you stay here after the war, Luca? If you didn't have to go back to Italy?"

"I could stay here; my mother was born here. But I want to get back to find her and my sister." He looked at the hills around the bay. "I cannot tell you how much I want to see my home again."

The MP held a sheaf of papers and shifted back and forth on his stumpy legs.

Nate jumped onto the dock. "What do you have, Stan? You look ready to do a dance."

"Yes, sir. I mean, no, sir."

Tomaso teetered as if the ground were moving under him and took some tentative steps up the path.

Luca put his hand on Tomaso's shoulder. "Go see your brother. You can tell him what has happened. Is that all right, Corporal?"

Nate nodded and turned to the MP. "Tell us."

"Parker, one of the men waiting to ship out to the Pacific, was outside the barracks the night of the fight."

"They told us they were all in the barracks."

Stan raised his eyebrows almost to his widow's peak, as if to say, *What did you expect?*

"After Lieutenant Wright talked to them, they decided to tell what they knew. I told them nothing would happen to them for stretching the truth the first time."

Luca wondered if the commanding officers of these men would take such an understanding view, but perhaps they *would* look the other way. Maybe some good would come of their fear of publicity.

"What did the witness see?" Nate rolled his hand in a get-on-with-it motion.

"He was trying to cool down. His brother is one of the Port Chicago defendants. He didn't want to listen to the talk in the barracks, so he hid in the shadows near the exercise yard. He heard a fight, then splashing and whispers down by the water. He didn't know if it was his friends or the Italians, so he crept closer to see what was going on. A big man had hold of one of the POWs. He pushed the guy's head under the water, then pulled him out and asked him questions. Parker couldn't hear everything, but he heard the man asking who else knew."

"Then what happened?"

"The big man said something to the other three, then held the man under the water. Parker heard splashing for a while, then nothing."

"You said the big man said something to the other three. Who were the other three?"

"A smaller man Parker didn't know—looked like a fisherman, with those high boots—one of the cooks from the camp, and another white soldier."

"Did he recognize anyone?"

"He got glimpses of them. He's not sure about the small man, but he would recognize the big man and he knew the cook."

"Is he fat? The cook?"

Stan's brow wrinkled in confusion. "He is. How did you know?"

"It's not important." Nate glanced at Luca. "Then what happened?"

"The men let the POW float in the water while the big man looked in a box. He picked something up and smelled it, examined it with a flashlight. They all argued, and then the fisherman helped the cook and his helper carry the body up the hill. He got in the boat with the big man and the box, then disappeared into the dark. Parker took off back to the barracks."

"Why didn't he tell anyone?"

"He said he didn't care what those white men did to each other. Besides, if he told, he figured he'd be in trouble for being outside, get blamed for something." Stan started dancing again. "There's more. The inspection Captain Buonarotti ordered this morning turned up a field tunic missing a button. And a pair of wet boots. Guess whose." Stan's smile faded when Nate didn't say anything. "The cook's, sir."

"I'm looking forward to talking to that cook." Nate's eyes narrowed, and his smile alarmed Luca. He would see that the corporal was not alone with the cook.

At first the cook didn't seem worried. So a Negro soldier said he saw him outside. Big deal—no one would believe him. But when Nate told him they had found his missing button in Fusco's stomach, he collapsed.

He hadn't signed up for murder, just a little black-market dealing. Those dagos didn't deserve sugar and coffee, or meat. He had noticed Fusco listening to him while he set up the rendezvous with his connection, and had begun to wonder if the POW understood English. The cook's helper waited to see if Fusco followed the cook when he went to meet the boat. When he did, they were ready for him.

The cook decided to hang Fusco's body so the Army would blame the soldiers who had gone after the POWs—just as it had done at Fort Lawton.

Nate leaned toward the cook. "Who were you working with?"

The cook turned his head away. "A civilian with connections."

"What kind of connections?"

"A place to sell whatever we took, and someone inside the legal system who knew when there would be inspections—stuff like that."

"Who is he?" Nate tried to hold the cook's gaze.

"I can't tell you. He has a whole group of people working for him." The cook pressed his lips together.

"Like the Mob?"

"Worse."

Nate leaned back and smiled. "You're doing time for this. It can be easy or hard. Think about how many bad meals you're going to eat in twenty or thirty years. You want us to want to help you, then give us his name."

The men waited. Luca was amused that Nate had gone to the cook's obvious weak spot. Maybe the cook would crack, maybe not. Finally he spoke.

"Sandy Slater. But he wasn't here that night. He couldn't fit in the boat with that fat butcher who wanted to inspect the meat before they paid for it."

The cook calling the butcher fat.

"What was the butcher's name?"

"George something."

"Who else?"

"That's all I know. Look, it was just food from the POWs. No big deal."

"It's a big deal when someone gets killed over it and someone else gets blamed." Nate shoved his chair back so hard it crashed to the floor.

"How are we going to do this?" Nate and Luca had returned to Harry's office in the Presidio. Luca stood to the side while the corporal briefed Harry.

"We finally have a reason to arrest Sandy Slater and get search warrants for his shop and house. We also have the names of the other people in the boat. The cook said someone in the legal system was helping them, but he didn't know who."

"My first guess would be Frank Slater or Paul Butler. When Peter died, we wondered if there had been a leak, someone who might have told the Klan what he was doing, but Peter would never have told anyone in the police department about the informant."

"Maybe it's someone in your department."

"A secretary burst into my office when Peter and I were talking about the informant. Maybe she was involved."

"You didn't suspect her then?" Nate's tone wasn't accusing, just curious.

"No. I suppose I should have, but she had no obvious connection to anyone we thought might have been involved." Harry wondered if he would have realized things sooner if he hadn't split his attention between the DA's office and JAG.

Nate interrupted Harry's self-recrimination. "Can you get the warrants without anyone tipping off our suspects?"

"We—the Army—will handle it. There won't be any leaks. I'll add the woman. Nate, you get the men we need."

Chapter 77

Oliver almost missed Frank's car. Was he inside? Stealth and surprise, or frontal attack? Who was he kidding? When he got out of his car, he heard voices behind the house. He leaned on his borrowed crutch and slowly made his way to the hill. How was he going to get up there? Something flitted through the fog and moved toward the sounds. He whistled the *forget everything else and come to me now* command. Nothing. If it had been Harley, he would have run to Oliver.

Getting up that hill wasn't going to be easy, but it sounded as if Oliver didn't have too far to travel. As he belly crawled through the damp, the wind passed over the hill and thinned parts of the fog. He froze when he saw Frank pointing a gun at Roan. He had to get up there.

A shadowy form seemed to waver in front of him. Then the arc of a bow sliced through the fog, and Zoe rose from the mist. Before Oliver could move, she yelled at Frank.

"Drop the gun!"

Frank laughed at her. "Oh, this is too precious. Did you think whistling would distract me?" Frank's voice turned ugly. "Put down the bow and get over here, or I'll shoot him."

Zoe held her pose, while Oliver willed her to drop to the ground and creep down the hill, under the cover of the fog.

"Fine. Which do you think is faster, little girl, an arrow or a bullet? I said put it down."

Oliver crawled closer to Frank.

Zoe turned away and started to run down the hill.

"Stop, or I'll shoot the freak. Get moving." Frank waved the gun, motioning her toward Roan, who was maneuvering himself away from the pit. Frank turned toward him. "No you don't. Move over—"

"Frank," Oliver whispered, his voice just loud enough for Frank to hear him.

Frank spun around. Once, then again. "No. Impossible. It can't be you. You can't keep coming back!"

Oliver rose from the fog and pointed the bartender's gun at Frank. "Over here, Frank."

Frank swung toward the voice and fired. Roan leaped on Frank's back and grabbed for the gun. It went off. The second shot echoed across the hill, and Zoe's scream joined the sudden cawing of the crows. Frank and Roan teetered on the edge of the pit, until Roan propelled them into the air. They disappeared into the earth.

Harley flew up the hill and almost knocked Oliver over as Harry's brother yelled, "What's happening up there?"

"Get an ambulance. I think Zoe's been shot. And Roan may be hurt. Hurry." Oliver held on to Harley and let the dog half drag him up the slope.

Zoe lay facedown. Harley nudged her, but she didn't move. When Oliver turned her over, a red blossom spread across her sweater.

Roan found himself on top of Frank, surrounded by a forest of pointed stakes. He pushed himself off and staggered to the side. Blood dripped from his sleeve, and the crowns of the trees spun into a blur, whipping around his head. He heard Emma and called to her. Finally, his voice penetrated her howls.

He looked back at Frank, who writhed, pinned to the stakes from the weight of Roan's body and the force of the fall. Frank lifted his head and tried to push off from the ground, but Roan saw that he could get no leverage. Roan picked up the gun, and Frank ducked his head to the side, straining to see what Roan was doing.

"Go ahead. You won't get away with shooting a policeman." Frank's face twisted as he stretched his arm back toward his leg.

Roan set the gun on the edge of the pit. He had never shot anyone, not even in the war. He could hear Oliver yelling something about an ambulance. Help would be here soon. It might be too late.

He looked at Frank's leg, at the stake piercing it. It was flat and thin, sharp like a knife blade. Roan let himself fall to the ground.

He welcomed the smell of damp earth and the coolness on his face as he crawled between the poles supporting Frank's body. The stake through Frank's torso might have pierced something vital, but the most life-threatening was the one near the groin.

Roan crawled under Frank and closed his eyes. He put his hand under Frank's leg and pushed upward. Roan could barely hear Emma barking over Frank's screams. Flesh and muscle clung to the stake, Frank's weight now working against Roan. He held his breath and heaved against Frank's leg with both feet until he ripped it off the stake. Beautiful bright-red blood spurted from the wound. Frank's arms stretched as far as they could, reaching toward the pumping vessel. He tried to raise his torso but failed. He was pinned like a bug.

"Help me."

Roan dragged himself to the corner of the pit and closed his eyes.

Chapter 78

Harry caught Sandy as he was closing up shop, minutes before MPs served warrants on the other suspects. Luca and Nate followed Harry into the garage.

"You're keeping me from my dinner, but if you have a warrant, go ahead. I've got nothing to hide. I'll call home, let them know I'll be late." Sandy turned toward his office.

"Forget the phone. Over against the wall." Harry drew his weapon and motioned for Sandy to move. If Frank had told the truth, Sandy was responsible for Peter's death. Harry felt a hand on his shoulder—Luca asking if he was okay. "It's under control. Don't worry."

The men took apart the garage. They searched in piles of threadbare tires, in the rag bin, in the desk, behind signs and photographs, between the pages of the pinup calendar, even inside the radio. Behind the garage, they found a pile of smoldering boots. Enough of the soles remained for Luca to assure Harry they would match the bruising found on Jonah and Steve.

Luca stood to the side and studied Sandy. He spoke to Harry in Italian, asked him to tell Sandy other men were searching his house and to watch Sandy's reaction. Harry did as he asked, then nodded to Luca. Sandy's lack of concern about his house being searched convinced Harry that what they were looking for was in the garage.

"Let's take a look in that pickup truck." Nate motioned to the MPs.

"Hey, that belongs to a customer. Watch what you're doing." Sandy quieted down when Harry waved the gun at him.

They took out the seat, looked under the fenders, inside the tires. Nothing.

Sandy seemed amused until Nate asked for the keys.

"I don't have them. The customer forgot to leave them."

Nate walked into the office, picked some keys off a board, and tossed them to an MP, who put back the seat and drove the truck forward.

Nate stood at the edge of the hydraulic-lift pit.

"Where's the last place you'd want to go in this garage?" He found the switch for the lift and raised it.

As he lowered himself into the pit, he called to Harry, "Captain, I'd be grateful if you made sure Sandy can't reach that switch while I'm under here."

"Got you covered, Corporal."

Nate gave a yell when he found a metal box stuck on a ledge under the garage floor. He told the others that it was packed in a thick layer of grease, hidden from the view of any mechanic working in the pit. Couldn't have been convenient for Sandy, but he had to retrieve the counterfeit gas-ration coupons only once a month or so. The Office of Price Administration had been lenient with petty violations, but the pile of multicolored coupons, counterfeit or stolen, would make sure Sandy Slater wasn't going to get away with a fine and a slap on the wrist.

But first he would stand trial for Peter's murder. A second box contained a list of names and the grant of immunity Peter and Regis Simmons had signed. It wouldn't be hard to convince a jury that Sandy could have gotten it only from the wrecked car. Harry thought Sandy must have kept it in case he ever had to justify Regis's death to the Klan, but if Sandy already had that, why the interest in Theo's briefcase?

Chapter 79

"What is wrong with you, man? You won't be any good to anyone confined to hospital with an infected leg." Doctor Carter thrust a finger at Oliver. "Remain there until you are attended to. Trust your niece to me."

Oliver wished Carter had made one of his bad jokes. Seeing the doc serious made him uneasy. He watched Zoe's gurney disappear through double doors at the end of the long gray corridor, then surrendered himself to the nurse. She squinted and wrinkled her nose as she looked him up and down. When she uncovered his knee, she called for a doctor, who whistled when he looked at the battered marine, as if he didn't know where to start.

"I'm going to clean up your cuts and wrap your knee. There's not much I can do except warn you that if it becomes infected, you'll lose the leg. If you want to keep what's left of it—and I'm not sure why you do—then come in daily for injections of penicillin, and I'll keep an eye on it. But you need to rest it. No weight-bearing activities."

Oliver nodded. This wasn't the first doctor who seemed to think the leg should have been amputated, but Oliver hoped someday someone would figure out how to give him a new knee, and they couldn't do that if he didn't have a leg. He was willing to live with the pain until then.

Later in the evening, Zoe sat propped up in her hospital bed with her arm in a sling fastened with a giant safety pin. She alternately sipped her chocolate milk shake through a glass straw and told her audience her version of what had happened behind the house.

"I knew something was wrong when I heard Emma barking, especially since Mr. Buonarotti's brother had stayed in the house overnight." She sipped. "I've known that Roan and Emma have been looking out for me and Theo for a long time, so I figured they might be watching the house, too, and I was afraid that something was wrong with Roan, because Emma wouldn't stop barking. Usually they stay quiet and out of sight, like they don't want us to know what they're doing."

Zoe's next sip allowed Jennie to ask why she hadn't woken Mr. Buonarotti's brother.

"He had fallen asleep in a chair, and I thought I could take a look and yell if I needed him."

While Zoe's cheeks were sucked in with her next sip, Oliver asked her why she hadn't let Harley out.

"He was whining and pawing at the door, but I thought it would be better for him to stay and guard Theo, because someone might have been trying to trick us into leaving Theo unprotected. Harley actually gave me a dirty look when I told him to stay." Zoe smiled at the dog, who sat by her bed, making sure nothing else happened to her on his watch. "For a minute I thought he wasn't going to listen. But he did, so I strung my bow and went out to see what was happening."

Oliver was so grateful Zoe was alive that he didn't have the heart to tell her how foolish she had been. It would be punishment enough that she would miss the archery tournament she had practiced so hard for; Carter said it would be quite some time before she would be able to string that bow again.

Luca arrived with Harry and his Aunt Lucy. The smells from the hamper they carried reminded Oliver that he hadn't eaten all day. While the group ate, Harry told Oliver what had happened on the island and what they had found in the garage. Sandy had killed Peter.

"I don't think I can sleep until we find out what Frank was looking for in Theo's briefcase." Oliver pushed himself out of the chair and tried to balance on his new crutches. "Luca, let's go see Theo."

The women stayed behind to watch Zoe through the night. Luca kissed her good hand and told her she was not only beautiful but brave. She smiled at him, then closed her eyes. Oliver pitied the teenage boys who would have to compete with Zoe's memories of the POW.

Chapter 80

Oliver didn't think Luca did it deliberately, but he seemed to enchant every woman he smiled at. Of course the nurses would be happy to get him more padding for the tops of Oliver's crutches. Oliver sat in a chair outside Zoe's room while Luca disappeared into a linen closet with a pretty blond nurse. *Hmmm.*

Oliver closed his eyes and rested, just for a moment. He heard footsteps and then his father's voice filled the hallway.

"Are you proud of yourself? Look at you. What did you accomplish, running off to the war? You left your brother to die so you could come home a cripple. It's what you do best, isn't it—abandoning the people who need you? And now you almost got my granddaughter killed."

Oliver tried to push himself out of the chair.

"Judge, Zoe's going to be fine."

The look of disdain on his father's face stopped him. Something turned over in Oliver, a physical tumbling in his chest. There was nothing he could ever say that would change how his father saw him.

"You know, you're right. I wasn't there for Elizabeth. I wasn't there for Peter. And Zoe almost got killed. You're right."

"Is that all you have to say? You're nothing but a disappointment to me."

"I know." Oliver looked his father in the eye. "I guess I've always known."

"You're pathetic." Judge Wright turned his back on Oliver and almost bumped into Luca, who stood by, holding the crutches. Oliver watched his father walk away and felt the guilt return; his dad was right. He wasn't there for the people who needed him.

"I heard. Forgive me for intruding, but you know none of it is your fault."

"I'm not one of your patients, Captain. Let it go." Oliver's voice forbade an argument, but Luca ignored it.

"If you were one of my patients, I would let you find your own way to the truth, but we do not have time to indulge ourselves."

Oliver reached out for his crutches, and Luca backed away.

"I will ask you this: Do you blame your son for your wife's death? From your face, I see that would be unthinkable. So why is it different for you?" Luca held up a hand to silence Oliver's answer. "Because you expect more of yourself than you do of your son? Because you are better than he is? No, I think he is so much like you that he almost drowned trying to save his mother. Does he blame himself that she died? No. Because he has no need to punish himself for surviving. I think he is very much like you, with one significant difference. He was raised by a loving man, not a 'judge.'"

Oliver looked at his feet. He understood where Luca was going with this. Oliver didn't blame Charley, was grateful Charley didn't blame himself. So why did Oliver think if he had been at the lake, things would have been different? Because he could have done what Charley couldn't?

"Think about it, Oliver. And think about whether you could ever speak to your son the way your father speaks to you. I suspect you have never spoken even to your dog that way."

"He was different with Peter."

"Not entirely. I am sure he judged your brother but approved of what he saw. The son who wanted to be like his father. Which only makes it more difficult for the other son, who knows love is possible but not attainable. In a way, your father's disapproval freed you to be the man you were supposed to be, however painful it was. Now you must learn to be as forgiving of yourself as you are of your son."

The men looked at each other; then Oliver nodded and held out his hand. "Can I have the damn crutches now? And your bill?"

"*Ehhh.*" Luca reached out a hand to help Oliver up. "I don't think you can afford me."

Theo emptied the briefcase on the table in his studio as Oliver and Luca watched. He carefully lined up pencils and pens, stacked sketchbooks, and sifted through assorted stuff a kid would collect. Nothing had anything to do with Jonah's death.

When Luca asked Theo if he had taken anything from the place where Jonah died, phrasing and rephrasing the question until Oliver's brain went numb, the boy reluctantly opened a cigar box and slowly removed one piece of foil at a time, lining their edges up neatly before adding another. He stopped at a piece with embossed writing, set it aside, and gestured toward it. He said it had never been in the briefcase. When he had picked it up, he had put it in his pocket.

It was the wrapping from a piece of *torrone*, the nougat candy Mrs. Forgione gave to customers. Oliver turned it over. No secret message. He didn't bother asking Theo if he was sure this was the right paper. It had nothing to do with anything. Frank's pursuit of the briefcase had been pointless.

Thursday
November 23, 1944

Chapter 81

Thanksgiving Day. Darkened windows reflected Harley and Oliver as they walked slowly up Park Place toward the Café Avellino. Oliver thought he should be grateful that he had graduated from crutches to his cane, but he would rather be grateful for a leg that supported him without one, that wasn't stiff from riding in the freezing cargo hold of an army plane all the way to Washington, DC, and back in less than twenty-four hours.

Oliver had stolen his son away from work long enough for dinner at the Willard Hotel. Just seeing Charley's smile when Harley raced to him and jumped up to lick his face made the trip worth it.

The maître d' guided them to their table for three and seated them with a flourish that signaled to other diners that he would brook no complaints about the dog who accompanied the limping marine and the man who was clearly his son.

When Oliver said they were ready to order, the waiter motioned to a busboy to clear the third place setting, asking, "Your guest will not be joining you?"

Charley told the waiter she was already there.

The waiter nodded and poured wine into the three glasses. Charley and Oliver silently toasted Elizabeth's memory, touched their glasses to hers, and in that moment, for that moment, Oliver believed she *was* there.

The conversation was pretty one-sided. All Charley was supposed to say about his work was that it was boring pushing numbers around all day, so Oliver talked about Jonah and the fire, Luca and the Angel Island POWs. He told Charley about his almost drowning, and about Just Tom. Tears filled Charley's eyes, and he looked down to touch Harley. He drained his wineglass, then smiled and shook his head. When Oliver looked at him quizzically, Charley said it was ironic that Oliver had been attacked by a man who should have been his ally, and saved by his mortal enemy—at the risk of the man's own freedom.

Oliver had thought often of the risk Just Tom had taken for him. He nodded at Charley, then asked him what he did when he wasn't working. Charley told him about a girl he had met, one of the coeds recruited from Wheaton to join their division. He said it wasn't serious, but the way he talked about her led Oliver to believe maybe it was more serious than Charley knew. Oliver talked about the K9 unit's efforts to bring the dogs home from the Pacific and retrain them. The military said the dogs were unfit to return to civilian life, but the men were determined to honor the sacrifice of the twenty-five dogs who had died protecting them on Guam. What better way to do that than by finding loving homes for the ones who had survived?

Charley asked whether Oliver would be able to help with the retraining, what he was going to do when the war ended. Oliver didn't have an answer. So much of what he did next depended on whether he could still be a detective with his injured knee.

When they held each other outside the restaurant, finding it difficult to say good-bye, Charley said he might be home for Christmas. He wanted to meet Oliver's new friends, the ones with whom he had solved the murders.

Oliver and Harley stopped outside the café. The streets were empty, the bars silent. Smoke escaped from chimneys on the hills surrounding them, weaving through a silver mist that smelled of salt and green. Oliver pictured women cooking in kitchens with steamy windows, children trying to keep their dress-up clothes clean, and men reading the paper in easy chairs. Charley was right: Pt. Richmond was home again.

He hoped Charley was also right about making it back for Christmas. If you asked people what they wanted for Christmas, the answer was the same. For the war to be over, for their men to be safe. Civilians were encouraged by the news that the Allies were nearing Germany, but Oliver knew the military anticipated a massive

German attack, a last-ditch effort to buy Germany time to regroup. If that did happen, Charley would be needed at work. At least he would be safe—not like Mrs. Forgione's sons, fighting somewhere in Italy and France. He didn't know how she managed to go on.

The café was closed to the public today, but Mrs. Forgione had invited the people she thought of as family to come for a special Thanksgiving dinner.

Oliver walked in and looked around. The men sat together and talked. He glimpsed Edna and Cora in the kitchen when Isabella bumped through the swinging door with a platter of antipasti.

At Enrico's wake, the café had seemed exotic, the men around the table as foreign to Oliver as the crowd at Carlton's. Now he couldn't imagine his life without them, especially Luca, who sat at the round table with Harry and his father. They spoke in Italian, no longer an enemy language.

What were they talking about? Probably about Harry's search for Luca's mother and sister. Harry was optimistic about finding news of them, because Sicily was in Allied hands. It would be far more difficult to find out about the Criscilla boys' grandmother in the north.

Oliver thought about the people who were gone. Peter, Ellie and Sammy Fleming, their uncle Regis, and Jonah, whose notes revealed that someone had been paying Sandy Slater to burn those crosses. Solving the murders had not been enough; Sandy had confessed to them but insisted they had been his idea. Oliver had been sure that eventually Sandy would realize he could do himself some good by admitting someone else had been behind it all and naming him, and maybe Sandy would have, if he hadn't died in custody. No one had seen anything; no one had heard anything. Hard to imagine, given that Sandy had been beaten and stomped to death. It had a certain poetic justice but had left Oliver feeling empty.

The chief said it was obvious the Klan had done it to punish Sandy for using the Klansmen for his own purposes. That it had saved them all a trial and the electricity to execute him. But it niggled at Oliver. He was sure Sandy had been killed to protect the person who had paid him to burn the crosses. The other men had insisted that they had never received any money for anything. If Sandy had, they hadn't known anything about it—he sure hadn't shared it with them.

Jonah had been closing in on whoever had been giving the orders.

The notes he had mailed to the *Courier* before he died documented that a single company owned twenty properties near the house the professor was supposed to buy—coincidentally, the same area the minister had been interested in. So far, prosecutors had traced the company back to a lawyer who said he had never met his client and was always paid in cash. Unless they could find something to link that company to the cross burnings, it was another dead end. For a while, Oliver had thought the butcher might be behind it, but it had become clear that he was involved only with the black-marketeering and Fusco's murder.

Oliver told the chief he would watch those houses, whether he was on the force or not, and one day, no matter how long it took, he would find the person ultimately responsible for his brother's death.

Something made Oliver hold back Jonah's notes about Regis Simmons, who had told Jonah that Regis had given Peter negatives stolen from the photographer who took photos of the Klan's activities. They showed the faces of some of the men who had burned the cross, and another group of men meeting in front of a Confederate flag. Regis had said he didn't know who all the men were, but Jonah hadn't believed him. Oliver bet the man giving Sandy Slater orders was one of the men in front of the flag. Maybe the negatives were what Frank had been looking for.

"Oliver, *buona sera*."

"*Buona sera*, Signora Forgione."

"You are becoming more and more Italian every day. Pretty soon you'll be taking time to sit and enjoy your food. Like Luca."

"I doubt anyone could enjoy their food as much as he does."

"Not to be disrespectful, but I think I know someone who does. One moment."

She scurried away and came back with two large knucklebones.

"These are for Emma and Harley. They also have something to be grateful for."

Oliver smiled at the dogs as they followed Mrs. Forgione. She laid the bones down in front of the fireplace, and the animals settled with their backs to each other and gnawed on their treats.

Oliver felt a tug on his sleeve. When he turned around, Cora took his hand. She looked much better now than she had at the hospital. After Oliver had sworn Frank was dead, she had admitted he was the one who had raped her. Twice. She felt so stupid for marrying him, for not knowing he was the man who had gotten her pregnant.

She put her hand in her pocket.

"Close your eyes and open your hand."

Oliver felt something cool touch his palm and opened his eyes. His grandmother's locket.

"I think this should stay in your family. Maybe give it to Charley one day." She closed his hand around it. "I found it with some other pieces of jewelry in a box Frank kept hidden in the garage. I think I know what they are, but I'd rather give them to you than to the police, if you don't mind coming by and getting the box. You can figure out what to do with it."

Oliver thought he knew where the other jewelry had come from, but he didn't think the women would want it back. He'd have to talk to Auntie Josephine.

The bell on the door sounded, and Nate walked into the café. He was a sergeant now. *Has an investigator's mind, that one.* Oliver had to get Nate alone later, tell him about Pappy from the Stop.

Pappy had asked to bury Frank. After the funeral, he had sought out Oliver. The old man looked nearly ready for a coffin himself; burying his son and his grandson seemed to have taken the heart out of him. He told Oliver he suspected Nate was Frank's son, and before Oliver could answer, Pappy went on. He'd let the boy and his family decide whether Nate needed a great-grandfather, but, one way or the other, he had to tell him about the illness that had taken Roy. Oliver thought he would let Nate recover from finding out who his mother was before giving him any more news about his relatives.

He almost didn't recognize the teenager who pushed through the door with Jennie and Zoe. Mia Fiori. It looked as if Jennie had taken the girl under her wing. Oliver felt a rush of tenderness toward all three of them—women to be reckoned with, like Charley's mother. And Ellie Fleming, who had died trying to save her brother.

The girls sat with Roan and asked him to play. He pulled a clarinet out of his pack and played the introduction to a song. One by one, the men joined in singing. Oliver was touched, and didn't even know what the hell they were saying, but he caught the repeated phrase *Santa Lucia*. Didn't take a genius to figure it out.

Luca left the singers and sat with Oliver. Harry picked up a bottle of wine and four glasses and joined them. Nate said hello to his mother—both of his mothers—then straddled a chair at Oliver's table and rested his chin on his arms.

"It's finally over."

"Is it?" Oliver looked at Nate. "We've caught some dirty cops, but we still don't know who was behind them."

"Enough." Harry filled the glasses. "We've done what we can for now. Be grateful. Whoever it is will make a mistake. We're not quitting; we're waiting."

Harry raised his glass. The men looked at each other, sharing the moment.

"Wait. Roan should be here, too."

Oliver put his hand on Nate's shoulder as he started to get up. "He's content there, with the girls and the singing. He doesn't want us to make a fuss over him, call him a hero."

Mrs. Forgione set down a basket of bread. "But he is a hero, Oliver."

"Yes, of course he is. He saved Theo and Zoe."

"Luca told me *you* saved Zoe. That she would have died if you hadn't been there." She tilted her head toward the musician. "Roan's been a hero for a long time. He never speaks of it, but his sister, Dorothy Brennan, showed me his Silver Star before she passed. Did you know he was a medic in the First World War?"

Oliver looked at Harry. They both shook their heads. Oliver wondered whether they were denying that Roan would have known removing the stake from Frank's leg would kill him, or just saying, *No, enough.*

Epilogue

Theo sat on the drafting stool and looked at the collage on the easel. It was finished. When he sat with it, he had no impulse to add an element, move one, color one, add words, a photo. The calm had settled inside him. He held the feeling in his chest and his head, closed his eyes, opened them. It still felt right.

He had started with a large charcoal drawing on a silver-gray canvas. White chalk lightened the fence edge and the grasses on the hill. A figure hid under strips of light and dark tissue paper that overlapped and formed a kind of jagged moon. Different-size buttons tumbled in a milky way of stars against the charcoal sky. They spilled down the sepia hill to the canvas's edge, where they danced like light on the water. A tiny speck of silver foil peeked out from under a bush made of paper, the partial words *Ralp* and *taur* barely visible through the layers of indigo glaze that threw the bush into shadow.

Theo scooted the drafting stool over to his worktable and opened his briefcase. He separated bottle caps, some straight, some bent, some printed, some plain. He disassembled empty cigarette packs, opened and flattened the cellophane outer layer, then the silver paper layer, then the paper part with the name. He knew that as he worked, carefully sorting and organizing them, they would tell him what to do and the ideas would come. String, a bird skeleton carefully contained in a jar, some pampas grass fronds from the pit on the hill, and tufts of Emma's beautiful golden fur joined similar items already in cigar boxes.

When the briefcase was empty, he laid it on the table with the overlapping flap extended. He had to decide what to do. He had almost lost everything to that Detective Slater. He had heard everyone talking in the commotion after the gunshots on the hill. Detective Slater had been after his briefcase. Something about what Theo had picked up from the ground by Jonah.

But that had never been in the briefcase. The only thing in the briefcase that mattered was what his father had left him. He loved having it with him all the time, but maybe it was time to find a better hiding place. Or work it into a piece. Not a piece, not yet. Inside the body of the briefcase, he raised the seam that appeared to be stitched down and slid his hand into the thin pocket between the stiff outer leather of the flap and the stiff inner lining. Their secret compartment, the place Theo left sketches for his dad, and his dad left him used movie tickets, or cigar bands, or lunch-counter receipts. It was their secret, just enough space for a few thin items. Even Zoe didn't know about it. Theo had discovered it years ago when he was exploring the briefcase. He had slipped a sketch in, then asked his father weeks later if he had found the hidden present.

Theo slid out a length of film in a paper holder. He loved the film, shiny on one side, dull on the other. When he tilted it in the light, the darks went flat, then glossy. It said *120* under the little holes that bordered the frames. He set it aside and with his tweezers eased a worn page out of the flap. He could picture his father's fingers gripping his tortoiseshell pen as blue words flowed from the golden point, ink glistening until it dried into squares and lines across the page. He closed his eyes and slid his fingertip across each square, each line of words—words his father left him.

Afterword

Readers of early drafts of *In the Shadow of Lies* often asked whether certain events really happened. Unfortunately, my answer was most often yes. The story is fictional, and the characters my invention, but I have tried to portray accurately the way people were treated in the Bay Area during World War II. It was a dark time, a time of fear—fear of invasion, of social change, of anyone who was different. Fear allowed us to close our eyes to injustices, to accept the excuse that regrettable actions were "necessary" for national defense or national security. We didn't *want* to do it, we said—we *had* to.

Everything I have written about the restrictions against Italian Americans is true. They are based on real stories told by the people who experienced them. I am most grateful for the people who told their stories in *Una Storia Segreta* and *UnCivil Liberties*, and to Lawrence DiStasi and Stephen Fox, who collected them.

The ugliness Nate Hermit experienced is based on the real experiences of black soldiers. I know good men in the military tried to circumvent the injustice against black soldiers, as Harry Buonarotti does in this book. *Taps for a Jim Crow Army* and *Fighting for America* are two of the sources for Nate Hermit's experiences in the army. The USO for black servicemen *was* blocked in Pt. Richmond.

Italian prisoners of war lived on Angel Island, collected garbage, and held dances in San Francisco, and the country was divided about their privileges.

An Italian POW was found hanged at Fort Lawton, Washington, and black soldiers were blamed. The entire story of the Port Chicago explosion and the subsequent mutiny trial and verdicts is also true. Black men passed as white reporters to cover stories, and Thurgood

Marshall, later to become a US Supreme Court Justice, did go to San Francisco after the verdicts to help the men.

Oliver's experiences on Guam are based on true accounts of the fighting there. The dogs did find men who had been buried to their neck in sand and abused for several days. Incredibly, all the men survived. The banzai attack and the attack on the field hospital happened, although there is no record of a dog's detecting the latter. (For that I plead authorial license.) The Marine K9 Corps saved patrols from snipers and guarded the men at night. Captain William Putney tells their story in his memoir, *Always Faithful*. It is a moving tale of bravery, sacrifice, and love.

In 1924, Ku Klux Klan members marched up MacDonald Avenue in the Fourth of July parade in Richmond. A photograph of them appeared in the *Richmond Independent*. Later, they held an initiation ceremony in the El Cerrito hills. The Klan was active throughout the United States then and continues in some parts to this day. Other references to news and editorials in the *Independent* are also true. The cross burning that killed the Fleming children did *not* happen, but it could have, as cross burnings were common occurrences throughout Klan history.

The references to corruption in the Richmond police department are also fictional.

During the war, college students from more than thirty colleges, including Mount Holyoke, Smith, Vassar, Wellesley, Princeton, and Wheaton, were recruited for secret classes in cryptology. Many joined the navy or WAVES after graduation and worked in Washington, DC, where they deciphered and analyzed the thousands of codes the government received every day.

I could tell only a small part of the story. The time, the place, are filled with stories of people suffering discrimination, abuse, and hardship, but also filled with stories of sacrifices, large and small, that touch me. Readers seeking more information on these subjects may refer to the bibliography.

I cannot express how grateful I am to the courageous men and women who lived through these times and left us their writings, their words, so we might understand and appreciate their sacrifices. I have done my best to tell some of their stories. Any mistakes in the telling are my own.

Acknowledgments

Encourage: to make someone more determined, hopeful, or confident.

I am not sure if anyone has ever had as much encouragement, from the most unlikely sources, as I have had while writing this book. People I barely know were excited about what I was doing and helped make me more determined, hopeful, and confident about writing it. To writers beginning their journey, I want to say, take heart and share your dream with people who will wish you well and share your adventure with you.

Among the people encouraging me were my first readers, Barbara Brown, Richard Jones, and Steve Osborn, who slogged through early drafts, and Karel Collins, who painstakingly read all of the book's "final" versions. Each of them made the book better and helped me to believe in myself and the project.

When I was tearing my hair out because I had read widely about the battle for Guam but couldn't "picture" it, my husband suggested I look on YouTube (not a place I normally go for information). To my surprise, I found History Channel reenactments of the battle and, most inspiring, interviews with the men who had been there. The interviews, conducted decades after the war, showed how immediate and painful their memories of that time still were. There are no words to thank them for what they gave, and for what men and women still give, in service to their country.

When I had gotten Oliver into a fix I couldn't get him out of, Chris Stribling, friend and Feldenkrais practitioner, brilliantly demonstrated how Oliver could use his injured leg to extricate himself from his predicament. Thanks, Chris.

I am grateful to Robert Schell, who interrupted his vacation to share his considerable knowledge about guns with a generally clueless stranger, and to D. P. Lyle, MD, author of *Forensics for Dummies*, who generously answered my questions about that subject.

Annie Tucker, my wonderful editor, applied her skill and logic to the book and helped make it immeasurably better. Thank you to Brooke Warner and Kamy Wicoff of She Writes Press, both for creating an alternative to traditional publishing and for selecting my book as part of their spring catalog. And a special thank-you to Jackie Good, who helped me find my voice. My thanks also to the Regional Oral History Office at the Bancroft Library, UC Berkeley, for details about life in Richmond during World War II.

My family supported me throughout this process and heard more than anyone would ever need to know about the history of World War II. Were it not for Brian Callahan, our talented winemaker, there would have been no CRUX wines to sustain us during that time. I give my thanks for and to my daughter Kim, who supplied moral support from across the sea; my daughter Heidi, for years of affectionate stories about children with Asperger's syndrome; my son, Aaron, for his insights about the battle for Guam and all things military, and for his careful reading of the manuscript; my son-in-law, Mathew Hall, for his discerning and insightful analysis of the book and the gentle way he discussed the things that did not work so well for him; and my husband, Richard, for his support, his belief in me, and his generous willingness to help me in any way he could. Thank you.

I have been blessed to have known and cared for many extraordinary dogs. From the time I was a child, they have protected me, comforted me, made me laugh, and taught me to see with my heart.

There are many beautiful spirits like Harley and Emma in shelters and rescues, longing to accompany you on your journey. If you enjoyed reading about them in this book, please think about inviting one to share your life.

Bibliography

African Americans in World War II

Allen, Robert L. *The Port Chicago Mutiny: The Story of the Largest Mass Mutiny Trial in U.S. Naval History.* Berkeley, CA: Heyday Books, 1993.

Hamann, Jack. *On American Soil: How Justice Became a Casualty of World War II.* Seattle: University of Washington Press, 2005.

McGuire, Phillip. *Taps for a Jim Crow Army: Letters from Black Soldiers in World War II.* Lexington, KY: University Press of Kentucky, 1993.

Moore, Christopher Paul. *Fighting for America: Black Soldiers—the Unsung Heroes of World War II.* New York: One World, 2005.

Guam

Lemish, Michael G. *War Dogs: Canines in Combat.* Dulles, VA: Brassey's Inc., 1996.

Putney, DVM, USMC (ret.), Captain William W. *Always Faithful: A Memoir of the Marine Dogs of WWII.* New York: The Free Press, 2001.

Rottman, Gordon L. *Guam 1941 & 1944: Loss and Reconquest.* Botley, Oxford, UK: Osprey Publishing Ltd., 2004.

The History Channel: *Pacific: The Lost Evidence: Guam.* 2004.

Italian Americans in World War II

DiStasi, Lawrence, ed. *Una Storia Segreta: The Secret History of Italian American Evacuation and Internment during World War II.* Berkeley, CA: Heyday Books, 2001.

Fox, Stephen. *UnCivil Liberties: Italian Americans Under Siege During World War II.* United States: Universal Publishers, 2000. Originally published as *The Unknown Internment: An Oral History of the Relocation of Italian Americans during World War II,* Twayne's Oral History Series. Boston: Twayne Publishers, 1990.

LaGumina, Salvatore J., ed. *The Italian American Experience: An Encyclopedia.* In *Garland Reference Library of the Humanities.* New York: Routledge, 1999.

Italian Prisoners of War

Camilla Calamandrei. *Prisoners in Paradise.* Documentary film, 2001. www.prisonersinparadise.com.

The Bay Area, World War II

Archibald, Katherine. *Wartime Shipyard: A Study in Social Disunity.* Berkeley, CA: University of California Press, 1947.

Bastin, Donald. *Images of America: Richmond.* San Francisco: Arcadia Publishing, 2003.

Camp, William Martin. *Skip to My Lou.* Garden City, NY: Doubleday, Doran & Company, Inc., 1945.

Cole, Susan D. *Richmond—Windows to the Past.* Richmond, CA: Wildcat Canyon Books, 1980.

Fabry, Joseph. *Swing Shift: Building the Liberty Ships.* San Francisco: Strawberry Hill Press, 1982.

Graves, Donna. *Mapping Richmond's World War II Home Front: A Historical Report Prepared for National Park Service Rosie the Riveter/World War II Home Front National Historical Park.* 2004.

Johnson, Marilyn S. *The Second Gold Rush: Oakland and the East Bay in World War II.* Berkeley and Los Angeles: University of California Press, 1993.

McLeod, Dean L. *Images of America: Port Chicago.* San Francisco: Arcadia Publishing, 2007.

Moore, Shirley Ann Wilson. *To Place Our Deeds: The African American Community in Richmond, California, 1910–1963.* Berkeley and Los Angeles: University of California Press, 2001.

Roselius, Donna, et al., eds. *This Point in Time: An Historic View of Point Richmond.* Point Richmond, CA: Point Richmond History Association, 1980.

Veronico, Nicholas A. *Images of America: World War II Shipyards by the Bay.* San Francisco: Arcadia Publishing Company, 2007.

The Home Front: World War II

Clinard, Marshall B. *The Black Market: A Study of White Collar Crime.* New York: Rinehart & Company, 1952.

Goodwin, Doris Kearns. *No Ordinary Time: Franklin & Eleanor Roosevelt: The Home Front in World War II.* New York: Simon & Schuster Paperbacks, 1994.

Lotchin, Roger W., ed. *The Way We Really Were: The Golden State in the Second Great War.* Urbana and Chicago: University of Illinois Press, 2000.

O'Brien, Kenneth Paul, and Lynn Hudson Parsons, eds. *The Home-Front War: World War II and American Society.* Westport, CT: Greenwood Press, 1995.

Starr, Kevin. *Embattled Dreams: California in War and Peace, 1940–1950.* New York: Oxford University Press, 2002.

Stickney, Zephorene. "Code Breakers: The Secret Service." *Wheaton Quarterly*, spring 2011.

About the Author

M. A. Adler lived in Point Richmond as a child and later moved to Ohio, where she became an attorney and an associate dean at Case Western Reserve University School of Medicine.

From time to time, Adler visited the Bay Area to refresh her spirit and research Richmond's history during World War II. In the late '90s, she returned to Northern California full-time to write, enjoy her family, and do canine scent work with her dogs. *In the Shadow of Lies* is her first novel.

SELECTED TITLES FROM SHE WRITES PRESS

She Writes Press is an independent publishing company founded to serve women writers everywhere. Visit us at www.shewritespress.com.

Watchdogs by Patricia Watts
$16.95, 978-1-938314-34-6
When journalist Julia Wilkes returns to the town where her career got its start, she is forced to face some old ghosts—and some new enemies.

Water On the Moon by Jean P. Moore
$16.95, 978-1-938314-61-2
When her home is destroyed in a freak accident, Lidia Raven, a divorced mother of two, is plunged into a mystery that involves her entire family.

Shanghai Love by Layne Wong
$16.95, 978-1-938314-18-6
The enthralling story of an unlikely romance between a Chinese herbalist and a Jewish refugee in Shanghai during World War II.

Clear Lake by Nan Fink Gefen
$16.95, 978-1-938314-40-7
When psychotherapist Rebecca Lev's father dies under suspicious circumstances, she becomes obsessed with discovering what happened to him.

Fire & Water by Betsy Graziani Fasbinder
$16.95, 978-1-938314-14-8
Kate Murphy has always played by the rules—but when she meets charismatic artist Jake Bloom, she's forced to navigate the treacherous territory of passionate love, friendship, and family devotion.

Trinity Stones by LG O'Connor
$18.95, 978-1-938314-84-1
On her 27th birthday, New York investment banker Cara Collins learns that she is one of twelve chosen ones prophesied to lead a final battle between the forces of good and evil.

CPSIA information can be obtained at www.ICGtesting.com
Printed in the USA
BVOW03s1048120514

353081BV00003B/15/P